Ron Sewell was born in Britain in 1944. He was educated in London, the Royal Navy and Glasgow University.

The great docks of London were an important influence on the author's childhood. Many a school holiday was spent travelling to and from Greenwich where he watched the multi-coloured cargo ships bound for foreign lands.

Having completed a successful career as an engineer in the Royal Navy, he left, seeking pastures new. After a short period of civilian life, the author enrolled in the Royal Navy Reserve as an Engineer Officer but switched direction, becoming a fully qualified Deck Officer.

The sea and its mood remains a part of his life. When at home, the sound of the waves tumbling and crashing on the shore vibrate the foundations of the house where he lives happily with his wife Sheila.

The Angel Makers

by

Ron Sewell

APOLLONIA

First published in 1998 by Apollonia
78 The Promenade
Joppa
Edinburgh EH15 2EL

ISBN 0-9534102-0-X

Typeset by Amolibros, Watchet, Somerset
Publication managed by Amolibros
Printed and bound by Professional Book Supplies, Oxford, England

I do not speak unless I have something to say.

Unknown

One

March 1993

Lieutenant Commander Adrian Viper, RD, RNR, the Commanding Officer of HMS *Blackbird*, sat relaxed in his bridge chair, almost mesmerised by the scene that unfolded before him. The air was unhurried and the sea had taken on an oily calmness. His ship disturbed the tranquillity as the deep frames of the reinforced bow split the black waters apart, leaving a frothing white trail in her wake. Lanky and muscular, and just less than six feet tall, Adrian's deep blue eyes were set in a weathered, yet well-tanned face. At the age of thirty-five he had fulfilled all his material aspirations.

Suddenly the radio blasted out "MAYDAY, MAYDAY, MAYDAY; this is Motor Vessel *Bristol Adventure*. My position is 55.10,05 North, 00.15,20 East. I am on fire, and unable to control the situation. MAYDAY, MAYDAY."

John Gittings, the Officer of the Watch, was already plotting the ship's position on the chart. The voice on the radio remained cool and calm, as it continued to repeat its cry for help; Adrian deliberately turned the volume down.

"How far are we away, John?"

"Twenty miles, Sir."

"OK, let me have the Closest Point of Approach." Without waiting for an answer, Adrian picked up the radio's hand-set and began to speak clearly on Channel 16, the frequency being transmitted by the distressed vessel.

"This is the Commanding Officer of HMS *Blackbird*. My position is twenty miles due west of the *Bristol Adventure*. I'm able to give assistance."

For a few seconds the radio was silent, then it burst into life. "This is Tynemouth Coastguard Station. There are no other vessels within fifty miles of you or MV *Bristol*. Take charge of this rescue until relieved by a superior vessel."

Adrian paused for a moment; "As the Captain of one of Her Majesty's Warships I'll take charge, unless relieved of that duty by a senior officer. Out."

The bridge team all smiled at his reply. They knew their boss well.

"Understood, Sir; good luck."

Adrian listened again to the desperate message of a captain in trouble that continued to fill the small confines of the bridge.

"This is Captain Kelly, Master of MV *Bristol*. I have a fire in my engine room. I have a cargo of nitrates. I intend to abandon ship."

Adrian realised that, having acted spontaneously on the instinct to save others and accepting the task without consulting and obtaining permission from his Area Flag Officer, he would soon be risking his ship and crew by approaching a floating bomb. If that fire reached the hold the resulting explosion would kill the crew, and seriously endanger his own men.

With the knowledge he would be in serious trouble

if this ensued he turned to the Officer of the Watch, "How far to go, John?"

"She bears green one five, we're making a good twenty-two knots and I would estimate another forty minutes."

"Sparks, send the following to our Flag Officer. Intend to rescue the crew of MV *Bristol* and, if possible, salvage vessel."

"Excuse me, Sir." It was Jim Potts, *Blackbird*'s First Lieutenant. "I've mustered the crew and have ready all the necessary equipment for fire fighting and salvage. The ship's boat is ready to pick up survivors."

"Well done, Number One. We've about thirty minutes before we decide which option to choose. What do you think?"

"My choice, Sir, would be to pick up the crew and get the hell out of there."

"I've a strong tendency to agree with you, but even if their lifeboat has a jet engine they won't travel far enough to escape any blast. Let's wait and see."

Adrian moved from the relative comfort of the enclosed bridge to the Port Bridge Wing and looked forward. The deck beneath his feet vibrated as the power of the ship's two huge diesel engines pushed *Blackbird* ahead. It would be at least another fifteen minutes before they were in position but his men were ready. They had dressed in their Fearnaught fire suits and all the ship's pumps were operating at full power. Hoses had been secured and trained over the side, each jet of water creating a large arc before it fell into the sea. On any other occasion it would have been a beautiful sight, but now it represented their protection and the salvation of others.

A dull explosion rattled the reinforced glass screen that protected them from the ravages of the wind and sea. Everyone, their faces showing the apprehension they felt, looked forward as the stern of MV *Bristol* lifted into the air tossing blazing sections in all directions as if they were paper in the wind. A huge plume of smoke rose across the watery sun, hiding it momentarily. The fire that was consuming the violated hull of MV *Bristol* was still over two miles away.

Adrian felt his hands tighten and his throat go dry as the thought of dying and damaged seamen filled his mind.

"Ready to drop the boat, Sir," came a voice from the deck.

"Wait," shouted the First Lieutenant.

Adrian's eyes explored the sea about the explosion. All on board were desperately searching for a lifeboat, or signs that anyone, by some miracle, might have survived. Adrian peered down at the deck again. Those on the fo'c'sle were motionless as they progressed at full speed towards the floating inferno and the blazing sea that surrounded it. All were now prepared to risk their lives to help others.

"Slow ahead both." Adrian tasted the stench of burning as he breathed deeply to calm his anxiety. Gently he eased his ship into the debris strewn waters where the acrid fumes of the burning nitrates seared their senses.

Adrian shifted his binoculars, trying not to stare at the dying vessel. The speed at which the fire was now spreading across the water startled him. "Number One, make sure those hoses keep our decks well washed. It's going to get a bit warm."

"The Buffer has it under control, Sir. I threatened him if the paint-work gets singed he'll spend all his off duty time redecorating."

Adrian smiled, for even under these conditions a sailor's bizarre sense of humour always came to the fore. He watched Jim light a cigarette and inhale deeply, before exhaling with the same passion. It had been a long day and it had all the signs of being much longer before it was over.

Forward, the Buffer bellowed orders as if it was his life that depended on a successful rescue. The Captain was aware that this hulk of a man used his fists on the odd occasion to settle arguments.

Adrian's attention switched when a gust of wind cleared the smoke directly ahead of them. There was the lifeboat, blackened by smoke and flame, steered by the scorched remnants of a man. He had no need to tell Jim what to do; he was already up forward ordering the fire parties to get hoses directed at the lifeboat. The small motionless craft drowned in a deluge of spray that instantly began to quench the flames that surrounded and were trying to consume it. With caution Adrian manoeuvred HMS *Blackbird* until the distance between them was close enough for thrown grapnels to pull it to safety. Even with the torrent of water that fell upon them, the steam could clearly be seen rising from the survivors' clothing. Adrian watched as the Petty Officer Cook and his mate, encumbered with their first aid kits, lowered themselves from the ship's deck into the gathering of bodies. They began to check each man in turn for other injuries that would, if neglected, cause further suffering. Those with the severest burns were placed with care into Neil Robinson Stretchers. Once securely fastened, the delicate task of lifting each victim began. Some screamed in agony as the coarse wooden slats cut deep into their skin, and relief came in unconsciousness. For the others any pain was ignored. They were thankful for their salvation from the mouth of death itself.

Adrian heard someone vomiting below the bridge and then the harsh tones of the Buffer, "You can clear that up now you messy bastard."

When they were all safely onboard, Adrian gave the order, "Both engines slow ahead." His whole body was shaking as he shoved both hands in his pockets.

"Hard to port. Steer north."

The First Lieutenant came to the bridge, still gasping as the nauseous vapour-saturated air hit his nicotine-filled lungs. He waited until Adrian was ready. "They're alive, Sir, but a few may not survive unless moved quickly to a hospital."

Adrian leant on his chair and motioned with his right hand for Jim to come forward. "Well done, Jim. Pass my thanks to the crew, but it's not over yet. Tell sparks to contact the Coastguard and get the SAR helicopters out here to take those poor sods off."

Jim walked away leaving Adrian to his own thoughts. He found the Buffer shouting at a group of young seamen who had failed to secure the sea-boat correctly. "Buffer, prepare the ship for flying stations."

"Aye, aye, Sir."

"You, you and you," the Buffer roared in his irrepressible roguish manner, pointing to the three youngest seamen. "Follow me."

As *Blackbird* left the immediate area of the tragedy, Adrian walked to the right-hand side of the bridge. The self-generated breeze helped clear his mind as he watched the spreading mass of oil, its flames even attempting to engulf the water on which it floated. It was all over - others had executed the dangerous tasks, but their safety had been his sole responsibility.

"Port thirty, revolutions ahead 200," he ordered. His eyes glanced at the gyro compass repeater as it started to swing. "Starboard ten, steer 340." The turn halted and HMS *Blackbird* settled onto the requested course. Those not involved with the treatment of casualties stood and stared at the dying ship, all knew that there was nothing they could do to save her. It was not a dramatic end. The initial blast had torn through the hull like a bolt of lightening and ripped apart most of the bulkheads that held her together. Those that had somehow remained intact were now buckling under the weight of water entering the wrecked hull. The ship began to lean and slowly she settled down. When the machinery broke loose and crashed through what remained of the bulkheads, her end was confirmed. Finally she disappeared in a cloud of black smoke and a flurry of steam. Only a few items floated on the surface of burning oil to mark the spot where a ship had died.

"Plot that position, John, and inform the authorities. First Lieutenant, Prepare a Dan Buoy to mark the spot."

"Ready when you are, Sir."

Without wasting a moment Adrian turned the ship and pointed its bow towards the area where the *Bristol Adventure* had sunk. At a much reduced speed, the red and white painted buoy dropped into the water marking the ill-fated ship's final resting place.

Blackbird turned again and continued north for a further twenty minutes until the radar screen showed three helicopters closing on the ship.

Adrian was aware that Jim had prepared for their arrival and when they were in view he ordered, "Hands to flying stations." The aircraft controller guided the first craft down. The others hovered to port, their down-draught flattening the sea as they moved forward at a steady ten knots. The difficult task of hoisting the casualties up and into the cargo hold was achieved as if it were a commonplace activity, comfortably handled as their rhythmic pulsing rotor blades penetrated the remotest corners of the ship. With the assistance of willing hands, it was not long before all the survivors were airborne and on their way to Newcastle Royal Infirmary. With the operation completed, Adrian returned to his cabin. He sat at the desk and attempted to concentrate. It was important that he wrote the report now while it was fresh in his mind but the muted noise of the ship tended to distract him and he found himself listening to the sounds of men carrying out their duties or just passing by. His mind wandered: the disaster he had witnessed reminded him of his own past sorrows. His parents had died in a car accident leaving him, their only son, as the beneficiary of a large steel foundry.

When the funeral was over, he had returned with the house staff but felt isolated in the stone-built Georgian Mansion. It was far too large and empty; a sad place where only memories remained. The silence in every room had been overwhelming. For days he wandered aimlessly around the house and the estate recalling the times he and his parents had spent together. To him it had been a waste of two good people. Why did they have to die? What God in his right mind allowed good people to die and the bad to live on?

It was old Joe, the local poacher, who had helped him come to terms with his loss. This wizened old man constantly puffed away like a steam train at a pipe jutting from his tobacco-stained lips. He always wore an old peaked cap to keep his head warm and draped over his thin frame was a paint-marked army combat jacket. It was an odd association, for he spoke to Adrian as an equal. Adrian took note of his advice to display his emotions and remember his parents as they were, to go home and think of all the good times, to look at old photographs and cry. Whatever the pain, he had to get everything out in the open and then learn to live again.

Adrian followed old Joe's guidance and wept openly until his grief subsided. At times, the feeling of loneliness was unbearable. Often he would leave the confines of the house and go for a long walk. On one of these forays there was an hour or so of daylight left as he wandered alone. A twig snapped and he turned round to see the welcome face of old Joe. Together they discussed countless subjects until it was dark. On many days thereafter, Adrian met with Joe and talked about his loss and the old man was always willing to listen. The common-sense counselling Adrian received found its way into his sorrow and began to ease the pain. Many weeks later, in the seclusion of home, his thoughts returned to the important matter of the future. He was eighteen years of age and on his way to Cambridge University. It was time to resolve what was to be disposed of and retained. And thus he came to sell off the foundry but retain the house and estate. Unfortunately all but two of the staff would have to go. For their previous service each member of staff would receive a satisfactory sum to tide them over until they found further employment. The proceeds from the sale would be sufficient to support him comfortably for many years to come.

Cambridge came and went and with it an Honour's Degree in Roman History. Now free of any restrictions, and a wealthy young man, the next two years were spent enjoying life to its full. He sailed and partied with the best of them, drinking and dancing his way around the globe. During one of his rare visits home, a chance meeting with Colin, a close friend, was to change his life. Colin had been wearing the uniform of a Sub-Lieutenant, Royal Naval Reserve. Inquisitively, he asked Colin when he joined the navy? It was over a few beers in their local that Adrian began to appreciate that Colin was a reservist. After attending a Wardroom Mess dinner, Adrian decided to enlist, although becoming a Naval Officer proved not to be so simple as he had first imagined. Multiples of documents had to be completed and there was also the mandatory medical examination. It was only after verification of all the relevant information that an interview with the Base Captain confirmed his acceptance. That was the beginning of a stretch of hard work, studying for the infamous "Admiralty Interview Board" that would decide whether he remained in the service or not. Adrian found the study to his liking and became a regular attendee at the many classes of instruction.

A commanding officer of a sea-tender was short of a trainee officer and asked Adrian if he would care to join his team. Adrian soon discovered that being part of John Donald's ("the Bull") team meant working all the hours God made, only to receive a bollocking at the end of it. "The Bull" demanded an efficiency from his officers that was impossible to meet. Despite being a bastard of the first order, Adrian thought the man was a good teacher. Many lessons he learnt were a direct result of the Bull's teaching. From his new-found love of the sea, and in a vain attempt to recoup some of his squandered inheritance, Adrian purchased an ailing sail-charter company. His lack of business acumen and inexperience in financial management were disastrous as he ploughed money into an almost lost cause. That patch of difficulty was now in the past as a result of the concentrated effort and unending hard work of his friend and business manager, Selwyn Churchill.

+++

Time had disappeared when he should have been writing the detailed report the Admiralty would be waiting for on his arrival at Leith docks. Adrian knew that, for not following the correct procedure, he would again be in trouble, but it was his opinion that the rules existed only for fools and the misguided.

It was after midnight when he had finished writing and for the last time that day he went up to the bridge for a final look around. "Glad to see it's all quiet—

I'm off to my bunk. Keep it steady. Call me if the weather changes."

As he discarded his clothing, the easy roll of the ship beneath him caused him to stumble. With one hand to steady himself he climbed into his bunk, made himself comfortable, then switched off the reading light. That night he slept sound in the knowledge that his ship and the men that lived in her had done their best. The remainder of the passage home was uneventful.

+++

It was Sunday morning. Adrian awoke, as always, half an hour before sunrise, looked out of the only window on the ship and saw, at least to starboard, that the sea was clear of any other vessel.

It was approaching seven when Adrian heard the First Lieutenant's deep voice broadcast, "Hands to Harbour Stations." He placed his empty coffee cup on the desk and stood up, instantly aware of the ship's movement as she headed up the river Forth to her home port. A framed photograph depicted *Blackbird* steaming at full power on trials. It was amazing how the Chief Engineer could manipulate those few extra revolutions on the homeward leg. At any other time, he would scream blue murder if they stayed at full power longer than was necessary.

Adrian dragged himself from the comfort of his settee, picked up his cap and binoculars before he stepped out of the cabin, and ran up the steel ladder that led to the bridge. Jim and the rest of his officers were waiting. "Special sea duty men closed up and the ship is ready for entering harbour, Sir."

Adrian nodded in acknowledgement.

Everything was prepared. As he sat in his chair, the Pilot presented his brief for entering harbour.

"Very good, Pilot. Number One, would you like to take her alongside?"

"Yes, Sir."

Adrian ordered the Yeoman to hoist Desig second sub or, as he referred to it, "the flags denoting the driver".

Adrian made himself comfortable in his chair while those around him adjusted their positions to enable the First Lieutenant to drive the ship. Through experience Adrian had learnt to delegate but he watched carefully as Jim stood behind the ship's gyro compass and gave clear precise orders. The initial operation was to enter the huge entrance lock to the dock area, a manoeuvre Jim had often undertaken.

Adrian always found it difficult to sit there, watch and say nothing. He knew that each man would complete the same task in a way different from himself. It went well but Adrian could not help but observe that Jim didn't relax until the ropes forward and aft held the ship fast to the dock wall. It took the dock pumps more than twenty minutes to balance the water levels. As they left the lock and entered the vast basin of the dock area, Adrian focused his binoculars on their berth to establish if the base staff had arrived to take the ropes.

"Jesus Christ. The jetty has a welcoming committee." Those who heard his remark grabbed the spare sets of glasses and looked forward. Gathered on the jetty were cameras and newsmen by the dozen.

Adrian was pleased when he heard Jim shout for silence. The thought of his alongside being filmed made him nervous but steadfastly he followed his instincts. The bows began to turn slowly to port as he began his final approach. With true professionalism HMS *Blackbird* came alongside without so much as a flake of paint being disturbed. Once the ropes were across and secured, Adrian quietly remarked into Jim's ear, "Better than I could've done with that lot watching. Nice one, Jim! No visitors, except those known to us, are to get on this ship until I'm ready to receive them. Is that clear?"

"No problem, Sir. The Buffer will be placed in charge of the gangway."

The ship gave a final tremble as the two large diesel engines stopped and went to sleep until awakened for the next patrol.

Adrian returned to his cabin to gather his thoughts and to write down a few notes as mental reminders before he met the press. Again he was breaking the rules. He should wait until the RN Public Relations people arrived and briefed him. "What the hell," he thought. "All that really matters is that my crew has risked their lives to rescue the survivors from that stricken vessel and they should receive the credit. To hell with bloody protocol!"

With his mind clear he left his quarters and made his way aft to the gangway. "OK Buffer."

The Buffer's huge frame moved away from the narrow gangway to allow the local and national media representatives to come onboard.

Adrian had moved aft to the sweepdeck, an area covered in minesweeping gear. "When you're ready ladies and gentlemen, I can let you have ten minutes, no more, and no less. After that I must ask you to leave my ship and allow the crew to get on with their duties." For a few seconds his eyes and those of an attractive blond reporter met. The questioning went well with Adrian controlling the situation; he carefully deflected those questions that had nothing to do with the rescue but answered fully those that were relevant.

The interview was over and the Buffer, who had been standing to the rear of the party during this time, moved as swiftly as his bulk would allow, stepping between the reporters and his Captain, enabling him to depart unhindered. Those present realised the futility of remaining any longer. Cameras and notebooks were hurriedly stuffed into bags and pockets; the meeting was over. The media left.

Adrian returned to his cabin and began to pack his clothes knowing that his First Lieutenant would be getting the ship ready for hand-over. Although he had plenty on his mind, somehow he could not forget those beautiful brown eyes that had belonged to the blond reporter; they seemed to penetrate his very soul. As Jim and the Coxswain approached, he picked up his cap, waited for the formal report, and then followed the Coxswain down the nearest ladder to begin his rounds. It was the end of another patrol. The messdecks were now lacking the life sailors gave them; even their bedding was now in a sack ready for the laundry. In the radio shack, the Operator was completing his shutdown of radio traffic.

As this party of three made their way aft to the stores and steering compartment, a dark green Jaguar

XJ10 screeched to a halt on the jetty. Adrian gave a friendly wave of recognition to the driver. It was Selwyn, his business manager, who, uninhibited by protocol, sounded the horn in recognition of his friend and employer. Once parked, he left the car and made his way towards the ship. Adrian's crew all knew and respected Selwyn. The six-foot-two black African's lean frame leapt across the short length of gangway. Adrian observed the Buffer and Selwyn exchange pleasantries before he made his way forward to the Captain's cabin.

With the formalities now complete, Adrian had Jim telephone the Base to inform them that they were ready to hand over.

The Base Staff Officer appeared in less than ten minutes. He did not bother inspecting the ship. He was aware of Adrian's standards which invariably surpassed his own. David, however, was not in his usual jovial mood. "The boss wants to see you. From the way he bent my ears, the Admiral has been giving him a hard time at you playing the hero. What's more that press conference you gave is already on the news. So stand by to get your arse well and truly kicked."

"Thanks for the warning, David. What did they want me to do, spend hours on the radio while innocent men died because of red tape?"

The hand-over concluded, Adrian turned to Jim: "Thank you, Number One. Carry on please."

The high-pitched shrill of a Bosun's call over the ship's broadcast filled the air. "Attention on the upper deck, face aft and salute." The White Ensign and the Union Jack were slowly lowered to their respective attendants, carefully folded and returned to the captain's cabin.

Adrian left the ship and, without looking back, walked briskly to the waiting car.

"To Rosyth Naval Base, Selwyn. Better get the dramatics over."

"Bet you a tenner you get away with it. After all you're a hero. Even Her Majesty's Navy can't change that."

"You're on, now shut up and drive."

Selwyn did just that and thirty minutes later they were approaching the dockyard main gate.

The duty Ministry of Defence "policeman" moved to the centre of the road and waited until the car drew alongside him. As the window wound down the waiting constable was momentarily speechless. "It's all right, I know I have to get a pass," commented Selwyn before the officer had a chance to say anything.

With the pass in place, the remainder of the journey to the Tenth Mine Counter Measures office took only a few minutes. The car slowed to a halt in the shadow of MCM10's Office.

The dockyard on a Sunday was comparable to a ghost town; everything was dormant - vessels large and small in various stages of repair, others ready to leave on the Monday morning. Adrian, still in uniform, got out of the car and glanced at the single-storey building, shrugged his shoulders and walked in. As it was Sunday only one office had its lights on - the Commander's. He had walked only a few yards when the voice of Commander North bellowed down the passage, "I'm waiting, Viper!"

Adrian looked at the man sitting behind the standard grey desk. He was in his late thirties, well-built with a weather-beaten face.

"Come in," the Commander roared impatiently.

Adrian entered and waited for the tongue-lashing to begin.

"I hope you realise you've ruined the first weekend I've had off in months. My wife's raging mad and the Admiral wants your guts for garters. I know you're one of my better officers, but a signal or two to let us know what was happening would've calmed his lordship. Anyway, is that your report of proceedings? Give it here."

North read the document as Adrian stood in silence.

"Glad to see you carried out the rescue almost according to the letter of the law. At least you did something right."

"Is that it, Sir?"

"Yes. Damn you, Adrian. Now let me go and calm down the Admiral. The next time you're in the area you can apologise to my wife and take us to dinner."

"That's OK by me."

As Adrian left the office, he removed a ten-pound note from his wallet. The ever-smiling Selwyn held out his hand and grabbed the note. It wasn't that he needed it, purely the principle.

"Let's go home."

The journey south was monotonous and Adrian, knowing he was in safe hands immediately fell asleep. Selwyn drove carefully, conscious of the fact that, had it not been for Adrian's good Samaritan act, his life would have been so different. Time had turned a chance meeting into a solid business partnership and a friendship. From their first meeting, Selwyn's intelligent chatter and cheeky character ensured that his new-found employer would warm to him. When asked, Selwyn would talk about the history of his ancestors - how the tribes, when raided for slaves, were forced to undertake basic tasks that were beneath their status. Occasionally Adrian had queried these remarks and was never in any doubt about the ensuing reply. Whereas European royalties were all-powerful and respected, tribal kings and queens were never officially recognised, unless it suited the ruling country for their own ends. To this he added that his own great-grandfather was a Zulu Witch Doctor, a member of the highest hierarchy and feared by all. This position was always passed on to the eldest son along with the secrets of the magic potions and remedies accumulated over many generations. Adrian had smiled as Selwyn went on to describe the strength that emanated from the witch-doctor, the good he bestowed on his own tribe and the contrasting evil with which he could smother their opponents.

The long journey from Rosyth was almost over when Adrian awoke with a start as a wheel found a large pothole.

"Where are we?" he asked, dazed.

"A few miles to go and we'll be there."

"Have I been asleep that long?"

"Six hours, to be precise."

The car turned up the gravel path that led from the main road to the house. Stones picked up by the tyres rattled against the steel of the bodywork. Adrian could see that everything was in perfect order. He had become used to the preciseness of the grounds; it gave him a sense of stability in contrast to a rapidly changing world. The lawns were as immaculate as any Crown green; even on the small lake the lilies were in perfect bloom. The car stopped at the ivy-covered entrance to the house as the large metal bound door to the rear of the stone porch opened. Mrs Duke, despite her age, moved quickly across the gravel drive towards him. As she approached, he held out his arms and they hugged each other; it was good to be home. This remarkable lady had chided him as a child and taught him manners. Now she and her husband were all that remained of the large staff that had previously served his mother and father. She managed the domestics, while her husband, Bob, tended the grounds and undertook any other chores asked of him. Adrian had adopted them; they cared for him more than anyone else ever could. When, after the death of his parents, he presented them with the cottage and its title of ownership, they swore faithfully to serve him as best they could. Security and a good master outweighed all other considerations.

"Welcome home. Did you have a good trip on your boat?"

Adrian smiled. Mrs Duke had no idea of the time, effort and hard work required to command even the smallest of Her Majesty's warships.

"Very pleasant."

"I've prepared a nice hot meal— it won't take a moment to serve."

While this exchange of formalities took place, Selwyn emptied their belongings from the boot and drove the car into the open garage. Bob Duke appeared from the garden and, although well into his sixties, carried all the luggage into the kitchen ready for his wife to sort for washing, cleaning, brushing and hanging up.

Adrian was home; now he could recover from his seventeen days of operational duty. This house held many warm memories of his parents and childhood. It was a restful place, well away from the pressures of the Royal Navy.

During the following weeks Adrian got up to date with his yacht-chartering empire. This now profitable venture had once been his personal nightmare until Selwyn pulled all the pieces together and made it viable. It had taken Selwyn some considerable time to untangle the intricately knotted ball of string that was Adrian's business perception, and then turn it around. Twenty-five yachts, each worth more than a hundred thousand pounds apiece when new, were now at differing locations cruising the Greek islands. Most were skippered by professional seamen, but on the odd occasion, by a qualified charterer. The bright glow of the computer screen displayed the latest positions of each craft as Selwyn painstakingly examined each journal. It was he alone who decided what maintenance was required and when it would be necessary. If a boat was in poor condition, lives could be lost.

Past and future bookings were shown in separate columns alongside each craft. It was important to know who was skippering what, where and when. Financial matters were left exclusively to Selwyn. The growth of the company satisfied Adrian as this meant that his lifestyle for the future was secure. He could still be an officer in the RNR, yet, when the mood took him, sail his own boats. It was a good life and he loved every moment, but he was acutely aware that fate could deal a cruel blow when you were not looking.

Two

June 1993

It was just passing ten o'clock on the Thursday morning when the phone rang. Adrian managed to answer it before Mrs Duke who always considered it her duty.

"Viper speaking."

"Hello Adrian, it's Charles, Charles Dawning."

"Long time no see. To what do I owe the pleasure? It can't be for old time's sake, what can I do for you?"

As Adrian listened, Charles became uncharacteristically quiet. "It's a bit difficult to speak over the phone, but I'm sure the company coffers could stretch to a decent lunch."

Adrian hesitated; it was unusual for this man to contact him unless it was important. If he remembered correctly, Charles had recently been taken on as a Marine Consultant by Lloyds, the company that insured all his craft, albeit at a heavy price.

"Can't you give me a clue what it's about?"

"Not really, but it could be to your advantage."

"OK, I've nothing on at the moment, let's fix a date."

The reply was as sharp as a butcher's boning knife, "Tuesday my office at twelve."

Adrian was taken aback at the tone of the reply but nevertheless agreed with the date and time. "I'll be there, look forward to seeing you again."

Adrian replaced the receiver and walked across the hall to an adjoining room that was used as an office. Selwyn was on the business line chatting away in a mixture of English and Greek to one of their suppliers who had, for some "unknown" reason, failed to receive an order. This agent was now attempting to negotiate enhanced terms for an emergency supply for two boats. The man had obviously lost the argument, as the phone was, without any respect for its delicacy, slammed into its cradle.

"Cheeky bastard, tried to charge us over the odds 'til I reminded him his contract was up for renewal at the end of the season."

Adrian smiled, then went on to say, "I've just had the strangest of calls from Charles Dawning. Wants to meet me at his office, and then take me for lunch. Didn't even give me a reason. Just said it could be to my advantage."

"Whatever you do, don't sign anything before I've read it."

"Anyway I've agreed to meet him next Tuesday. I'll go by train."

+++

Tuesday duly arrived and Adrian woke early for his journey to London. Mrs Duke had prepared a continental breakfast and insisted, in her motherly fashion, that he eat something before he left. To satisfy her he quickly ate a warm croissant and gulped down half a pint of fresh orange juice. Selwyn was waiting in the Jaguar and, despite Adrian's protestations, insisted that he drive him to York station. When they were approaching the parking area Selwyn advised Adrian that he felt the meeting wouldn't go smoothly.

"What makes you say that?"

"Last night I didn't sleep well and when I eventually dozed off, a beautiful woman kept entering my dreams. As much as I tried to make some sense of it, I couldn't. Adrian, be careful what you say and do today."

It was an odd reply but Adrian understood. "I'll be on my guard. OK. I'll ring you as soon as I know what train I'm coming back on."

After a tedious two hours, Adrian found himself looking out of the carriage window at the inner city of London as the train arrived at its destination. He stepped off into the diffused sunlight that struggled in its progress through the years of London dirt and pigeon droppings that had settled on the glazed roof of a crowded King's Cross station. He looked smart, tie neatly knotted, a striped shirt freshly pressed. All the signs were there that he had travelled first-class, the exact way he now wandered through life. He was at his best and after a short taxi ride Adrian was standing outside the ultramodern edifice affectionately nicknamed "the espresso machine" because of its unusual design that rose dramatically from the ground. This was the famous Lloyds Register of Shipping. Hesitating for a moment before entering this monolith of glass and stainless steel, Adrian wondered what the original underwriters would think about their new offices. Once through the entrance he approached the reception and introduced himself to a prim and proper middle-aged lady who proudly wore the badge of head receptionist as would an Olympic winner a gold medal.

"Can I help you, Sir?" came the polite but hollow request.

"I have an appointment with Charles Dawning. My name is Adrian Viper."

"One moment, please. I'll check those details with Mr Dawning's secretary."

She punched in a number, spoke for a few moments then turned to him, while in synchronous motion with her right arm, beckoned to a messenger on call a few yards away. With her left hand she gave Adrian a numbered security tag. A flicker of a smile crossed her face as the pin dug into Adrian's finger. "Security and fire safety, needs must," she remarked. Turning away she spoke at the messenger, ordering him as she pointed with a bony finger towards Adrian," Escort this gentleman, to Mr Dawning's Office, room 507."

"Would you please follow me, Sir?"

The blunt politeness that accompanied the corporate image and the business face of the organisation shocked Adrian. Everything was automatic, without truth or emotion; the Americanism, "have a nice day", was comparable in its sincerity.

Charles was waiting for him at the door to his office and with a nod dismissed the messenger, welcoming Adrian simultaneously.

Adrian looked at his host carefully and as always Charles was faultlessly dressed in an obviously newly purchased suit. His shirt was stiff with starch. The narrow collar, if he moved suddenly, gave the distinct impression that it would be more than capable of decapitation. The brilliant display of the pale blue handkerchief peeking out of his breast pocket matched the colour of his tie exactly.

He spoke with a well-educated accent, his voice soft in timbre. He always appeared calm and in control. The office wasn't empty; in one of the three armchairs sat a very attractive woman.

Adrian instantly remembered Selwyn's words a few hours earlier.

"Let me introduce you. Janice Porter, meet a good friend of mine, Adrian Viper."

She paused for a moment then smiled, her tongue moistening her lips before speaking. "Hello. I've heard so much about you from Charles. I doubt if you'll recall, but we've met before."

Adrian remembered well and was taken aback by her presence; it was unexpected but he could not forget those eyes - they were full of life and a hint of mischief. They were close enough to feel the warmth radiating from each other. He could not resist the temptation to take more than a casual look. She was wearing a white polo neck top that clung to her, leaving little to the imagination. Her pale green skirt was short, exposing her beautiful long legs. She said nothing about his prolonged gaze but moistened her lips again with the tip of her tongue in a tantalising gesture. She in turn examined a well-proportioned, good-looking man in his mid thirties.

Dawning walked across and sat in another armchair, placed one leg over the other and admired his gleaming black shoes before suggesting that Adrian should sit in the remaining chair.

Adrian listened as Charles began to speak. "There's something you should know about Lloyds, that is something apart from what everyone else knows. What I'm about to reveal is not to be repeated."

Adrian was at once intrigued and stopped staring at Janice's legs.

"You may have read that this bastion of London is in some difficulties. Well, our analysts are set to announce record losses of at least two point four billion pounds. Over the last four years it's estimated that accumulated losses may even exceed eight billion pounds sterling. Lloyds will of course deny this as pure speculation. Unfortunately these facts are correct, but we'll continue to pay out all valid claims from both company and personal reserves. The first responsibility of the corporation is that Lloyds owes a duty of care to its members and is not exempt from having to pay damages. You may not have noticed as you gallivant around the seven seas, but across the dinner tables, the bars of golf clubs and the rolling hills of Britain, the despair is noticeable. As we speak, five thousand names already owe about £550 million, a figure that is likely to double or even treble in the coming year. Lloyds has rocked the establishment, achieving in a few short years what each socialist government fantasised over: an unprecedented redistribution of wealth. An undeclared sum will be required from the estates of deceased names, that's how bad it is. Over the past five years there have been many disasters; typhoons in Japan, tankers ablaze in the Channel, floods in Wales and aircraft destroyed by extremists. Most of these calamities were covered by us and we've had to pay, but for the 'names' it's been another nail in the universal coffin.

"The loss of shipping over the last few years has increased dramatically and the organisation requires me to discover if each loss was legitimate. Strange as it may seem, everything appears to be above board except five vessels that have disappeared without trace during the last decade. These ships were a vague assortment of bulk carriers and container ships operating independently wherever a cargo could be found. In my day they were affectionately known as 'tramps'."

Adrian looked intently at Charles: "What do you mean without trace? There must have been some wreckage or survivors? Ships these days don't just disappear."

"If you would let Charles finish, you might begin to learn something," interrupted Janice.

Adrian smiled at her and nodded for Charles to continue.

"Those five individual losses, although of no singular significance, amounted together to over two-hundred and twenty-five-million pounds. At first they appeared to be no more than a coincidence. But you know me. I beavered away as ever until I could recognise a connection and I think I've found it. With the aid of computers, extensive research and Janice's assistance I've recognised a common thread. Each of these vessels was purchased by a minor Greek shipping company then towed extremely long distances only to be refitted and extended at the Poi Loo Shipyard, Inch'on, Korea. When they were returned to service they pursued a legitimate trade and were insured by us. This in itself is unusual, as the present climate has created a surplus of vessels in world shipping. Simply to survive, costs have been cut to the bone. No-one insures ships with Lloyds any more unless they are a prestigious passenger line and certainly not a small shipping company with a tramp-steamer. The other interesting factor is that all the missing vessels made money - they were always given a cargo, and not once did they travel empty."

Adrian couldn't remain silent any longer. "Perhaps the answer is the crew scuttled each ship for its owner and pocketed a neat pension to see themselves into old age. If my memory is correct wasn't it about 1980 when some African countries allowed the dumping of cargoes free of charge before the ship was sunk? It took the authorities years to figure out that scam."

"That's preposterous. Don't you think that, with the thousands of contacts we have at our disposal world-wide, someone somewhere would have noticed something?" responded Charles.

"OK, so you have all the answers, where do I fit in?" Adrian knew that Charles had to reply.

"Ah! Now you're interested?"

Adrian chuckled to himself, "I'm not concerned at the plight of people who make millions by sitting on their fat backsides collecting their bonus cheques each year, then scream poverty when the going gets tough. I run a business and if it goes under there's no-one to bail me out of the shit. But I must admit I'm curious about these missing ships and when you've told me what you want me to do maybe I'll give you a hand."

Adrian wasn't prepared for the verbal onslaught from Charles. "You're just like your father, difficult.

If there was another man with a private income I could trust, with your knowledge of the sea and ships, then your arse wouldn't touch the ground as you left. I remember when you were a cheeky brat running around shipyards while your father and I did business. So just for once shut up and listen."

"All right. All right, what do you want me to do?"

"I have identified what I think will be the next ship to disappear."

"Wait a minute. If you know this why don't you just cancel the insurance, say it was unseaworthy or something."

"Sometimes I wonder if you have the intelligence others credit you with. What I want you to do is take passage on this ship as a tourist looking for a novel way to travel the world. Whilst you're on board, you check it over. If you find nothing what have we lost?"

"What if I find something? What do I do then, go down with the ship?"

"If you can't be serious for one minute we can finish this conversation right now."

"OK, continue, you're the man with all the answers. Tell me."

"The present Captain of the *Kia Hua* went to the same nautical college as myself and over the years our paths have crossed. I actually made a point of meeting him when he was last home on leave. Although we're the same age, life hasn't been so good to him as it has to me. Don't get me wrong, this is the last voyage he'll make as Captain. Hopefully after his retirement he'll live out his remaining days in moderate comfort. We had lunch and chatted about old times, but he appeared as rigidly set in his principles now as he was as a young officer. I believe he's trustworthy."

"If he's as honest as you think why not ask him to do your dirty work?"

"Will you listen to what I'm saying, I said I *believe*. If I told him what was going to happen to his ship, this man wouldn't wait for it to happen, he would go straight to the authorities. They in turn would undertake to carry out a cursory examination and find nothing. Any chance of finding out what's going on would disappear. If I was in charge of running contraband or whatever, this would definitely warn me."

"Gentlemen!" interrupted Janice. "How about including me in this discussion? Don't forget that I'll be on that vessel as well."

Adrian looked directly into her eyes. "What do you mean as well?"

Janice clearly was not in the mood to be ignored. "Let me make this abundantly clear. Charles, either I go on this assignment or you get another expert. I've put too much time and effort into this project to back off now."

"Janice, Adrian, let's have some lunch and discuss this like adults."

Before either man could say another word, Janice walked out. Realising that to lose her temper would not be to her advantage, she took several deep breaths and regained her composure.

Charles was still talking to Adrian when she returned.

"Janice," said Charles, "Adrian will have to be told everything we know. This beating around the bush is getting us nowhere."

"All right," her voice vibrated with power and confidence. "Let's forget lunch and get down to the nitty-gritty. The five ships that have disappeared were not worth much to Lloyds, about fifty million apiece including cargo. One, a Greek freighter, sailed from Piraeus for Rio. It never arrived. It just disappeared into thin air. Others amounting to much more have been allegedly hijacked by nationalist Chinese gunboats and their crews imprisoned or murdered. Where this has been the case, and our investigations have already revealed several such occurrences, the company doesn't have to pay out a penny. If the vessels remaining on our list were not sunk for their own worth, what were they carrying and why? Charles and I have our suspicions but nothing to confirm them one way or another."

Impressed at her ice-cold presentation of the facts, Adrian asked politely what the suspect cargoes could be.

"Nuclear waste, one cargo of that would empty someone's dustbin and save them a mint in reprocessing or storage. Dangerous chemical by-products for the same reason."

The *Kia Hua* has generally operated out of third world ports where the security is a joke and anyone or anything can be bought at a price. We, Charles and I, have assumed that she'll soon load up with her dangerous cargo. I doubt that even the crew will know what they're carrying. Maybe they'll change the crew, we don't know. The best we can hope for is to be there when it happens."

"It's that 'we' business," commented Adrian. "Would you mind explaining?"

"I'm a freelance reporter and I was investigating large losses of shipping when my research crossed that of Charles. It seemed at the time that two people could cover more ground than one, so we joined forces. The plan is that we, you and I, pose as a slightly eccentric couple who, as we said earlier, are indulging in a different approach to seeing the world."

"OK, Charles you also mentioned that this could be to my advantage. At the moment I can't see why."

"Free insurance for your vessels and any extra you may purchase for the next two years."

"Can you do that?"

"This organisation can do absolutely anything if it saves money."

"All you want me to do is spend some time on an old tramp steamer with—" Adrian looked at Janice dubiously "—her, and report anything suspicious."

"That's all I want."

Adrian pondered the thought. "Let me think about it and I'll be in touch. When do you need an answer?"

"The *Kia Hua* is due to dock in Mombassa in eight days' time. So that the necessary arrangements can be made I need your answer in less than four."

"Very well, if I decide to go, I'll have to make plans of my own. One addition to the party would be my business Manager Selwyn Churchill; his local knowledge and colour could be very advantageous in an African Port. Naturally I assume this is all-expenses paid?"

"Within reason, we'll pick up the tab and I emphasise, within reason."

Adrian decided to push his luck. "I take it that

'within reason' allows the extravagance of first-class air tickets?"

"Every man has his price," Charles responded, "so if that's yours...?"

" I'll be on my way. Goodbye Miss Porter," Adrian added as an afterthought, "And thank you for lunch," as he opened the door and left.

Charles looked at Janice, "What do you think of my expert?"

"Arrogant, self-opinionated but with the ideal credentials."

Adrian walked towards the lift, thoughts of Janice filling his mind. There was something about her that bothered him. Distracted, he almost collided with people waiting. When it arrived one of the new occupants pressed the button for the next floor down and Adrian speculated why they hadn't used the stairs for such a short distance. He pushed the green neon that indicated the ground floor. The journey was swift and in what seemed like a few seconds he was out of the lift and passing through the main entrance doors as he remembered his security tag. Even as he turned there was the messenger behind him: "Your tag please, Sir. It activated electronically when you passed through the main entrance."

Adrian handed it over, at the same time apologising for his forgetfulness.

London was in the middle of a severe June heatwave that had already lasted two weeks. After the cool freshness of air-conditioning, the hot suffocating air hit him full in the face. "God, this heat," he thought, as he wiped the back of his hand across a sweaty brow. It was mid-afternoon and tourists were trudging under the blazing sun along the Thames Embankment to the Tower of London.

With time to spare he removed his jacket and tie. It made a pleasant change to wander along with those who had nothing better to do than enjoy the weather and relax in its radiance. After a quick telephone call home, he bought himself a refreshing drink of ice-cold orange and a sandwich from a kiosk to make up for the lunch he had missed. Adrian used the remainder of the afternoon and the return journey to ponder over a myriad of questions. What was this old tramp steamer carrying? Why was it so important to find out? When was the sabotage planned? The chances of being in the right place at the right time were slight. Even if Charles had selected the right vessel, how could he prevent it being sabotaged and sunk? Surely they would have to get rid of those who were not participating in the fraud. The captain—was he as honest as Charles supposed? Was this last trip his opportunity to secure a better pension? The idea of finding the right ship intrigued him. His mind was still wandering around in a quagmire of uncertainty when he heard the conductor announcing the arrival of the train into York station.

As he left the station entrance, there, as anticipated, was his friend Selwyn.

After dinner the two of them sat down and discussed the probabilities that existed if they agreed to take part in what seemed a senseless undertaking. If they boarded the ship at Mombassa, would they be able to check on the cargo and discover its final destination, and if so, what if it proved legitimate? Obviously they would have to remain at sea until they docked. A covert search of the ship was likely to reveal nothing. Their final strategy would be to befriend the crew in an attempt to discover something that just might prove to be significant. Simple seamen, knowing that they would soon be coming into a large sum of money, invariably spend it before receiving it. The officers would be a different matter, but chatter over the dinner table with a glass of wine to release inhibitions could also give some substance to the theory of sinking for gain.

Selwyn looked at his friend; "Then it's agreed, and we must be stark raving mad to get involved with this. At worst we could be killed."

"That's looking a bit on the dark side, my friend. Let's play the game and have an all-expenses paid break. Kenya has sunshine and beaches for us to enjoy."

"Why not? If time allows I might be able to look up some of my relatives."

Adrian laughed. "I don't think your kin will be staying at the Mombassa Beach Hotel—no offence but didn't you tell me they were existing somewhere around the borders of South Africa and Namibia?"

"That shows how ignorant you whites really are. The Zulu race is the most revered of African tribes and can be found almost everywhere."

"OK, take it easy, I take back my white remarks. I'm only winding you up and you went for it like a duck to water."

"What about this Porter woman?" asked Selwyn.

"Headstrong, self opinionated and good looking. Do a bit of research on her tomorrow. Best to investigate our travelling companion. Mind you, she is attractive and has a lovely pair of legs, and you never know what a drop of fresh sea air could do to her libido."

"What you mean is, given half a chance you wouldn't mind getting her between the sheets."

Adrian looked at Selwyn and laughed.

+++

The next morning Adrian telephoned Charles Dawning. He tried to persuade him that it would possibly be easier without Janice but it was a futile attempt. After a few minutes Adrian altered his approach, accepted the job but demanded first-class flights to Nairobi and, whilst waiting for the ship to arrive, the best suite the Mombassa Beach Hotel could offer.

Charles conceded, and arranged to meet them four days hence in the departure lounge at Heathrow Airport, terminal four. As part of the contract, Adrian was to check out the dockyard storage areas prior to the ship arriving. Adrian yielded to this, but made no guarantees.

All that day Selwyn busied himself with phone calls to all and sundry in an effort to acquire any snippets of information he could collect on Janice. The more he researched, the more impressed he became. When he had compiled a satisfactory dossier he presented it to Adrian.

"What's the verdict?" asked his friend as the document was laid on a nearby table.

"Good at her job and obeys orders only when it suits her. Sounds very much like someone I already know," came Selwyn's mocking reply.

"There must be much more to this woman than I had imagined. It'll be interesting," he told himself.

Three

The massive air-conditioning plant located on the top of Seoul's Commodore Hotel ensured a constant supply of cool air to those who could afford it.

Four men sat in sumptuous armchairs while the slowly rotating fans gently agitated the air around them. These men dealt in the supply and distribution of prohibited drugs to the world's marketplace. If conscience was ever a measurable commodity, theirs would register a minus factor on a scale of one to ten. Although Greek by birth, Angel Andrias spoke perfect English, a language common to them all.

"Then we're in agreement, it's time to harvest the *Kia Hua*." For an instant he paused to study the eyes of his accomplices. He continued his delivery, outlining a plan that had to date served them well.

The thin American waited, saying nothing, tapping his gold-topped pen as he watched and waited for Angel to finish. With the reflexes of an attacking cobra he struck. "In my opinion gentlemen, we've used this plan far too often and should look for a different approach."

Angel was acutely aware that Terry Rouse was an FBI renegade who in recent years had only just escaped arrest by the authorities. Angel's eyes reflected his contempt: "It's a plan that has paid dividends time and time again. You know how I operate—use people until they've served their purpose, then dispose of them."

The other two men, the suppliers, remained silent but were aware of the competition that raged between the American and the Greek. They had always been prepared to gamble a year's harvest on Angel's ideas; after all he had made them unbelievably rich. The risk of being connected was minimal—once they had delivered the goods. Anyway there was always another crop next year.

There was a sharp knock on the main door, which stilled all conversation.

Angel smiled as he moved towards the door. "Our guest has arrived. Good afternoon, Captain, I respect a man who's punctual."

In the doorway stood a hard-faced, well-built man whose attire had certainly seen better days.

"Be at ease, Captain, you're amongst friends." He gestured to a chair. Angel turned to the others: "May I present Captain Vaughan, the man who will reclaim the *Kia Hua* for us. He's a man who needs money and will obey my orders. That is correct, isn't it, Captain?" Vaughan did not have a chance to answer as Angel continued, "My assistant Chung will brief you on the details, Captain; it has been nice to meet you."

Vaughan was no fool; he stood up knowing the meeting was over. Angel made a phone call, shortly after which Chung appeared at the door, beckoned to Vaughan and escorted him away. An evil smile crossed Angel's lips: "A desperate man who for a price will do anything we ask of him."

The formalities were soon completed and three men left leaving Angel alone with his thoughts. The next time they would meet would be in a year to plan and agree the disposal of another lethal harvest. From now on the recovery and distribution of this project was the responsibility of Angel. Failure had only one reward—death.

Angel languished in his hotel suite. He enjoyed the challenge of another assignment and the ultimate power of life and death it gave him over others. Adrenaline surged through his veins at the mere thought of what lay ahead and he longed for the sexual excitement of a woman. He quickly keyed in the number and waited. His pimp answered and listened carefully as Angel gave his instructions.

The women he used were easily controlled and they were acceptable as a fringe benefit to boost his ego. Later that evening two elegantly dressed young ladies conversant with his needs knocked gently on the entrance to his suite. For Angel this was the definitive touch to a successful day. The girls meant no more than that. Although both well into their eighteenth year and experienced in the art of seduction, they hated this animal. Bruised and bloodied from his treatment, their recompense came in a very generous form. To be in Angel's favour meant good food and up-market accommodation. To fall from grace invariably resulted in their rapid descent into the clutches of the brothel keepers. Once reduced to this level, only a short period of time elapsed before a once youthful form became haggard, disease ridden and worthless. Those who for a while managed to survive this enforced regime soon found that their life was short lived.

As he lay spent on the bed the two whores had vacated, Angel remembered the events with a quiet smile. They had been so obedient, their performance almost perfection as they undertook things no European could even imagine. He wasn't stupid and knew they used him as surely as he used them. For the moment he closed his eyes and thought of what the future required of him.

Vaughan and his ragged bunch of seamen would be well on their way to the rendezvous planned weeks ahead.

+++

MV *Kia Hua* was on passage from Pusan in South Korea to Mombassa on the east coast of Africa. According to the log she had been making a good eighteen knots since departure. If the weather held, which was unlikely for this time of year, she would arrive two days early. No penalty clauses this trip. With the merchant marine full of specialist carriers and container ships it was becoming harder and harder for tramps to survive, but somehow their agent always managed to obtain another shipment to fill the holds. This time it was bulks of aluminium, a nightmare to secure. With the abundant use of steel chains and blocks, it was positioned in the centre of each hold. The Cargo Officer and the Bosun swore that only a hurricane could move it. Captain Ian Hope, a meticulous mariner in every way, always made a point of checking the hatch notebook and the disposition of the freight in the holds in order to facilitate the cargo plan. It had now become more of a tradition than a requirement, for the entire crew knew his standards. Captain Hope loved the sea. He believed that a ship was a living thing and the oceans of the world no more and no less than a conflict of quarrelsome elements. Now more than anything else, his heart belonged to this tired old lady who ploughed her passage with dogged determination.

This was his last command; soon he would reach the age of compulsory retirement. Hope continued to fill in the ship's log in the section marked "Captain's comments," finally signing his name and dating it in black ink that issued in a fine line from a Parker fountain pen. Once this daily ritual was completed he stood in front of the full length mirror that was fitted to the back of his cabin door. When he was satisfied that his appearance was immaculate he donned his cap. The cloth cover was as white as snow, a fact his steward was well aware of, for this had to be changed daily. Straightening his back and with a final tug to the base of his jacket, he opened the door and left his day cabin to step onto the rear of the bridge. As he stood there, his eyes wandered slowly from one side of the deck to the other; it met his strict requirements. Hope noticed that the officer of the watch, Jenkins, the second mate, was unaware of his presence.

Without making a sound he stood there waiting. "How goes it?" was the first warning that he was not alone. Jenkins swore quietly under his breath. He hadn't heard the Skipper arrive and that was unacceptable.

"Fine, Sir. The Satellite Navigation equipment is playing up a bit but sparks reckons it's a loose aerial coupling and will have it fixed sometime today."

Hope was used to the mass of electronics that now festooned the back of his bridge but having mastered the art of celestial navigation he was still unable to accept that technology had completely defeated a compass and sextant.

"Anything else to report?"

"Nothing of real importance, Sir but we have two small craft directly astern of us at a range of thirty miles. They've been in the same position since I came on watch."

"Doubt if they're worth worrying about." Hope stepped forward and stared out of the forward bridge windows to survey his kingdom. The company pennant flying from the forward mast was up and stiff, the ever increasing gusts tugged viciously along its length.

"The weather's changing. Keep me informed on the hour."

"Roger, Sir, I'll note your order in the log."

For the remainder of that day every time Hope came on the bridge he enquired as to the exact position of the two boats; it never varied more than a cable or two. The wind had begun to increase in its ferocity and he ordered that all hatch covers be checked every four hours until it abated. It was late into the middle watch as they cleared the straits of Formosa when the duty deck officer called his captain.

"Sir, I have those two small vessels at a range of fifteen miles abaft the beam and approaching rapidly."

The seas were becoming steep and short and the wind was whipping the top of each wave into the air. Hope took his time reaching the bridge for, like his ship, age was beginning to take its toll. In his younger years a disturbed night's sleep never seemed to matter, but now he needed time to dress and gather his thoughts. The ship was beginning to roll dramatically, a fact he hadn't noticed whilst asleep. He put out his hand and grabbed at the safety rail. Another wave attacked the ship from the beam, lifting and rolling the massive weight of steel and cargo as if it were a feather in the wind, until its force was spent and it let go. Tumbling like a lump of lead into the trough, her aged hull twisted and battled to find the correct stability before the following mountain of black water hit her. There was no time for the bow to lift and climb over this one. The ensuing wave was well formed from its passage across the open sea and it engulfed the fo'c'sle and deck with white surging foam. The old lady was having none of it and broke free shaking a deluge of water from her skirts. During this rapid see-sawing motion Hope became soaked by the spray that showered the bridge. He positioned himself on the Port bridge wing with a pair of binoculars and painstakingly scanned the area directly astern. He was aware of the possibilities that existed, they could either be pirates or the despicable Chinese Navy who supplemented their meagre earnings by arresting the passage of lawful shipping and removing what they always referred to as "contraband". Each possibility was a dilemma. The *Kia Hua* could not outrun either of these adversaries and, with not another steamer in sight, there would be no witnesses to any unlawful assault.

Hope decided to continue his course and direction. There was no point in capitulating early, and perhaps the storm would worsen. The bows dipped again into another seemingly bottomless trough and the ship began to shudder violently. As much as she wanted rid of her burden the weight of water was too much. The bow didn't rise and a wave much broader than it was high was bearing down on the bridge with only the superstructure barring its progress. "Brace yourself," shouted the Officer of the Watch. Instantly there was a darkness surrounding them as the deluge blotted out their entire world. That moment seemed an eternity until the water cleared and three men stared forward. All the hatch covers were intact and everything was where it should be.

"Maintain full power—it's just possible we'll leave our friends behind if this weather continues."

"Aye, aye, Sir."

Hope, albeit soaked to the skin, settled into his chair and prepared himself mentally for a long night.

The storm exhausted itself two hours later; spray still covered the fo'c'sle but the worst was over and Hope returned to his cabin.

The early morning sun was masked by dark clouds. Hope could now clearly identify the two vessels closing from astern. They had waited for the daylight. His ship now had an unwelcome escort, a pair of fast motor gunboats. Although being smashed and covered by the sea as they powered up from one trough to face another, they were closing fast. One craft leading the other, its dark grey painted hull formed a direct line like a shark homing in on helpless prey. Hope stared at the rust streaks that ran from stem to stern; he despised this lack of basic ship husbandry, it indicated a distinct lack of discipline. As the foremost vessel drew near he could see the Commanding

Officer had wedged himself tightly into a corner of the open bridge. This man was resting his elbows on the bridge screen as he levelled his binoculars and gave them the once over.

His contempt for men such as these boiled up inside him but he knew that any attempt at resistance would be suicidal. As he continued to stare aft his thoughts were rudely interrupted by the Communications Officer, Merridith.

"Sir, the vessel astern has demanded we slow down and prepare for boarding. They say they have information that we're carrying contraband and unless we heave to they will be forced to open fire."

"Any excuse," thought Hope.

"Very well. Ring on slow ahead Mr Davis, get the watch on deck to lower the accommodation ladder for our guests."

"Roger, Sir."

Although small, compared to the super-tankers, the old *Kia Hua* soared over the approaching gun boat like a huge mountain. Having slowed to five knots the lee created by her bulk enabled the craft to come alongside with apparent ease despite the heavy swell. Hope could see the group of armed men ready to jump the gap that separated them but, even as the distance closed to less than one yard, they waited. Then they moved. All were fleet of foot as if crossing the gap were an everyday event. Once these men were up the companionway and on the deck, a defensive circle was formed. Not a word was said; they just stood, their weapons ready to use, in threatening silence. It was not long before their leader appeared. Hope had previously broadcast to his crew that they had better get up and be dressed to receive their visitors. He knew that they would now be ready and waiting for their cabins to be searched. Some would be attempting to hide items of value hoping that they would not be found. Others would be more open.

Hope considered the situation, and aware that even the Chinese enjoyed formality, he walked forward to meet his uninvited callers. The leader was short and had a dark unemotional stare. This alone caused those present to become troubled with their own predicament. Hope realised that the man's eyes were studying every detail and seemed to miss little. "Captain, I am Chung Loi." His voice was effeminate and high pitched, but his pronunciation of the English language was understandable. "You will muster your crew on the main deck and wait for further instructions. My men will search your ship."

Hope recognised that the situation was futile and this man would take what he wanted. "May I inform my crew of your request?"

"Yes."

The loudspeaker gave out the message but it also amplified Hope's fear.

"Can I leave an officer on the bridge?"

Chung pointed to Davis. "Leave him."

In his own language his voice sounded harsh and cruel as he issued instructions to his men. Hope's crew had arrived in dribs and drabs much to the annoyance of their visitor. He seemed to lose his temper and by shouting at his men motivated them into using their rifle butts to move people along. Most meandered around the main deck, waiting for it to end. Hope, having been soaked to the skin and feeling the effect of a long night, ordered the Bosun to move the men into the shelter of the superstructure and for them not to oppose anyone, no matter what. He was tired and perspiring far more than he should. Following his men, he took up the rear of the group. It was becoming difficult for him to breathe and he collapsed to the deck clutching his chest. The world for him was becoming vague. He felt the strong hands of the Bosun lift and support him; for this he was thankful. From what seemed far away the soldiers were shouting but he could not understand. Even in pain a sharp dig in the back with a rifle butt had little effect. Hope was gently helped to a side bulkhead and laid on the green painted steel deck. Those with coats gave them up to make a pillow. The medic tried to find a pulse—it was faint but there. Hope looked with staring eyes at his men. As he lay there unable to move or speak, he watched the Bosun walk towards their captors and try to make them understand that they needed help. The soldier looked at the Bosun who towered over him, grinned, bowed, then without blinking an eye smashed the rifle butt into his groin. Hope felt a fear rising up inside him as the Bosun fell screaming to the deck. He knew that these were no ordinary pirates. When the crew moved to help, the Chinese soldier levelled his rifle, the snap from a released safety catch creating a dread in them all.

It seemed an eternity as they waited. The cold wet air penetrated their clothes. Nobody had dressed to stand and wait on a wind-battered deck. As Chung returned, Hope inwardly prayed that it was over and they would leave. He watched the man stop, give some orders, then walk to the side of the ship. His men were disciplined and quickly surrounded the shivering crew. Hope stared up at him and tried to listen as he spoke.

"Your Captain is unwell." Without any indication of compassion showing on his face he drew his revolver and shot Hope three times. A hail of bullets scythed the crew down where they stood.

Chung signalled with his hand to one of his men, who ran swiftly across the deck and up the ladder to the bridge. Two shots rang out in succession; Davis died not knowing why. Chung went to the starboard side and motioned to the waiting craft. 1205 came abreast only for the interval of time it took to toss a bundle of black canvas body bags onto the bottom of the gangway. These were swiftly retrieved by two men. After 1205 had manoeuvred away to a safe distance of about 1000 yards, the other vessel began its approach. Once correctly positioned alongside, it transferred a group of poorly dressed and unkempt individuals, who for three days had been crammed into its tiny accommodation.

Kenneth Vaughan was the first to reach the deck and see the carnage. "Good job, Chung, that's what the boss wanted."

He nodded acknowledgement and went with Vaughan to the bridge. Those who were not required immediately for specific duties went below to make themselves comfortable in the now vacant accommodation.

The soldiers had not been idle during this period of transition, for they had encased each corpse in a weighted body bag. With this grisly task complete they pitched each bundle unceremoniously over the side. As each sack hit the water it floated for a minute or two before the air escaped, then vanished beneath the surface.

Chung waited until he was alone with Vaughan; "Our mutual friend ordered me to remind you that to avoid any suspicion the ship's present passage schedule isn't to be deviated from unless you're told otherwise." With that he left the *Kia Hua*.

Vaughan and his crew had been selectively recruited, although not personally by Angel. His agents had scoured the bars and seedy haunts of Hong Kong to locate these dregs of the earth. The men chosen were those who, if paid enough, would pledge their allegiance to the devil. They were the trash, the unwanted of the Merchant Marine. Most had turned to petty crime to survive but still retained those skills that were necessary to operate a ship.

Kenneth Vaughan was different. He had been in front of a tribunal for gross misconduct, then disciplined by the United States maritime authorities. His punishment established in him a hatred for authority and those who administered it. He knew that the crew of *Kia Hua* were to be slaughtered but it did not bother him. Now was the time to make some serious money and get back to a life of luxury. The Chinese vessels were now a mere speck on the horizon, as he wandered around the ship that was his to command. He passed amongst the crew, and was inordinately conscious that he would have to handle these creatures with an iron fist. They studied him and saw a man who was capable of looking after himself. In his well fitting uniform, he was an impressive figure, over six feet tall, wide shoulders and heavily muscled. The set of the mouth in a long face gave a mere hint of the cruelty that lay beneath the surface. His eyes expressed an utter contempt for all those beneath him. The ice-cold stare that emanated from them confirmed each man's worst fear.

The future was looking better than he had ever imagined, thanks to the Angel.

FOUR

The flight tickets and hotel bookings arrived at Adrian's house by special delivery. In the same envelope were details of the ship, and every officer on board.

Selwyn noted a departure time of 1345. Allowing for the nine hour flight, they should land in Nairobi at 2045 and, if all went well, they should arrive at the hotel before midnight. Selwyn handed Adrian the information on the ship and its crew, but retained the travel details.

Before they left, arrangements had to be implemented to ensure that the business would operate without Selwyn's guiding hand. These took time but so well oiled were the wheels of the organisation that the changes were effected without too many levels of authority having to be delegated.

Adrian spent most of his time in the library. He scrutinised the details and memorised the photographs of the *Kia Hua* and her officers. Each had achieved satisfactory results at the many maritime schools they had attended. He scanned each summary meticulously.

Adrian examined Hope's photograph, and attempted to analyse his thoughts. With the study of each individual concluded, the whole package was returned to its envelope. With time to spare before dinner, he went in search of old Joe. He didn't find Joe, Joe found him. Adrian respected this man, for he was an incorrigible scoundrel who scratched a livelihood by pitting his wits against the land and man-made laws to supply all and sundry with good fresh meat at a reasonable price. There was even a judge on his far-reaching list of customers who never said no to a well-hung flank of venison.

"Joe, I need some advice and you're just be the man to give it."

With his pipe jammed between his lips, Joe sat on an old tree stump and smiled. "What kind of advice can I give? You've got money, a successful business and a lovely house to live in."

Adrian paused for a few seconds saying nothing as he formed the question in his mind. "How can you tell if someone's lying?"

"Watch their eyes, son, watch their eyes. If they look directly into yours it's unlikely, but if during the conversation they wander away, it's a good chance they are. When you talked to me I could always tell, especially when you were a brat but as you got older you became more honest and then I trusted you."

"Are you sure that it always works?"

"It does for me. Anyway I've things to do, can't sit 'ere all day chatting to you. I'll be on my way and you take care."

Adrian stayed where he was and watched as Joe simply melted into the forest. Not a sound did he make. One minute you could see him clearly, then he was gone.

+++

13 June 1993

The whole household rose early on the day of departure. Mrs Duke made a good old-fashioned English breakfast, commenting more than once that they didn't know when they would next have a decent meal. Mr Duke drove them to the station, an act that always frustrated Adrian as he never drove at more than thirty miles an hour irrespective of the road conditions or permitted speed limits. "More haste less speed," was his customary remark. As always, they arrived on time.

The journey was as monotonous as all train journeys are and both men became lost in their own thoughts, Selwyn in the depths of a Douglas Reaman novel and Adrian in the tasks that lay ahead.

They arrived at Heathrow at exactly twelve a.m., checked in their luggage, then walked the short distance to the first-class lounge. Charles Dawning and Janice were already there and obviously enjoying each other's company as her laughter could be clearly heard over the general hubbub.

Whatever the joke was, on seeing Selwyn and Adrian, they quietened down.

"Good, you're on time; at least the Royal Navy taught you something," commented Charles.

Adrian looked at his father's friend sitting there. He felt a sadness for this man and his upper-class attitudes. The system this man and many like him represented was falling apart at the seams. People now had more respect for those who came from different backgrounds, those who had clambered up the tree of success without the assistance of the "old school tie." "God," he thought, "I could have ended up like that." It had been the RNR that had made him realise that the world was full of real people who worked and played hard but got nowhere fast.

Time passed quickly as they chatted about the arrangements. Adrian was not amused at having to play the role of Janice's partner and she in turn teased him for all it was worth.

"It'll only be for two weeks, *darling,* then we can separate and, with luck, we'll never have to see each other again," she taunted.

"It's not sharing a cabin that bothers me, I've seen the female form many times—I'm sure yours is nothing special, or is it?"

"Darling, just try touching and it'll be more than your fingers that get burnt. In fact your masculinity will be permanently damaged."

"You think you're something special, well, time will tell, my *darling*."

Selwyn sat in silence, smiling occasionally as he secretly kept score. Charles made the odd attempt to intercede but was always pushed aside by one combatant or the other. Frustrated, he went to the bar for a stiff gin, said goodbye to Selwyn and left them to it. When it was time for them to board, Selwyn decided it had been game, set and match to Janice.

Once they were airborne, Selwyn glanced forward to where Janice was sitting. She was on her own and had obviously planned it that way when the flight had been arranged. She was dressed in a tight-fitting denim outfit that highlighted the curvature of her body. He laughed inwardly; she was all woman and he was well aware that Adrian was licking his wounds from her verbal attack. It was going to be an interesting "vacation".

Selwyn stared out of the window. The air was clear, the sky blue with only a few sparse clouds to shroud the ever-changing perspective. From fifty-five thousand feet his homeland to all appearances was a barren wasteland. The scene constantly changed from desert to large forested areas, then back to scrub and the occasional river that seemed like a pencil line drawn over parchment. He checked his watch. They would soon be approaching Nairobi.

The aircraft began its descent and the cabin staff drew attention to the "seat-belt" and "no smoking" signs which had just been illuminated. Janice looked out of her window; at first there were only a few signs of human habitation but quickly the outskirts of a city that held two million people came into view. Nairobi airport was much like any other, in the tropics - a large sweep of sun-bleached concrete. Only the black scars of aircraft tyres hitting the runway differentiated between one area and another. There were buildings that embodied at least four decades in their design and use. The most predominant of these was the modern three-storey central concourse that served as departure, arrival and control tower. The landing was smooth but once they were inside the terminal building "Manyana" became the order of the day. The queue at passport control was prolonged by the one and only duty officer. Once clear and through customs they made their way to the air-conditioned transit lounge. This brief stopover enabled muscles to be stretched and a meal to be eaten in relative comfort before the flight to Mombassa.

Due to a minor defect their flight was called twenty minutes late. On completion of the security procedures, all the passengers were ushered through an external door and into the warm night air. Within a few minutes Janice began to feel tiny rivulets of perspiration running down her back. The passengers and flight crew were directed by armed airport employees towards the waiting aircraft. The temperature was twenty-two degrees centigrade; by comparison Mombassa would be humid and hotter. The plane, a thirty year old veteran Dakota, was in pristine condition but lacked the opulence of major commercial airlines. Only when everyone had been counted onboard by the only male steward, and baggage secured, was the safety brief commenced. The take-off defied description as the pilot toyed with the warm upward flowing air currents and gentle cross winds. The craft seemed to rattle its way down the runway for an eternity until finally, free of the ground and in its own environment, it soared as a bird, almost silently, into the sky. Adrian admired this "seat of the pants" style of flying and the courage of the pilots who were often required to land anywhere, whether it be a good solid runway or some hastily cleared dust-covered stretch in the middle of nowhere. For him the roar of the engines was music to his ears, the smell of the exhaust perfume to his nostrils and the style of this machine, classic. "This is flying," he thought.

The sun had set some hours before and the only signs of life in the area below were the occasional flecks of light that seemed to twinkle like fireflies, then, as quickly as they appeared, were gone, disappearing into the darkness. The descent to Moi International Airport was swift and the landing as unpredictable as the take-off. The higher ground temperature gave less lift as the density of the air beneath the wings decreased. The wheels grabbed at the runway but the speed of the descent tossed it back into the air shaking the aircraft and its passengers furiously. Those who had travelled this route before gripped the sides of their seats and grimaced at the pilot's antics but some shrieked loudly with fright. When the cabin door was opened, the cool air of the interior rapidly dissipated. Strange smells invaded the atmosphere of the cabin as the humid environment took over.

Adrian and Selwyn had changed into loose-fitting cotton clothing in Nairobi but Janice, who had remained in her London clothes, again began to perspire. It was not long before her tight denims became uncomfortable and her form-fitting jacket was hastily removed. Adrian could not help but notice that Janice's denim shirt was saturated front and back, revealing the outline of her breasts more than it should.

Passport Control took well over thirty minutes as each person's identity was checked and in some cases, double-checked. It was apparent to Adrian that Janice was feeling the heat and should have changed her outfit. As the petty delays continued she became irritable.

Adrian looked at her and smiled almost contemptuously as she struggled with her bags. It was Selwyn who eased some of the burden by placing her luggage on a baggage trolley along with his, leaving Adrian to carry his own. For once she was grateful of male assistance, having already made up her mulish mind that if Adrian had offered, she was going to tell him where to shove his help.

As they made their way to the taxi-rank, Janice followed in angry silence. The driver of the first car waiting in the ragged row of vehicles got out to help Selwyn but left Adrian to his own devices. Aware that in some areas whites were only tolerated because of the money they had, Adrian disregarded the snub and climbed in the front passenger seat. The driver waited for a moment and then turning his head asked Selwyn for the destination: "Mombassa Beach Hotel, please."

Adrian said nothing, but wound his window down. The tired old Mercedes diesel roared into life, leaving a choking cloud of black exhaust smoke in its wake. The road from the airport to the hotel was once well founded but the ravages of heavy transport and disrepair had taken their toll. Potholes assumed the identities of mini-craters as the wheels dropped into and bounced themselves out, much to the discomfort of the trio. The driver only seemed to slow down when they reached speed ramps, but was soon completing a hundred kilometres an hour despite the traffic and road conditions.

Janice was in a foul mood and sweating profusely. "Adrian, for Christ's sake close that bloody window."

He attempted to ignore her, smiling wickedly at her distress but having won the battle he relented and closed the window. It was as they passed under the huge metal elephant tusks at the entrance to the city, that the stark reality of life in an impoverished African state was plain to see. There were a few shops and an abundance of bars. Here men and women could purchase and act out their wildest fantasy for a few paltry shillings.

The large expanse of land that surrounded the hotel was out of bounds to those who worked the bars. Tall palms with coloured lights encircled and complemented the entrance. The road surface was smooth and well illuminated. Sounds of laughter could be heard coming from the beach. The moment the taxi drew to a halt, four porters in immaculate white shirts and perfectly pressed black trousers were in attendance. Armed guards postured lethargically around the entrance, engaged in what appeared to be idle chatter but all the time their eyes checked every individual, black or white.

Adrian walked directly to reception and addressed the young girl behind the counter: "I am Mr Viper, you have reservations for us."

Without even flickering an eyelid she replied in an equally curt manner, "Your party have suites—315, and 316 which is a double."

Janice was in the foulest of tempers. Leaning across the counter she snatched key 316 and, without a word, disappeared into the lift. Adrian had to admit that he had sanctioned the sharing of accommodation to create the correct image. The thought of sharing a room for three whole days was unbearable. Aware that Janice would not be in the best of moods, he wandered over to the bar and ordered a large whisky and soda. For a while he leaned against the polished surface and sipped at his drink. When it was finished he made his way to suite 316.

Adrian paused for a moment in the corridor and decided that a truce would be the most sensible thing to declare, but to his amazement the door was locked. He hesitated, walked a few yards down the corridor and knocked on Selwyn's door.

"Excuse me but I must use your balcony." He carefully swung himself around the dividing partition and entered suite 316 via the balcony.

Janice was revelling in a cool shower and was unaware of his entrance. Now that she felt more human and was dry she looked at herself in the full length mirror. Her body was slender; a few more inches on her breasts would make it even more desirable. Her bust, although petite, was still firm as she gently felt and examined every inch. Why was it, she wondered, most men had a mammary fixation? - something akin to suckling babes, no doubt. The rest of her was as near perfect as age would allow, plus beautiful thick long blonde hair. Her legs were firm but not muscular and as shapely as they had ever been. Now feeling refreshed she wrapped a huge fluffy white bath robe around her body and walked into the day room. Adrian, was lounging on the broad balcony in a wickerwork chair enjoying the cool breeze that wafted off the sea. It was a good feeling, a sensation that brought hundreds of memories flooding back.

The serenity of the moment was only disturbed when the sight of two legs protruding from the chair surprised her: "You found your way in then?"

Adrian calmly replied, "Yes, thank you."

She walked towards him and looked straight into his eyes: "Don't you think we should sit and talk instead of fighting each other?"

"My sentiments precisely."

She pulled her bath robe tight around her and settled down into the remaining wicker chair. "OK, first, it may help if I tell you about myself. Once I was married to a very wealthy man who beat the shit out of me when things went wrong with his life." For a moment she remained silent, then she drew her knees up to her chin and resting on them she gave a deep sigh and continued. "His death caused me to have more relief than remorse, a maniac who spent good money on fast cars. After one of his regular drinking sprees with his so-called friends, he decided to show off his driving skills but had a disagreement with a bridge support on the auto route and killed himself. I promised myself there and then no man would ever get that close to me again." She paused and her face expressed a far away look as if she was with someone else. "Fate had other plans for me though, and I met and fell deeply in love with a Naval Officer. Gregory was murdered whilst on active service but he left me with the only human being I truly love, my son. Today I'm recognised and respected in my own right, I've broadened my social scene by being an opportunist and I still grab every chance with both hands."

Adrian remained silent but listened intently, his body language indicated he understood how she felt and was interested in her.

Janice continued talking so softly that Adrian had to concentrate to hear. "Do you realise that my job didn't exist over fifty years ago? Now attitudes towards female reporters have been stood on their heads. Discrimination still exists but today there are many women in newsrooms and even more as foreign correspondents. The only thing that prevents others duplicating my skills is an unfounded lack of confidence. Most people can achieve anything so long as they put their minds to it. Hard work and long hours have earned me the power to make decisions. I'm not seeking fame, but success. My intellectual prowess and audacity have accomplished this, not my femininity. I don't apologise for being a woman but I am the best at what I do."

"Well it seems we have something in common," commented Adrian.

"What's that?"

"I am the best at what I do."

"Very droll."

"Anyway, from what I've discovered, you're quite a remarkable woman."

"How can you say that?"

"That you've spent the majority of your life in places where most men would fear to tread and came through relatively unscathed. You were voted Journalist of the Year for your coverage of an IRA incident."

"Oh! So you were the person asking questions. My friends told me someone was inquiring into my background."

Adrian nodded; "Well how about calling a truce until this is over? I'll respect your professionalism if you honour mine. With your journalistic inquisitiveness and my knowledge of ships, if there's something wrong then I'm sure we'll find it."

"Agreed, but I'm not going to share a bed with you."

"No problem," said Adrian pointing towards the day room, "I'll sleep on the sofa, it looks comfortable enough. You can have the luxury of cold sheets and an empty bed. That way we have separate rooms except for the facilities."

It was well past two in the morning when they finished talking. The long journey and the heat were beginning to take their toll as tiredness gradually overcame them. The balmy air and relaxed attitude that now invaded the night almost found them falling asleep on the balcony. Adrian recognised the lethargy from having spent many a long night on the bridge of a warship. Although not wanting to break the spell, he suggested that they had better get some rest. They moved from the balcony to their separate rooms. As Janice shut the door she whispered, "Good-night, sleep well."

Adrian had already removed his clothes and was nestling his body into the contours of the couch.

Janice went to bed with the wrong thoughts running around her head. She had enjoyed talking to Adrian. He was intelligent and good looking. Many men in a similar situation would have tried to take advantage but he had behaved as a perfect gentleman which she had wrongly assumed he wasn't.

Adrian slept well that night and it was the rising of the sun that woke him. Rested, he went to the window, stretched, yawned and looked out at a flat calm sea. The clear blue sky guaranteed another burning day. He took deep breaths of fresh sea air; it felt good to be alive. Determined not to waste any more time, he showered and dressed in a loose-fitting shirt, white shorts and sandals.

When presentable, he knocked gently on the bedroom door. There wasn't a sound from within. Without thinking he opened the door but she was still fast asleep. Both pillows had found their way to the floor and at some time during the night the thin cotton sheets had been kicked aside. As she lay there curled up like a baby with her knees almost under her chin, the sunlight, filtered by the net curtains that covered the balcony doors, shimmered across the bed giving her an almost angelic charm. She must have sensed his presence for she straightened out and rolled over onto her back.

Disgusted with what he was doing, he quietly shut the door. To redeem himself he telephoned reception and ordered a continental breakfast for two along with a large jug of freshly squeezed orange juice. As he replaced the receiver Janice walked into the lounge wearing a wrap-around sarong. He couldn't help but notice the woman who stood before him, even though she had just got out of bed—the blonde hair and roundness of her face were captivating. Through the thin material he could make out her firm thighs and shapely frame. It would be very hard for him not to desire this woman who retained the strength of character to shut him out completely.

"Good morning, did you sleep well?" Adrian asked. "I died when my head hit the pillow."

"Yes thank you; I didn't realise how tired I was. Have you finished with the bathroom?"

Adrian thought that despite her hair being a mess she still had, even at this hour, that something men desired. "Yes, but don't be long, I've ordered breakfast."

He walked into the bedroom and out on to the balcony where they had made their pact. On a day like this, the sun was warm and a cool ocean breeze wafted across a clear blue sky. Not far away was the beach of sun-bleached sand where local children were already playing. A few Arab dhows were at anchor off the beach waiting for their chance to offer the use of their craft to tourists. He looked down into the hotel grounds; the tennis courts were full of the obese and aged keep-fit brigade who were making the most of the temperate airs. Later the heat would become unbearable.

His mindful meanderings were interrupted by a knock on the door.

Selwyn was standing there.

"Breakfast, boss."

Adrian smiled at his friend, removed the tray from his hands and walked out to the balcony and placed it on the wickerwork table.

"I've had mine and I'm off to get some wheels. Walking around in this heat will be hell. See you later."

Adrian waved as Selwyn left.

"That looks good." Janice was still wearing the sarong but had now adorned her head with one of the hotel towels. The combination of her wet skin and fresh fragrance incited his animal instincts.

The freshly baked croissants filled with lashings of jam and butter dissolved readily in their mouths.

As they sat in the bright morning sun, Janice pondered on what would have been if they had met under different circumstances. Would they have argued or just passed polite conversation? He was rich and attractive - many a woman must have attempted to seduce him for that fact alone, and yet he had never married.

"What shall we do today?" asked Adrian.

She was lost in thought. "Pardon?"

"*What* shall we do today?"

She thought for a moment before replying, "While it's still relatively cool let's go and have a chat with the Harbour Master. This afternoon we can relax by the pool."

"Sounds good to me. When Selwyn returns we can travel in comfort and inspect the docks at our leisure."

"OK, I'm off to get dressed."

Janice returned, her long hair tied back into a pony tail. She was wearing shorts that exposed her shapely legs to the full and a loose blouse that, when the breeze drifted across her body, confirmed she wasn't wearing a bra.

Adrian was impressed at her nerve and didn't fail to notice that she had a perfectly flat stomach between the shorts and top.

"Now we're ready I suggest we go and wait for Selwyn."

As they entered the large expanse of the entrance area, a stranger stared lustily at her legs, but his companion, a rather plain girl interrupted his thoughts with a savage jab to the ribs.

Adrian smiled.

As if ordered, a hand-painted, black, open-topped Land Rover drew up outside with Selwyn at the wheel.

"To the docks, and don't spare the horses," Adrian shouted above the noise of the engine.

Janice settled herself on the back seat and asked, "How long will it take us to get there?"

Selwyn turned his head: "About thirty minutes, all being well."

The narrow road was virtually traffic-free. As they entered the outskirts of the town they drove by dilapidated wooden houses which at one time belonged to the white colonialists who had governed and managed all the business in the area. Now they were painted in gaudy colours and the numerous rooms divided into homes for more than one family. Children stopped their play and watched them, their large white eyes shining from round black faces.

The town itself was busy but the dock area was almost deserted. A few rusting coasters and tugs lay at anchor offshore. The stooped heads of a dozen cargo cranes hung like giant flamingos waiting to feed from the ships. The harbour itself shimmered in the sunlight, the few small boats that moved on the water gave a breath of life to an otherwise indifferent scene. A handful of people were gathered by the doors of the empty sheds. Selwyn drew the vehicle to a halt, got out, leaving the others to sit and wait. He walked briskly across the concrete roadway and began talking to the waiting men. Janice and Adrian couldn't hear what was said but there was much waving of arms and laughter. Selwyn was away for a good ten minutes and on returning was in a sober mood. He leant on the door and spoke softly. "The *Kia Hua* is due in this afternoon. She will begin unloading on arrival and from what those men have been told, load her next cargo as soon as possible. They intend to work non-stop to turn this ship around.

Adrian got out and walked to the edge of the wharf. The only sounds were the shrill cries of sea birds and the gentle splashing of water against the harbour wall. At the extreme end of the jetty, where twin concrete towers rose towards the clear blue sky, a large coaster could be seen loading hundreds of sacks of cement from the Bamburi Portland Cement Company. He stood there staring out to sea, his mind wandering from one thought to another. From the cursory look of the warehouses as they had entered the yard, most had appeared empty. He remained standing on the same spot for almost ten minutes. Janice wanted to get out but Selwyn had motioned her with his hand to remain in her seat.

With the rudiments of an idea sketched in his mind, Adrian returned from the water's edge and settled himself behind the wheel; Selwyn climbed in. Adrian started the engine and quickly drove down the jetty. "We don't have time to mess about, I'll check with the Harbour Master and confirm the *Kia Hua*'s arrival. You drive around and see what's happening. Selwyn, you stay with Janice. Talk to anyone and everyone but don't let her out of your sight. An attractive white woman on her own would not be a wise move."

"Well at least he considers me attractive and is bothered about my welfare."

They stopped outside a whitewashed concrete building that served as the dock control office. As Adrian got out, Janice moved swiftly from the back to behind the steering wheel. With a screech of tyres she began driving at forty to fifty kilometres an hour along the jetty.

"We can cover more ground this way," Janice shouted above the roar of the engine.

Adrian entered the building and was greeted by a clerk.

"Can I speak to the harbour master, please?"

The clerk left Adrian while he made a telephone call.

After he had replaced the receiver he beckoned Adrian to follow. They went across the office to a back room, and as soon as he entered, the door was closed behind him. Adrian looked at the man standing in front of him. He was in his early forties, tall and had maintained a healthy physique. He had a long face with deep set eyes and beneath a large nose was amassed a straggly black beard. It was his offhand manner that bothered Adrian, as it was quite unusual from a man whose prime objective in life was to give assistance.

"What can I do for you?" The voice was deep and guttural and the English fragmented. Adrian introduced himself and then continued, "Two friends and I are booked on the *Kia Hua* which I gather is arriving today. It would be appreciated if you could notify the captain that we'll remain in our hotel until she's ready."

"Certainly. It will be my pleasure and if there's anything else I can do for you during your stay in Mombassa ***don't hesitate*** to ask. I'm busy, so you'll have to excuse me."

Without another word being spoken, the man moved forward and to prevent an entanglement Adrian found himself backing out the door and into the outer office.

As he left, he glanced up at the sun. It was going to be a scorcher and it wasn't even midday.

He started to walk down the jetty towards the entrance gate when the Land Rover came out of a side opening. The smell of burning rubber filled his nostrils as all four wheels locked alongside him.

"Jump in, it's too bloody hot to play detective. Time for a drink and a swim."

Adrian got into the back behind Janice, the fragrance of her perfume tantalising his senses. The Land Rover moved off rapidly, causing him to hold on. A sharp bend was negotiated much faster than was wise, and Adrian's eyes were drawn to the paleness of her legs. The white shorts she was wearing had ridden up her thighs leaving little to the imagination. A bump in the road brought him down to earth as he realised that he couldn't be such a bastard as merely to use her. What was making him think like this? She wasn't a cheap tart to be had for a few gin and tonics. He didn't have more time to examine his confused thoughts as they halted abruptly at the hotel entrance. Janice let them both out, then moved the Rover from the driveway of the hotel and parked in the shade of some magnolia trees.

Once into the cooler confines of the hotel Janice made straight for the bar and ordered three large fresh orange juices with plenty of ice. The waiter delivered the drinks and they sat in silence until he was well out of the way.

Selwyn looked at his companions: "We could be in trouble—Daniel entering the lion's den was easy compared to this. At least, he could see the lions."

Adrian knew something was troubling his friend. "You feel uneasy about this whole business, don't you?"

"Last night I had a vision of the mountains and all I wanted to do was drink water but the guns kept us moving forward."

Janice laughed: "What are you going on about?"

Selwyn explained in simple terms what he believed.

"Don't tell me you actually believe that witch doctor stuff. The worst that can happen is we'll get on that boat."

"Ship," interrupted Adrian.

"OK, a bloody ship, and find nothing, just like those God-forsaken docks."

Selwyn smiled at her: "What you think is of little significance—I accept what I see in my mind. The problem that remains is translating the message."

"So how do you propose to do that?" asked Janice.

"Simple, I go and see another witch doctor."

"Oh, just like that. Pop down the road, make an appointment and wait your turn."

Selwyn wasn't ruffled by her sarcasm. "Well not exactly like that but almost. Mombassa is set at the cross-roads of numerous cultures. Some are fascinating and others more crudely barbaric. These operate together like two roads going in the same direction but still satisfying the needs of the people. If the white general practitioner doesn't prescribe the answer to remove a curse they go to the seer. As I explained, the best and worst of both cultures. The main difficulty for me is to locate a skilled practitioner. The government has outlawed them in favour of a Christian society, the punishment for practising is death. It will take much searching to ferret out the right person."

Adrian sat silently as his friend cast his own strange spell over Janice. By the end of the conversation she was convinced that Selwyn had a power over others but what it was she could not understand.

"Well I'm off for a swim in the pool—who's going to join me?"

Selwyn nodded to Adrian and rose from his seat: "You two enjoy yourselves, I'm off to find a confidante—I'll take the Land Rover as you obviously won't be needing it."

Adrian and Janice went to change.

He left her in the bathroom and made his way to the pool barely stopping to throw his towel down before plunging into the clear refreshing water. The coolness of the pool cleared his brain and helped relax his body, but he was still disturbed by what his friend had portrayed.

Janice arrived a few minutes later and gingerly slid her body into the water, desperately trying not to wet her hair, which was now tied in a bun.

Adrian swam over to the white tiled side and with one movement pulled himself up onto the edge. It was now well past midday and over eighty in the shade.

The heat rose from the paving stones in unseen waves that encircled the fresh breath of the pool. Janice loved the heat, soaked it up. Although in her early forties, she had retained the fresh figure of a twenty-five year old. She basked in the freedom her occupation gave her, the thrill, the adventure.

"Well, what do you think?" asked Adrian as she slowly swam near to where he sat.

"About what?"

"This whole affair."

"For what it's worth, the whole situation doesn't seem right for the sinking of a ship. The cargo isn't worth much, even the vessel has seen better days and the claim wouldn't amount to a great deal. I feel, call it female intuition, that it's the right vessel but we're missing something. Don't ask me what."

She gazed at Adrian as he sat there dangling his feet in the water. She forced herself to swim away whilst attempting to dismiss the fact that the nearness of him was beginning to bring to the surface feelings she hadn't experienced for some time. He was good looking. His body was splendid, there wasn't an area invaded by unsightly fat and the muscles of his arms and legs were well defined. His intelligence and maturity were a combination rarely found. His old-fashioned attitudes sometimes infuriated her, but he made her laugh.

Adrian's response was an affirmative nod. "I think we should visit the harbour again tomorrow and make our presence known to the Captain."

"OK I'll go with that, but what do we do if everything seems normal?"

"Head for home." She was close to him at that moment and Adrian felt the need to cool off again. The resulting wash covered her as his body hit the water.

"You beast!" she screamed, as she swam towards him and tried to push him under. As their bodies touched, he grabbed her, feeling the firm flesh in his hands as he dragged her down. She in turn felt secure in his grip and enjoyed the thrill that ran through her body. They surfaced together, laughed and for a few moments behaved like children.

"Tomorrow I fancy a dip in the sea; it looks so inviting. Is it safe?"

Adrian looked at her: "Wouldn't count on it. Some years ago a honeymoon couple had a disastrous experience. They went to an isolated spot on the beach; he was a strong swimmer while she stayed close inshore. She heard him scream as his body was hurled out of the water, then he disappeared. I found what was left of him washed up the next day. It wasn't much."

"Oh my God, how horrible!" Janice began to dry her hair, rubbing it energetically. "I must go to the bank."

"What do you need money for? I'm paying all the bills."

"No you're not; I'm an independent lady and I prefer not to be obligated to anyone."

"Fine—suits me. If that's the way you want it."

Their relationship reverted to normal and for once she was hurt on the inside. What was it with this man that she found so fascinating one minute and irritating the next? She was beginning to like him. There was much to desire and respect but also much to confuse. He was a mixture of indifference and understanding, and his warped sense of humour left much to be desired. He obviously cared about many things, but his depth of feeling seemed protected by a barrier that no-one could penetrate.

They lazed away the rest of the afternoon barely saying a word to each other.

It was just after three o'clock when Janice got up and went back to their room.

Adrian remained by the pool.

+++

Selwyn drove slowly into town and then up and down the numerous tracks that radiated from the centre until he ended up in what had once been an up-market neighbourhood. Then he saw the sign, discreetly hidden from the uninitiated but abundantly clear to those who could read it. Strangely, the gardens were still well tended and the house, although aged, had neat curtains at each window, but there was an atmosphere of disrepair. Selwyn parked some distance away as a precaution and walked back to the house.

He knocked on the door and waited.

An old crone bent with the years opened the door and looked at him, her eyes scrutinising every detail.

"What do you want?" she asked roughly.

"To see a friend."

She wavered for a moment but judged him not to be a threat and motioned him into the dark hallway. As his eyes accustomed themselves, he could see that her scrawny right arm was directing him to a solitary wooden bench.

As Selwyn sat, she shuffled away, disappearing into the darkness.

For what seemed an eternity he sat there and waited; he knew his every move was being observed. Soft footsteps came to his ears, and he waited, wondering if this was whom he was destined to meet. His eyes peered into the blackness. A shrivelled old man came into view, his face was primeval; deep lines radiated from a face with dead eyes; anaemic lips covered a toothless void.

"You come in search of the truth?" he asked.

"Yes."

"You already know the truth."

"I have dreams."

"Follow me."

They walked along the dark passage and then down a winding stone staircase into the basement. Flickering candles, set in recesses carved into the walls, cast an eerie yellow light, the overpowering fragrance of incense filled the air. All around were the artefacts that represented the man's craft.

"You're not frightened? Those that still have the courage to visit are always afraid."

"I have some of the skills, but not the wisdom."

"We will dispel your fears and reveal the truth as it is and as it will be."

For more than two hours Selwyn listened whilst, with the shaman's skill and the insight of a true visionary, the wise one muttered ancient charms, his eyes never leaving the talisman laid in front of him on the earthen floor.

"I advise that you go home, but you will not and much pain will be inflicted on your body. Death will not come but it will wave its dark cloak across your path. Follow the way of the light and you will survive."

"What of my friends?"

"They will survive but only if you are close."

When he was finished, the old man stood up and motioned for Selwyn to leave. He still felt confused, but left, leaving a sealed envelope as payment on the floor. The crone was waiting by the open door which she shut as soon as he had passed through. The bright sun irritated his eyes causing him to stumble along the path. He did not see the old woman crossing herself.

+++

Janice, wearing a loose fitting dress suitable for the temperature, picked up her camera and bag of accessories. Undeterred by the distance she decided to walk into Mombassa. The heat of the afternoon was subsiding but she was grateful for the shade provided by the trees and numerous flowering shrubs.

The township was waking up, the afternoon siesta was over. The bank was easily identified by its well-known logo. Janice pushed open the glass door and shivered as the ice-cold air surrounded her. The air-conditioning was obviously at its maximum for the visiting Europeans—the locals wouldn't relish it at all. It took only a few moments for her to complete the transaction and with time to kill she wandered down to the docks. To her amazement, the *Kia Hua* was making its approach to a nearby berth. Her camera was unslung and with telephoto lens fitted she began to take photographs of the vessel as it turned to come alongside. Satisfied that if anything unusual was to be seen, it was now captured on film, she returned to town to have the spool developed whilst she waited. To her the pictures revealed nothing out of the ordinary—it was simply a ship and a very old one at that. On arrival at the hotel she found Adrian relaxing on the balcony, having already showered and changed into slacks and a white short-sleeved shirt.

He stretched out his arms and legs, then checked his watch. "Dinner at seven if that's all right with you. Selwyn will meet us in the dining room. I thought it best to eat early and then get a good night's sleep. We can take a trip down to our ship at first light; that way we may gain the advantage of surprise."

"Thank you for asking me, kind Sir," she replied sarcastically, throwing the photographs into his lap.

"What are these?"

"Take a look."

"The *Kia Hua*, well I'll be dammed."

Adrian studied each picture carefully but none of them revealed anything of significance and, like Janice, he wondered why such an old ship would be worth so much trouble.

Janice said nothing, but disappeared into the bathroom, feeling disheartened. He had offered no comment on the photographs, not even a thank you. She knew he was right about having an early night but was damned if she was going to admit it. The shower was turned from hot to cold and then back to hot again until her exasperation was consumed.

They went down to dinner in silence. Janice wore a sleeveless white dress belted at the waist. Adrian looked at her admiringly; her teeth matched the white of the dress and on her lips was just a hint of pink lipstick. Whatever she chose to wear seemed to suit her to perfection, highlighting the fact that she was a stunning full-blooded female.

Selwyn was waiting for them and had pre-empted the evening apéritif by ordering a moderately inexpensive Muscadet. This was in the process of being chilled and an Australian Claret that he personally recommended was warming to room temperature.

Janice complimented him on his choice of wines, as they engaged each other in sociable conversation. Adrian remained quiet but could hear the clink of glasses and the murmur of voices as other guests chatted in between courses.

The meal over, they decided to have coffee on the veranda. The darkness was rhythmically broken by the sweeping beam of the harbour entrance lighthouse. A cool breeze came in from the sea and somewhere deep in the hotel grounds came the distant throb of popular music. The sounds of the African night filled the air - the continuous droning sound of cicadas and the swish of bats as they landed in the nearby trees. Monkeys could be heard rummaging in the kitchen dustbins and then the rude comment of a chef chasing them away. One of the staff came and spoke to Adrian.

"Excuse me Mr Viper, there's a Captain Hope at reception wanting to speak to you."

"Please give my compliments to the Captain, and ask him if he would care to join us for coffee."

The man nodded in a subservient manner and left.

They didn't have long to wait until the Captain strode in. He was wearing the full tropical uniform of a Merchant Navy Captain and marched towards them. "Mr Viper." Adrian stood, held out his hand, but the offer was ignored. "My apologies for disturbing you but the Dockmaster informed me that you were staying at this hotel and I considered it my duty to come and talk to you."

"Captain," interrupted Janice, "please don't stand on ceremony. Join us for a coffee."

He turned, his cold eyes dismissing her with contempt.

"My vessel is loading and it's my duty to be there. I'm here to save you the trouble of joining my ship. A few days ago we suffered a minor fire in the crew's quarters which has resulted in a reduction of accommodation. Consequently and regretfully, I must advise you that your scheduled passage cannot take place."

Adrian shook his head in a manner of acceptance: "I fully understand and thank you for apprising us of the situation. We'll naturally make other arrangements. It's a minor nuisance to our travel plan but of no real significance."

"I'm pleased you understand."

Selwyn studied the man intently. He knew he was lying.

Adrian thanked him again."

Without another word the man turned and walked towards the reception area.

Adrian left the table and followed at a distance ensuring he couldn't be seen. The captain stopped at the desk and spoke to the receptionist. She smiled, then picked up the nearby telephone and spoke to someone. Seconds later the Manager appeared. The Captain motioned with his right hand in the direction of Adrian's table. The conversation lasted for a few minutes.

Adrian's suspicions were confirmed. Realising that whatever their actions were now, they had to be careful. He returned to the table and re-occupied his chair.

Janice seemed relieved as she said, "Well that's the holiday over and I must say I'm glad we're not going on that ship. I didn't like that man at all. His eyes were ice-cold. I'm sure there was something quite sinister about him."

"The man was lying through his teeth," said Selwyn.

"Wouldn't you, if you weren't Captain Ian Hope?"

Adrian's bombshell astonished them.

"How do you know?" demanded Janice.

Adrian crossed his legs and drank a mouthful of coffee: "When I accepted this, let's call it a quest, Charles gave me a file that included not only the names and a brief summary of all the officers, but as many up-to-date photographs that were available."

"And what other little gems have you been hiding from us?" Janice asked, re-filling her cup.

"None that I know. You acted the part because you didn't know, therefore it's just as well that the photographs remained my secret. Despite the fact that you didn't like the man, you had no reason to believe he wasn't who he said he was. If you think about it, this whole charade was coming to an end until our friend walked in."

Selwyn interrupted: "I don't like this."

"The question is what are we going to do. Any ideas?"

Selwyn suggested, "Go home and leave this to the authorities."

"My friend, what have we got? We know he's not Captain Hope, I'm sure he has documentation that says he is. So why show our hand while he holds all the aces?"

"We should try and get on that ship," butted in Janice.

"Don't be so bloody naïve, woman," retorted Adrian.

"Don't scorn my suggestion—all you want to do is give up and go home. Some bloody navy hero you've turned out to be. The first sign of trouble and it's back to your lordly manor and the servants."

"Janice, ***shut up***."

This startled her and, temporarily subdued, Janice pushed her empty cup away. "Maybe you feel concerned about my safety, is that it?"

"Don't flatter yourself by emphasising the bloody obvious, woman."

Adrian didn't want to get into a bitter discussion, it was hot enough as it was. Looking directly at Selwyn he winked, stretched out his arms, checked his watch and stood up. "Well, it's an early night for me."

Janice looked at him with disdain, poured yet another coffee and stared across the grounds and out to sea. This man had seemed everything she wanted, the thought of sharing a bed with this wimp now disgusted her.

Both men left Janice to her thoughts and went to Selwyn's room.

"Janice was right, we must get on that ship and have a look round. Tonight may be the best time."

"I think we should leave well alone. The omens for this excursion have already indicated there'll be trouble unless we change direction. You've always believed me before so why not now?"

"True, but this time I think we should continue."

"You're crazy and how do you intend boarding that ship?"

"When they finish loading, it's a good bet they won't leave a gangway watch."

"You can drive me down to the docks."

It took over thirty minutes to reach the far end of the jetty where the *Kia Hua* was berthed. The ship could be seen but there was a dilemma he hadn't anticipated. She was still loading, and the dock area was glowing in an excess of floodlights.

Adrian's face showed disappointment: "This is a waste of time."

"What do we do now?" came the sarcastic statement.

"I don't know; let's wait a while—it may get quieter."

They sat and waited as an endless convoy of large transports discharging their loads came and went. From a distance neither noticed the taxi arrive and leave.

They had waited for more than an hour when Adrian made a decision. "Let's use the psychological approach."

"What on earth are you whittering about?"

"The best form of defence is to attack. We are going to visit our bogus Captain."

"You've got to be joking, if he suspects anything we're dead."

"Why should an honest man doubt our motives? All we want to do is visit the man who so kindly advised us our passage was cancelled."

Selwyn shrugged his shoulders and started the engine. The short journey was completed in silence. "I'm not coming with you and if you're not back on this jetty in thirty minutes I'm off to get the police."

"Don't worry, you won't get rid of me that quickly."

Adrian walked to the foot of the gangway and, looking up, saw a man in his late twenties barring the way. Watchfully he clambered upwards. This deckhand was tall and lean with brown shoulder-length hair. The sun and wind had tanned his face to a golden brown. The once dark blue denims were faded and well worn. In a broad East London accent came the challenge: "You want somefink, Mate?"

Adrian shouted above the clamour of cranes and the bedlam that surrounded them. "I'd like to see Captain Hope."

"Who?"

"Your Captain. The governor, your boss, comprendi?"

"Don't be funny, or I'll knock your fuckin' 'ead off."

At that moment a short plump man with a Hitler style moustache came across to see what was happening. "Having trouble, son?"

"Nofink I can't 'andle. This—" he poked Adrian hard with his middle finger "—wants to see the skipper."

Fatty looked Adrian up and down: "Two visitors in one night. The old man must be popular. Follow me."

They walked forward, keeping clear of the mass of ropes and discarded hatch covers that festooned the deck. Adrian noticed the officers' uniforms were either badly fitting or were well worn.

Once clear of the main deck, they entered the superstructure and began to wind their way up to the Captain's day cabin. *Fatty* beckoned him to wait as he knocked on a cabin door and walked straight in, closing it behind him.

Vaughan opened the door, smiled at Adrian as if he had been expecting him. "Ah! Come to collect your lovely lady?"

Adrian was flabbergasted; grasping at the momentary respite, he followed Vaughan into the cabin.

Janice was wearing the most provocative of dresses that left little to the imagination.

"Darling, glad you decided to come. I've had a wonderful evening."

Adrian attempted to smile: "All good things must come to an end, darling, and Selwyn is waiting. Remember we must have an early night—it will be a long flight home tomorrow." He was beginning to come to grips with the situation but knew the conversation must have sounded stilted.

"Surely, Viper, you can stay for one drink? Davis will inform your man you'll be along shortly." *Fatty* took the hint.

"Your wife has told me that you're a navy man and if she hasn't exaggerated, something of a hero. What would you like to drink? Pink gin is the normal Naval Officer's tipple isn't it?"

"Gin and lots of tonic is my preference."

"And I'll have another 'Horse's Neck' if you're offering," piped Janice.

"Please be seated—you look most uncomfortable standing there." Vaughan motioned to a chair alongside Janice as he poured himself a double Scotch. Then he settled himself in a chair on the other side of the cabin and lit a cheroot.

The next ten minutes were hard work - Janice eyeing Adrian uneasily, the latter commenting on the abruptness of the Harbour Master. Vaughan suggested that this was typical of minor African bureaucrats, as they like to parade their own importance over the whites.

Janice butted in with, "Does it really matter?" ending that topic of conversation.

His drink finished, Vaughan stood up: "As you have your own transport you shouldn't keep the hired help waiting. I'll escort you to the gangway and see you ashore."

Again they entered the chaos of the main cargo deck. A multitude of voices could be heard, each shouting over the other, as tons of freight were being lowered.

"What's your cargo, Captain?"

"Peanuts, one thousand tons of them."

The same man was still standing at the top of the gangway but he moved to one side when he saw Vaughan.

"Good night. I doubt we'll ever meet again."

Adrian uttered a polite farewell and walked down the gangway holding Janice's left arm tighter than he should. A fresh breeze had begun blowing off the sea, and she was forced to use her free hand to prevent her dress from blowing up and giving the crew a sight reserved for husbands and lovers.

On the jetty, an agitated Selwyn stood by the Land Rover: "You took your time. What she doing here?"

Adrian pitched Janice roughly into the back seat of the car and slammed the door with a resounding bang. She tripped and collided face first onto the hard leather seating. Selwyn had the engine started and they began the journey back to the hotel. Janice eventually managed to sit upright. Not a word was said—none were necessary. The air was filled with indignation and rage.

Even before the car stopped Janice was out and running through the foyer, her action startling the hotel guests, the expression on her face attracting even more attention.

Selwyn looked laughingly at his friend, "Your room or mine?"

"I have the feeling that I won't be welcome in mine but I'd rather face her now and get it over with. If this situation is left until the morning it might be more than a spoilt brat we have to deal with. In her present mood she could do more harm than good and we could all end up in trouble. It's been a bad night, God knows what else can go wrong!"

Five

Janice was in a foul temper as she kicked her shoes into the air and fell onto the bed. How could he treat her as if she were a child? She began to sob uncontrollably until it was apparent that someone was standing by the bed. In the darkness she turned her head slowly and could just make out the silhouette of a man. She swung her legs so that they would catch this intruder in the crutch. He was fast and grabbed them as they passed but he didn't move in any other way.

"Right little tom cat, aren't you?"

"Oh it's you, you arrogant bastard." Again she tried to hit him with her arm but he deflected the blow so that it fell away harmlessly.

"How the hell did you get in?"

"Over the balcony, I thought we had agreed a truce."

"We had until you left me sitting like a lemon and when I returned to our room you weren't there. It was that smarmy receptionist who told me you and Selwyn had left."

"Look, you stupid bitch, you could have been killed on that ship and no-one would have given a damn. Men like those take it in turns to use women. Your body would have turned up on some deserted part of the beach for the shitehawks and sand crabs to feast on. Did that ever occur to you? The whole crew of that ship are impostors. Or were you thinking about how you could improve your position with your media friends?"

That insult hit the mark and she flew at him with fists flaying and legs kicking. It was true, but for the moment all she wanted to do was hurt him where it was most painful. Adrian grabbed her arms but managed to turn as a knee connected with his right thigh. With no alternative he threw her to the bed and fell on top, holding her arms over her head and her legs together, clamped tight by his own. They were face to face and he could feel her body twisting.

"I can stay like this all night if I have to. It's quite pleasant for me."

"Go to hell. You're disgusting."

"I probably will."

One of her legs came free and she raked her toe nails like a feral cat down his shin. Adrian winced as the flesh split, then felt the warm flow of blood as it trickled over his skin. Suddenly he rolled off and walked away into his own area of the suite. Janice followed but before she managed to say a word Adrian stopped her short: "Tomorrow we fly home, this whole thing is much bigger than anyone ever imagined. It's out of our league."

Janice went in for the kill. "Not only are you an arrogant bastard but a quitter as well. You know what—you're a first-class fucking wimp. I'll have you know I phoned Charles this evening and he was more than pleased with the news."

" You did what? You stupid cow. What phone did you use?"

She was taken aback by his rebuke. "I phoned from this room when you were out."

"Good God, woman, you may have just signed our death warrants—get packed while I rouse Selwyn."

"Who's being stupid now? I've never heard anything so ridiculous."

"Look, I didn't tell anyone which hotel we were in but they tracked us down, and, in case your roving reporter's eye failed to notice, this hotel still has a manual switchboard."

Adrian left her standing with her mouth open as he went to his friend's room. Selwyn was awake and fully clothed and agreed that the sooner they left the better.

"Where are we going to make for, Selwyn? Nairobi would be too obvious."

"I would suggest Dar Es Salaam—better roads and regular flights to Europe."

"I agree. How much fuel have we got in the car?"

"More than enough. I filled the tank this morning and there's two five gallon jerry cans."

"What on earth made you do that?"

"Voices."

"Did you know this was going to happen?"

"Not exactly; I followed my instincts and prepared for any eventuality—I'm already packed."

"I'm not, but give me five and we'll meet in the car park. As a precaution toss your bags out the window. There's no need to tell the world we're leaving."

"A bit melodramatic isn't it? They'll know in the morning."

"Yes but hopefully by that time we'll be far away."

Adrian returned to his room where he found Janice sitting on the floor in front of the full length mirror, tossing her head with anger as each stroke of the brush passed through her hair.

Her eyes said it all: "Well get on with it," she shouted. "Tell me I've ruined everything."

"Look, we can't waste time bickering about who's right or wrong, get packed we're leaving *now*."

"For God's sake, kindly remember I'm not one of your ratings on board your bloody ship."

Adrian looked at her as he rammed clothing into his suitcases and then started to deal out the same treatment to hers.

"Stop that! I'll pack my clothes properly."

"Suit your bloody self, you've got four minutes and then we leave."

Janice remained silent, but the look she gave would have made a stone bleed. She picked up her denims and a blouse before disappearing into the bathroom.

On her return, she meticulously packed the dress she had worn on the ship.

"Right! Are you ready or would you like half an hour to put some make-up on?"

With deliberate intent she stopped, fumbled in her handbag and withdrew a lipstick. It took a second to apply the slash of pink to her lips. "Now I'm ready!"

"Typical bloody woman!" Adrian snatched their suitcases and from the balcony tossed them out into a thick bush.

They left the room, locking the door behind them. Adrian deposited the key into a large fern as he passed.

So as not to be seen, they left by the fire escape. Adrian was so engrossed in getting clear of the hotel, he failed to notice the Manager standing in the shadows. Two minutes later, Selwyn was behind the wheel and heading at the best possible speed for town. Once away from the localised illumination of the hotel the car's headlights struggled. Janice only broke her silence to ask where they were going.

"Dar Es Salaam," came the rapid retort from Selwyn as he concentrated on the road ahead.

"Well I might as well make myself useful, give me the map and I'll navigate." Janice sat with her back to Selwyn and stretched out her legs whilst checking the route with a pencil flash.

Mombassa was wide awake, the bars were open and the whores and their pimps were openly plying for trade. After twenty minutes of wild driving through the packed streets they reached Kenya Ferry Services terminal. The craft was on its way to the far side. Their arrival encouraged a swirling crowd to descend. These were the people who scoured a meagre livelihood selling, at highly inflated prices, cheap bric-a-brac to unsuspecting Europeans. The blind beggars led by sighted children came and went, pickpockets eyed potential targets but chose the less vigilant. The ferry arrived and even at this late hour it was crammed to capacity by varieties of the human race - African, Indian, White South Africans, Arabs - all were to be seen in greater or lesser numbers. As they drove down the steep slope and onto the ferry, the entire quayside could hear the master of the vessel proclaiming in Kiswahili, English, German and other languages for all to mind their wallets. At the far side, the main coastal route to Dar Es Salaam was well signposted. Initially its surface was good but as they progressed, it gradually deteriorated. Potholes jarred the tough suspension. Selwyn slowed down to prevent any damage, maintaining a steady forty-five to fifty kilometres an hour.

Adrian had calmed down and asked the question which had been nagging him: "When did you phone Charles?"

"Janice's voice was soft and amiable as if she had done nothing wrong: "A few minutes after I found out that you two had left the hotel."

"Shit, there is a good chance our Captain already knew we were on to him. I'll say one thing for him—he's a cold calculating bastard. I wonder why he let us go?"

The twisting road embraced the coast. Immediately to their left was a wide ribbon of palm trees that helped conceal the tourist hotels. A dark belt of noisy grinding surf pounded the reef before it washed onto the white sands. Further out, white-capped rollers moved relentlessly onward. To the right there was nothing but scrub, bush, and acacia trees, the untamed Africa. They had not seen a soul since joining the main highway. Every mile they travelled south was a mile closer to safety.

"While I think about it," Adrian said, "slight change of plan. When we get to Kilindini we'll take the inland route to Vango."

"Sounds as if you're expecting trouble," declared a now curious Janice.

"It's called working the percentage. There are three main routes out of Mombassa, and if our friend does know we're on to him it wouldn't take much to cover our exit."

"Sounds a bit far-fetched. What could he do if he did know?" responded Janice.

"One telephone call could have us eliminated. He's only a pawn in a powerful empire which, I'm sure, has far-reaching tentacles."

"There's a lorry coming up fast behind us," Selwyn warned.

Janice turned in her seat to see the vehicle. It was big. "A juggernaut with trailer catching us up like a bloody steam train. He's careering all over the road as if he's out of control." She looked at the dimly lit speedo as she noticed that they were moving much faster than was safe.

Selwyn glanced in the rear view mirror. The madcap juggernaut was still bearing down on them as if they were not there, far exceeding the speed limit for a road such as this. The trailer behind the lorry was swaying violently from side to side. Then it was almost upon them, its immense size towering over them as it began to overtake. For no apparent reason this Leviathan began to move closer. Scared stiff, Janice moved away from the side nearest the lorry and waited for the impact that was certain.

There remained roughly eighteen inches between both vehicles but the gap was swiftly diminishing.

To the right of them was bush, the unknown. To turn into there would be disastrous but alternative options were limited. Selwyn gripped the steering wheel hard with both hands as he concentrated on his driving and looked ahead. The road was empty. This would be another unfortunate accident caused by tourists who did not know the road and who had ventured out at night. No-one would question their deaths.

Selwyn's eyes went rapidly from the road to the front wheels of the lorry and back again. He was waiting for that movement that would hurtle them into oblivion. As the gap between them closed he shoved his left foot hard down on the brake pedal, locking all four wheels instantly. The lorry driver, expecting the Land Rover to cushion his move, realised too late that it was no longer there. Travelling far too fast the mammoth overshot and, now committed to its direction, careered savagely into the scrub demolishing everything in its path. The Land Rover, with three people holding on for grim death, slithered to a halt. The fact that the brakes were defective caused the vehicle to veer to the right. Finally it stopped some fifty or more yards into the bush, on the edge of a gentle slope. Three shaken but unharmed people sat very still, each composing themselves as they breathed slowly and deeply. They had been lucky.

Adrian jumped from the car. "You two all right?"

"All in one piece," responded Selwyn in a spirited manner.

Janice complained about the mosquitoes which appeared from nowhere and were biting her in places she rather they didn't.

"You have been taking your malaria tablets?" asked Selwyn.

"Yes I have. What about the other driver? Maybe he can tell us something?"

They followed the path torn through the bush by the lorry until they found it. From what they could see it was apparent that the vehicle had plummeted into a dry riverbed and the trailer, under its own momentum, had landed squarely on the top of the cab. Selwyn clambered down to where the driver should have been. After a cursory check he returned to the others. "Not a lot worth worrying about down there. He didn't know what hit him."

"I don't give a damn about that bastard. I'm concerned about our survival. Let's get back to the car and see if we can drive it on to the road. Then we'll get the hell out of here," responded Adrian.

"I'll second that but if you don't mind, I need to go."

"Typical bloody woman, when all else fails, they go and powder their nose. Come on, let's sort our wreck out and get moving."

Selwyn got into the driver's seat and engaged the four-wheel drive whilst Adrian, torch in hand, checked their way. Initially the wheels spun in the dry soil. Undeterred, the two men gathered twigs and small branches, jamming them under all four wheels. Slowly they began to grip, and the Land Rover inched towards the road. Adrian moved around and looked under the bodywork checking that any damage was no more than superficial. Janice returned and curled herself up on the back seat. She had been in some serious situations in her time but in each case she was conscious who the enemy was. Her thoughts were a worrying clutter. What if it had been her telephone call that had endangered them? She remained silent, keeping her feelings to herself.

Adrian realised he had been very abrasive and had treated her appallingly, turned, and in a calm voice asked if she was OK. Having been emotionally bruised by his previous indifference, she ignored him. Selwyn engaged first gear and they were once again moving south. The only reassurance he felt was that if that lorry had been dispatched to kill them, its failure would not be known until much later. He was worried for different reasons. Nothing was making sense. Adrian wondered if the driver had deliberately attempted to kill them or had it been just a lunatic having what could have been loosely described as "fun". It wasn't too far fetched to assume that, having exposed the crew of the *Kia Hua* as impostors, someone was out to eliminate a possible leak.

Running southwards, they reached Kilindini in less than an hour but lost some time looking for the inland route. The town was quiet and devoid of life. Only a few mangy dogs could be seen rummaging in dustbins for scraps. A traffic light flashed amber, then red; Selwyn ignored it. They drove on at a steady rate through the sleepy town but the sound of the old engine and the hum of deep treaded tyres reverberated off every building. Once on the right road they were surprised that the surface, although only hard packed earth, was reasonable and they began to make good time. The glow from the single dashboard light illuminating the speedometer gave the whole interior of the cab an eerie effect in the darkness. Every now and again a dog, or possibly a hyena, would lope across the road, but wild animals generally would avoid areas frequented by man.

Once in a while they stopped and checked the map and gave the opportunity for Adrian to take his turn at the arduous task of driving. Janice, despite the rough terrain, was fast asleep. One thing her nomadic lifestyle had taught her was to grab sleep whenever the opportunity presented itself. The night sky was beginning to lighten and Venus, the evening star, was disappearing into the morning glow. The shadows were beginning to disappear as each minute passed. Once the sun was up over the horizon, driving became more of a pleasure and less of an ordeal. Janice had woken with the sun but her body was stiff and her muscles ached. The brightness of the day gave them hope that they could now reach their destination. The sooner they were out of this country and on their way home the better.

"We might as well stop and have a breather and stretch our legs for a while. Madam, no doubt will want to powder her nose," Adrian remarked sarcastically.

"If you mean I want to pee, why don't you say so instead of being so bloody patronising."

Adrian stopped the car under a giant acacia tree, disturbing a family of monkeys who had been preening themselves; young and old screeched as if terrified.

"What's worrying them?"

"Nothing," said Selwyn; "just a family squabble."

As their confidence grew they began to leap onto the bonnet. Janice, seeing at least a good picture, retrieved her camera and used a whole roll of film on this screeching hoard that now seemed to have taken over the area. "Don't touch them, they'll bite your fingers for the sheer hell of it," commented Selwyn, "and their teeth are like razors."

"At the next village can we stop and get something to drink? I'm thirsty," muttered Janice.

"I'll soon remedy that. Come with me." Selwyn set off towards a clump of trees about four hundred yards away. He approached one that held a meagre foliage but many sausage-shaped seed pods. With the use of a stick he prodded some until they fell to the ground.

"What are you doing?" asked Adrian.

Selwyn removed the husks and placed two of the seeds in his mouth, and with a cheeky grin offered some to Janice. She accepted and trusting his judgement placed them on her tongue and was instantly amazed at the refreshing taste of lemon.

"Suck these and not only will your thirst be quenched but you are also giving yourself the most natural source of vitamin C."

"Where did you learn that?" asked an inquisitive Adrian.

"From my grandfather."

"Good old granddad," remarked Janice.

It was then, their arrival unheard, that four Africans in ragged combat clothing appeared. They carried AKM47s with the distinctive curved black magazine, the woodwork scarred from use, while numerous bulging ammunition pouches adorned their carriers.

Selwyn spoke quickly but softly, "Don't move, and leave all the talking to me."

The largest, his combat clothing faded by constant washing but now dirty from the dust of travelling, approached cautiously, his weapon held in the ready position. Adrian noticed that the safety catch was off, which made him anxious. Selwyn began talking in English but it was obvious that none of them understood. They simply shrugged their shoulders whilst all the time they grinned ridiculously at each other and stared perversely at Janice. Selwyn then began to speak in a language that was alien to his companions but it brought a smile to the faces of the four men. The leader stopped him with one word as he stood without fear of contradiction. The men moved forward, forming a circle around the one who spoke their language. Selwyn was not smiling for he was very much aware that it was unwise to offend these men.

All the time Janice and Adrian were being visually scrutinised with a mixture of interest and distrust. These were professional warriors, political rebels, subject to their own laws and proud of their abilities in the art of killing. Their skills came from ruthless survival. Each had undoubtedly been confronted with a kill-to-exist situation in the abundant tribal wars that had inflicted the African continent. It would be advantageous to gain the respect of these men in the period that lay ahead. They would kill easily and without conscience someone they despised, but being a comrade could make all the difference. Having been taught their tribal rituals and their social conventions as a child, Selwyn knew how to flatter enough to please but not too much to make them scornful. Adrian started to move forward and the bolts on four AKMs were immediately cocked and the weapons pointed in his direction. He froze where he stood and raised his arms in the air. The Africans laughed at him.

"Selwyn, what the hell's going on?"

"Shut up, Adrian."

Recognising the serious tone in his friend's voice, he did just that. His shirt was soaked in perspiration - they had been standing in the full morning sun for over thirty minutes. Selwyn was eventually allowed to walk away from the group and explain.

"It would appear that there is a change in our plans." He paused for a moment and spoke again to the men whose gaze had not left his back for an instant. "We're going to drive Kumu and his friends across the border into Tanzania and then on to Rwanda. I've told them that I'm your guide and that you're tourists taking photographs of wild animals. The choice is simple—you agree or die; for once my ancestry has helped me but condemned you. I suggest we wait for the right moment but with four of them our chances are slim. I'll do what I can but these men are mercenaries, the remnants of one small Zulu tribe that were almost eradicated a hundred and fifty years ago. Another murder or two makes no difference to them, especially if those lives are white. These are terrorists of the worst kind. They bring about political change by violence. For a price they'll commit any atrocity that you can imagine and some that you never will."

Janice realised that he was trying to allay their fears. Having seen tribal warfare at first-hand, she was aware that he had spoken the truth.

"Let's get on with it," whispered Adrian.

Selwyn turned to the four men and told them that

his friends were only too pleased to help the fighters of Africa rid the world of fascist governments. Adrian and Janice moved slowly towards the Land Rover; he jumped into the driver's seat whilst she sat alongside him. Selwyn waited for the others to get in the back before he joined them.

"OK, which way is Rwanda, my friend?" asked Adrian. An AKM prodded the back of his seat. Selwyn spoke to the men and in the same manner to his friend. "Drive due west, it's about six hundred miles. The terrain gets worse the further inland we go. We have gas for about four hundred miles. They're aware of that."

Without further hesitation the car was turned until the compass on the dashboard read west and the journey began. There are no roads in the bush but the broad undulating plain they were traversing ensured, initially at least, that many miles were covered without too much difficulty. Although past its best, the vehicle was designed for this terrain and enabled them to average about thirty miles an hour. Dried up riverbeds, the occasional curious lion, minor detours and three hours of arduous travel located a tarmacadamed road. Kumu, the leader, pointed with his rifle that they should go to the right.

A loaded weapon precludes any questions. Janice finally drained the last morsel of refreshment from the seeds. Her mouth was now dry and desperate for a drink of water. Slowly she turned and faced her captors and with her middle finger pointed toward her open mouth, "Water, water." They laughed at the gesture, copying it.

Selwyn remained silent until they were ready to listen. "My friends. We must have water or we'll perish in the heat and you'll not be fit to fight for freedom."

Kumu looked at him and smiled, but said nothing. Now and then trucks covered in red dust and loaded to the brim approached from the opposite direction, their drivers waving in acknowledgement as they sped by. The road surface improved and in the distance they saw the beginnings of a small settlement. Kumu began to shout orders at Selwyn, who in turn tapped Adrian on the shoulder telling him to stop the car.

"What the hell's the matter now?"

"Shut up Adrian, just do as I say." Selwyn began to speak to Kumu and during the conversation raised his voice. It became obvious from his tone that he had lost the argument.

"They want us to drive into the village and buy food and water while they take Janice and skirt around the perimeter. Don't argue, they're not prepared to listen."

Janice put out her right hand touching Adrian's arm. "It would seem I go with them. Get some water, I'm dying for a drink."

Janice and the soldiers got out and soon they had disappeared into the bush. With his foot hard down on the accelerator Adrian drove like a maniac covering the few miles that remained between them and the settlement. Although not a helpless female, Janice was not dressed for jogging through such territory during the hottest part of the day. Only a mile had been covered when her heart and lungs began to hurt more than she had ever known. The two men who had been detailed to trail behind could see she was struggling. Without a word being spoken they moved up beside her and grabbed an arm each, and at a murderous pace dragged her along. Several times she stumbled and fell full length onto the dust covered ground. The men shouted at her and each time it required a supreme effort to continue. Every now and again they would stop for a few minutes to regain their breath, before they were once again running like young gazelles.

Abruptly they stopped and fell to the ground, dragging her with them. Janice lay there at first, thankful for the rest, but then she saw the lioness and three cubs, at most four to five weeks old. If they antagonised this lady they would be forced to shoot and reveal their presence. The lioness had stopped for the cubs to suckle. The men whispered to each other and all the time looked at their captive. One moved so close she could smell his unwashed body and the foulness of his breath. He lay alongside Janice and with sign language made her understand that they must move very slowly and quietly but above all so as not to threaten the cubs. Janice nodded, and without a sound they began to move downwind and around the animal as it lay on its side feeding its young. Without warning the beast stood up, shaking its cubs from its teats, and began to look around. The group froze, the lioness roared, shook herself again and continued on her journey with the whelping cubs following. Janice had never been so close to such a creature before and it left her in a cold sweat.

Meanwhile, Adrian wasn't happy at having to leave Janice at the mercy of the soldiers. Selwyn assured him that for the moment, as they were useful to them, she should be OK."

"What causes men to behave in such a way? It's not even their war," asked Adrian.

Selwyn thought for a moment: "Ever since I can remember, Africa has been at war with itself. People are fighting for their right to live." The Land Rover entered the village and drew to a halt at its centre. Selwyn got out and went to obtain food and, most needed of all, water. Adrian remained, preventing what possessions they had from being stolen by a group of smiling children that surrounded the car. It was not long before Selwyn, with his arms laden, returned and they drove away in silence to a point some five miles out of town. They pulled off the road and parked just inside the grass line and waited for the wanderers. Adrian continued to quiz his friend on African politics and soon began to realise that this open land was as politically corrupt as the so-called civilised countries and that multi-national businesses had joined the destructive bandwagon just to accrue a fast profit. The native African was suffering much the same fate as the American Red Indian. Selwyn continued to emphasise that slavery still existed in some regions of Africa. Unfortunately it was in areas far removed from the world's eyes. He pointed out that if the right people were contacted it was easy to purchase a child for use as a herdsman in return for nothing but the crumbs from your table. Young girls were more often than not used for the sexual pleasure of their owner and, when they became pregnant, sold to a brothel. He continued to open Adrian's eyes to the lack of morality that existed amongst the various tribes. Villages were still being raided, old men murdered and the women and children carried away to enslavement. "There are bad people who mistreat their slaves, and there are good people who allow their slaves to live well. Europeans have this vision of Africa, bare-breasted women pounding maize into flour in a scene of pastoral timelessness, young men fishing from dugout canoes, swimming and washing, their chatter filling the air. This masks the harsh reality of life and is not believed by those who think they know Africa. The reality for any slave is invariably enduring squalor."

It was another harrowing two hours before the grasses parted. The dishevelled soldiers and an exhausted woman clambered into the back of the Land Rover. Janice, covered in dust, had several large cuts on her hands and knees. Blood and a mixture of dust had bonded together. This needed cleaning before infection set in. Selwyn had purchased three gallons of drinking water, some tins of corned beef to be eaten with local maize bread. This he distributed first to Janice who grabbed at the water and began to gulp it down by the mouthful, spilling it as she quenched her extreme thirst.

One of the Africans tore it away from her and began to shout at Selwyn, "If you drink too much, you will want to drink all the time."

With a few well chosen words the man was thanked for his concern and handed some bread and a tin of beef. Adrian was worried about Janice. If they continued to use her in this way, he was aware that this alone would drain her reserves of energy until she was no longer physically capable of moving. When she recounted their meeting with the lioness, that disturbed him more than he cared to admit.

Without a weapon she could have easily been mauled and left for dead whilst the men escaped. Selwyn had tried to obtain a weapon in the village but there was either none to be had or they were not selling. When they had eaten and drank some of the precious water, the leader shouted at Selwyn for them to drive on. Adrian started the engine and engaged first gear. Slowly the aged vehicle moved from its screen of tall grass onto the tarmacadamed road. Silence encompassed them for the next sixty miles; only when they were forced to stop did conversation begin again. "We'll need more petrol, this will last two hundred miles at most," declared Adrian.

Selwyn was peering at the petrol gauge. "I know."

The sun began to cast long black shadows across the road as they wound higher and higher into the mountain range that spread itself across hundreds of miles in front and now began to encircle them. Mosquitoes were starting to swarm as the temperature at this higher altitude began to drop rapidly. Inevitably, after having made good time, the road began to deteriorate. The heavy rains had taken their toll and the once acceptable surface had been severely rutted by the heavy trucks that constantly abused it. Janice had fallen asleep but woke as Adrian changed gear. The engine raced as they were compelled to negotiate the landslides that confronted them. It was hard work and at sunset, exhausted, they stopped. The only light came from the moon and stars. Through the thin air of the mountains they could be clearly seen, illuminating the starkness of the landscape. Adrian and the others realised that driving by night would be easier than they had at first imagined. One of the

Africans, used to improvising, lit a fire and, with a piece of sheet metal found by the side of the road, fried the corned beef with what remained of the bread, and equal shares of this concoction were distributed to everyone. Despite its burnt and tattered appearance, as food it was welcome.

Selwyn looked at Kumu as they studied a map of the area. "It would appear that we are here—give or take a mile or two."

Kumu had begun to trust Selwyn, "You are correct but these places, Mushi and Arusho could be troublesome. I don't like towns—they are full of people." This fact seemed to irritate him.

Selwyn raised the point: "If we're to get you to your destination there is no alternative, and we do need food and diesel."

Kumu accepted this and agreed that one stop would be necessary.

Selwyn and Adrian drove for periods of two hours at a time. Three hours had elapsed when they reached the outskirts of Mushi. Kumu banged the butt of his rifle on the floor and in his native tongue said, "Stop here. If anyone raises the alarm, I'll have no hesitation in shooting you and anyone else. Drive on."

Mushi was the only decent looking town they had seen since their rapid departure from Mombassa. There was a hotel on the main street but they drove on until directly ahead was a garage and general store.

Kumu again banged his rifle on the floor: "Stop there, and don't forget one wrong move and you'll all die."

Adrian drove directly into the beam of a harsh floodlight and stopped beside the solitary petrol pump.

It being very late, the owner was in bed and being disturbed gave him a foul temper.

The steel door groaned on its hinges and opened a fraction: "What you want?"

Selwyn leant against the door frame: "My friend, we are weary travellers, who being stupid have run short of provisions and fuel."

The man laughed: "You wait for morning."

"What if we make it worth your while?"

The door remained open, greed was a good bait: "How much?"

Selwyn was aware that he had to convince this leach that they were desperate but not fools. "Twice the asking price."

The door started to close: "OK—three times."

The door shut to and a chain rattled before it opened fully. The rifle Kumu held on the nape of Adrian's neck remained hidden. The storekeeper was dressed in a pair of bright red overalls emblazoned with the Amoco livery. His English was adequate, but Selwyn was sure that he understood more than he was making out. With much pointing and words they soon obtained all their needs. Selwyn operated the fuel pump and Janice, more by intuition than anything else, found a toilet.

Adrian sat motionless and said nothing. If anyone made a wrong move all hell would erupt, not that he would know much anyway. The Land Rover's fuel tank and two jerry cans were filled. Janice gathered the food and water and carried it to the rear of the car.

When they were ready Selwyn removed his wallet and gave the man what he considered sufficient.

"More. More."

He gave him all the money he had: "You robbing bastard."

The man laughed. "No problem." Fortunately for him, he did not know how close he was to being shot.

Adrian's blood pressure reduced dramatically when the transaction was completed and the AKM was removed.

It was past four in the morning when Adrian pulled in to an opening and stopped. Kumu had ensured that one of his men was always awake, and this one shouted and jabbed his rifle for him to drive on. Adrian got out and shouted back, "I'm stopping. I'm tired and I don't even know what day it is; I can't drive any more."

Kumu was now wide awake and screaming at Selwyn. Janice stayed silent but was acutely aware that anything could happen. After much shouting and pointing of rifles it was agreed between Selwyn and Kumu that two hours' rest would be allowed but then they would have to move on. Relieved, they made pillows out of their suitcases and attempted to put their heads down. Janice positioned herself near Selwyn, a point Adrian noticed. He also saw that one of the Africans was left on guard. Worn out, her physical resources depleted, Janice indulged in the luxury of a quiet weep. For what seemed a long time she lay watching the star-filled sky listening to the strange noises that invaded the night. Despite the cold, it was not long before she had fallen into a deep sleep.

The hours passed far too quickly and the guard, the most arrogant of the four, seemed to relish the act of kicking his captives awake. Adrian sat up, rubbed his eyes and stared at the sun that was just beginning to cast its warmth across the still cold mountains, painting the clouds and sky a fiery red. He looked at his captor, smiled and, as fast as a cat, pivoted his legs around, sweeping the man off his feet. The noise of his weapon falling alerted the others but it was too late, Adrian had a stranglehold around the man's neck and was throwing all his strength into the muscles of his left arm as he attempted with his right to find the fallen rifle. As his hand grasped the cold metal his spirits rose. Kumu was alert and swift on his feet but, instead of moving towards Adrian, dived to the ground, and lay protected behind the body of Janice. He had left his AKM but in his right hand was a long, serrated-edge hunting knife. It was pressed hard against her white throat, the droplets of blood falling onto the ground giving a clear indication that he was not bluffing.

Kumu smiled, his teeth glowing white, and shouted at Selwyn as Adrian assessed the impasse.

Adrian, if luck were on his side, would kill or seriously wound his captive but Janice would die.

"Adrian, drop the weapon or Kumu says he will happily cut Janice's throat and drink her blood."

He tossed the rifle towards its owner.

Kumu walked across towards where Adrian lay. Holding the barrel of an AKM47 he drove the steel butt into Adrian's middle, the impact forcing the air out of his lungs and causing him to curl up with the pain into a tight ball. The others then set about kicking him savagely. The first kick connected with his ribs, those that followed failed to cause any more pain, only the deep wish that it would stop. A shout from Kumu ended the attack. He was bleeding and his chest was suffering with pains that defied description, but he was alive; he had survived.

Kumu laughed out loud as he dragged Adrian's mutilated body to its feet. His pain showed as he screamed out loud and hugged his ribs. Despite his suffering, he was pitched unceremoniously face down into the back of the Land Rover, where his hands were bound. Kumu ordered Selwyn to get in the car and Janice to drive.

Clutching at her throat she did not hesitate and when they were all on board the engine was started. She was exhausted, mentally and physically, and to argue with these psychopaths would be suicide. To ease the torment, she thought of the hotel they had passed, clean sheets and a soft bed. What she wouldn't give for such things at this moment defied belief. Selwyn began to chat to their captors in a vain effort to restore the balance that had existed before but he was well aware that they would not be caught by such a simple trick again. Sleep would be where you sat or not at all. The conversation became one-sided and eventually the only sound to be heard was the roaring of the engine and the tyres as they ground along the boulder-strewn and rutted road. Adrian managed to wedge himself under the metal seat, but with each bump the pain of his injuries caused him to gasp for breath. They were in trouble and it was his fault. Next time, if there was one, he would have to make sure before acting independently.

Janice was beginning to tire—her arms ached from the continuous buffeting they were receiving from the steering wheel. With each jarring movement it strove to wrench itself from her grasp. The mountain road doubled back on itself and continued to climb steeply. In places it had deteriorated into a barely passable track and its edge fell away to a three thousand feet drop. The river, which threaded its way through the gorge below, seemed as a strand of silver stretched out along a well worn path. Janice stopped the car and Kumu immediately began to shout.

Selwyn pointed: "Look at the road ahead," he shouted back, "there's been a rockfall."

Again Kumu shouted.

"Sod you bastards," screamed Janice as she tightened her hand on the steering wheel and crashed the gearbox into four-wheel drive. Slowly she began to move the vehicle forward towards the edge of the fall. What remained of the road was minimal. As the wheels neared the edge, stones fell into the chasm and what remained began to disintegrate slowly.

"Well come on, shout now, or would you like to drive this bloody wreck?"

Kumu and his henchmen remained silent. Inch by inch Janice negotiated the loose rubble until all four wheels were clear and back on solid ground. She stopped the car and turned off the engine. Despite Kumu's shouts, she walked back along the road until disappearing behind a large rock. It seemed an eternity before her reappearance and return to the driving seat.

"What the hell do you think you were doing?" asked Selwyn.

"Having a pee, even in this wilderness a lady must have some privacy," Selwyn told Kumu, who managed the barest of grins.

They continued, each mile of buffeting taking its toll, each pothole jarring every nerve. A lorry approached, obviously being driven by a lunatic as it shifted from one side of the road to the other. It was full of men with shovels and picks who waved with tremendous gusto as they passed. For safety Janice stopped as close to the cliff face as was possible until they had gone by. The road ahead was obviously clear; with a grimace she accelerated and despite the never-ending potholes they were making fifty-five kilometres an hour. As Kumu and his men had to hold on tight for fear of falling out, Selwyn smiled at her determination.

Finally, as she attempted to avoid a large boulder, there was a sharp crack. The punishment the aged vehicle had tolerated ultimately took its revenge. The steering wheel turned hopelessly in her hands. Whatever she did was useless. The Land Rover was out of control and its momentum drove it directly towards the unprotected edge. For a brief instant, as the chassis caught on the hard earth, it hung suspended before toppling over onto a steep slope. The initial drop was sufficient to pitch its occupants and contents in all directions. Then it fell almost one hundred feet to a boulder-covered ledge. Those that managed to scream went unheard as the sounds of disaster were absorbed by the mountains that surrounded them. Kumu and his warriors landed with bone-breaking thuds onto the rock-covered surface.

When the vehicle finally came to rest not a sound could be heard, not a body stirred. Adrian, having been wedged tightly under a seat, had survived the horrors of the crash. Only when the side panels were torn away had he been thrown clear. He lay unconscious on the hot rocks, his body battered and bruised. It was the pain in his ribs that dragged him back to reality. After a few minutes he managed to focus his eyes and come to terms with what had happened. For a while he struggled to push himself into a sitting position. Cursing, and swearing, he eventually managed to slide his bound wrists under his body and with his teeth pull at the knots that held him. It took ages, but eventually the ropes loosened. He rubbed his wrists viciously until circulation returned. This gave him time to think before beginning the search for the others. Loose rocks made his ascent difficult and every time he slipped he cried out loudly as his chest hit the ground but he had to know the fate of his friends before he could rest. The first corpse he saw was Kumu, his skull had smashed open and was divesting its contents. The next had bones protruding from numerous torn orifices in his frame. As he sat alongside the third African, Adrian found a rifle and gathered up a pocketful of ammunition. His scramble up and along the rocks in search of the others was continuing to hurt, but now mentally rather than physically. The fourth African was still alive but his right leg was impaled on a stump of brush and, having pierced an artery, had for some time been pumping life-giving blood over the ground on which he lay. Adrian knew that this man would soon be dead.

No-one knew they were in this ravine and it would be by pure chance that anybody would survive without help. He began to traverse the slippery slope looking for Janice and Selwyn. The rock face was becoming more vertical with each move he made, his recollections of outward bound weekends whilst at school flooded back. Slinging the rifle across his shoulder he began to traverse slowly across the ever-increasing slope. At first, foot and handholds were solid and he made good progress; before every move, each was tested before he reached for the next, the minimum of weight applied as he passed. In small recesses trees and brush grew profusely in large clumps which gave precious shade. As he continued his search and neared an outcrop that seemed to hang horizontally from the hillside he heard a whimper from below.

He stopped and held tightly to his tenuous grasp of the rock face and looked down. Twenty feet below him, in the branches of a tree that appeared to grow horizontally from the rocks, lay Janice. She was alive. Adrian almost lost hold in his excitement, but quickly regained position. Making his way down was more difficult than it had originally seemed. Each move was repeatedly tested before he placed his weight on it and again bore down. Inch by inch he made his way towards the prostrate form. After what seemed an eternity he was on the steep slope and moving cautiously on all fours towards the clump of vegetation. This collection of bushes and a solitary tree were more dense than they had first appeared. It was strange that these growths survived in the most inhospitable of surroundings. Most of its lower branches were devoid of foliage; the upper area, however, comprised a lush arrangement of spreading branches that had miraculously stopped and held her. The rifle was going to be a hindrance so it was wedged between two rocks before he made his move. Warily he straddled the thick trunk and moved slowly forward—below him was the direct route to heaven or hell. When he was in a suitable position he leant forward and held onto the strongest looking branch to pull himself up. This enabled him to climb quickly into the upper limbs where the branches were thick and coarse. His head broke through into the sunlight almost alongside Janice. She looked like a little girl asleep.

At first he dare not touch her; in many places her clothing had ripped to reveal her pink flesh on which large weals were forming. Apart from these superficial abrasions, nothing appeared out of place, no blood stains or protruding bones. Making sure that he would not slip, he began firmly but gently to run his hands over her arms and legs, again checking for any sign of broken bones - there were none. Gently he turned her head; if her neck or back were damaged he knew that he was about to kill her or paralyse her for life, but under the circumstances there was no choice. Her face was covered in small cuts but on her forehead was the beginning of a large bruise. If he did not move her soon, the sun would burn and cause dehydration but it would be difficult and dangerous—one slip and they would both plummet into the gorge.

Cautiously he moved around until her still form was positioned over his right shoulder. As he pushed upwards the pain that stemmed from his ribs hit his nervous system like a thunderbolt. He clenched his teeth, biting hard but he knew that there was no other way. He was also acutely aware that if she had any internal injuries he was about to cause even more damage. Eventually her prostrate form was lying across his shoulder and held in position with his right arm. As he began the descent, each branch was tested before moving to the next. At last, after much swearing and cursing loudly to the world, he reached solid ground and, most importantly, shade. Carefully he laid Janice against a rock that would give her head and back some support and then he waited. For over two hours she lay there breathing evenly, but not moving. Adrian made himself comfortable in the confined space and rested. The next problem was to get her off this ledge. Her moaning quickly brought him back to reality and he moved across to her.

"Where the hell am I?" were her first words as she rubbed her forehead.

"Lie still, we're on a ledge with not a lot of room to spare."

"My head feels like that bloody truck hit me."

"At least you're in one piece." Adrian went on to explain what had happened and how he had carried her down from the tree. "If I hadn't found you, one move and you would never have woken up."

"What about the others?"

"Apart from Selwyn who must have gone clean over the edge, they're dead or might as well be. I thought you were too. The problem now is to get out of here and the only way is up."

"You must be joking, I've never done any climbing in my life."

"There's no choice," explained Adrian. "If we stay here we'll die from lack of water. You don't have to look, but going down even with the correct equipment would be bloody impossible. For the first time since we met, you'll have to do as you're told. Will your jeans stay up without a belt?"

"Yes. Why?"

"To tie you to me, it will act as a sort of safety harness."

Janice removed her belt and handed it to Adrian who fastened it through his and then secured the free end to her right wrist. "What I want you to do is copy my every move, where my feet are will be where your hands go and so on. For God's sake don't try to be clever and do your own thing."

Janice looked up and over to the left where she could just see the remains of the Land Rover. "What have we got to lose? Let's get on with it."

"Adrian picked up the rifle, slung it over his shoulder, and began to contemplate the climb; when he was satisfied that he had identified what seemed the easiest route back, they began. As he climbed, Janice followed his orders precisely, not wavering an instant from the footholds which were her handholds. Slowly they made their way up and across the face, Adrian shouting encouragement all the time. His strategy worked and she found confidence in his voice. She remembered the time she had thought him a wimp. It took them over an hour to return to the comparative safety of the wide ledge and regain their breath.

Janice looked up towards the road: "What do we do now? There's no way we can climb that."

"First things first. Look around and see if any food or water survived the crash."

Together they carefully explored the slope, each checking to see what there was, picking up everything and discarding most. After what seemed an eternity they discovered a few battered tins of beans, some clothing but no water. It was unbearably hot on the rock face, so collecting their salvaged items they changed position to the furthest end where a slight breeze disturbed the dust. Here they made themselves comfortable in the shade of a few sparse bushes that had somehow germinated and grown from a crack in the rock. The paltry provisions they had collected were neatly stored near the top of the ridge. Adrian salvaged the four AK47s and busied himself making a primitive shelter out of retrieved combat clothing. It would never have kept out the rain but it provided valuable shade. He ordered Janice to keep as much of her body covered, especially her head.

At first he intended to leave the dead to the savagery of the vultures but his Christian upbringing gave way. Painstakingly he began the process of covering each corpse in turn with stones. Who will bury us, he thought?—without water they could last up to forty-eight hours; with the few provisions they had, maybe a little longer. Adrian looked into the sky, shading his eyes. He saw nothing to relieve his uneasiness. He made his way back to Janice who, despite the heat, appeared to be sleeping. The uneven surface caused him to slip, and for the umpteenth time he let out a curse.

She turned to face him. "I'd forgotten all about your beating—let me have a look."

"It's my ribs, those bastards either broke a few or badly bruised them but it's my guess they're busted."

"Give me one of those shirts and a knife." With the deftness of a seamstress she began to cut the material into long lengths until it resembled a handful of rags. "Off with your shirt and I'll bind your chest, it'll help to ease the pain and give some relief. Tell me if it's too tight."

Adrian removed his shirt to reveal numerous cuts and dark blue, almost black, bruises all over his body. Janice tenderly wound the cloth around him until his chest was covered. It had taken three shirts to provide a satisfactory job and even Adrian had to admit that it felt better.

"Thanks."

"What do we do now?"

Adrian glanced up to the road, "I'm going to try and find a way out of here."

She looked at him with tenderness; "Be careful."

"Don't you worry about me, I've no intention of meeting my maker just yet."

Leaving her in their makeshift camp, he moved to the base of the cliff. There were numerous foot and handholds near the bottom but each time he approached the overhang they either disappeared or crumbled as he touched them. With a rope, pitons and a good pair of climbing boots he would have chanced securing himself to the fragile rock but without them he didn't have a hope in hell to move higher. His arms and legs were beginning to ache so it was a common-sense decision to return to the base and rest before trying again. It was then that he saw the crack in the face that would, if he had the strength, help him get to the top. His legs were beginning to shake and his feet and hands were numb from the strain—it was madness to continue. Retracing his route, he returned to the base of the cliff and pondered.

He was aware that time was their immediate enemy. If there was a way back to the road he must find it or their chances of survival were limited. Janice was sensibly lying in the shade and, by moving a few of the larger stones, he lay alongside her. Resting uneasily, an idea began to form in his mind. Without harping on the danger it involved, he voiced his thoughts to Janice.

She fully understood just how hazardous this was all going to be, but appreciated that he was doing it for her and not just for himself. If he failed, she might as well be dead. Thoughts that should not be there flowed as a flash flood around her brain; she wanted him more than anything else. Her body longed for his touch—a touch she had previously repelled both mentally and physically.

Shaking herself back to reality and gently holding his hands in hers she saw that the tips of his fingers were raw and bleeding from gripping the sharp rocks that formed the tiny handholds which would have defeated many a climber. "Let's have another look around—maybe we missed something useful."

"What I need is a hook and a length of rope."

"Can't we make something?"

"We could if we had the right tools and suitable materials."

Looking into his eyes, she whispered, "Come on we can't give up now."

Once more they walked the slope but found nothing. On their return to the shade of the shelter it was Adrian that first noticed the knives and canvas belts he had removed from the Africans. Janice looked at the belts: "You have your rope—not very long, but beggars can't be choosy."

"I have my hook—if we can fasten two of these knives in the form of a cross it might work. Just a minute. Where's the rope they used to bind my hands?"

Adrian got to his feet and began another methodical search of the slope until he found it. Would it be enough he wondered? With the proficiency of an experienced sailor he bound the strongest of the knives together. Near the base of the cliff he forced the home-made crucifix into a crevice and tested its strength. For the moment it appeared to hold no matter how hard he attempted to dislodge it. Next he braided the belts together; they formed a rope of approximately six feet in length. Janice's belt secured this makeshift apparatus together. He passed the free end to her and told her to pull as hard as she could; the line remained intact.

He looked at his watch. It was just passing five; they had been down here for nearly seven hours and it would be getting dark soon. There was no time to waste. "Janice, there's a slim chance this will work and I'll get to the top. There's about an hour or so of daylight left—as it gets dark it'll begin to get cold; whatever happens stay where you are, eat the food sparingly and you'll be OK."

She looked at him. What was he telling her?—that it could go wrong? Without a thought for his wounds she pulled him close until their lips met. The kiss was intense and as much as his mind craved for more, it was neither the time and definitely not the place. He eased her away: "Wish me luck."

This time she watched him depart up the slope and begin his ascent. Carefully he retraced his route up and across the face until he reached the point where he had first identified the crack. It was now or never. Making sure his feet were well placed, his left hand formed a pinch grip around a projection. His hand squeezed the rock hard—it was a good hold. With his free hand, the hook was removed from the safety of his belt and the cord lowered to its full length. Slowly he began to swing it in an ever-increasing arc. This improvised grapnel overlapped the crack by about a foot. The fingers of his left hand continued to grip the rock, as Adrian stretched his body to the limit. His timing had to be perfect; sweat was running down his face and the pain was becoming unbearable as he cast the cross. It was on target but the blades failed to enter the crack and rattling against the stone, they fell away. To regain his breath he drew close to the wall before trying again. Three times he tried and failed but on the fourth attempt it dropped into the crevice as if made to measure.

Adrian's left arm was beginning to shake uncontrollably with the strain. For the moment he moved closer to the face to rest, breathing deeply to recharge his energy levels. His left hand took a few minutes for the circulation to return. Time to gather his thoughts was needed for the next move—it could be his last. The moment of decision arrived; there was no alternative.

Janice's eyes never left him for an instant. If mind over matter was feasible, she was willing him to succeed with every ounce of her existence. What she had failed to understand was Adrian's next move: in her naïveté she had thought that the hook was to help him climb. Now that his breathing and circulation were back to normal, he turned and looked down at Janice. Appearing not to have a care in the world he waved, counted to three, and swung out from the face. For a moment his life hung in the balance as the cross shuddered and moved but the blades dug in and the apparatus held fast.

In the distance he heard a scream but he wasn't sure whether it had emanated from his lips or hers. That intense pain, which is impossible to understand until you suffer it, erupted in his chest as he swung like a pendulum back into the rock face. It reminded him that he was still very much alive. He hung on, his legs acting as buffers to stop the swing. It worked - adrenaline, initiated by absolute fear, was pumping through his veins. Slowly and deliberately he pulled himself up until he could place his right hand into the crack and jam it solid. For the moment he knew he was safe but he had to find another good hold. With his legs wrapped around the rope he pulled himself up and stretched his left arm to its full extent, feeling and searching for it. A cavity allowed him the luxury of a good pocket, his feet remained dangling.

"Well I got away with it once," he shouted at the inanimate rock face, moving his right arm ready to jam it again. His whole bodyweight was transferred to a hold he could only feel. Now totally reliant on the grip of his left hand, he began to pull himself upwards but then the hold failed. Fingers clawed desperately at the rock face, a scream filled the air as he fell and the serrations ripped his flesh. His right hand by instinct formed a fist and jammed into the crack with a force never before imagined. Pain and desperation made Adrian achieve in the next few minutes what many would consider impossible.

Torn fingers searched for a secure hold, and then another and another, as inch by inch he moved up the face. With determination from reserves never before realised, he pulled himself higher into the break until it became wide enough to hold his body. Exhausted and gasping for breath, he rested: contact with the rock had torn the skin off his knuckles, and blood dripped from both hands. Having beaten defeat twice, now was not the time to think of giving up. For a minute or two he hungrily gulped air down into his lungs to deliver oxygen to muscles that ached from such unaccustomed work. Despite battered fingers and aching ribs, the knives were retrieved and secured to his belt. It was great just to be alive. Time was running out and without food and water, his body would lack the energy to carry on. With his back firmly against one wall and his feet against the opposite side of the chimney he paused, and composed his mind for the next stage. Slowly he began to push himself with his hands upwards an inch at a time. The pain was overwhelming but the fear of failure and death forced him on.

As he moved higher, the fissure opened wider and wider until he was able to bridge it. His left hand and foot were on one wall and right hand and foot on the other. Adrian found this to be less strenuous as a way of progressing the climb. Then it funnelled outwards. A narrow ledge remained the only positive way to go. The going became relatively easy until the ledge all but disappeared. Above his shoulders a mantelshelf ran to his left, giving him no choice of direction. Again he rested for a few minutes. When he was ready, he straightened his arms and slowly pulled himself up, until he could twist his body and place one foot on the shelf. Once his bodyweight was over his hands, he rolled onto it. At the narrowest point it was eighteen inches wide and standing became easy. For the first time since the ascent had begun he could, unaided, stand upright.

He continued upwards into an area of loose water-washed rock. Secure holds became hard to find and the further he travelled, the harder it became. Desperately he ran his hands across the surface looking for the barest of holds; he found a small split in the polished surface and drove one of the knife blades deep into it. This enabled him to move slightly higher. With his body grasping the surface he edged his way until he was halfway up the slope, only the blade of a knife separating him from the fall to oblivion. With the right equipment the most average of climbers could have negotiated this with the minimum of difficulty. He looked right and left, it was as smooth as glass. The road was at most twenty feet above him and he was helpless; one false move and he would join those that he had buried earlier.

Janice was still looking at the figure who had clawed its way up that face and initially thought that he was just stopping to regain his breath. It was only when he was still in the same position thirty minutes later that she realised something was wrong. The sun was beginning to set but it still had the warmth of a small furnace as it reflected off the rock and burnt into Adrian's flesh. He was sore and beginning to wish that fate had been merciful and killed him outright but he shook his head and shouted at the sun, "You can't beat me—I'm still alive!"

He began to sing, his parched throat barely able to produce the words. When it was too sore to make any sound he played "I spy" with himself—anything to maintain consciousness and hope. As the sun fell below the horizon the coolness of the evening air lifted his spirits and he started to think, that if he moved down into the funnel, just maybe he could get some rest but the idea evaporated as fast as it formed. He struggled to stay awake, each look at his watch only revealing that a few minutes had passed. His legs were numb from the constant pressure they were forced to apply to the hilt of the knife. He tried one leg at a time in a vain attempt to rest the other. It worked and tired muscles screamed as blood flowed freely to them but the changing of feet on such a small object was fraught with its own problems: several times he experienced the danger of slipping but still he clung to life. He tried to remember all the good things he had experienced but aching limbs continually returned him to reality.

Janice did not sleep; Adrian was in trouble and there was damn all she could do about it. She sobbed until the tears dried up, then prayed to an unfamiliar God. This could not be the end, not this way. Adrian's energy levels were draining rapidly but he continued to believe he would find a way. He had to return to the chimney or fall. It was then he heard the sound of a large diesel engine and a vehicle moving slowly along the road. He tried to shout but only a hoarse croak came from his mouth. The noise the engine made filled his ears and he knew it would be unlikely that he would be heard above such a din.

Suddenly strange voices radiated all around and the bright beam of a powerful torch was being shone down to the slope: he watched as it moved methodically down to the edge, then onward to another sector until it finally found Janice standing at the base. She had not dared to move as she had guessed they were looking for something even if they were scavengers out to rob the dead.

The engine was stopped and a familiar voice echoed down: "Janice."

The joy of hearing his voice defied belief and she shouted, "Selwyn, Adrian's on a ledge just to your right, he's in trouble."

The torch moved away and her eyes followed the beam until it found him. A gaggle of voices erupted.

One of the rescuers began to climb into a body harness. The engine was restarted and slowly the winch began to revolve, releasing a thin wire as it lowered a man over the edge. Once clear, the speed was increased, and small stones began to rattle down onto Adrian; he didn't care, someone up there liked him.

It seemed ages until the man was next to Adrian and methodically fastening a harness around his body. Once secure, they began the ascent: his rescuer smiled, the mouthful of white teeth against his dark skin acting like a beacon in the darkness. Adrian did not understand a word his saviour uttered but he knew enough to relax and let him do all the work of avoiding the cliff face. As they neared the top willing hands reached down and dragged them both away from the edge.

Without pausing to rest, the man grabbed another harness and began his descent to Janice. Adrian tried to stand as helping hands assisted him but his exhausted legs buckled beneath him. They carried him to the back of the lorry and sat him on the tailboard. Selwyn was waiting there, his right arm in a sling and his head wrapped in bandages. In the moonlight the stark whiteness of the cloth stood out against his dark skin as does the white in a zebra crossing at night. Not a word was said as the two men embraced, ignoring the pain of their wounds. Adrian felt the warmth of tears running down his friend's face. "Thought you'd gone over the edge with the Land Rover," whispered a croaky Adrian.

"No chance: when it went out of control I dived out, smashed my head on some rocks and broke my arm. It appears I was found lying in the road when the gang of workmen that passed us earlier came back. Even then the gods were smiling; they took me to the hospital in Arusho where the staff patched me up and watched over me until I came round. It took some time to explain what had happened, but once it was understood they moved heaven and earth to get back here. Seems we only just made it in your case."

Adrian grimaced a weak smile; "Oh I don't know, I could have survived for a few minutes longer. Can I have a drink of water?"

Selwyn moved to the front of the lorry and returned holding a water bottle and a clean cloth; using this he soaked it and bathed his friend's face and lips. When he had finished he told Adrian to lean back and he squeezed the soaked cloth, letting the liquid slowly enter his mouth and soothe a parched throat. This was repeated several times until he heard the amiable tones of Janice.

"Here comes trouble," murmured Adrian, "and I think I'm in it."

Still covered in her odd array of clothing, Janice kissed her rescuers one by one and then walked around the truck to Adrian. "You stupid bugger, you could have killed yourself." Her tirade was not malicious, simply showing care for the man that had risked everything in an attempt to save her. She held his hands gently and felt the torn flesh.

Adrian did not flinch, but removed his hands slowly from hers. There was a look in her eyes that sent only one message. As he leant forward to kiss her, darkness overcame him and he fell to the ground. The men, having recovered all their ropes and equipment lifted him into the rear of the vehicle and laid him on some sacking, Janice sat beside him, cradling his head in her lap. Selwyn let her lean against him as they began the fifty mile journey towards Arusho, leaving behind their forsaken attempt at conquering an unforgiving precipice.

As the truck proceeded, the breeze induced by its movement wafted the smell of sweat-covered bodies—the result of days spent in the same clothing. She promised herself the luxury of a really hot bath once they reached the hospital. That was her top priority after getting Adrian settled in.

For him the rest of the journey was like a dream, and, had he been able to gather his thoughts, he would have been thankful just to be alive. Selwyn and Janice tried to talk but the roar of the engine and erratic movement of the lorry made it impossible.

The hospital consisted of two single storey white washed stone buildings with corrugated iron roofs, one for men, the other for women. There was not the luxury of porters or a huge medical team; one doctor and half a dozen nurses covered the medical and surgical needs of a district that was equivalent to the total expanse of Wales. The men assisted Janice and Selwyn to the ground but one disappeared, returning in seconds with a stretcher. They lifted the unconscious Adrian on to it and carried him into the ward. The doctor, who lived in a one-roomed bungalow adjoining the compound, had been awakened by the arrival of the lorry. He joined them as Adrian's clothes were being removed and each cut and abrasion examined. When all the wounds had been cleaned and bathed in an antiseptic solution and his ribs bandaged, the doctor turned and left the rest to the duty nurse. As he walked out into the cool night air he spoke gently to an anxious Janice: "Wait a few minutes, then you may go in—but do not stay. You need rest as well."

On entering, she could barely see Adrian, his bed being surrounded by a huge mosquito net. He was awake and, satisfied that he was in the most able of hands, she kissed him gently on the lips and left. The nurse advised Selwyn that, to ensure complete rest, Adrian would be sedated. The doctor returned and gently pushed the fine point of the needle into Adrian's arm. The powerful sedative entered the blood stream and began to work.

To everyone's amazement Janice's wounds were limited to severe bruising, although there was some possibility of concussion. A bath and a good sleep were ordered. She luxuriated in the hot bath for some time until she was reminded by a nurse that it was getting late and they all needed to sleep.

Adrian was in a perfect world, dreaming of the future and all he believed it to hold.

Six

Captain Vaughan was in a bad mood and worried; Angel had ordered him to sail immediately his fuel bunkers were full. He roared at his crew constantly from the bridge but despite his protestations, it took over an hour. Renegade he may be but he had no intention to sail for the Cape with an unprepared vessel. With the engines ready, he warped his ship methodically off the jetty until the bows were clear.

When satisfied he bellowed, "Let go forward, Let go aft, and slow ahead." As the old engines began to deliver power, MV *Kia Hua* slowly nosed her way forward.

"Steady as you go, Helmsman." The tall deckhand with brown shoulder-length hair, still in the same faded denims, made a barely audible but contemptuous reply, "OK Mate."

Vaughan demanded respect, and his foul mood did nothing for his temperament. For him it was the last straw, so he struck the boy hard in the back, knocking him to the deck. The ship started to veer towards a sand bar but Vaughan grabbed the brass-spoked wheel and steered her past the danger whilst kicking the man viciously. As he retched over the deck the young man shouted that he would kill Vaughan. Another kick to the head silenced him. The Bosun came on the bridge as the final boot was administered. His own fear forced him to drag the helpless wretch away from further harm before taking over the wheel.

"Bosun," roared Vaughan, "you can inform this rabble that that we may be mercenaries but they'll still pay the proper marks of respect to all officers. Is that clear?"

"Yes, Sir."

As they cleared the harbour, the men, organised into watches, took their positions and a sort of normality resumed. They had seen the condition of the man that had annoyed Vaughan. For the time being they were not ready to end up the same way, although the hate was spreading like the Black Death in a crowded city. It was only a matter of time before Vaughan's power ended. Until then, time was on their side. They had been at sea for ten hours and making a good speed when their destination was received: *You are to proceed at best possible speed to the Bonaparte Archipelago in the Timor Sea. Further instructions will follow if your arrival remains undetected.*

Vaughan understood the orders and went to his cabin. Once there, from his desk drawer he removed a small manila envelope. Slowly he read his orders again just to be sure that he had not missed any important point which, if left unattended, could jeopardise their objective. They were very precise: whilst on passage, change the look of the vessel so that it could appear as another. Various comments were made on how to implement the changes; an overriding factor was that all works, including course changes, were to take place at night. Vaughan left his cabin and went up on the bridge, feeling the warm wind sweeping over him as he made his way to the chart table. He shouted for the Bosun, and pointed to the flag fluttering at the masthead. "Get rid of that, change it to something less conspicuous."

"Yes, Sir."

Vaughan half looked towards the masthead on top of the main cabin deck. The Red Ensign had been replaced by one of convenience, Panama. Satisfied, he continued with the task at hand. A quick mental calculation told him they had about five and a half thousand miles to travel before reaching their destination. At best possible speed, taking into account changes in direction, it would take about eighteen to twenty days. Each night the men would have to work hard to alter the appearance of the ship. "God help us if we hit bad weather," he thought.

He summoned the Bosun and detailed each night's workload and how he expected it to be accomplished. The look this man gave him said it all: "Why?"

Vaughan read him correctly and standing at full height so that he towered over him screamed into his face, "Look you bastard, I didn't make these orders but when I give them that's the end of it."

The Bosun wanted to reply but he valued the bones in his body more than enough not to argue, so he nodded and left.

Night after night the men worked to the arduous schedule, burning away at the superstructure and the vast array of deck fittings that distinguish one ship from another. Vaughan seemed always to be watching them from the sanctuary of the bridge peering through the salt smeared screen as the *Kia Hua* lifted then fell into the dark sea, slicing her way towards her fate. The disposal of the cargo and much of the top weight had increased their speed by two knots, they were making good time. Every night, and then again before the sun rose, the violent changes of course baffled the crew but none dared ask the question. Vaughan had taken over the navigation and revealed nothing of their whereabouts. It was his responsibility alone. They were aware that it was getting hotter by the day and that working at night now suited them. Each time the radar indicated another vessel, Vaughan would alter course away from it. The *Kia Hua* was losing itself to the world. Gallons of paint covered the scars inflicted by cutting torches until Vaughan was satisfied with the changes. High in the water and devoid of deck gantries and superficial lockers she could have been any type of tramp but not one that would appear in any book of reference.

Vaughan was tired; he had to rest. With the work now complete he could pass the routine running of the ship to his First Officer. He called him to the bridge and gave him the order, "Steer this course, avoiding all other shipping by a minimum of ten miles, we must not be seen. Understood?"

The First Officer just said, "Yes, Sir."

Having left the bridge, he entered his cabin and fell onto the bunk but his mind was still active enough to realise that some of the crew would, given half a chance, like to see him dead. He got up and went across to the door and threw the two bolts that would make it secure. For good measure the back of a chair was placed under the handle so that it would fall if the door was forced open. Satisfied with these simple precautions, he removed the pistol from under his mattress and laid it alongside him as he fell into the welcoming comfort of the bunk. Sleep evaded him for some time until pure fatigue overwhelmed him and he fell into a restless but much needed slumber.

The First Officer and the Bosun kept the ship running as instructed but, with the main task now over, the crew began to relax and think of the money they would receive when the ship was delivered. One man still resented the severe treatment dispensed by Vaughan but was content to wait for a better time. Having slept for over ten hours, Vaughan awoke fuddled and confused, but a cold shower, followed by a shave, shocked his system back to reality. He dressed and combed his hair in the large mirror on the back of the door. Feeling better, he retrieved the pistol from the bed and placed it in his jacket pocket. Now he was ready.

Unlike his predecessor, he opened the door with a crash so that those who were on the bridge were immediately aware of his presence. With deliberation he surveyed the empty horizon. Even on the radar the nearest ship was thirty miles away. Turning to his First Officer, his voice short "What's the closest any vessel came?"

"Twenty miles, Sir."

"Good, get some rest; I'll need you later. The Bosun can continue this watch."

"Sir, the Bosun has been with me since you retired to your cabin."

Vaughan realised that to keep the Bosun on the bridge would be foolish and ordered that the Second

Mate keep the next six hours in his company, whilst he fixed the ship and ensured the correct course was maintained. The Mate arrived, Vaughan looked at this man who had, he believed, been dismissed from his ship for battering a man senseless. The irony was that now they were the same. The only power he had was his fists and the knowledge of where they were going. "Steer a steady course and keep your eyes open for any shipping."

Tomorrow he would transmit their estimated time of arrival. Ten minutes before noon and with a sextant held tightly in his right hand, he walked out to the bridge wing and took three sun sights, writing down each angle and the time recorded on the bridge chronometer. In ten minutes he had the ship positively fixed, the Satellite Navigation system had been surprisingly accurate.

Happy with the progress made, he drew a thin line from their present location to the Bonaparte Archipelago, stopping it some twenty miles off shore. "Mate," he shouted, "this is the course you will follow and return to if other shipping is in the area. Whatever you do, don't go closer inshore than ten miles—there are some dangerous reefs around, and now we've come this far I would be very annoyed to run aground."

The Mate was more than surprised when Vaughan finished with, "I will be in my cabin if you need me." Without waiting for an answer he turned on his heel and left the bridge. Once in his cabin he removed the folder that gave precise instructions. He read aloud to himself, "When twenty-four hours away from the rendezvous point you are to send the following on frequency 192SW—'Am in position.' When this has been received, a homing device will be activated on a frequency of 120SW. This will direct you to where the ship is to be anchored and sunk. As arranged, you and your men will remain on the ship. When advised, you will leave the ship using one of the boats."

At noon the next day Vaughan left his cabin and checked the time of high water yet again. Satisfied that his calculations were correct he strolled into the radio shack and told the operator to send the message. He waited, and then, as a precaution, he ordered it to be sent again. Unbeknown, the message was no more than a trigger to activate a homing device. On completion of the second transmission the operator was ordered to change the frequency to 120SW. Almost immediately a high-pitched tone could be clearly heard over the speaker. "Right sparks, get me a direction on that and keep me informed if we stray off course."

"The course required is 090, Sir."

"Thank you."

Sparks was taken aback at Vaughan's apparent civility but continued to monitor the signal relaying the direction of the beacon to the bridge over the intercom. When they veered from the designated course, corrections were reported immediately. They were closing the land fast. At a speed of five knots the *Kia Hua* cautiously approached the shore. What a few hours before had been a thin dark line was now a seemingly unending panorama of cliffs and trees. The crew was becoming nervous at the sound of the surf which could be clearly seen crashing onto the beach.

"There it is," shouted Vaughan. "Steer for that gap in the cliff."

The man couldn't see where he was supposed to go and asked for a mark to steer by. Vaughan pushed him aside and proceeded, with a skill born from years of practice, to move the ship gently against the flow. He guided the old lady towards what appeared to be an impenetrable ridge of red rock and earth covered in vegetation. Even he had his doubts, but followed the signalled course purposefully. They were travelling along a line of muddy-coloured water that flowed from the shore. The gap was beginning to show itself more obviously but as they came closer, it still seemed too narrow. The channel was well-founded but all could see that only a few yards away were rocks with breakers tumbling over them. Vaughan's concentration never wavered for a second as he directed the *Kia Hua* towards its final resting place. Without its cargo and top weight the ship was high in the water and answered its helm sluggishly.

"Increase speed to fifteen knots for two minutes only," screamed Vaughan.

The surge of power as it reached the propeller enabled the rudder to centre the bows directly on the entrance. Then they were in and amongst the undergrowth pushing their way through. The tropical vegetation that had concealed it from humanity gave way to the force that fell upon it. The bows entered the dense growth at eight knots, shattering the branches of the overhanging trees and causing a myriad of different birds to soar screaming into the air. The huge structure of the bridge shuddered as branches, torn from their parent trees, cascaded on the deck. Steadily they moved forward, brushing aside that which had remained undisturbed for so long. Once through, a natural deep water harbour revealed itself to all who had dared remain on deck. Towering red earthen cliffs surrounded them on all sides; the only way out was the way they had come in. Once clear of the entrance and its encumbrances the order was: "Full astern." The single propeller bit deep into the water and began to reduce the forward momentum of the vessel until it was almost stopped.

"Bosun," shouted Vaughan, "let go the anchor, we've arrived."

On his way forward he had ordered two men to accompany him; when they were ready they looked at the bridge and saw Vaughan nod. With the command given, one of the men released the brake on the capstan. At first it remained still, but the Bosun kicked the cable viciously. Slowly it moved until the weight of the anchor overcame any resistance and it began its descent into the murky depths. The Bosun judged the depth of the water correctly. He signalled to the bridge that the ship was held by its anchor. The crew returned to the deck, sighing with relief at the end of a long journey. One of the men noticed a movement on the small beach and then in horror drew back from the guard-rail. There, swimming towards them, were three of the largest crocodiles he had ever seen. Others gathered by the side and witnessed these huge beasts from the dark ages circle the ship until, one by one, they returned to the shore to bask in the sun. Every man was acutely aware that to fall in the water would mean a horrible death.

Vaughan returned to his cabin and removed his orders from his desk: "when in position send the following message on a frequency of 120VHF—'*Home and all's well.*' When our contact receives this, arrangements will be made to get you out. Do not attempt to leave the ship or send your men ashore."

The message was transmitted.

+++

Concealed from those onboard, wandering in the forest away from the confines of the bay but not far from the edges of the cliff, was a single aborigine who caught venomous snakes to supplement his meagre livelihood. These were eventually sold to those who milked their venom to produce antidotes for the stupid white men who strayed into the wilderness and got bitten. Most died, as they wandered haphazardly in delirium around in ever decreasing circles. His own tough hide had been pierced many times by those razor sharp fangs, even as he placed each snake with care into a separate sack. He was immune to such poison and played with his captives as a child would a toy. This day, his concentration had been disturbed by the sound of chaos as branches were broken and trees torn from their roots. His natural inquisitiveness led him to the top of the cliff that overlooked the cove. He knew the bay well but had never ventured down. The water dragons that lived there devoured his people. His ancestors had declared this as the place of the sea devils.

As the *Kia Hua* entered the bay he watched in wonder, not knowing why such a vessel would want to visit this place. When the commotion stopped he left the scene and continued with his business. It was not his problem to worry what others did if it did not affect him.

+++

Vaughan had the crew gathered in their messroom and explained that they would have to wait until whoever from wherever arrived to take them away. The orders also stated that it was necessary to place explosive charges and that this would be completed by their expert. Volunteers were asked to help and two men offered on the understanding that when the detonators were set they would be elsewhere. The man laughed, explaining that detonation required a specific radio signal from close range.

One man still bore a grudge for his beating and was planning his revenge. Patiently he had waited for this day. No-one would care; the crew despised Vaughan's arrogant manner and the way he had worked them since leaving Mombassa. The captain's execution was planned for later that night.

The meeting over, Vaughan returned to his cabin to rest. It was dark when he awoke and, feeling drained by the heat, he decided to freshen up with a cold shower. The spray of the water as it hit his body, preoccupied him, and he let his mind run over other times—bad ones, profitable ones. He did not hear his cabin door open or the man enter holding a razor sharp rigging knife. It was by sheer chance that a fleeting shadow caused him to turn. As the knife came arcing down he punched out blindly; the blow hit home but the knife cut his right forearm from top to bottom, severing the artery. Vaughan acted instinctively;

ripping the curtain from its rings he tossed it at his assailant. Then, motivated by the fear of death, he lunged forward, kicking and punching as he did so. The attacker fell to the floor and Vaughan jumped on his chest killing him instantly. His heart was pumping fast and blood from his wound was now splattering the bulkheads. He was in serious trouble: if the bleeding was not stopped he would soon join his attacker.

Stumbling across the cabin he grabbed the intercom and called the Bosun. The first-aid box was ripped from the wall by his left hand as he searched for bandages to stem the continuous flow of blood. He attempted to clean the cut but the outpouring was unrelenting. With perseverance he tightly wrapped bandage after bandage around the wound but each one rapidly changed colour. The Bosun eventually arrived and between them they reduced the spillage to a weep but without proper medical assistance there was little they could do. With his arm strapped to his chest, Vaughan walked across to his drinks cabinet and removed a bottle of Johnny Walker whisky and two glasses. He placed them on his desk and poured two large measures, "Bosun, drink with me. If I am about to die I don't want to know about it."

"Captain, if you relax and we leave this place within the next twenty-four hours you have a chance."

"Bosun, thanks but it's my time. I know that and so do you. That bastard in there's the lucky one; he died quickly and with little pain, though in the end it's the same nothingness. Help me die with some dignity at least. The orders for the termination of this voyage are in the right hand drawer of my desk, read them and follow the instructions precisely."

The glass was offered and both men sat and devoured the whole bottle of whisky and then, to ensure oblivion, a bottle of brandy. The Bosun was drunk but his mind still managed to function at a reduced level. Without any real concern he dragged Vaughan across the deck and unceremoniously dumped him on his bunk. He threw a blanket over the still body mumbling: "Fucking bastard, you'll survive—the devil looks after his own." He left the cabin, turned out the light, laughing as he did so. The Bosun did not want the responsibility, but accepted the fact.

The next morning Vaughan and his attacker had joined company—both were dead. The flies had already found the mess of bloodied sheets and were busy laying their eggs in the festering carcasses.

The Bosun, suffering from an almighty hangover, was overcome by the stench that saturated the air, and vomited over the desk as he retrieved the documents. He staggered out of the cabin, knowing that the old man had been right, his time had come.

Once in the fresh air the documents were quickly studied and he realised that all they had to do was wait and then, just prior to leaving, set the explosives. The men were becoming restless, they wanted out of this hell hole. Bored and irritable, many watched the huge crocodiles as they waddled from the searing heat of the sun into the shade and eventually into the water to keep cool. Feeding time was twice a day when the flood tide roared in through the gap bringing with it an involuntary entanglement of fish and weed. Once the first rush of water began, these beasts moved swiftly, devouring everything in their path. It was a meagre diet, they always returned to the beach hungry.

It was passing two in the afternoon of the second day when the FM radio on the Bridge burst into life. No-one was there; a further five minutes elapsed before one of the hands passing on the deck below heard the chatter. He ran up the ladder and grabbed at the hand-set. This had the action of silencing the message. Realising his mistake he spoke into the mouthpiece. "This is the *Kia Hua*."

The reply was swift and abrupt: "Time to leave. Complete the mission."

By this time all were on the bridge listening. They made their way to their accommodation area to pack the few personal possessions they had either brought with them or acquired. Within ten minutes they were on the cargo deck. From far away the sound of a helicopter could be heard. They waited as the reverberations of the rotor blades grew stronger and stronger then suddenly a Sea King Variant, with its bright red fuselage, appeared over the edge of the cliff. The men cheered at the sight of their ticket home. The pilot operated the fixed loud hailer and asked if everything was ready. The Bosun acknowledged and indicated that the charges were set and in place.

Suddenly, without any warning, the explosives began to detonate, the ship appeared to leap in the air as it twisted from stem to stern. Heavy steel plates buckled and were ripped by the force they tried to contain. Large sheets were tossed like paper in the wind with men still clinging to them. Those felled by the shock waves and uninjured began to pick themselves up and rush for cover. It was foolhardy for there was no escape. Fire raged out of control at the aft end of the ship forcing those seeking refuge elsewhere. Dazed and in a state of confusion some ventured onto the open deck. The helicopter was hovering close by and Chung diligently operated the heavy calibre machine gun, its awesome fire power cutting men to shreds as they ran. The Bosun and two others were hiding in the forward rope store and witnessed every horror of the massacre as it happened. Slowly the ship began to settle in the water: others knew that, before long, water would flood their shelter, forcing them into the open. If the madman in the helicopter failed to kill them, there remained the crocodiles. Life—so precious to all—suddenly seemed pointless. The beasts, having sensed the panic of dying men, had already begun to feast on those unfortunates thrown into the water. These creatures from ages past swam effortlessly around the dying ship, waiting. The stern went down first, and, with the engine room flooded, bloody water now tumbled through damaged bulkheads into the empty holds. The Bosun looked through the small round window in the rope store door. As water rushed over the deck, he witnessed the pitiful efforts of the injured as they floated into the bay. The crocodiles seemed to wait for the men to reach them before, with a movement of their tail, they moved in. Most men were dead before the crocodiles reached them. Some still had the strength to scream in agony when those massive jaws clamped tight to a limb or trunk, and what remained was dragged below the surface. As they feasted, these monsters spun wildly until a piece of carcass tore away, others grabbed at the remains. The Bosun covered his ears and looked away in an attempt to shut out a fate that would soon be his. The screams reverberated around the cliffs as the beasts enjoyed their banquet. As they swam, men were cut down by the rapid fire that continued in sporadic bursts to end their existence. This primeval carnage continued until not a scrap of living tissue remained.

"At least the skipper died in his bed," thought the Bosun as the bows began to settle but still he and the others remained where they were. Any chance was worth the effort, no matter how small. The helicopter continued to hover until the bow finally plunged into the depths. With a quick sweep of the bay, Chung fired at anything that resembled a man. With one final circuit the magazine was emptied and then they headed westward across the sea towards the sanctuary of Indonesia. Chung had achieved the objective of eliminating any witnesses.

The Bosun and the two men with him were about to dive into the water when the movement of the ship slammed the door shut. The pressure of the water on the outside held it fast as the forward section of the hull fell uncontrolled to the bottom of the bay. The youngest of them screamed at the blackness that surrounded them but the Bosun and the other man were prepared to die in silence. When the bow of the *Kia Hua* hit the bottom, tons of mud and silt were disturbed, causing the waters to turn a dirty brown. They were in trouble; the door remained jammed, but what kept the water out, kept air in. For the moment, fate had given them a chance, slim by most standards but still a chance.

The Bosun calmed the others down and spoke to them in reassuring tones. "We know the helicopter's gone and if those creatures have sated their hunger we could make it."

Bart, a deckhand was not so easily convinced but when the alternatives were considered he realised that death was close whether it was by drowning or as a snack for the monsters that swam above. The air pocket was reducing slowly and what remained was beginning to taste foul.

The Bosun had an idea. "What we'll do is increase the flow of water so that we can get the door open. If we stay here much longer we'll die anyway. When you get to the surface don't, whatever you do, splash about. Swim gently to the opposite bank away from the crocs. Don't try to help each other, it's every man for himself. Once you're ashore find a way up that cliff. OK?"

They agreed.

"Right, get your shoulders to this door and push before we drop dead in this metal box."

Thompson, the youngest, had found a metal bar and between them they began to pry the door open. Initially any movement was barely discernible but they knew it had moved as the force of water entering increased. The level rose rapidly and in moments their heads were covered but still the door remained fast. As the pressure equalised, it opened enough to get the bar into the gap. With lungs bursting they gave up and surfaced, each gasping at the little air that remained.

"Well, my friends we make it this time or we die in this ready-made coffin," asserted the Bosun. "On the count of three, fill your lungs and good luck. One, two, three."

Taking a large gulp of air they pulled themselves down to the door and with all their remaining strength shoved. At first it held fast but with brute force and desperation it began to open wider until the gap was enough for a man to squeeze through. The Bosun grabbed one of the men and pushed him through. He repeated this action with the other. The pain that now inflicted his lungs almost cost him his life but he clawed his way into the murky water. With the depth of water each man cleared the surface by half a body length but, despite the splash, they followed the Bosun's instructions and almost without a ripple made their way to the far shore. The crocodiles were sunning themselves with full stomachs and would remain that way until their huge meal had been completely digested. Even so they had reserves stored beneath the water rotting for another day.

The three men could, for the moment, consider themselves fortunate. Each made for the base of the cliff, but, exhausted by their endeavours, collapsed and waited. Only the Bosun chivvied them along for he knew that to stay could mean certain death from an inquisitive beast. With a boot up their backsides he forced them to find a way up the steep embankment. They clawed at the soft earth, moving slowly up until a narrow ledge some twenty feet above the water gave them a place of safety.

The Bosun looked around: "We'll get our breath back and then make our way to the top."

Two minutes stretched to half an hour but they did not seem to care. With no money or possessions their future lives were destined to be short-lived. To surrender to the authorities as shipwrecked mariners was the only sensible course of action; no-one would know that they were accessories to murder. Still they were alive and so far the only survivors.

The Bosun stretched his arms, looking at the others: "Let's get going."

"Where to?" asked Bart.

"I'm fucked if I know but it's got to be better than staying here."

Again they attacked the soft cliff face and inch by inch moved towards the crest. It took over three hours, moving up three feet and sliding down two, but, eventually, weary and covered in dust, the top was reached. Looking down and amazed at their own tenacity, they were relieved at having achieved a miraculous escape from death.

"I don't bloody believe it," screamed the Bosun. "Look at that."

The three men stared down into the bay and where there had been a huge water filled basin full of terror there now remained a wide but shallow lake. The superstructure and a large section of the hull were in fresh air. With the muddy waters having washed away, the *Kia Hua* could be seen lying slightly to one side. On its own, some yards away, was the bow section.

"That's why the bloody door jammed," stated the Bosun as they stared at the wreck.

"What do we do now, Bosun?"

"Get away from this place and find somewhere safe to rest for the night."

"Where the hell are we anyway?" asked Thompson.

"Australia." The Bosun stood up and looked around and realised that at sea he may have been more than capable but in this inhospitable land he was no wiser than the others but a decision had to be made. "We'll walk north hugging the coast until we reach a settlement."

"What then?" asked Bart.

"We'll make that decision, when we have to."

The Bosun started to walk in a northerly direction, the others, covered in dry mud, followed in silence. Not more than fifty yards away, the aborigine, his sackful of snakes equivalent to a month's drinking money, followed without making a sound. His curiosity had for once got the better of him. Who were these men and where did they think they were going?

Seven

The morning had arrived bright and sunny; wisps of white cloud drifted overhead, promoting the blue of the tropical sky, its filtered light staggered through the hospital windows as the net curtains moved gently with the breeze. Adrian stirred, opened his eyes, and with every movement felt the pain that tormented his nervous system. Then he began to remember and was grateful to be lying between white sheets. A noise to his right forced him to turn his head. Standing with her back to him was a nurse, her uniform crisp with starch. It rustled with her small movements as she busied herself.

His voice sounded far away: "Nurse."

In passable English she managed, "Good morning."

Adrian attempted to explain how he felt without success, but fortunately for him, as frustration began to set in, Selwyn arrived, and he instantly felt better at the sight of this familiar, smiling face. "

"I bloody ache everywhere."

Selwyn looked at his friend lying there covered in bandages. "That's not surprising—you're lucky to be alive."

"How's Janice?"

" Better than you. She has a mild concussion, multiple bruising and some superficial cuts. Anyway there's some good news—a light aircraft should arrive in a few hours to take us to Nairobi. Once there a RAF Hercules Transport will take us home."

"Who arranged this?"

"Charles Dawning."

"How the hell did he find out where we are?"

"The doctor reported us to the local police and as we were on the missing persons list, they informed headquarters, who in turn told London. It would appear the whole damned world has been looking for us while we avoided every living soul."

"What about our ship? Has it been searched?"

"Charles asked me about that. I told him nothing."

Adrian had now, inch by inch, moved himself to a sitting position and was puzzled at his friend's reply.

"Why didn't you tell him what we know?"

"Simple. Tell him, you tell the world. If we have avoided the bad guys I'd rather they didn't know where we are now."

"Good morning everyone. How's the walking wounded?" Janice was wearing a blue cotton dress that one of the nurses had given her. It was at least two sizes too large and hung loosely from her shoulders, but she looked refreshed and ready for anything the day might bring. The only visible signs of the previous day's experience were the large black bruises that covered her forehead and numerous scratches on her arms and face. She walked over and kissed Adrian gently on the lips. "How are we?"

"I think he'll live," commented Selwyn, "but with tender loving care administered in that fashion his blood pressure'll have gone sky high."

"If that's all that's gone up, I must be losing my appeal."

Adrian blushed a bright red.

Janice looked at him and laughed. "I'd never have believed that a man of the world, especially a sailor, could be so sheepish over such a small matter."

Whatever his reply Adrian knew he would lose: "Janice, shut up. Would you please leave while I get dressed?"

She laughed as she left.

"Selwyn, help me—I intend to walk out of here."

At his first attempt, the muscles that had worked so hard only hours before screamed at being woken and failed to support him. Selwyn moved to give him a hand but one look from Adrian stopped him. Stubbornness prevailed and with some vigorous rubbing of leg muscles, circulation was restored. Gingerly he stood up and remained standing.

"There you are!"

"Is that why you're sweating like a stuffed pig?"

Adrian looked at his friend: "Please help me get dressed."

With the pain from arms and legs that didn't really want to move, it took over ten minutes to help him. The clothes provided by the hospital were not a perfect fit but they would suffice until Nairobi. The doctor arrived and was determined that his patient would not leave without a final medical check. As he poked and prodded in a methodical manner and listened to a good set of lungs, not a word was spoken until he was satisfied.

"Thanks, Doc, for everything. If there's anything you ever need, just let me know."

The doctor looked at him quizzically: "If you mean what you say, how about getting our antiquated generator repaired? It's frustrating when the lights go out, then stay that way until a mechanic can fix the damn thing."

"Doc, I'll do better than that. I'll arrange for a new machine to be sent out here with the engineers to install it."

The doctor smiled. "That would be appreciated. Thank you."

Janice wandered across the compound with a tray of bread and boiled eggs. Each of them was ravenous but good manners prevailed as they attempted to eat like civilised human beings. It was a lovely morning, they were alive and going home.

The meal over, Selwyn went away to obtain details for the generator, leaving Janice and Adrian. There was a strange silence between them, before Janice eventually spoke. "You risked your life for me yesterday and I owe you an apology."

"Consider the debt paid."

"What do you mean?"

Adrian looked with adoration at the woman who sat beside him: "The kiss you gave me before I passed out was payment enough."

She searched his face, expecting him to say more. "What do we do now?"

"Don't you know that I love you?"

She looked at him with tenderness, but her eyes were sad and tearful. Then she leaned against him and he felt her hair brush his face. She hesitated. "You can't love me Adrian. I'm not available for anyone to love. Every man I've ever got close to has died and I don't want you to die. I couldn't take it."

The shutters that came down over her eyes were unmistakable, she was deeply troubled. Before he had a chance to interrupt, she continued, "I've wanted you since the first day we met and life will be dull without you. I'll even miss you and your old fashioned ways. I don't know how to love. When we get home I'll return to my life and you to yours and we'll forget this ever happened."

"Janice, please listen. Do you think I'm just going to walk away? You can't tell me not to love you." Adrian was hurt and retaliated. "Just get one thing straight—you don't have the monopoly on heartache. Some of us actually get it together and get a real life with real people who bleed, dream and care about others. All you think about is work. When you fall, the world you live in will cease to exist and no-one will be there to pick up the pieces."

Janice listened to what she didn't want to hear and without hesitation screamed: "Are you bloody finished?"

Adrian knew he had done it again; his shoulders stooped in rejection and he stood up and walked away. If he had waited he would have seen the sadness in her face.

She knew he was right but the mould had been fashioned long ago and, it would take a stronger love than Adrian's to break it.

Selwyn found Adrian sitting on a chair outside the men's ward, "The car's here."

"Thanks. You'd better tell Janice."

"You two been arguing again?"

Adrian looked at his friend: "Why is the only woman in the world I care about as cold as ice?"

"I doubt if she's that. You two are always trying to prove who's right or wrong. As a mutual admiration society you fail miserably. If you give up without a fight she has won and will remain behind her protective screen whilst you become a bloody miserable sod for God knows how long. I believe she loves you but just hasn't realised it yet. Seize the moment, now's the time; don't lose it or waste it."

The conversation was interrupted by a nurse who informed them that the car had arrived. Both men walked towards the waiting car. The doctor was talking to Janice who was in the front passenger seat. This told Adrian all he wanted to know. The goodbyes said, the young driver engaged first gear and they lurched forward. It took fifteen minutes to reach the airstrip. In this mountainous region it had been hacked out of the mixture of undergrowth and hills by hand many years previously. It had a distinct slope down and to the left and its flatness compared favourably with the road. Where the rains had washed away the arid earth, someone had filled in the holes but not very well. The car stopped at the highest point, the driver told them that they should get out and wait as the plane would soon arrive.

"How do you know that?" asked Adrian.

"People are coming—the Doctor has told them to be here."

"OK, you know best."

The young man pointed to a fallen tree: "Sit there."

A crowd of some twenty Africans gathered at the

side of the runway and their voices filled the air. After a few minutes the bee-like drone of a small aircraft could be heard. The babbling from the crowd stopped as they all waited for the aircraft to appear. There was no point in wondering about the wind direction or which way the aircraft would land—for the terrain defined there was only one way. If the pilot got it wrong he would end up in the trees and, if he really screwed up, as part of the hillside. They all watched as the tiny speck in the sky grew larger and larger. It was on its approach course and losing height rapidly. The pilot had obviously performed this manoeuvre before, the wing angle matching the irregular slope of the ground perfectly. Whoever was flying this machine completed a series of slow passes over the makeshift runway, each lower than the previous one. Flaps were lowered, the engine throttled back and the final approach began. With the mastery of much practice the pilot put the Cessna down. The three wheels caressed the hard-packed surface simultaneously, each issuing a trail of red dust in its wake. The brakes were applied at maximum pressure and at less than two hundred yards from the end of the prepared area it turned sharply right. So unpredictable was this gambit that the starboard wing tipped over and almost touched the ground. With its engine still running, the crowd of Africans ran forward and with nothing but physical strength grasped the wing struts, preventing it from rolling down the incline.

The pilot seemed but a boy in comparison to the waiting trio as he jumped out of the cockpit and strolled, unruffled by the landing, towards them. "I'm

George. You the passengers for Nairobi?"

Selwyn answered, "Yes and I must congratulate you on that landing."

"No problem."

"Where did you learn to fly like that?" asked Adrian.

"Out here you fly like that and make a living—if you don't you die or go broke. Must admit the first time you see these dirt tracks you want to give up but when you've done a couple of bumps and grinds it becomes normal. I have more problems with large airports and air traffic controllers who tell me to wait. Anyway, the sun is getting hotter and the air thinner, better make a move."

Janice went ahead and sat in the rear of the cockpit; Selwyn joined her, leaving the remaining seat alongside the pilot for Adrian. Once they were strapped in, the engine revolutions were increased to maximum, creating a minor dust-storm behind them. The pilot waved his hand out of the window, the crowd let go, and the craft began to career down the bumpy track. The whole structure of the plane vibrated as it struggled to climb and then suddenly only the smooth reverberations from the engine could be felt as they were assisted by the steady hot air currents wafting upward from the valley below. Speech was almost impossible but the views were splendid as they winged their way over the mountains.

Janice leant forward and shouted, "Can we go lower?"

The pilot eased back on the throttle and put the Cessna's nose down. At two hundred feet he levelled off, the country beneath them rushing past at an alarming rate. The heat of the day was now causing air currents to rise and fall and the aircraft tossed in the turbulence. "Lonely hills we call them," said the pilot as he pointed. "Not much water and mosquitoes by the million. That's wild country over there—" he pointed far into the distance "—mostly bush. Africans know how to live off it when things are normal but now its ravaged by drought. People kill the game to survive until it's gone then the poor devils starve."

There was a touch of pain in his voice. Then he saw a small herd of wildebeest in a clearing beside a dry riverbed and some miles further on, female elephants and their calves. He dropped to just above the height of the tallest tree and did a series of figure eights around the animals. The aircraft startled them and they trumpeted into the sky. Adrian could see the beasts clearly and found himself gripping the sides of his seat. The pilot tapped at the fuel gauge and shouted, "Home!"

It was not long before the outskirts of the city were drifting below them. Nairobi air traffic control gave permission to land and George, guiding the plane down as if it were filled with valuable glass artefacts, could not have bettered the landing. They were directed to a less congested area of the airport where two police cars were waiting. The engine was switched off, the three-bladed propeller jerked to a stop and the aircraft handler put chocks under each wheel.

A uniformed officer walked towards the cockpit door and opened it. "Mr Viper, airport formalities have been waived and we will take you directly to the British Embassy."

Adrian was somewhat taken aback at this priority treatment, "Fine."

All three said goodbye to George and thanked him for the guided tour.

He looked at them and the police: "Whatever trouble you're in, I hope it sorts itself out."

An officer moved forward and, taking Adrian by the arm, guided him towards a black BMW with tinted windows.

"What's happening?" questioned Adrian. From the corner of his vision he could see that similar civility was being bestowed on Janice and Selwyn.

"We have transport, these cars. You and your friends are being driven to your embassy." He opened the door of the front passenger seat, closed it again as Adrian settled himself. Selwyn got into the rear of the car with another officer. There was no sign of Janice and no point in debating the issue.

In a few moments they were travelling at high speed along the busy streets of Nairobi. It took over half an hour of dodging traffic before they arrived outside a typically colonial building, the British Embassy, where the police guided them towards the main door. It was opened by a uniformed Marine. As they mounted the steps, a woman in her late fifties nodded politely to the officers and then in a cultured English accent invited them in: "Welcome, I've heard all about you."

They were led in silence through the corridors, eventually ending up in a comfortably furnished room which overlooked the croquet lawn. It was very quiet. The lady turned to them: "I am Anne Swithenbank, the wife of a minister. I'm aware of your ordeal but our security staff are required to debrief you. When that's over, rooms will be provided and a meal served. I apologise for this, but these are the rules we have to live by."

There was a knock on the door and two men and one woman, all in civilian clothes walked in.

"Well I'll leave you in capable hands. Oh by the way, I have ordered tea and coffee—it'll be here in a minute." The door closed and she was gone.

"Lieutenant Commander Adrian Viper."

Adrian, surprised at his rank being used, nodded to a stocky man who stood with his hands behind his back. The other was a thin faced, studious looking much younger fellow who said nothing. The woman was round-faced, tall and well proportioned; what could be mistaken for fat was solid muscle.

"Sir, I am Major Tomlinson. This—" he pointed to the thin man "—is Captain Arnold and last but not least is Sergeant McAdams. We are the mainstay of the security staff attached to this and other embassies in Africa." Adrian introduced Janice and Selwyn whilst he studied the Major. He was in his late forties, overweight, and red-faced, but nevertheless dressed smartly in a dark blue suit—a retired officer who could not let go. "This formality is the best method of obtaining the facts of the incident which beset you. Would you all please sit down? Commander, tell me why you came to Kenya."

Adrian looked at this imperial relic who more than likely believed Britain was still all-powerful. Hairs protruded from his nose and merged with his waxed moustache and reminded him of an old pig. And pigs when riled were dangerous creatures. Sergeant

McAdams smoothed her skirt after preparing pencils and opening her notebook to record the interview.

Adrian began the tale from the moment Charles had contacted him. His story was briefly interrupted when the refreshments arrived. Sergeant McAdams asked what each preferred and poured as requested. What had taken days was related in just over two hours. Selwyn filled in those incidents which were relevant. Janice added the top dressing to the whole scenario as a reporter would. Her memory was faultless. She remembered details as if looking at a film of the whole affair. The thin-faced Officer Arnold then asked a few personal questions and when finished left the room.

The major looked at them. "You've all been very stupid. What you don't know is that there's been another bloody tribal conflict. Thousands of refugees from Rwanda have escaped into Tanzania from the latest uprising between the Hutu and the Tutsi. As you'll know—" he looked at Janice "—this is the eternal conflict between pastoralists and tillers. In Africa people are fighting for the land and existence, more often than not in areas that are only marginally equipped to barely support one tribe. These people are now starving and bring with them diseases collected along the way from polluted water supplies and inadequate personal hygiene. The men who captured you were mercenaries of the most barbaric sort. They would have murdered you. Killing is their only purpose for existing—they change sides as many times as the sun rises. Anyway, you're safe now and more importantly, alive. Thank you for your information. It agrees with what we were able to piece together after your disappearance. I'll let you go and wash up. Temporary passports have been arranged and, looking at you, some good food is what you want. What you all need is a good night's sleep. Commander, I have arranged for a doctor to attend your wounds. Would Mr Churchill and Mrs Porter like treatment for their injuries?"

Both replied that they were well and thanked him for his concern.

"My sergeant will show you to your rooms, dinner will be at eight."

Janice moved towards the Major touching him gently on the arm. "Could I have a word with you in private."

"Certainly, my dear. What can I do for you?"

Adrian and Selwyn followed the sergeant.

"Here's your room, Sir. The doctor will be along shortly. Mr Churchill your room is adjoining. All your needs have been met and some casual clothes are in the wardrobe. If you require anything, press the button alongside your bed and a member of staff will attend. Is there anything else I can do before I leave?"

"Thank you, sergeant. You seem to have thought of everything."

"Just part of the job, Sir." For a moment she hesitated then turned smartly and marched away.

Adrian smiled at Selwyn, "As brainwashed as they come—I bet she makes love by numbers; her whole life will be for the honour of the regiment."

"I'm sure you're right. Anyway I could do with a nice hot bath."

"I'd better wait for the doctor before I can enjoy that luxury. When you're ready come and get me."

Adrian had only just entered the room when there was a sharp wrap on the door. Before he had a chance to move, in walked a small man who had a large nose that resembled the beak of a parrot. At university his fellow students had nicknamed him "Beaky", a name that had remained with him when he joined the army. "Hello Commander I'm Captain Beaky Wallis, your friendly quack. What have you been up to then? Would you please get undressed?"

Adrian obliged and reiterated the basics of the story while the bandages were removed from his hands and chest.

"The Doc who patched you up did a good job, but the dressings need changing. While I'm at it I'll put some antiseptic ointment on those abrasions. It will help them heal a bit quicker. A good hot bath is the doctor's order for the moment. Be back in half an hour to treat the damage."

It felt strange without the bandages, but the bath was deep and the water hot. It felt good and he relaxed, forgetting the time. As his mind wandered, he thought of Janice and wondered why she wanted a chat with the Major.

The bathroom door opened with a bang; Beaky was waiting. "Better get out—you don't want your skin to get too soft or those cuts will never heal."

Adrian dried himself carefully; his ribs were now beginning to hurt, if only a little.

Beaky applied the new bandages with the utmost care and for Adrian's hands he had what amounted to gloves made of fine surgical gauze. "These will protect those cuts but enable you to use your fingers."

After about twenty minutes he was satisfied with his handiwork and said he would be back to check the dressings in the morning before Adrian left for home.

"What do you mean 'home'?"

"Oh! Haven't they told you? You leave tomorrow."

"Thanks for the news, Doc, and the treatment."

Captain Beaky was already on his way out of the room; it was doubtful whether he had heard Adrian's thanks. Although off the peg, the clothes fitted well. They were what the service classed as smart but casual: grey flannels, white shirt and navy blue blazer. The shoes were of local black leather and pinched a bit but the overall appearance was satisfactory. Adrian was having trouble with his tie when Selwyn, dressed identically, walked in.

"Snap. Seems our tailor has only certain items in stock. I wonder if they supplied the same to our Janice! Ready? Let's see if we can find the dining room."

The Duty Officer, Graham Penny, was passing and introduced himself as he led them to the dining room. Here was the remainder of the duty personnel. All were officers or senior civil servants, the lower ranks ate elsewhere. Graham indicated where they were to sit. Adrian asked if Janice was going to join them. "Mrs Porter has left, Sir."

"Thank you, thank you very much."

Adrian ate the meal in a stunned silence, answering the few questions he was asked with a yes or no. Those around him assumed that he was suffering from shock.

Selwyn won the hearts of all those present with his mild banter and pleasantries. As soon as it was polite to do so Adrian made his apologies and left.

He found his way to his room but there must have been something wrong with the air-conditioning for the heat persisted. He had trouble sleeping, tossing from side to side, covered in sweat. Janice would not leave his mind. Why he had to fall in love with her remained a question he could not answer.

Next morning he went for breakfast but picked at the food. "Damn the woman," he thought; "the sooner she's out of my life the better." This time it would take longer, but eventually she would be replaced.

Moments after returning to his room the doctor arrived and proceeded to give him the full once-over. "You're fit to travel but when you get home take it easy for a week or two. I doubt if I'll see you again." He packed away his ointments and with a wave left.

Adrian sat on the edge of the unmade bed; it was ten o'clock, he had half an hour to kill. It took him two minutes to pack one dirty shirt and underwear into the small travelling bag provided. This done he made his way to reception.

Selwyn was already there and he sat opposite his friend. "You'll be pleased to know I have your temporary passport."

"Good, because I couldn't give a toss about anything at the moment, all I want to do is go home."

"Ah! Good morning, gentlemen." Graham Penny was glad they were early. "The kitchen staff have prepared a packed lunch for you; I hope you enjoy it." Selwyn took the lunches. At exactly ten thirty a black Cavalier drew up outside the main door to the embassy and a driver in RAF uniform entered the building.

"Corporal—" Penny beckoned "—here are your passengers. If you would, gentlemen."

Adrian and Selwyn stood up and thanked him for the assistance they had received. Selwyn shook the man's hand, Adrian just raised his and waved.

They arrived at the airport, entering via a military gate and stopped close to the waiting Hercules. Adrian looked at this beast of the air and knew that it was going to be a very long flight. The Load Master, a Flight Sergeant, came down the steps and introduced himself before directing them onto the aircraft. The hold was empty. The sergeant handed them a set of earplugs and explained that this was necessary to deaden the noise of the engines and that with the exception of going to the toilet they should remain strapped in at all times. As soon as they were seated, the engines started, the whole plane shook from nose to tail as this giant made its way towards the main runway. The engines roared to full power and then they were trundling along. It seemed ages before the angle changed perceptibly to indicate they were in the air. Adrian had always compared these craft with that of a swan leaving the waters of a lake. Lots of noise but hardly any lift until, like the plane, in the air it became graceful. With nothing to do or see, Adrian relaxed and let the drone of the engines send him to sleep. It was a restless slumber but time vanished.

"Adrian, Adrian, wake up." It was Selwyn's smooth voice he could hear but it seemed muffled. Slowly the world of dreams transferred to reality as his mind and body stirred. He ached from cramp and his injuries, having been in practically the same position for many hours. A soft bump and the mighty reverse thrust of the engines told them they had landed at Larnica Airport, Cyprus. The Hercules, while capable of delivering heavy loads, only had a range of 4700 miles. This stop was for refuelling only.

Soon they were again at 30,000 feet, lumbering along at approximately 300 knots. Adrian and Selwyn dozed for the remainder of the long flight. The landing was textbook, and, only after the craft had remained stationary for five minutes, did the Load Master give them permission to leave the craft. An RAF staff car was waiting to whisk them off to Passport Control. The formalities were brief and within a few minutes they were clear and able to leave the airport. Adrian commented that it all seemed a bit of an anti-climax.

Selwyn looked at his friend and said, "Let's go home. Who knows what tomorrow will bring?"

Eight

Janice talked convincingly until the Major agreed to help. In less than an hour she had left the Embassy and was on her way to the Nairobi Office of *The Times* Newspaper. The Consul managed to arrange a three month visa as a British news correspondent. What strings he had pulled in the local hierarchy of ministers she did not know or care. A few scraps of paper gave her access to the area of the latest tribal massacre. Again she would be the first reporter on the spot. Clothes and money were the next priority and her editor would fax that without question, once contacted. The offices of *The Nairobi Times* are as efficient as any western newspaper. As soon as Janice entered the nicotine-stained door marked "Editor", she recognised the thickset, red faced man, Jock Moir, sat at his desk in his khaki shorts and short sleeved open necked shirt. What always made her smile were his white socks and highly polished sandals. "Typical bloody colonial," she thought.

"Long time no see, my darling. What the hell happened to you? Did you walk in front of a bus?"

He offered her a drink of ice-cold lemon and water which she accepted gratefully. Jock tilted back his chair, took a cigarette from the packet of Capstan Full

Strength lying on the desk and lit it, blowing smoke rings into the air. He puffed at his cigarette waiting for the woman that stood before him to say something. Janice grimaced and told him of her "adventures".

Their conversation was interrupted when one of the three telephones on Jock's desk started ringing. He picked it up. "Yes," he snapped, frowning as he listened, his eyes raised to Janice who sat opposite. With a blunt "No way," he slammed the phone down.

When she had finished talking, he stubbed out the cigarette and wrote a fax which Janice signed. They sat for a while discussing the recent uprising and a deal was struck. A local cameraman, fluent in the native dialects, would accompany her into the area and the story would be a combined effort for both papers.

"I need a vehicle, preferably with air-conditioning, and a few changes of clothes. Can you lend me some money until Fred my editor clears that fax?"

"As always you don't beat about the bush, do you? Here—" from his right-hand desk draw he tossed the equivalent of five-hundred pounds, "—and I want it back."

"If I had a bottle we could have a drink for old time's sake."

"Off the stuff. Haven't had a drop for almost two years now."

"Anyway, time is money and I need clothes. Have my car and that photographer ready to leave by the time I get back. You couldn't get someone to drive me to the nearest clothes shops, could you?"

"Anything else I can do, while I'm at it, madam?" Jock replied with a hint of sarcasm.

"Yes, make sure there's a good supply of Malaria and Water tablets. Wouldn't go down too well to get the best story this year, then spend time in hospital for God knows what."

Janice left Jock leering at her lovely backside. From leaving his office and arriving at the main entrance, an open-top jeep was waiting.

Without any hesitation she jumped into the front seat and ordered the driver to take her shopping.

"What sort of shops do you want?"

"As I need everything, let's start with somewhere that sells rucksacks."

With a bemused look on his face, he swung the vehicle into the flow of fast-moving traffic and accelerated away. Within ten minutes they were drawing to a halt outside a row of shops. Janice looked around and decided that with luck she would be able to obtain all that she needed in the immediate area. Having had to prepare hurriedly in the past for many assignments, the gathering of her immediate needs was no different. Her first stop was a chemist, where she obtained those items necessary for her personal hygiene. The next was a clothing store that contained all she wanted. This emporium suffered from a direct attack that startled the owner. Never before had he witnessed an English woman choose so much so quickly. With her arms overflowing, she dumped the whole shebang on the front desk.

"Please total that up and I'll be back in about five minutes."

At full tilt a nearby store was scoured for a good pair of walking boots, a large rucksack and a lightweight, waterproof cloak.

On her return to the clothing store she paid for the now neatly bagged pile of clothes, rammed them into the rucksack and left.

The driver had waited patiently, but had carefully monitored where she went, just in case there was any trouble. As she got into the car he smiled at the bulging rucksack and asked, "Where to now, Mrs?"

"A gun shop."

With a squeal of tyres, they roared down the road and for a while said nothing; then the driver asked why she wanted a gun.

"Just in case, that's all."

They stopped outside a small shop in the suburbs and the driver got out and stopped her moving from the jeep.

"I don't care why you want a gun but even here you can't just go and buy one. They like you to have a permit signed by an official. This shop will sell me what I want but not you, please wait."

"OK James."

It wasn't long before he returned and handed over a shoe box. "Everything you want is in there but don't tell Jock. Reporters are not supposed to be armed you know."

"Of course I know, but after what happened last week, I'm going prepared. Hopefully I won't have to use it." As they arrived back at the office, Janice jumped out, hoisted her new belongings over her shoulder and wandered up to Jock's domain. He was lighting another cigarette as she entered the room. Looking up at Janice he smiled: "How did you get on with Jacob?"

"Who the hell's Jacob?"

"Jacob, my dear, is the best photographer in Africa and has just been driving you all over town. At the moment he's standing behind you."

"Oh shit." Janice turned.

Jacob smiled, "When do we start, boss?"

Janice, somewhat embarrassed, looked at her travelling companion. He stood there, his thin frame towered over her, but a beaming smile from a ebony coloured face gave her the confidence that he was a man to trust.

Jock looked at Jacob: "A Range Rover is round the back and ready to go. The team haven't forgotten anything, travel permits, your visas and some money are in the glove compartment. I supervised the loading myself. Extra fuel cans and plenty of fresh water plus all the essentials for a two week trip. The radio works and there are cassettes of film by the dozen, so get going and get me a story."

Jock fussed around like a mother hen while two members of staff collected her purchases and transferred them to the waiting Range Rover. Jacob climbed in, settled himself behind the wheel. Within thirty minutes they were leaving Nairobi behind them. It was getting dark and Janice offered to drive but Jacob insisted that he would get them on the road to Kampala, some 350 miles distant, the halfway point.

"Won't we need some diesel before we get there?" she enquired.

"No way, this beast has extra large tanks and a thousand mile range but we'll top up before the bad country."

+++

They drove westward all night, the whine of the tyres on the road reminding Janice of another journey. The orange glow from the multitude of dashboard lamps was the only illumination that broke the darkness. She did not want to sleep and Jacob remained silent except for the occasional grunt—his every action and thought was concentrated on the road ahead. Every now and then the broad beam of the headlights illuminated a wild animal but they were too swift to be seen clearly. Realising that without sleep she would not be able to drive, she moved to the rear of the Range Rover. Two cots were slung from the roof and with one smooth movement of her body, she swung neatly upwards and into the thin but soft mattress.

+++

The morning light roused her but the hubbub from outside brought her back to reality.

Rubbing the sleep from her eyes she asked, "Where are we?"

"Kampala," came the brisk reply.

"Why the hell didn't you wake me? You must be knackered."

"Didn't feel tired."

"My! We are talkative this morning, aren't we?" The hint of sarcasm was not missed.

"With this wagon and the power under the bonnet I need to concentrate on what I'm doing. We aren't on a Sunday school outing, you know."

Janice clambered into the front and peered at the hoards of people that meandered around the vehicle. They were about their own business and the intrusion into their lives of a Range Rover meant here was someone with a great deal more money than they would ever have.

Jacob finally spotted a filling station: "I'll fill this beast with diesel and you go and get freshened up. Then we'll get some food and be on our way. By the way, you'll be driving the next two hundred miles while I sleep."

They drew into the station and Janice, as ordered, went for a wash and felt better for it. On the way out she purchased two Mars bars, one for each of them.

"Right, Mrs, we're ready, get in."

Without thinking she got into the passenger's side but Jacob yelled, "Oi! You're driving, remember?"

Janice slid across the seat and spent a few moments adjusting its position. Jacob guided Janice through the maze of congested roads until they turned right and stopped.

"We eat here."

"What is here?" she asked, looking at the outside of a run-down building.

"My uncle's house."

Jacob knocked on an unlocked door and walked in. A haggard figure stood over an ancient wood burning Aga cooker. His hair was white as bleached cotton and he merely glanced up as Jacob stood in the doorway.

"Joseph!" Jacob cried and embraced him lovingly. The old man had been his stepfather and mentor for twenty years. The smell of home-baked bread filled the air as Joseph disentangled himself from Jacob's embrace.

"Who is this lady you bring to my home?"

Jacob introduced Janice as an associate who was

working with him on a great story. She said nothing to spoil the illusion.

"I suppose you're hungry?" Joseph guided Janice to a chair alongside a huge wooden table. "It has been many years since a woman graced my table. It is a pleasure to give you food. My meals are better than you will eat in any restaurant."

Jacob butted in: "Joseph was a cook in the army for twenty years and his food is good."

The two men chatted incessantly in their own language, while Janice nodded approvingly at the mountain of bacon and fresh eggs laid before her. The bread from the oven was the best she had ever tasted. Any thoughts of calorie counting disappeared when the tantalising aroma invaded her nostrils.

The meal over, all they wanted to do was sit and relax; it was Joseph who made them move. "You have a long way to travel. It is best you be on your way or the night will overtake you. Be careful where you spend the night—there are many who would seize your belongings and leave you for dead."

"The army will take care of us," interrupted Jacob. "Arrangements have been made."

The old man looked at him and frowned, "Which army?"

"The Government's army of course."

"Take care, Jacob, and trust no-one until you return. I've a few years left and I'd like to see you again."

"We'll be back soon, old man. Don't worry yourself." Janice moved towards the door as the old man and Jacob embraced. There were the beginnings of tears in both men's eyes and she knew that there was a love there that no-one could ever change. When

Jacob came out of the house there was much bravado in his statement: "Silly old bastard, always makes a fuss."

Janice started the engine and the next phase of the journey began. It took over an hour to clear Kampala. Once free of the hindrance of bullock-drawn wagons, they began to cover the miles between them and the Rwandan border. It was a blistering day; the heat rose in shimmering waves, causing phantom puddles to appear then fade as they drew near. From the sun-baked ground there erupted clouds of choking dust that hung motionless in the air. Dust-covered trees and bushes wilted as they waited for life-giving rain to revive them. The air-conditioning worked overtime to keep the temperature of the interior bearable. Jacob slept for over five hours while Janice drove the beast like a professional rally driver.

The further they progressed into the heart of Africa the worse the road became. From a reasonable surface it changed into a track, sometimes difficult to determine from the land it crossed. The morning moved into afternoon and still she managed an average of fifty miles an hour. Jacob had returned to the passenger seat and was staring at a map. "We're not far from the Zaire border. You'd better slow down."

"What for? The sooner we get there the better."

"Because we're staying on this side tonight. It's safer."

"We'll be wasting time. I can drive for a lot longer and so can you," shouted Janice.

Jacob looked at her sharply, searching for the woman, not the reporter, "I'm sure you can, but once over the border there are people who shoot first and ask questions later. I like living and no story is worth losing your life for."

"Of course." Janice placed her hand on the back of Jacob's. "Tomorrow is another day."

They were entering a township and at the end of the dusty potholed main street Jacob directed her into a small compound where she stopped.

"Where the hell is this?" she asked.

"This is where I was brought up until Joseph and his wife took me away. It was an orphanage."

A white man and a black woman came out of a small corrugated hut, showing all the signs of old age; the man was deeply tanned and the women as black as night.

"Father Morrison, it's Jacob."

The couple embraced him for a long while, ignoring Janice. After a few minutes they asked why he had come. Briefly he explained the situation. They nodded at his reason and then told him that to travel in Zaire at the moment was dangerous and only allowed if accompanied by a military escort. Jacob looked despairingly at Janice. "We have wasted our time."

Father Morrison saw his disappointment. "A convoy leaves tomorrow, maybe you can get permission to join them. There's nothing you can do tonight. Come and eat, a good night's sleep will do you good."

They entered the small two-roomed bungalow and ate the meal of maize and meat placed before them. Conversation was limited to Jacob telling the Morrisons of his exploits as a photographer. They always seemed to nod at the right moment or on the odd occasion grunted a yes or no: politeness at the extreme—they were old and well set in their ways. The orphanage had been shut down some years previously when the church authorities in England had withdrawn funding when Father Morrison married his black wife. Since then they had survived by farming their tiny plot and administering first aid to the locals.

Jacob left the room and returned after a few minutes. In his hand was an envelope. "Father, you took in a young boy and found him parents, it is now my turn to repay your kindness." He handed over the packet.

Father Morrison took it but did not open it, merely placing it on the table. "Thank you, it will be used to help others."

Jacob spoke softly: "Use it as you see fit."

It was getting late and Father Morrison directed them to the equivalent of a garden shed. "This is dry and safe, you will find blankets and a bowl for your use. Sleep well, and I'll call you in the morning."

Janice lay on the blanket and for no reason began thinking about the men in her life and acknowledging that they had not been that spectacular—numerous affairs that had always led to disappointment: one dead husband, one dead lover and a son she adored but never saw. It wasn't much of a love life to remember. Tomorrow and the next day, these were all that mattered, not recollections of past relationships. Thoughts of Adrian came and went; he had saved her life and she wanted him but did she need him? The night passed in torment as she dreamed. The minutes passed like hours and when she finally slept the hours vanished like minutes. Startled awake, for a moment she sat upright—she was so sure he was near that she called his name out loud. The silence that filled the hut was so oppressive that she ran out into the open; it was pitch dark, only the night stars illuminated the compound. She sat on the ground and for what seemed a long time she heard her own voice speaking but was not sure what was said. Exhausted and confused, she returned to the hut and fell asleep. Meanwhile Jacob slept soundly and was not disturbed by either her or the mosquitoes.

Father Morrison woke them at first light and advised that they move quickly as the convoy was preparing to leave. With sleep in their eyes they walked towards the border post and asked to see the officer in charge. They were ordered to wait. After a few minutes a tall, black bearded man in combat uniform, with what appeared to be officer's insignia glistening on his epaulettes, arrived.

Janice was taken aback at what looked like a hostile reception. The smooth cultured voice broke the illusion; "How can I help?" It was a tone that could have only been cultivated at Sandhurst.

Janice spoke quickly explaining who they were and what they wanted to achieve.

The officer scrutinised the two people who stood before him, his eyes lingering on Janice a touch longer than made her comfortable. He then pointed into the distance: "This is dangerous country, but if your papers are in order you may join us."

Jacob quickly produced the visas and travel documentation, passing them to the officer who in turn handed them to his sergeant.

"Please wait here—my sergeant will issue additional papers."

While the exchange was taking place Jacob observed that these were Government soldiers of a high calibre. Their uniforms were in good condition, the weapons and vehicles almost new. The officer nodded to Janice, turned smartly on his heel and marched away. The sergeant returned some minutes later and handed their documents back. Janice asked if it was OK for them to travel. He looked at them: "It's OK."

Without wasting a moment they ran back to their Range Rover, Jacob disappeared into the house and hurriedly said his farewells. When he returned, Janice rapidly drove across the border. They waited until they were noticed by the sergeant, who gave the Range Rover the once over. His cursory inspection complete, he directed them to place their vehicle between two Armoured Personnel Carriers. There was more to the patrol than they had first thought - six APCs, four open trucks, one mobile radio lorry and four stripped-down Land Rovers equipped with heavy machine guns. Several other private cars were slotted into position along with an old army half track. In all, there were about one hundred men milling around, each with ammunition pouches bulging and carrying the familiar AK47s. The waiting seemed endless but at ten o'clock precisely the officer gave orders to move out. The NCOs passed these on to the troops. Two armed men positioned themselves on the front of a

Land Rover, the officer and his driver waiting patiently while a corporal checked the action of the machine gun.

With a wave of the officer's hand the convoy moved off. Some soldiers had to run and jump into the APCs much to the amusement of the others. The vehicles followed the rough road, the progress was slow but sure. All the time the soldiers manning the machine guns scanned the bush for any activity. This ragtag outfit of new and used vehicles followed the main road such as it was. It was rough and deeply potholed; at times they stopped and scanned the route ahead before proceeding at a snail's pace. Janice wondered at the caution but was advised by Jacob that the Rwandan border was barely five miles away and bush wars often drifted across man-made boundaries.

The journey seemed endless, the Range Rover shaking and bouncing, turning and twisting, as it fell in and crawled out of miniature chasms gouged between natural rock and the soft earth of the road. The APC remained close behind, the roar of its diesel engine destroying any chance of normal speech but in its own way a reassurance that the army was close by. The uncomfortable journey continued with nothing to detract the attention other than the occasional glimpse of zebra and impala. Some wildebeest blocked the road at one point and while they stared with questioning bewildered eyes, one of the soldiers positioned on the front wing of the officer's car took aim and fired, killing one of the animals instantly. The sound of the weapon caused the remainder to bolt into the bush. The carcass was dragged by six men and loaded onto the nearest lorry. Tonight there would be roast meat to supplement their meagre rations.

In time the bush changed; large trees lined the edges of a river, after running parallel to them for a short distance the scenery altered dramatically as Lake Kivu opened up before them. The officer stopped the convoy, looked at his watch, and then gave orders that they would camp by the water's edge for the night. If necessary it was a position that could be well defended.

NINE

The survivors from the *Kia Hua* were hot, tired, hungry, and lost. The vegetation seemed to change without reason from dense to non-existent. Any attempt to walk in a straight line was blocked by deep chasms. Their skills as seamen were useless.

The Bosun stopped and looked at the sun and then his watch. "I know where we are! Somewhere in Western Australia. How far from civilisation, I haven't a clue."

He had their attention. "I guessed that by walking north we would've come across a road or something."

They all knew if they could reach a medium-sized town without being caught they had a chance but first they had to find food and water. At the moment he had two men who were worse than useless and he certainly was no wiser.

With an air of bravado, he looked at the others. "We must attempt to maintain a direct route even if that means climbing up and down these bloody cliffs. There's no other way. You can of course sit down on your backsides and die but I say we keep moving. The further we get away from the *Kia Hua* the better."

They knew he was right. The Bosun led the way, as the sun begun its slow descent behind the horizon. They were desperately thirsty. Ahead the Bosun noticed a small clump of rocks that afforded some protection from the warm dry wind that was drawing every ounce of fluid from their bodies.

When they reached this natural shelter the Bosun looked around: "We'll stop here. It's as good a place as any."

Bart was looking the worst for wear: "When are we going to find some water?"

"Tomorrow," came the harsh reply. "If you want to wander around in the dark be my guest; I'm staying put."

Thompson was feeling the strain mentally and physically. He curled himself into a foetal ball and fell asleep. Bart started to walk around but the rapidly fading light forced him to return.

One man, who was camped not so far away, was perfectly at home—his ancestors had survived in this region for forty thousand years. Food could be found everywhere and his water supply came from fresh water springs just below the surface of the ground. Their location had been passed from father to son over countless generations. Despite his non-committal attitude he remained close. This solitary aborigine was at home and, once he had secured his load, he lay on the dry red soil and fell asleep becoming one with the earth.

The sun rose and the air was soft and sweet. The three men lay as if dead. The trials of the previous day and the lack of water had drained their will to carry on. Unaccustomed to sleeping in the open, the sounds of the tropical night had often awoken and petrified them. Thompson, the youngest and fittest, was the first to wake. Despite the cramp in his right leg he did not feel too bad but he knew they had to find water. A little knowledge can be a dangerous thing but thirst will overcome fear. He wandered off in what he thought was a northerly direction looking for anything that might be edible. In his ignorance he vaguely remembered the film, *Crocodile Dundee,* and began to look for berries or any small creature he could catch. If he had been a native he would have known where and what to look for. God sometimes helps fools and sinners and he was both. As he scrambled over a small rocky outcrop he found fresh water; it was the merest of trickles from a spring but enough for him to cup his hands and quench his thirst. It was surprisingly cold and tasted sweet but it was water. He washed the dry dust from his face and felt the building of a new resilience inside, they would survive.

Climbing higher, he had a good view of the land for miles around. In the distance the forest began to thin and his hopes were raised when he saw what looked like a road. Returning was easier than he anticipated, even though he had left a trail that any fool could follow. The aborigine was glad the young man had found the water.

Meanwhile the Bosun was getting more and more agitated by the minute as he considered the available options. He could wait for the boy or move on. Thompson returned just as they were about to leave.

"Where the hell have you been, boy?"

"Bosun, I've found water."

"Where?" The Bosun and Bart instantly forgot their fury and wanted water more than anything else.

Thompson felt important: "That way, about half a mile."

"Well, what are we waiting for?" shouted Bart. "Show us where we can get a drink."

Their spirits were raised more than they had thought possible. If nothing else they would not die of thirst today. Thompson followed his own footprints in the dust and in less than ten minutes he was back at the spring. The Bosun and Bart almost came to blows as they struggled to quench their thirst. They drank their fill, were refreshed; life felt good again.

"Bosun."

"What now, Thompson? Don't tell me you managed to find a restaurant as well?"

Thompson felt hurt by the remark but he played his next card slowly; "Not exactly, but if you climb to the top of those rocks, you can see a road."

The Bosun pushed him aside as he scampered up the rocks causing some of the loose rubble to fall. "Where's this road of yours?"

Thompson was now beside him, pointing into the distance. Bart saw it first. "Right, let's drink our fill before the sun gets up and get to your road before it gets dark."

With their stomachs bursting they began walking. The cliffs were steep and the route down treacherous but with careful planning they negotiated the first ravine. The sun was now overhead, their thirst critical once more and their elation was draining away. The Bosun felt a sense of despair. It had taken them the best part of two days to get this far and where were they? The Bosun called a halt. "If we keep this up, we're going to die."

Bart looked at him with a touch of contempt in his eyes. "We're already dying. Unless we find some more water we won't have the strength to make another climb."

Realising the futility of pressing ahead, the Bosun nodded in agreement: "Let's rest." Bart and Thompson made themselves comfortable in the shade of an overhanging rock.

"How are we doing?" Thompson asked almost cheerfully.

Bart who had removed his shoes responded, "My feet are killing me, I'm starving and I'm dying from lack of water. How do you think we're frigging doing?"

The sun had began to lose its heat and the Bosun kicked out at the two men. "Come on, if we don't find some water by nightfall we've had it."

They descended a gentle slope to the base of the gorge only to discover dry red dust. Walking in a ragged line they kept moving along the riverbed. The heat, even from a dying sun, was causing rapid dehydration. Long ago the desire to find the road had disappeared. Monotonously they placed one foot in front of the other as waves of heat rose in shimmers that distorted all around. Night came and this scruffy trio had to stop. Bart suggested that they would find water if they dug into the ground. Tired, hungry and desperate, where they fell they remained. Thompson dozed, his mind wandered through strange dark corridors. In sleep he remembered his brother and how he must have changed since he had last seen him. He suddenly felt very young again, and wished he was home, a little boy shielded from the cruel realities of life by an understanding and kind mother. Thompson's mind drifted in and out of reality.

The rough voice of the Bosun cut through his half-dream, "It's daylight—time to move on."

Shaking himself awake, Thompson stood, and started walking down the gorge until a swift rebuke from the Bosun stopped him. "I can't wake Bart, something's wrong."

Thompson rambled back and stood looking at the body that lay still on the ground. "The bastard's gone and died on us. Why did he go and do that?"

"God knows. Anyway if we stay here we'll end up the same way."

Thompson had lost interest in everything. "Let's get going before that sun gets too high."

They left Bart where he lay; neither noticed the mark of a snake bite on his right arm. Now they were two in this God-forsaken land. Within an hour of sunrise, the air turned hot. The Bosun knew that this would be their last day unless they found water.

The aborigine stared at the corpse and then covered it with stones. It wasn't that he had any religious beliefs, it was simply to prevent wild animals from feasting. When he had finished, he collected his own writhing bundle and followed the two men. The Bosun and Thompson were close to the end. Both scanned the way ahead: to them it remained the same. Thompson spotted birds souring and diving in the distance. "Look," he croaked. "Birds have to drink, don't they?"

"You must be seeing things." The Bosun's voice was rough.

Thompson started walking towards his birds. An hour later they reached the end of the gorge but now, in the blinding light, it was difficult to see. They entered an area of deep grassland which added a lift to their depleted spirits. Thompson bent and picked a blade of the tough, dry grass and rubbed it between two fingers. It turned to dust, for in this environment even grass failed to survive. What chance was there for ordinary men? Even so the change of terrain gave them hope. They attempted to move a little faster and with a sense of purpose. Both knew they were close to knocking on death's door.

Thompson was in the lead. At a staggering, lurching run, he forced his dead legs along an animal track and then he saw it. A spring! He ran, stumbled into a depression. A few birds shrieked and took instant flight as Thompson plunged face down into the brown shallow water. The Bosun was but a moment behind. He took a long drink and rolled over. He pushed at Thompson. Slow down or you'll be sick. Let your body savour the water and drink slowly."

Thompson let the warm liquid run down his face. When both had sufficiently recovered, they studied the adjacent area. The water-hole was screened on all sides by tall green grass and without the birds they could have walked right passed it. Refreshed, they made the decision to find a resting place for the night. There was only the shade from an unusual tree, it had a large bulbous trunk and very few branches. The Bosun realised that if this was the only water for miles around the only safety lay in its branches. His thoughts were confirmed as dusk approached, when many strange animals appeared and drank, departing quickly into the grasslands. Wild dogs sniffed at the air knowing that a strange odour existed. The sparse branches of the tree were uncomfortable but here they felt safe. The night passed and the men, still wary that some wild animal could be lurking in the grass, went to the water's edge. Taking it in turns, they drank and washed the sleep from their eyes.

Thompson sat by the edge of the pool: "What are we going to do now?"

"Get out of here," came the irate reply. "How long do you think we can survive without food and hoping each day to find water? First things first; let's scout the area and see if we can spot anything before we wander off into the unknown."

Desperation was becoming a good teacher. Together they walked in a northerly direction for one hour, marking the path clearly. Thompson climbed the first tree they found and studied the surroundings. Large unclimbable cliffs seemed to encase the area, the only logical way was to go north. He told the Bosun, who simply shrugged his shoulders and without another word they wandered on. To their utter amazement within a short distance they found a small pool. As they sat and let the water freshen their bodies, the Bosun realised that they had been walking along a dry riverbed and that the water holes were the remnants of a river or stream before it finally dried out and turned to dust. They left the pool and continued on their way. Maybe it will rain thought the Bosun as they proceeded along the natural path leading to God knows where. The grass was becoming rich as they moved forward but their direction was subtly changing. The walls of the escarpment had, over the last few hours, begun to close in. Now there was less than one hundred yards from face to face. Without talking, the Bosun attempted to maintain a rugged pace, forcing the younger man to search for reserves from deep within.

The sun was at its peak but they were now sheltered by the shade from the high rock walls: they continued on and on. Without warning there was damp sand underfoot, then, a few yards further on, the ground became saturated. After a while they were tramping as playful children through a narrow and shallow stream. The further they moved up the canyon the deeper the stream became until it was above their waists. It was clear and cool and full of small fish that nibbled at their ragged clothes every time they stopped to bathe. They were tired and again they searched for a tree to rest in. There were many young saplings by the water's edge but only high up the embankment were there any sufficiently strong enough to hold both men.

That night they slept soundly—even the sound of wild dogs baying in the distance failed to disturb them. With water they could survive but without food their strength was rapidly waning. The old aborigine saw they were safe and slept on the moist earth. Early in the morning he trapped some fish and began to cook them over a fire. He was aware that the aroma would soon reach the men. Leaving some of the fish in leaves around the ashes to keep warm he speared the remainder and left them gently toasting over the dying embers. Content that the men would survive he made a clear trail for them to follow and headed home. The Bosun woke and was certain he could detect the smell of a fire in the air but put it down to his imagination. It was only when Thompson mentioned that he could smell cooking that they began to look around. It took them two minutes to find the fire and its tasty offering. Without considering who had lit the fire and prepared the fish, they ate as ravenous dogs.

It was only when the last morsel had disappeared down Thompson's gullet that the reality of the situation struck home. Each looked around but no-one could be seen or heard. They regained some courage and began to shout, only the dull echo of their own voices could be heard and the chattering of birds disturbed by the intrusion. Leaving caution behind they ran around like lunatics, scouring the area and noticing nothing. The markers left by the aborigine were scattered. As time passed, they decided to move on. Where there was water surely there must be some form of civilisation. They kept turning and hoping that whoever had prepared the food would show himself and guide them out of this hell hole. The river deepened and the gorge became narrower until the only way was up. A track made by animals guided them as they scrambled up the steep sides. It was hard to find the path sometimes but after a few hours they were sitting on the side of the gorge looking down. The sight was breathtaking for a tourist but to men trying to survive it was just another hurdle to overcome.

Thompson looked at the Bosun, "What the hell do we do now?"

"Why do you keep asking me? I don't fuckin' know."

They sat on a rock in silence, Thompson staring

across the red boulder-strewn plateau looking for any sign of life. He thought that prison would be a blessing compared to this.

"Look!" he shouted. "It's that road. We must have been walking the right way after all."

The Bosun turned, and, now that the sun had altered its position, the road could be clearly seen. "What are we waiting for? Let's get going."

The heat hung over them like a fiery furnace, draining any reserves they had. Forced to rest they remained fearful that their goal was unattainable. The day grew longer and the relentless, savage sun tormented them with an unmerciful ferocity. With dogged determination they trudged, one staggering step in front of the other, their shirts and shorts saturated with stinking sweat. Where it had burnt and blistered, their skin was red raw. By late evening a stretch of rough dusty road was finally only a few yards away. They stopped, relieved by the hope that civilisation could not be far.

The Bosun glanced at Thompson who was looking at him for guidance. "We go this way."

Thompson didn't care; like an obedient dog he followed his master. As darkness covered them, they pursued the track northwards. Their eyes were well tuned to the night when moonlight suddenly shone brightly on buildings in the distance. Elated at their good fortune they attempted to run, exhausting the remnants of their energy, until they were standing gasping in front of the first building. It was derelict. Still gasping, they examined every structure—all were deserted. A slight breeze began to rattle the corrugated sheet metal roofs; an old wind pump groaned as it turned, but it was long past supplying water. Thompson sat on the steps that led to a larger property and screamed at the night sky until his rage subsided.

The Bosun searched in the half-light for any signs of water. With nowhere to go, both looked desolately for a place to spend what remained of the night. Where they found themselves, some old chairs still remained and with a bit of inventiveness two crude beds were constructed. Exhausted, it was not long before they fell into a deep sleep. The sun was by now high in the sky but the cover given by the building prevented it from waking them.

Thompson was still in a buried slumber, when the Bosun got to his feet, stretched and left the comfort of the shade. Water: he must find it or all their efforts would have been wasted. With the height of the sun he reckoned it was late morning; they would last for a day or two but then it would be over. He began a methodical search: each shack revealed the same answer—no water. As he looked around, he reasoned that it had been built by miners searching for something, and to prospect you needed water. It had to be somewhere. In his rage he hurled a stone at a timber frame leaning against the rock face. The wood was rotten and on impact the fragile structure disintegrated. Intrigued, he moved slowly towards the opening. As he drew near, it was evident that this was man-made. Cautiously he entered into the darkness. It felt cool compared to the exterior, that in itself was refreshing. He stopped after going only a few yards, waiting for his eyes to grow accustomed to the defused light. Slowly he began to make out the outline of a tunnel that disappeared at a gradual incline down into the bowels of the earth.

"Should I go further," he wondered. The need to find water overcame the fear of the unknown. With a shuffling step he started to inch his way down the slope. Time seemed an eternity but eventually he reached the point where he could see no more. The darkness was now complete. Without a light it would be sheer stupidity to go on. Disillusioned he leant against a side wall and relished the coolness of it and the way it made his shirt feel damp. It took ages for it to occur to him that his shirt was wet. The rocks were sweating—life-giving water—not a great deal and after he had wrung the shirt into his mouth he knew it was not enough to survive on. He dried the surface and had to wait for ages before enough accumulated to gain another mouthful.

Thompson needed water and the Bosun almost ran out of the mine shaft to get him. Together they returned and indulged in the coolness whilst waiting for water to gather. The Bosun knew it was the end; they would die in this mine. Wild animals would feast on their remains, scattering their bones far and wide. No-one would ever know they had existed.

+++

After his return home, Adrian was unable to sleep and thus regularly went walking in the woods. Here as a child, he had felt safe within its boundaries. He paused for a moment and took several deep breaths. It felt good after the hot arid air of Africa.

He walked, not caring in which direction; Janice was still foremost in his mind. A dog was barking a long way off and many thousands of miles away was the woman he loved.

"Good morning. You're up early." The sudden appearance of old Joe startled him but then nothing this man did surprised him.

"I heard you were back and been in the wars."

"I wanted to be alone with my thoughts. Please stay. I didn't mean that you're not welcome. After all, you know more about these woods than anyone." They continued to walk along narrow animal tracks, neither disturbing the peace of the other.

Joe broke the silence: "What are you thinking about?"

"A woman."

"Well it's time you found a nice girl."

Adrian turned and faced his friend: "I've found her, but she doesn't care about me."

Joe chuckled: "Rubbish—if you want her that much go and get her." Adrian struggled to reply, Joe waited and said nothing.

They started walking and paused by a small stream that snaked its way between the trees.

"I meant what I said; if you think she's the one, go get her and don't take no for an answer. Your father went and married your mother against the odds. Why should you be any different?"

There was silence for a moment. "I'm thirty five and until a few weeks ago I thought I knew everything. She proved me wrong in almost every aspect of my life. I'm losing the only woman, with the exception of my mother, that I have ever loved—but then she was never truly mine to lose."

Joe looked at him closely: "So what's the problem? If this woman has had such an effect on you, she must be special. I've never seen you like this before. Adrian, there are only a few good women out there. Take her, grab her with both hands, convince her that you need, want, love her and only her. If my senses tell me anything, she'll believe you."

Adrian smiled: "I feel better already," but old Joe was already disappearing into the morning mist.

When he reached the house, he knew that if the opportunity presented itself he would not let Janice escape again. First he had to find out where she was. Mrs Duke was waiting for him and chastised him for going out without an overcoat on such a damp morning. With her homely manner she informed him that the doctor was waiting in the library.

"Thank you."

Doctor James Leitch was a small-built man with a crazy mop of curly black hair. His glasses were so thick that without them he was nearly blind. He had, however, practised in the village for all of his life. The local children had nicknamed him "the mad professor", but their mothers trusted him implicitly.

"Mrs Duke telephoned last night asking me to have a look at you. Do you mind?"

Adrian removed his shirt, wincing at the pain: "Not at all, Doc. I was coming to see you anyway."

The Doctor examined the chest dressing, muttering under his breath as he prodded and poked. Adrian didn't utter a sound but his eyes showed the evidence of pain that Leitch couldn't fail to notice. Next, the bandages that covered torn fingers were gently but methodically cut away; here he was more impressed, the healing process had begun. "Keep your chest coverings on for at least another week; your fingers need fresh air to aid their recovery but keep them clean, I'm not in the business of amputation, so do as you're told."

Adrian laughed: "If that's what the doctor orders. Would you like some tea and one of Mrs Duke's famous cakes?"

"Thought you'd never ask. Don't get up—I think after all these years I know my way to the kitchen. Take care of yourself; I'll come back sometime next week."

Adrian was left alone with his thoughts, and, as he stretched his arms, battered ribs reminded him of pain. His solitude was interrupted by Selwyn.

"Are you busy?"

Adrian waved him towards a chair; "Take a pew."

"We have a business to run and we need to talk."

He realised that Selwyn had said something. "Just day-dreaming about Janice."

"If you want to talk about it, please do," remarked Selwyn. He saw his friend's uncertainty and uneasiness. "If I told you it will all work out for the best, would you believe me?"

Adrian eyed his friend: "Thank you but it's my problem and you're right, we have a business to run."

That day was spent pulling the strings of their livelihood together. During their absence a few minor problems had occurred but they were most impressed when they discovered that Mrs Duke had solved them with good old-fashioned common sense.

After dinner, Selwyn was reading *The Times* when he came across an article about the latest uprising in Rwanda. The paper's correspondent was none other than Janice. Adrian tore the paper from his hands digesting every word on the page. "I must get out there."

Selwyn glanced at his friend. "Wait a minute, that area will be closed to the likes of us. Why don't you telephone the paper tomorrow and arrange a meeting? As a matter of fact, we still haven't any passports so we're stuck until they arrive."

"Stop being so bloody right," shouted Adrian. He realised that he was making a fool of himself.

Selwyn laughed at his miserable face, Mr and Mrs Duke joined in. Even Adrian began to laugh at his own foolishness. It was the first time he had laughed since they had arrived home. Dinner was soon over and as the table was cleared Adrian looked at Selwyn.

"We must find a way to get out there, once we have our passports."

"As I said, we haven't a hope in hell. So forget it and wait till she comes home."

Adrian wasn't convinced but he knew that Selwyn was, as always, right and he would have to wait.

Ten

The officer of the convoy invited them to dine on roasted wildebeest. "Tomorrow you will cross the river into Rwanda."

During the night there was a rumble of heavy vehicles toing and froing, their headlights cutting a swathe of light across the camp as they went.

In the morning they were awakened and told it was time to go. One army jeep accompanied them to the river and border crossing. Once across they were on their own and followed the rough road for over an hour. Painted signs indicated that Goma was some distance ahead, but, long before they reached the outskirts of the town, they came across piteous groups of refugees huddled around fires. The cold of the night had sapped the life source from their bodies as they waited. Janice named it the "Road to Hell" - for many it was the final journey. This was obvious from the many corpses wrapped in tattered shawls and blankets. These unfortunates were treated as garbage waiting to be collected.

Those that arrived seeking refuge only added to the diseased and starving. Wherever they fell, young or old were left to die. Those with the energy to move barely gave the Range Rover a glance, the stronger ran towards them holding out their hands. The camp was a mass of makeshift tents and people in a dream-like trance. In the distance a Red Cross flag rose above this tragedy. The air had about it the putrid smell of death. Slowly they traversed the tents and groups huddled on the black cinders and volcanic ash. Piles of bodies wrapped in rags had been stacked awaiting burning or burial. Two cameras worked non-stop. When they reached the hospital compound Janice leapt from the car and made her way towards the temporary office and medical centre. Sat around a makeshift table were four men and two women. When they saw Janice, one rose to greet her: "What can we do for you?" asked a tall, thickly bearded man.

"Janice Porter, *Nairobi Times*. What the hell's going on here?"

"I hope you've had your cholera vaccinations, these people are dying in their hundreds. If you had a couple of tons of food, some drinking water and medical supplies, then that might begin to have some impact."

"What can we do to help?" asked Janice.

"Get us what we need and the Zairian Government to allow these people to go home."

"What do you mean?"

"The border's been closed. As you know, Zaire is an ally of the defeated Rwandan government and is carrying out this strategy at the request of those leaders who have survived. You could say these people are being used as pawns in a political game of chess."

"Well it's about time the world heard about it."

With determination in her stride she returned to the Range Rover where Jacob had already set up the transmitter and fax machine. Jacob grabbed his Polaroid and snapped a few pictures of the chaos that surrounded them.

The link and the transmission began, "Jock this is Janice—don't interrupt—just listen. This is the refugee camp near Goma which I can only describe as a living hell. The Black Hole of Calcutta would be luxury in comparison. I have no idea of numbers, but this illustration of human misery in a diabolic terrain is quite complete. Cholera has broken out and would appear to be spreading rapidly. As we approached the camp the road was littered with the dead. I gave up counting when I reached a hundred. There's no food, no shelter, the world must do something. Jock, I'm faxing some pictures, standby."

In Nairobi Jock looked at the pictures. "It seems you've uncovered a story that will shock the world; stay with it, out."

The equipment was shut down and Jacob locked the Range Rover. He slung a camera over his shoulder and began to make his way amongst the never-ending human misery.

Jock Moir was flashing a scoop across the airwaves via Reuters. He knew that Janice was right, the world had to do something.

Janice stopped and attempted, through Jacob, to talk to groups who sat amongst their pitiful possessions, straw mats used as bedding and a few personal items. It was useless, what these people needed was a miracle. Disillusioned, they returned to the medical team.

"Why don't you do something instead of sitting there on your fat backsides?"

The big man raised his head and looked at her, his eyes were sunken from lack of sleep. "Lady you've seen the problem. We know the answer. It would take twenty million litres of good water and four hundred tons of food to feed these wretches for one day. We have not eaten for days and our water runs out tomorrow. Give us the wherewithal and we'll get up and do something—and perhaps you didn't notice but they're still coming."

"I'm sorry, but why aren't the supplies being sent?"

"We are told they're on their way but it's too late. Everyday there's more discussion and every delay means more death on the ground. There's over six hundred thousand refugees, thousands will die. Alone and lost in this madness there are children searching for parents; they rarely find them. Young and old are beaten by the rebellious troops on both sides. You couldn't begin to believe the horrific brutality. Without seeking to sound insensitive the lucky ones will get shot stealing a scrap of food. Many will die from starvation, cholera and dysentery. The politically correct wording is "ethnic cleansing".

"How would you feel about telling my editor what you've told me?"

"I'll try anything."

"Jacob set up the transmitter."

"My name is Dr Derek Cumberland and the others are all suitably qualified. You have seen why we feel so despondent. It's so bloody pointless."

Jacob interrupted, "Jock is waiting and has set up a direct link to the world's news agencies. Give them hell, Doc."

Doctor Cumberland was about to let the world know of the plague of human misery, when a bullet struck the transmitter dead centre. Janice turned to see three soldiers, two were Africans carrying AK47s, the third was a heavily perspiring short, fat, white man in jungle greens who wore thick-rimmed glasses and a peaked commando cap. A wisp of smoke still issued from the heavy calibre pistol held tightly in his sweaty hand. The white man spoke to his protectors, who moved swiftly forward and began to destroy the communications equipment. Jacob attempted to intervene but a rifle butt in the groin stopped him in his tracks. Janice helped him stand, then in silence they watched helplessly as any chance of contact with the outside world was savagely ripped apart.

"You bastard," screamed Janice.

"I may well be, I never knew my parents." The cultured English accent stopped her rebuke dead. "Madam, my government pays me very well to assist the unfortunates in Africa." He gestured with both hands: "These are the less favoured. They don't pay my wages. If they were all to survive then the tribal conflict would only escalate and drain the limited resources of a poverty-stricken country. I assist in helping the conflict to continue, a bomb here, a few killings there—it keeps the momentum flowing. The nice thing about it is no-one really cares whether these people live or die. Yes, a few will pontificate and raise it at the United Nations and the 'goody-two-shoes brigade' will send some tents and old cast-off clothing to appease their conscience."

"Tomorrow you will be escorted to another area, held for a few days until my government tells me that they are ready to assist these poor people, most of whom will be unredeemable from the gates of hell. Then you can take all the pictures you want. It's a pity your radio equipment was damaged." He spoke quickly to the Africans who ushered Janice and Jacob into their Range Rover and shut the doors.

Doctor Cumberland was escorted back to the table where he sat and sobbed his heart out. The others looked at the white man with utter disgust.

"Prisoners in the midst of devastation and we can do fuck all about it." Janice smashed her fist against the dashboard.

"Look, get some rest: at least we have food, water and a place to sleep. Count your blessings, you're alive. That fat pig could have easily shot us."

The daylight was fading fast and with nothing better to do, they laid in their hammocks and rested, whilst all around them they could hear the cries of people dying. Janice tried to cover her ears to diminish the sound but it was useless. She was undecided as to what they could do, when the rumble of a heavy vehicle engulfed the sorrowful cries. When it stopped they could see it was a heavily armoured personnel carrier; about twenty fully armed men jumped nimbly out.

There were orders shouted at the new arrivals whilst those already there came to watch. The white man appeared and pointed. The sergeant of the new squad screamed an order at two men who swiftly moved alongside the Range Rover. The sounds of death and darkness returned as the engine of the APC and the lights died together.

That night it started to rain and then without warning a deluge of water fell, soaking those who were not under cover. The refugees drank copiously at the fresh clean water but were chilled to the bone by the tempest that attacked them. As the sun rose, the devastation caused by the rains had covered frail unmoving bodies in soft mud; most had died in the night, others were soon destined to join them. A new sound filled their ears—the wailing of relatives throughout the camp.

Refreshed by the rains, the bush was more alive, more vital, the bird song louder, the smell of the undergrowth stronger. The mood of the African guards was different; they seemed happy and ironically their laughter filled the air. Only the sergeant remained unaffected. An early start was made and he shouted at the soldiers, who had stood sentry all night, to get into the APC. He clambered into the Range Rover and before a word could be said, the engine was started and with his right foot hard down on the accelerator it screamed in protest. With a loud crunching of the gearbox the vehicle moved erratically down the unmarked track and into the bush. The APC followed at a distance of a few hundred yards. Janice and Jacob remained in their hammocks as they were driven further away from the camp.

Late in the afternoon the convoy entered a large open area. Here they stopped and the sergeant got out, bellowing more orders at his men. Four men stood guard as he walked towards a single-story stone building some fifty yards away. Janice and Jacob both lowered themselves from their hammocks and looked at their surroundings. It was a camp that had been cut out of the bush. Temporary it might have been, but it appeared at first glance to be highly organised and professional. There were heavy machine guns in dugouts ringed with sandbags. New APCs were lined up in perfect rows; there must have been at least forty of them. All the gun emplacements and vehicles had been meticulously camouflaged against discovery from the air. Jacob's brief look gave him the impression that this was only a small part of a larger military base. Who was funding this? The Zairians didn't have the resources to build such a staging post. Jacob moved to open the door, but the menacing thrust of a rifle butt into the metal warned him to stay put.

"This is another fine mess you've got me into, Stanley," mimicked Janice.

The sergeant came out of the building; with a sharp retort to the guards, he jumped back into the driver's seat. Janice asked where were they going but he ignored her. They were driven to a palisade; then the guards and the sergeant left them alone.

Jacob looked around: "This doesn't make any sense. They bring us here then leave us alone. Did you see the defence network of machine guns, dugouts and APCs?"

Janice looked at him: "What of it?—in a couple of days we'll be out of here and on our way home. It's my guess that this is the base that's been supplying the Rwandan Army. Let's go for a walk."

They moved towards the entrance of the compound and the moment their bodies crossed that imaginary line, two troopers moved out of the shadows. A spurt of dust erupted some two feet from Jacob scaring the hell out of him. They were prisoners.

"We must wait and see what tomorrow brings. Janice, keep yourself covered up, these men would do almost anything for the taste of white flesh."

"Thanks, that makes me feel so much better."

Janice plunged her hand into her backpack and removed the gun, concealing it inside her shirt and under the waistband of her trousers. It felt cold and horribly uncomfortable but somehow reassuring in this hostile environment.

It was getting late so they shared the contents of a tin of corned beef, washed down with tinned pears. With nothing else to do, they rested and chatted. Jacob did most of the listening whilst Janice, in answer to his questions, talked. As night came, the camp developed a dark foreboding atmosphere; only a few guards were noticeable as their new weapons reflected the moonlight.

Jacob was asleep and Janice dozed until she heard a noise. Raising her head from the pillow she saw macabre images at the side window. Two men were trying to get in; she moved to lock the door, but it opened and an arm reached in, grabbing her by the wrist. With brute force she was dragged kicking and screaming from the Range Rover. The strength of her attacker overwhelmed her and once out of the vehicle he forced her to the ground. She lay on her back, the weight of her attacker holding her down. Her heart was pounding so heavily that when she opened her mouth to scream nothing happened. Her anger suddenly overcame terror and with a deep breath she shouted venomously, "You fucking bastards."

Her attacker laughed.

Jacob, roused by the commotion moved towards the open door. The steel base plate of an AKM47 hit him squarely in the chest and then twice full in the face.

Unable to prevent further injury the senseless body was wrenched into the open and flung to the ground. The attack continued as blood poured from open head wounds and pooled in the dry dust. Satisfied, Jacob's attacker placed his AKM47 against the side of the vehicle and began to remove his trousers. Janice was still pinned down and struggling to release herself. Fear concentrated her mind, and for a moment her attacker relaxed his grip. It was all she needed, her knee connected with his crutch and she was free. With the speed of a striking snake she slipped loose and sprang to her feet. Escape was impossible so she prepared for the attack, screaming obscenities at the top of her voice. This man was no novice and recognised the stance—his charge was a ruse. She missed the opportunity and he was quickly behind, tripping her down and holding her face in the dust. Weight and size were his advantage as with one hand he tore at her jeans. Being brand-new made them difficult to remove. Her right hand held the pistol jammed between her stomach and the ground. She knew that once her jeans were below her backside he would violate her one way or another.

Janice was petrified—she had to do something; she could not bear the thought of this creature inside her. From somewhere deep within came the instinct to survive. The adrenaline surging around her body made her head ache but still she attempted to concentrate. As if in an act of submission she stopped struggling. This was enough for him to alter his grip and roll her over. His breath was now mingled with hers as he tore at her top, and dragged her jeans and panties down. There was no time to mess around; as he was about to penetrate her, with the quickest of movements, she shoved the pistol barrel into his crutch and pulled the trigger three times. Acrid smoke filled her nostrils and the odour of burnt flesh contaminated the air. The man shrieked in uncontrolled agony, the sound hung in the air, as it reverberated around the walls of the compound. The other trooper, shocked by the cry of his comrade, stared in disbelief as two bullets made neat holes in his head. Behind her, her rapist was in his death throes. It was over and the realisation of what she had done hit her with full force. She covered herself as best she could as the sounds of the dying man ceased. For support she leant against the Range Rover and vomited. She was shaking uncontrollably, and tears of relief were running down her cheeks.

Suddenly the area was lit by the headlights of a jeep. Behind it an officer in full uniform marched towards her. He looked every inch the army officer, his uniform immaculate from the peak of his cap down to the tips of his brown shoes. In a perfect imitation of a Sandhurst accent he began, "I apologise for the behaviour of these animals." He drew back his right foot and swung a vicious kick at the head of the dead man. "Pig!" he shouted and kicked the head again, smashing the skull. He pointed: "If that one lives, I'll be able to question him. Of course you'll be charged with murder."

Janice, trying to cover herself, stared him straight in the eyes, "What are you saying? These animals attacked me and tried to rape me."

"I only have your word. For all I know you may have tried to sell your body for a chance to escape. At the moment he cannot answer."

"Sod off, you're disgusting."

"Your opinions are of little consequence to me. You shot two soldiers. A court of enquiry will be convened in the morning. Just be warned that this army and many others will join forces and people like you will run from the tide of power that will, in the future, govern this country." In his anger he had said more than he should have and as an afterthought ordered: "Give me your gun." He removed the weapon from her hand, turned and walked away, giving orders to his own men.

Jacob still lay on the ground. The Range Rover's interior light revealed a forehead split to the bone in several places; a mixture of dust and blood had congealed around the swollen wounds. Janice bathed and treated each laceration and after a while he began to come round. Jacob knew he was in bad shape and attempted to get to his feet. He swayed, wobbled, then fell back to his knees. "Sorry, my head feels as if it doesn't belong."

"Stay still—the back of your head is a bit of a mess." She knew that it was far worse. "You must have caught it when you fell."

An over-generous application of antiseptic caused Jacob to flinch, but it dulled the pain. When he was ready, together they managed to get him into the Rover and his hammock. He was in a bad way, and the irregularity of his breathing and weak pulse bothered her. There was very little she could do with the limited resources she had at her disposal. Having done all that was possible for Jacob, her thoughts now turned to herself. Digging deep into her rucksack, she removed a full set of clothing and changed, discarding her torn underwear. Her only thought was to leave this place as quickly as possible—the chances were that tomorrow they would be shot. They had to seize the opportunity and make a run for it. Jacob required a doctor and they needed a stroke of luck. In the past few weeks she had survived more ordeals than most people would encounter in a lifetime; this time she was more than scared and in it right up to her neck. Scrutiny of the maps gave little, if any, indication where there were passable roads. Her decision was to drive north-east; at best she would eventually reach the border. The guards would be at their least attentive around three in the morning. She rested, then started the engine; it took the guards thirty seconds to arrive.

This process was repeated every half an hour. Her plan was working; they were becoming bored, and the record was now one and a half minutes. Feeling pleased with herself, she started the engine again. This time it was the sergeant who appeared. Reaching into the cab he removed the keys. With a huge grin he put them in his pocket and walked away. Jacob remained oblivious. Being an Oscar winning actress was not Janice's strong point but she shouted abuse at the sergeant until he disappeared. From under the dashboard she retrieved the spare key. It was approaching two-thirty and, hopefully, they would think she had fallen asleep. The way out was firmly imprinted in her mind. One mistake and they were as good as dead. The dull red glow from the dashboard clock indicated two thirty-five and it started to rain. At first a few spots splattered on the dusty windscreen, then within a few seconds it became a tropical deluge.

She engaged the four-wheel drive, started the engine and was moving rapidly forward as the first crash of thunder reverberated around every inch of their surroundings. The guards did not notice the Range Rover—they were more interested in escaping the storm. Janice was out of the camp in a few minutes and, without lights, driving recklessly along a jungle track. Only the frequent lightning flashes allowed her to negotiate the way ahead. When a few miles had passed, she turned on the headlights and drove at maximum speed despite the terrible conditions. The direction was north, but what the hell, she thought, she had to put distance between them and the army. The storm continued for just over the hour. The air-conditioning was working well, the controlled environment inside the vehicle was a blessing. The sun began to rise, its first rays casting long shadows over the hills to the east. She stopped to check Jacob. "Good news. We're out of the camp and on our way home."

He nodded; "That's good."

She told him what had happened and how the storm had aided their escape.

He smiled; "Clever girl. But don't stop for long." His speech had thickened and altered the sound of his voice. "We'll be sighted from the air before long. They'll be out looking for us." He was very drowsy and she didn't tell him what she feared most.

"Janice, could you get me a drink? I'm thirsty."

"Of course. I'll get the container." The canteen was full so she held it to his lips. He gulped, the liquid spilling from the sides of his mouth. The trickle of blood from his wound continued to stain the bandages that covered his forehead. "We'd better get going. You rest and maybe later you can give me a break from driving."

He was already unaware of her presence, his breathing no better than before. Janice turned off the road and drove in the general direction of where she thought the border should be. After a few hours she stopped in the cover of a small copse and fell asleep, her head resting on the steering wheel.

Janice woke with a start as a family of monkeys bounced on and off the vehicle. Her back ached and she had the beginnings of cramp in both legs. It was time to make a move. Jacob moaned in his delirium, causing her to go and look at him. The top of the hammock was red. What should she do? With cotton wool soaked in disinfectant she gently washed away the congealed blood that covered his face. Then she began to saturate the dressings before attempting to remove them. Bright red blood was seeping from the wound. Jacob stirred and began to protest, but his voice was thick and he had a tendency to ramble. As she examined his injuries she realised that the damage was far worse than she had suspected. Carefully she applied a fresh dressing, using white tape to secure it as best she could.

Quite suddenly he put his hands to his head, winced and opened his eyes wide. For a moment he returned to life in the real world. Smiling he looked at Janice: "I feel a lot better today apart from this damned headache." That was all he said before he returned to his own world. Realising that she could do no more, Janice began to drive as fast as possible along an animal path between the trees. She felt safe as the branches brushed the metal sides. It was likely that, if she couldn't see the enemy, they couldn't see her. The progress was slow and even with power-assisted steering the roughness of the track battered her to and fro. After what seemed an eternity she stopped for a rest and something to eat and drink. Jacob was sweating and in the cool of the air-conditioning she realised that this was not a good sign. With a hunk of bread in one hand she began to drive again. Hour after hour she forced their way forward; when she crossed large open spaces it was done at great speed. To Jacob nothing seemed real, the motion of the journey had ceased to bother him a long while ago. The throbbing headache had all but disappeared. The bright light and a strange feeling of floating in warm air was comforting. It seemed somehow that he was detached from his body. His mind was recollecting every incident since leaving Nairobi. Suddenly he was screaming at the darkness that shut out the light; it went very cold. Janice slammed on the brakes and was quickly by Jacob's side but she knew, as soon as that gurgling sound had erupted from his lungs, he was dead. It was her fault, if she had gone home with the others, Jacob would still be alive. For a moment self-pity, a commodity rare in her life, grabbed hold but it was soon gone. The determination was back; she had to get Jacob home and tell her story.

The brightness of the sun was fading into the twilight of the evening and Janice was tired. Hours of driving through the bush along paths and tracks had taken its toll. She wanted to stop; it had been well over forty-eight hours since she had a good night's sleep. "The border must be somewhere around here," she thought; "I've covered the distance." Dusk had given way to darkness by the time Janice decided to stop. Enough was enough; driving at night when half asleep was paramount to suicide. The internal lights illuminated Jacob's body; the sight of him at peace and no longer in pain prevented her from covering his face. It was a somewhat macabre situation, in the middle of nowhere with a dead man as your only companion. With one movement she clambered into her hammock and turned the light off. Sleep came from exhaustion and soon the only sound that could be heard in the Range Rover was the gentle breathing of a sleeping woman.

Janice wasn't sure what woke her but as she peered into the darkness she was positive that she was no longer alone. Then she heard the sound of large lorries not far away. It was a dilemma, but she was, for the moment, safe in the confines of the Range Rover. She had no idea of her whereabouts and whether these vehicles were driven by friends or associates of the mad officer. Cautiously she lowered one window and listened. Sure enough the noise increased as the glass went down. For a moment she hesitated but, friend or foe, in the morning she would be discovered. The bush in daylight can be dangerous, but at night it is lethal. Once outside the safety of her refuge, she began to walk guardedly towards the sounds. Moving forward very slowly, she felt ahead with her hands to prevent her walking into hanging branches. After a few minutes she glimpsed the glow of a fire. She went down on her knees and crawled cautiously forward until she could hear voices speaking in an African tongue. She stopped to listen, then moved again until she could see the fire more clearly. Sitting around it, so far as she could determine, were ten Africans in full combat camouflage. The conversation came predominately from one man; the others seemingly agreeing with his comments. The fire crackled, tossing sparks into the air as fresh wood was thrown onto the dying embers. In the flickering light she could see some of their vehicles. A few had been well covered, whilst others seemed ready to leave at a moment's notice.

She was watching, curious and scared, undecided as to what she should do. The rumble of a heavy lorry caused her to lie flat and hug the ground. Its headlights lit up the night as it drove into the camp. It stopped and more combat-dressed Africans jumped out. There were shouted exchanges between the new arrivals as the men who had been around the fire picked up their weapons and jumped into the APC. With a roar it turned around and disappeared into the night, the clamour of its diesel engine could be heard for a few minutes longer.

As she lay in the dark, an accent familiar to her gave the boost of confidence she needed. Reassured by the presence of an Afrikaner and observing that this was certainly a disciplined outfit, she stood up. Abandoning any attempt at concealment or silence she made for the fire and the light. Within a few seconds she was surrounded by armed men shouting at her. A man walked towards them and the soldiers cleared a path as he approached. He was an African and, as he started to speak, Janice interrupted his flow to say, "I need your help."

The man looked her up and down and then in reasonable English asked, "What are you doing out here? This is bad country for us; for you, it is suicide. Come, have some tea and tell me your story."

One of the men produced a crude stool for her to sit on while she sipped warm stewed tea from a chipped enamel mug. Janice told the story of the camp and her abduction. For the moment she considered it better not to refer to the men she had killed. The soldier listened in silence, after which he announced he could help her. She was given a hot meal, while two men were sent to retrieve the Range Rover. The food smelt good and tasted even better. It consisted of meatballs in a thick soup.

She said nothing during the meal but noticed men moving to and fro around the camp and eventually the arrival of her transport. They removed Jacob's body complete with hammock and were busy filling the latter with vegetation. "Do not worry," came the voice; "Those wild herbs will stop the body from putrefying, at least until we get you and him out of here."

"Whose army are you?" she asked. The man laughed.

"For you we are the right army, the Ugandan Army. From what we heard on the radio, the RPF have not stopped searching for you. We were ordered, along with other small detachments, to keep a look out for you and patrol this part of the border. By going missing you alerted the world to the human misery not so far away. Whoever kidnapped you chose the wrong person."

Janice heaved a sigh of relief, it was all over and she could go home. The next morning the officer in charge told her that he had spoken to Kampala. "A military convoy will be leaving for the city this afternoon. You will meet it at midday. Two of my men will take you to the meeting place in your Range Rover—there will be no problem."

"Hope you're right." Janice sounded uncertain.

Shortly before she was due to leave, she removed some soap and a flannel from the back of the Range Rover and started to wash herself. The officer shouted to his men to erect a screen which seemed to appear as if by magic. As the dirt began to wash from her face she realised that her appearance the night before must have been slightly comic to her rescuers. Washed, she began to apply some make-up to her face.

The officer scrutinised her as she did so. "When the cuts and bruises have faded and your hair's been fixed up you shouldn't look too bad by the time you reach Kampala."

"If you were an officer and a gentleman you would not notice such things."

"My apologies, it was meant to be a compliment."

She stopped doing her face, turned to him, "Will there be any difficulty getting me out of here?"

"You should be safe enough. It's about two hundred and ninety-five kilometres to the city. Most of it's bush track but by tomorrow you will be on your way home. Two men from your paper will meet you on arrival and I understand that a flight has already been arranged. Maybe this time tomorrow you will be back in the cold wet climate of your England."

ELEVEN

Adrian was disheartened by the article he had read in *The Times* that their correspondent Janice Porter was missing. A message had been received in Nairobi that she had been removed from the area for, "her own safety," by a military force believed to be the Rwandan Patriotic Front. He did note that it had not been corroborated. He was not in the mood for being told that everything would be all right. Janice was in trouble, God knew where, and there was damn all anyone could do about it. Even if he managed to get to Rwanda or Zaire, where would he start? Fed up with himself and the lack of purpose that seemed to surround his life at that moment he went for a walk. Adrian paused halfway up the hill on the path that led to a small copse. He was breathing hard and the silence that surrounded him only heightened his thoughts that somewhere, thousands of miles away, was Janice.

A twig snapped and he turned; it was old Joe. Strange that in all the time he had known this scoundrel he had never given his position away like that. Joe halted and faced him, the smell of tobacco filling the air. "Thought you might need some company, seeing as how that lady friend of yours has got herself into a bit of trouble." Joe waited for him to start walking and then strolled beside him.

Adrian walked in silence, only some dogs barking in one of the nearby houses spoiled the tranquillity of it all.

"What you going to do about it then?" asked Joe.

"There's not much I can do, is there?"

"Well my instincts tell me that what's meant for you won't go past you. If she's half the woman you've said she is, you'll see her again. Mark my words, I'll be right."

Adrian continued to stroll down the hill but when he turned to speak, Joe had gone. By the time he arrived home he was in a better frame of mind. Old Joe had reassured him more in his manner than by words alone. Why was it Joe always knew the answers to things that mattered? His shoes crunched on the gravel driveway as he walked briskly. For a change he made his way to the old stable yard and entered the house via the kitchen. The aroma of his favourite meal, steak and kidney pudding, filled the air. Every word of *The Times* was read and re-read as he looked for the positive rather than the negative. "Yes," he thought, "if anyone can survive, Janice will."

Mrs Duke entered the room. Absorbed in the paper, he was momentarily startled by her appearance. "You look a bit brighter now. The fresh air must have done you some good."

"I bumped into old Joe and had a chat with him. He always looks on the bright side of life and somehow it becomes infectious."

Mrs Duke looked puzzled, and wanted to ask a question but decided that if Adrian was happy, so be it.

+++

Selwyn poked his head into the kitchen: "Mrs Duke, where's Adrian?"

"Last time I saw him he was busy in the office."

Adrian was collating the list of new equipment the boats would need for the next season when Selwyn walked into the room. "Janice is on her way home. Her flight arrives at Heathrow tomorrow at five p.m. I've booked you a suite in the International; here's your rail ticket. Mrs Duke's packing all the clothes you'll need, and your car's in the drive."

Adrian was stunned by the news. His emotions were playing a game of tennis. One part of him was telling him to go, whilst the other was asking why. They had no commitment or agreement. He thought of how she had felt in his arms, how much he wanted her, needed her. It was a dream that he wanted to become reality. He was convinced in his own mind that she had feelings for him but if she rebuked him this time he would retire from the field of play.

"Selwyn, will you come with me?"

"No. You have to sort this one out on your own."

Adrian knew that either he went now or stopped deluding himself. The decision was not difficult. The journey to the station was the same as ever except old Joe was walking along the road. As the car drew near, he turned and waved; Adrian shifted his position to wave back, but Joe had vanished.

Four hours later Adrian was sat at the bar of the International Hotel. For the next twenty hours he had nothing to do except wait. What would he say when they met? It was important that he was there.

+++

It was nearing four in the afternoon, and although the wind had dropped and the rain gone completely, there was a suggestion of a storm in the air. Adrian left the hotel and made his way to Terminal Four. Once there, he stopped to study the Arrivals monitor. Janice's flight was showing thirty minutes late. With time to waste he went and purchased a cup of coffee and found a seat that gave him a clear view of an Arrivals monitor. The time passed slowly as he watched hundreds of arriving travellers dragging their heavy cases to taxis and buses. It was five-thirty when her flight landed. With his heart pounding, he walked towards the International Customs exit and waited.

A large group of media people was standing to one side, Adrian wondered who the celebrity was that would be plagued by these vultures. What would Janice say when she saw him? The last time any words of importance had passed between them had been at the hospital. Now, like a love-struck fool, he was nervous and waiting. He knew that he loved her - she was vibrant, bursting with life. When his parents had died he had lost the part of him that was hard to define. Through her, Adrian had recaptured those emotions which he had come to believe were long withered by unhappiness and the matter of fact of living. With her he had a reason to live; there had been many women in his life but none had stirred anything like the passion that now burned within him.

Suddenly she was there; he moved forward but the mass of reporters blocked his path. Flashlights filled the air, reflecting the tiredness in her eyes.

Janice's eyes met Adrian's. It was a profound "help me" gaze. Adrian had rehearsed a hundred things he wanted to say but could only mime a weak "hello".

He looked back into those eyes—something was wrong. He was not sure. She tilted her head slightly, and it left him with a feeling of uncertainty. Adrian Viper did not relish that sensation. Without any consideration or thought, he charged headlong into the mob. As unsuspecting journalists flew left and right, he lunged forward and grabbed her arm tightly. His momentum carried them clear and into the open; together they ran and lost themselves in the morass of travellers. When they eventually stopped, she placed both arms around him, laid her head on his shoulder and sobbed her heart out. Not a word was spoken as he held her tight and let whatever troubled her release itself. When it had passed, she pulled away and looked at him, her eyes moist from the tears that had flowed freely. "Why are you always around when I need a shoulder to cry on?"

"If you'd let me, I'd like to be around all the time."

She suddenly saw him hanging onto the cliff face and then jumping into the air only to hang like a rag doll from that precarious tether. She shuddered at the thought, as the feeling of need for this man overwhelmed her. For years work had become her only pleasure—no-one was allowed to see the real Janice. There were a few close friends that had penetrated her armour, and only in their company was she free to be herself.

"Come on, Adrian, I'll let you buy me a cup of coffee."

Adrian hesitantly asked, "Why not come and stay with me?"

Janice looked at him and holding both his hands very gently asked, "Why?"

"Because I love you."

"Do you know something, Adrian?"

"What?"

"Life's a bitch and so am I."

"I can put up with that. You don't have a very high opinion of yourself, do you?"

"At this moment I don't."

"That makes a change. Look all I want is for us to have a chance to get to know each other. I have a house with plenty of empty rooms and I'm sure Mrs Duke would welcome the chance of having some female company. Janice, trust me."

She was tired and as much as she wanted him, she was frightened by the thought of spending time alone with him. Her emotions were in turmoil. Pondering the moment, she looked into his eyes and saw a tenderness there. She had nothing to lose and needed to get away from the world for a few days. With not a hint of emotion in her voice she replied, "Yes, OK, but I need to make one telephone call and post this to my editor."

Adrian slightly taken aback at her answer, gulped, then glanced at the airport clock; it was a quarter past six. "If we hurry we might make the seven o'clock train to York. Whilst you're making your call, I'll telephone Selwyn and ask him to meet us, then post your letter. What is it?"

"It's Jacob's story. I'll tell you about it later."

Janice telephoned her son, Gregory. Briefly she explained that everything was all right and that for a few days she would be staying with a friend. Gregory asked, “Old or new flame?”

She laughed and felt happier that he always understood. Her mind was still confused by what was happening and she had to warn Adrian not to build up his hopes.

“I’ll stay in your house but promise no more than that. Give me time—I’m fond of you but whether I can ever love you, I don’t know.”

Adrian almost dragged her to the taxi rank. Whether there was a glut of taxis or they were just lucky, there was no queue. As they entered the rear of the cab and flung themselves on the worn leather seat, Adrian shouted, “King’s Cross and as fast as you can. There’s a twenty quid tip in it for you if we’re in time to catch the seven o’clock train.”

The driver looked at his watch and decided it was worth the extra effort for the money. With the ease of a professional racing driver the cabby negotiated his way through the entanglement of incoming and outward bound traffic. Every few seconds another aircraft thundered overhead, deadening all sound. Once on the M4 the taxi began to eat the fifteen miles that stretched between the airport and the centre of London. Janice closed her eyes and made herself comfortable.

The roads were becoming decidedly busy but, undeterred, the driver forced his way past slow and wandering traffic. It was just passing six forty when he roared down the Edgware Road and into Marylebone Road. Adrian looked at his watch and then the meter. Realising that it would be touch and go he took three twenty pound notes from his wallet and passed them to the driver. The man looked at the notes, swerved, swore at some fool of a driver, before stuffing them into his top pocket. At three minutes to seven they drew to a halt outside King's Cross station. Not a moment was wasted. The two of them, one still half asleep, grabbed their bags and ran as if their lives depended on it. The guard was about to shut the barrier but thought better of it as they raced the final few yards before clambering into the last carriage. As they paused for breath, the door shut behind them.

A whistle shrilled, the guard waved his hand. The train gave a jerk forward, then began to glide out of the station. A group of four seats was empty so they sat facing each other. Janice remained silent and watched this man, who for a moment was lost in his own thoughts. She moved her hands towards his and held them softly. They were warm; why were men's hands always warm and women's cold she wondered? Her touch brought him back to reality. The ticket collector lurched towards them. Adrian paid for her ticket, and in that brief moment Janice had fallen asleep.

As the train began its approach to York Station, he gently woke her.

"Where are we?" she asked, half asleep. Her face had lines where it had rested against the material of the seat. "I bet I look a right mess."

"Well, I can honestly say I've seen you looking a lot worse." He smiled; "But you needed the sleep."

As they walked out of the station into the cool night air, the Jaguar, its paintwork gleaming from hours of polishing, pulled up in front of them. Selwyn's beaming smile radiated through the window as he waited for them to get in. Adrian held the door for Janice, only closing it when she was well inside. Selwyn was puzzled when Adrian opened the passenger door. Seeing the expression on his friend's face, Adrian laughed, "Janice is very tired, so, being the gentleman that I am, I'll let her stretch out." Selwyn was full of questions but decided it would be better to ask later.

It was as if she needed to tell someone and it was the right moment. Hesitantly at first she began to tell them what had happened and, once she started, the words began to flow as a river in full spate. The killing of Jacob had obviously affected her more than she knew, the level of her voice dropped significantly when she spoke about him. It was very dark as the car rolled up the drive, its headlights illuminating the pathway to the house.

"I'm impressed," she said with a cheeky grin on her face. In the few moments it took for Adrian and Janice to get out of the car, Mrs Duke was there waiting.

"Janice, this is Mrs Duke, my second mum. Whatever she says about me is all lies."

"You're still and always will be a little boy to me, young Adrian. Now, my dear, I suppose you'd like to have a wash and change into something fresh after your long journey. My husband's running a bath for you this very moment. I've opened up your parents' room for Miss Porter—it's about time it was used."

Adrian was speechless; Mrs Duke had, in her own unique manner, broken the spell that had closed that room all those years ago. He had thought of letting Janice use that room but had been frightened to suggest it. It was a woman's room and had the added advantage of an en suite facility.

Selwyn returned from garaging the car. With a smile on his lips he stood watching as the procession of Mrs Duke, Janice and Adrian trooped up the stairs. Adrian followed them into his parents' bedroom and glanced around; it had been a long time since he had crossed that threshold. He knew that once a week Mrs Duke aired and cleaned the room from top to bottom. The décor was still quietly tasteful. The matching wallpaper and curtains in a delicate floral pattern had been chosen by his mother. In fact the whole room was his mother, his father had merely slept there. He clearly remembered as a child sitting under the canopy of the brass four-poster bed whilst his mother combed his hair. He went and sat on the edge of the bed and looked through the large bay window. The sprawling Yorkshire moors, which had always run through his veins, were now pitch black and seemingly devoid of life. A door in the far wall opened and Mr Duke appeared, followed by a cloud of steam.

"Your bath's ready, Miss Porter."

"Please call me Janice; no-one calls me Miss Porter."

Mrs Duke looked at her husband and then Adrian. Both men got the message and left.

"Well, now those two have gone, I can show you your clothes. Selwyn came with me to buy them yesterday but for good or bad he had to guess your measurements. I managed to get most things on a sale or return basis. There's size ten in the top draw and twelve in the next one down. Your bathrobe is an old one of mine, so I hope you don't mind."

Janice sat on the edge of the bed and for the second time that day she broke down and sobbed.

Mrs Duke moved forward, touched her arm and then held her as a child. This had the desired effect; it gave reassurance and much needed comfort. The tears subsided as quickly as they came but the pain remained. "I'm sorry, I'm making a fool of myself." Emotion still quivered in her voice.

"Better out than in I always say."

"Mrs Duke, you're a remarkable woman."

"The three men in my life have been known to sing my praises now and then. You must remember my husband's easy to please. I've looked after Adrian since he was born and Selwyn needed someone to care for him. It's easy to please if you love them."

"You make loving people sound so easy."

"It is when that love is returned. Anyway, you get yourself into that bathroom and have a good soak. When you're ready, come downstairs and we'll have a late supper. Oh, by the way, we eat in the kitchen."

Mrs Duke left, shutting the bedroom door behind her. Janice undressed, tossing her clothes into a heap at the side of the bed. The bath water was very hot; slowly she lowered her body into it. The aroma from fragrant herbs in the water filled the air and tantalised her senses. The warmth and the whole atmosphere of her surroundings began to envelop her, infiltrating the very pores of her body and enabling her to relax at last.

Adrian and Selwyn were in the kitchen reading the evening papers when Mrs Duke returned.

"How is she?" asked Adrian.

Mrs Duke continued to make some sandwiches as she answered his question. "Battered and bruised emotionally and physically; it will take time to heal the wounds. I don't think she realises how close she is to a breakdown. Adrian, I'm aware how you feel about Janice but go easy on her; if you push her too hard you'll only hurt each other. If it's going to be, it will be, but if not, try and remain friends. Janice needs real friends more than anything at this moment."

Selwyn waited for her to stop. "I had Mr Duke place some aromatic herbs in the bath water that will help her relax and I would suggest that a good night's sleep will aid the healing process."

Mrs Duke looked at him with wide eyes, "You and your potions, Selwyn—where did you get these from?"

"It's called aromatherapy these days but it's existed for centuries and all the oils and herbs are available from most chemists. The mix is the secret."

It was approaching midnight when Janice entered the kitchen. Mrs Duke had gone home but left the table set with enough fresh sandwiches to feed an army. Selwyn asked Janice if she would like a drink.

"Hot milky chocolate, please."

Adrian picked up the plate of food and handed it to her, asking if she felt better. The atmosphere was slightly strained; both men wanted to ask so many questions but heeded Mrs Duke's advice so the conversation was reduced to small talk. Janice nibbled at a sandwich; she felt exhausted. When her drink was finished, she excused herself. Adrian suggested that he show her the way but in a firm but polite tone the offer was refused.

Janice found her bedroom with more ease than she had imagined. As she removed her robe, the large four poster bed became very welcoming, the white sheets glistening in the shaded glow of the bedside light. As she snuggled down and was surrounded by its feeling of comfort, the world began to dim and sleep overcame her. Recently she had found it difficult to sleep properly—nightmares had lain in wait to torment her. Sometimes it was as if she had been reduced to playing the part of the fool in some ridiculous farce. Many times, waking in a cold sweat she had attempted to come to terms with it, but instead found herself with only unanswered questions that remained, come what may. This night was different—only good dreams seemed to come and go. Gregory, her son, was there to help and guide her along—he always said the right thing—but Adrian remained distant, forever there in the background. Then the mist that separates one dream from another cleared but only to return, and the darkness of deep sleep finally overcame her.

+++

For Janice, the night was unbelievably comfortable as if she was floating on a bed of soft down. When she woke it was light. She lay there, her whole being encompassed with the feeling of protection and comfort. She listened to the sparrows outside the window fighting over some scraps of food and heard people wandering about the house. For a while she dozed, until, with a concentrated effort she decided to leave the warmth of her bed. A glance at her watch caused her to gasp out loud; it was past midday. She went to the bathroom for a wash and returned to brush her hair and then quickly dressed in a pair of jeans and loose sweater and scurried down the stairs. Mrs Duke was there in the kitchen preparing some vegetables. Without any hesitation she remarked, "It's a bit late to call it breakfast but would you like something anyway?"

"I would love a cup of coffee but don't cook anything for me. It's far too late—I should have got up earlier."

Mrs Duke looked at her: "My dear, you were exhausted when you arrived and a few hours' sleep isn't enough to get you back on your feet. Adrian brought you here to get some rest. Cooking you a breakfast will take me only a few minutes."

Janice started to refuse but the bacon had somehow began to grill and eggs were already being cracked into the pan. Perhaps it had been the long journey, maybe it was the jetlag, possibly it was this house. Janice found herself staring down into the cup and her tears began overflowing. Mrs Duke looked at her with understanding in her eyes as she skilfully negotiated two eggs from a frying pan onto a warmed plate. Her charge's soul-searching was deepening, she was becoming aware of the change in herself. Chances in the past had been lost—the tide of time seemed to be ebbing faster than she wanted—she was beginning to feel vulnerable. She jolted herself back to reality with the thought that such feelings were ridiculous. It had been foolish and irrational to come to this house and again become involved with Adrian.

Just as she was finishing her breakfast, Adrian wandered into the kitchen. "Did you sleep well?"

She was confused: "I did, thank you, but if you don't mind I need some fresh air to clear my head—I'm going for a walk." She looked directly at him: "And I would prefer to be alone." Adrian had decided to let her do as she wanted and not to press the home advantage. Janice went and examined a burgundy coat she had seen hanging in her wardrobe. She tried it on; the material was pure wool and the fit almost perfect. It was draped over her shoulders as she left the house by the front door. Her feet crunched on the gravel path, disturbing the chirping birds momentarily. She turned left onto the road and after a few hundred yards crossed over and turned right, taking a rough trail through some trees. The path meandered uphill through a wood, emerging a few hundred yards later in a small misty clearing. It was peculiar, even the birds were silent. She became strangely troubled by the loneliness of the place, the feeling of not belonging overwhelmed her. For a long time she stood remembering her life; the pages of the book kept turning, stopping at relevant moments of sadness and happiness. The longing for something or even someone to fill that void, which had been there most of her life, caused her a lot of pain.

She didn't hear the old man approach and was startled when he asked, "You staying at the big house?"

The blackened pipe that hung from his mouth emitted a foul smell as he spoke. Janice couldn't decide whether it was a question or a statement of fact and answered politely, "I am."

"Well, you must be Janice. Last I heard you were lost in Africa."

"Excuse me, but who are you?"

Old Joe looked at her and taking a large puff from his pipe filled the air with tobacco smoke. "Everyone knows me and I know everything about them." As he spoke he moved towards a fallen tree and propped himself against it.

"OK then, what can you tell me about Adrian Viper? Is he a good, kind, generous man and a fantastic lover?" asked Janice, being deliberately outspoken and speaking in such a manner as to intimidate and shock.

Old Joe didn't flinch at her remarks. He puffed at his pipe, as if deliberating, then shook his head. "What you want is for it all to be perfect. You want him to be the ideal lover but life isn't that way. I think you should stop looking for perfection. He's a good man who would, if you gave him the chance, love you more than you deserve. You let your heart rule your head once and for a moment found true love—why not do it again? You could be surprised at the outcome. We're all blended by love, especially that one great love that changes everything."

Janice was becoming annoyed at the impudence of this stranger who seemed to know her every intimate thought. She was about to say something but the old man was already walking away into the woods. Bewildered by the actions of this stranger she wandered on down the hill. An inconspicuous circle of rusted black railings and a flight of stone steps led to a small unkempt graveyard. Nearby were the remains of a long forgotten chapel that must have once served the local farms and their workers. What intrigued Janice was the new grave and the white marble headstone that seemed to shine in the dim light of the trees. Slowly she read the inscription:

> Joe. Died… Age unknown. He lived off the land he now lies in. He provided food for the hungry. A friend to all who had the pleasure of knowing his artful ways. This headstone was given by those who loved him.

"How sad but very touching," thought Janice. "I wonder what my headstone will say—'A bitch who deserved all she got.'"

It suddenly went very cold, causing her to shiver; the smell of tobacco smoke filled the air but the old man was nowhere to be seen. She drew her coat around her and at a fast pace made her way back. Her feet disturbed the stones on the path as she almost ran into the house. Mrs Duke had heard her coming and was in the hall to meet her. "Are you all right, dear? You look very flushed."

"Nothing that a nice hot cup of tea wouldn't put right. Where's Adrian?"

As they walked to the kitchen Mrs Duke answered her question: "In the office with Selwyn, discussing boats." The tea was going to take a few minutes; Mrs Duke stood at the worktop with her back to Janice, arranging the cups and saucers.

As if to break the silence of waiting, Janice commented on her meeting: "I met a strange old man when I was out. In some ways he was quite rude, well not exactly rude but very personal."

"What did he look like?" asked Mrs Duke as she carefully poured out two cups of tea.

"Very scruffy, smoked a revolting pipe that must have had cow dung for tobacco."

The sentence ended as two cups crashed to the floor, their contents scalding Mrs Duke's right leg from the knee to her foot. Janice grabbed a tea cloth and soaked it with cold water and quickly wrapped it around the affected area. The cold water instantly reduced the pain. Selwyn arrived, closely followed by Adrian. Neither had to ask the obvious.

"I'll telephone for the doctor," exclaimed Adrian with a sense of urgency.

Selwyn bent down and gently lifted the leg; "Don't bother," he replied; "It's scolded but not bad." He walked over to the fridge and removed the ice cubes that had settled in the ice maker. He placed them in the wet tea towel and wrapped it around the leg. Mrs Duke could feel the heat and the pain diminishing. "Leave that on until all the ice has melted, then call me."

"How did it happen?" asked Adrian.

Mrs Duke looked at him and smiled. "Just an old lady beginning to drop things. It happens." She had decided not to mention that old Joe had been found dead in the woods whilst they had been in Africa. If Joe's spirit was still around, she was not going to be the one to disturb it. Janice felt awkward and asked if there was anything she could do.

Mrs Duke looked at her: "Adrian, Selwyn, get out of my kitchen."

Janice prepared the evening meal under the watchful eye of Mrs Duke. Mr Duke did not seem over concerned at his wife's injury once she had explained that Selwyn was treating it. Before they sat down, Selwyn removed the tea towel and examined the red welts that had formed. From his pocket he took a dark green bottle and poured a few drops of a brown sludge onto the leg. With two fingers the liquid was very gently massaged into the skin. Mrs Duke exclaimed that there was no pain. Selwyn wrapped it in a sterile dressing and bandage, advising her to go home and rest the leg and he would look at it again in the morning. The casserole was eaten and the dishes washed. It was nearing nine o'clock as they sat down to watch the news. Selwyn excused himself. For the first time since she had arrived, Janice was alone with Adrian.

"Now," she said, "tell me about yourself and start from the very beginning."

Adrian laughed: "What would you like to hear? My school days were the same as any young boy, then I went to Cambridge."

Janice interrupted: "No. Tell me about your mother and father, what were they like?"

He looked at his hands—they were trembling. It wasn't that he had forgotten his parents, he could never do that, but not once since their death had he spoken about the love between them. He found it difficult to explain how the loss of that love and attention now left him with an empty inside. He tried to explain the anger he had against the lorry driver for killing them. Janice listened to the outpourings of someone who knew love but had rarely if ever given it. She felt in many ways it was like listening to herself. They had so much hurt in their lives; loving and trust had become difficult, yet she knew that if she let this man love her it would be returned. Still she remained the wrong side of the bridge. One step was all that was needed to bring them together. It was nearing eleven o'clock when Adrian declared he had talked enough for one night and that they should get some rest. As she got up to leave, Janice leant forward and gently kissed Adrian on the cheek.

"What's that for?"

"I felt like it."

For an hour longer Adrian sat cradled in the comfort of the old armchair and reflected the moment of her leaving. Could she lower those barriers that separated them?

Twelve

It was dark and cool when the two men stirred and drank from the wetness of their own shirts. The Bosun couldn't see Thompson but he knew he was there. "Is this the end? We don't know where we are, there's no food and scarcely any water. Out there it roasts you alive, in here it's all right. You can do what you want but I'm going to stay here."

Thompson was not in the mood to debate life or death; he just wanted to be left alone with his own thoughts and dreams. For him the world was becoming idyllic—it was nice to be allowed to wander where you wanted with no-one to tell you what to do. It was cool and the fresh breeze that seemed to waft across his body reminded him of being at sea when he was a lad. Sleep was the answer. Time became meaningless as they lay in the mine. With no food, sleep was a respite from the misery that surrounded them. Eventually it became a constant companion that took away the will to live.

The noise was ruining his dream, the sun hurt his eyes and who was screaming and shouting at him? "I wish you'd all bugger off."

They wouldn't go away. Noise, tons of noise pounded away at him and the wind tugged his hair.

Why his hair? What was happening? The world was turning itself around and he was in the centre trying to stand still.

As soon as the helicopter landed, nurses whisked both men into the air-conditioned and sterile environment of the small Derby hospital. The priority was liquid to combat dehydration. The cool blackness returned; it was nice when they left him alone.

The Bosun and Thompson had been fortunate, for an off-road tour had stopped for a break in the old mining town. The guide had wandered into the mine to urinate. Only when his eyes had become accustomed to the darkness did he notice the two men. All Safari Land Cruisers must be fitted with two-way radios as a matter of safety. The flying doctor service had a helicopter winging its way towards them before the message ended. The doctor looked at the strangers, wondering where they were from, but until they regained consciousness they would remain as patients number one and two. Strangely, at that moment, the snake-catcher was walking down the main street to sell the poison, which he had extracted, to the hospital for cleaning and processing into serum. Once the venom was safely deposited and the snakes sold, the old aborigine strolled towards the local bar and began to drink his fill of dark Australian rum. Drink has the distinctive quality of loosening the tongue. Nobody ever listened to the aborigine as he slavered about exploding ships and men being eaten alive by dragons. Having had his fill he staggered to the far end of town to sleep off his alcoholic stupor.

David Jones, the local police sergeant, sat in front of Dr McCready's desk: "I don't like strangers turning up like this. These men from the Kimberlies, have they said anything?"

"Not a thing."

"Come on—" David looked at his friend "—they must have said something."

"I'm not here to get answers to questions. That's your job. I have two men who are suffering from acute dehydration. Maybe they were in an accident, plane crash, anything. How the hell do you expect me to know?"

"OK, Doc, I'll come back tomorrow; maybe our visitors will feel more like talking then."

"Sorry I can't help you, David. See you later for a beer or two."

"Yeah—sure." One police officer left the hospital none the wiser.

Both men were recovering and the Bosun had overheard one of the nurses and decided that a loss of memory was as good a ploy as any. Life was being generous for a change. No-one knew them as gutter-rats or pirates; for once they were being treated as human beings. When they were feeling stronger, they could steal some clothes and travel. The Bosun had pinpointed Derby in his mind and was aware that they had to head south where there would be harbours with boats.

When a nurse entered the room, Thompson remained fast asleep; the Bosun was wide awake.

"How are you feeling today?"

He looked at her with pure lust radiating from his eyes.

This caused her to shiver.

Surprisingly, his answer was polite. "I feel OK, thank you. Where am I? How did I get here?"

She moved across and adjusted his pillow: "Don't worry about it. After some rest you'll soon recover. She placed a tray of food in front of him. "Your friend's sleeping. I'll keep his hot and bring it back later. Sleep is the best thing for him now." The nurse left the Bosun to his meal.

+++

Doctor McCready was doing his morning rounds before the outpatient surgery began. He entered the small ward housing the Bosun and Thompson, to find them chatting away like old friends.

"You seem happy."

"Well, it's like this, Doc, we both keep getting these flashes and we're comparing notes. You know what they say, two heads are better than one."

"That's a good idea, who thought of that?"

"Don't know, it just seemed to happen, Doc," replied the Bosun.

Peter McCready left the ward amused by the charade he had just witnessed. Knowledge warned him that these men had recovered most, if not all of their memories. He strolled back to his office and telephoned Sergeant David Jones. The instrument at the other end seemed to ring for an eternity before it was answered.

"David, it's Peter; my two patients are ready to see you. They were as thick as thieves, but clammed up the instant I walked in."

"Thanks Peter—I'll pop over sometime this afternoon. Our drunken snake-catcher has been at it again."

"What's he been up to this time?"

"Just dead drunk and found sound asleep in the Reverend's front garden. I think a few rose bushes are lying just a little flatter than they were yesterday."

Peter laughed at the remark, but commented he had an in-grown toenail to whip off before lunch.

+++

"I think the Doc's realised our memories are back," whispered Thompson.

"We get out of here tonight," decided the Bosun.

"Where do we go? If it's back to those bloody hills, get stuffed—I'd rather go to prison."

"Get real," shouted the Bosun into his face; "we're murderers and if they find out the truth they'll put us away forever. On the run we stand a chance and it's got to be better than prison."

"OK, but we need food, money and a car. Where do we find these?"

"Leave it to me."

David Jones locked up the aborigine for the rest of the day and made his way down the main street to his local bar for lunch. Terry Ward, the bar owner, saw David enter and nodded to Rachel, his one and only waitress. David never paid for lunch and he turned a blind eye to what went on in the back room. It was mutually convenient for both parties. Rachel fancied David but he performed his duty in public and kept his private life as just that.

"Steak and chips, Rachel."

"You have that every Wednesday, don't you ever fancy a change?" Her eyes lowered sulkily in a sexual manner.

"I'd order something else if I wanted a change; now shift your pretty little arse and get my meal," smiled David, dismissing her lustful intentions.

Terry wandered across. "Had that bloody abo in here last night getting stoned. It's not that he ever bothers anyone but I think he's going a bit simple. All night he was going on about great metal monsters breaking through the forest and devil fish eating white men. The way he told it fair put the wind up some of my regulars. Had to throw him out."

David rarely said much, but as a good policeman, listened a lot. Tomorrow, when the aborigine had recovered, he would ask him a few questions. His meal over and it being a nice day, he decided to walk the short distance to the hospital. The two strangers were not, from what he had been told, educated men and police records had drawn a blank. Their clothing had revealed nothing of interest, and they were of English origin, something quite common in the area. If they didn't want to co-operate there was very little he could do except wait for them to make a mistake. For two hours he asked pertinent questions and for two hours was given the same answer: "I can't remember."

Before David left he asked Peter to keep a special note of what the two men did or said. "They'll make a mistake. You mark my words." He didn't return to the station but reported in by telephone that, if required, he would be at home. The antics of an alcoholic aborigine were temporarily forgotten.

In the early hours of the morning the Bosun and Thompson waited for the right moment. Clothes, money and a set of car keys were stolen from the locker room. It took a few minutes for them to find the right car. After leaving the hospital, time was wasted looking for the road to Port Headland. Once clear of Broome, the Bosun increased the car's speed to ninety miles an hour. The Great Northern Highway was empty. Apart from the occasional Road Train, the journey was uneventful and they reached Port Headland in good time.

"We need petrol," said the Bosun.

With a full tank Port Headland was soon behind them as they headed for Perth. The car's headlights did nothing but illuminate the Great Northern Highway and the odd animal that darted through the beam. Time seemed to stand still as mile after mile relentlessly vanished. The morning light began to shimmer on the sunburnt scrub and the ever distant hills. It merely gave the country size and they were in the middle of it. A single-engined plane flew overhead, shaking the ground on which they were travelling.

"Bloody crop dusters, nothing better to do out here except put the fear of God into people," shouted Thompson. Neither had noticed the markings on the plane. Another hour of boredom reduced the two men's alertness to the minimum. It was more by luck than skill that the Bosun managed to stop the car before it ploughed into the side of a stationary Road Train.

"What the hell!" screamed Thompson as he was rudely flung into reality. As the dust settled, it became apparent that they had come close to oblivion. The men got out of the car to find that the driver of this huge monster had apparently abandoned it in the middle of nowhere. A voice rang out: "Stand still and place your hands in the air, one wrong move and you'll be dingo bait."

The order required little understanding and they remained perfectly still with both hands held high. From behind the vehicle, led by the sergeant from Derby, walked half a dozen well-armed constables. David Jones, swinging his rifle across the front of his body, moved towards them, smiling as he did so, "Go on, please be my guest, make a run for it and see how far you get with at least six bullets in your back. I wasn't sure about you two but baited the trap with clothes and a car and you went for it. Only an idiot or in this case, two idiots, steal a car. There's one road out of Derby, two roads out of Broome and three out of Port Headland. You had nowhere to go, so we had a good night's sleep and waited until daylight. What took you a whole night to drive we flew in a few hours. Anyway, mates, so much for the cordial conversation. We can let you cook in the sun for a few hours until you talk or you can do things my way. I don't care which option you choose but we'll get the right answers or my mate over there—" he pointed to a six foot hulk in uniform "—will rip your arms off, one by one. So what's it to be mates - pain or more pain?"

The Bosun was not intimidated and being fairly sure of some justice, sneeringly replied, "You can't want to beat the shit out of us because we stole a car?"

"No mate, you're right about that. We want to know who you are and where you came from? Once we know that, we still might want to beat the shit out of you for spoiling our day."

"Very funny, ha ha, I'll die laughing," jeered the Bosun. With a nod from David, three constables moved forward and stood in front of Thompson.

"Show this Pommy bastard how we play cricket!" In unison their rifle butts hit chest and knees. Thompson fell in agony and vomited over the ground.

"You can't do that. We have rights," roared the Bosun.

David nodded to his men and the butts struck again, Thompson screamed in agony as the pain of damaged kneecaps raced around his nervous system.

"You have no bloody rights until you tell me who you are and where you come from? My men will inflict pain on your friend until you tell me. Out here—" he gestured with his arms "—you can scream as much as you want, no-one will hear you. If you die, your body will be tossed over there—" he pointed with the rifle "—as dingo meat. Now are you going to talk to me?"

The Bosun realised that this man wasn't really bothered whether they lived or died. As he considered the situation the constables clubbed Thompson into unconsciousness.

David looked at the body lying in the dust. "My men are more than happy to start on you."

Thompson was not moving. The Bosun started to talk. The story was not a lie, but a fabrication of the truth. They were shipwrecked sailors and they did lose their memories. David and the constables listened patiently to the story. "That's a good tale, almost believable, but I don't."

Thompson was propped up against the front wheels

of the road train and the deputies were preparing themselves.

Before the rifle butts had a chance to inflict more damage, Thompson came to and screamed, "I'll tell you. I'll tell you! Please don't hit me again."

The story was told, not a solitary detail was omitted. After a while David told him to stop. "Now that at least was a better story, some of it is even possible. All I can charge you with is car theft, all that other rubbish just tells me you Pommy bums are chancing your luck. Well, you'll be taken back to Derby and no doubt get bed and breakfast at the state's expense for at least six months."

The hulk picked up Thompson by his shirt and merely looked at the Bosun as he escorted them down the road to where the light aircraft was parked. The car was driven onto the trailer of the Road Train and two of the constables drove the beast to Port Headland. In less than three hours David and his prisoners were inside the cool confines of the police station.

+++

"Gentlemen," shouted Sergeant David Jones at the top of his voice, "you slept well? The beds aren't as comfortable as the hospital but beggars can't be choosers, can they?"

The Bosun and Thompson looked from beneath the coarse blankets at a man, this man who had treated them as scum.

"Today, gentlemen, is statement day. You will write in your own words where you came from and how you arrived here. Providing your stories are identical you will get food and be allowed a wash."

Jones smiled all the time he was talking. It had been a long time since he had real villains to deal with. In this town he was the law and it was never questioned. He turned the key in the lock of the cell door and dragged Thompson by his shirt out of bed and across the floor to an adjoining cell. The Bosun went to make a move but the cocking of a rifle stopped him in his tracks. The constable laughed loudly which infuriated the Bosun all the more. Jones stood back and explained that they had an hour to write, in their own words their account of what happened. He turned and left the jail in the hands of his constable. As he strolled down the main street the story he had battered out of Thompson tended to crash into the tale told by the bar owner, Terry Ward. The coincidence of men being eaten by crocodiles was rare even in this part of the world. "Where was that sodding abo?"

He went back for his car and began a slow tour of the places the snake-catcher was known to sleep. It was over an hour later when he found him dead to the world in black Mary's shack. David picked up a bucket and filled it with water from the outside tap. With a sweep of his arms he flung the contents over the prostrate form. The shock, more than anything else, roused the snake-catcher to physical wakefulness but his brain was still subjected to alcoholic contamination. David dragged the aborigine to the car and flung him onto the back seat. What existed of this wreck of a man curled up into a ball and quickly returned to his drunken stupor. David drove directly to the hospital and deposited the bedraggled body into the arms of the nursing sister.

Tracey Munden was never a Florence Nightingale but a professional hospital administrator who demanded that everything had its place and it should be there. Drunks were to her the lowest form of life. David did not wait, he pointed to the sodden heap on the floor. "Sober him up and feed him; any trouble call me. That might just be an important witness for the State."

Tracey had the utmost respect for the law, especially when it came in the form of a handsome sergeant. It had to be important as David was not usually so abrupt. She shouted at the porter to take the aborigine to a cubicle and strip him, then wash him. Once satisfied that the well-oiled machine was moving, Sister Munden retired to her room and changed out of her soiled uniform.

Life had been very unkind to Tracey; she was barely five foot in height, with short shoulder-length red hair. Her over-plump figure always gave the appearance that somehow she was pregnant. Men respected her but given the choice on a dark night any other woman was preferable.

The porter knocked gently on her door and announced that the patient was ready.

"Very well, I'll be out in a minute."

Her crisp uniform appeared to crackle as she marched briskly across the tiled floor. With as much gentleness that was possible on such occasions, she removed the last dregs of any alcoholic beverage from the man's stomach, all that was now needed was for him to sober up. Recognising the poor condition he was in, she acknowledged it would be at least twenty-four hours before the creature's liver rid itself of the raw alcohol that had damaged it beyond repair. Sleep was the answer, but first she fed him a cocktail of drugs and pain killers. It was the doctor's favourite brew for curing most ills. What was in it no-one knew but the doctor and the sister. The aborigine received a double dose. Its sedative powers knocked him out. A porter was ordered to watch and to let the sister know when he woke up.

"He's important." She pointed to the unconscious form; "He'll need a good meal inside him before the sergeant sees him."

For what remained of the day and all of that night the porter saw a man whose nightmares no-one could ever describe. The aborigine screamed until he was hoarse, then shivered and sweated the night away. One ill, but relatively alcohol-free snake-catcher watched with blood-red eyes as the sun rose through the window. He couldn't remember arriving at the hospital and considered it strange that he was even there. Usually he was left to sleep off the effects wherever he fell unless someone complained. As he went to get up, he realised that a restraining strap held him fast. Having been advised the patient was awake, Sister Munden marched in and shouted loudly at this wretched creature to lie still. His brain may have been unresponsive but the mere sound of her voice caused him to flinch with terror. The stench from the bed was evidence enough that the aborigine had soiled himself.

"You'll remain lying in that until the sergeant has finished." She left the room closing the door behind her. It took her ten minutes to locate the sergeant and a further five for him to arrive. As he was about to enter the room the sister handed him a mask: "It'll not get rid of the smell but at least it's germ-free."

The aborigine, being used to the freedom and his own choice of resting places, realised that the sooner he was out of here the better.

David stood at the end of the bed, trying hard not to vomit. "Snake-man, what's this story about men being eaten by monsters?"

With the strangest look of abject despair the aborigine looked at his straps and then at David.

Sister Munden saw the look in his eyes. "Tell the sergeant what he wants to know and you can have a shower, a change of clothes and a drink."

The word drink did more for this man than anything else. In a whisper he recalled in his own way how he had been up in the Kimberlies and how a ship crashed into the dragon's nest and stopped: then how a day or so later it had blown up and sank while the men who jumped in the water were eaten by the dragons.

"Anything else?" pressed David, knowing that the man's befuddled brain was only operating in a limited capacity.

"Yes, big birds from the sky shoot at the men as they run. Three men—they come to the shore later but one—he die. They get lost in the hills—never see them again."

David had heard enough to realise that between the two car thieves and the aborigine's story there were too many coincidences and, as one had never met the other, there had to be an element of truth in it. Before he relayed all this to Perth, he would need to find the ship as confirmation.

He walked out of the room with Sister Munden close behind him. “Sister, clean him up and have one your staff bring him to the jail; our friend in there is soon to take his first helicopter ride.”

As he strode away, she motioned to the waiting porter: “You know what to do. Let me know when ‘it’s’ clean and can be moved to the jail. Burn those sheets and the underblankets.”

The man went about his business, cleaning the aborigine and the room, leaving the windows wide open to let the smell of strong bleach dissipate. The sister, true to her word, gave the snake-catcher a large measure of cooking brandy before he was escorted to the jail.

THIRTEEN

Two Sea King helicopters swayed in the strong breeze and, amid the clamour of the rotor blades, gently lowered themselves into the jungle clearing. Angel's people had finally arrived at the small uninhabited island in the Sawu Sea; it lay approximately 400 miles from the *Kia Hua*. Fuel for the helicopters and diving compressors, stores and provisions, had been landed under the cover of darkness, all of it manhandled to the site. For a month, a few men had laboured to construct this short-term encampment. Their skill was in making it invisible from the air and obscure from the sea. The island was abandoned but passing fishermen would be curious if they noticed occupation. Angel had selected the location as it provided an escape route to the Indonesian mainland. When the helicopter cargo bays had been emptied of men and stores, they were pushed into tented hangers. The pilot and engineer had orders to ensure that one was, at all times, ready for departure. That night more fuel would be arriving so that the task could be completed.

The camp boss, Chung Wahh, knew that some time would elapse before the operation to recover the drugs began. Angel had been explicit in his instructions - if the camp remained undiscovered for a period determined by him, it was safe to assume that they were secure. The whole evolution of harvesting the drugs was planned to take no more than six days. It was late in the evening when Chung came out of the accommodation tent; he had a notebook in his hand. Meticulously he moved around the camp completing his inspection of equipment. The high humidity caused untreated metal to rust rapidly and provisions, if not kept in sealed containers, to grow mould. They had been ready for well over a week.

The two pilots were professionals who enjoyed danger and hoped that their lives would end in a blaze of glory, the last big one. They had nowhere else to go. That was the problem with people like these. The sooner the word came the better. If you stay too long with murderers your values are guaranteed to get distorted and the sinister becomes commonplace. Monotony was beginning to have its adverse effect on the men. This day had passed as the day before, utterly depressing. The men had spent most of it trying to keep dry. Miserable weather and the tedium of routine made them irritable and dull of mind.

"What a shitty place," the men were saying. In this they were all agreed as they lay on their makeshift beds, reading for the umpteenth time the same book or magazine. The tension was building. It wasn't the thought of being caught, rather it was sharing a hunk of rock with men who had nothing but contempt for each other. It was a well-trodden path that led deep into a grey area that is way beyond accountability and the law. Only the thought of a large cash payment bound these men together

Chung finished a tour of the camp and returned to his tent. He was satisfied that the men had maintained their readiness for the ordeal to come.

+++

The flight from Seoul to Singapore was nothing out of the ordinary except that it carried Angel Andrias, a man with the potential power to kill or make thousands of people dependent on drugs for the rest of their lives. His decision as to when the lethal cargo would be retrieved from the *Kia Hua* was imminent. He always travelled first-class, enjoying the ultimate in luxury and service that wealth granted him. Even when his right hand brushed the breast of the attractive air hostess as she served lunch, she smiled and courteously asked if there was anything else he required.

After his arrival in Singapore, he arranged for the duration of his stay to be spent in the company of associates enjoying what this reputedly "clean" city could offer. Angel knew that something special would have been arranged for his entertainment. This group had already delayed the punishment of a female informer just to amuse him. At first they teased, then injected her with heroin, not enough to kill but sufficient to place her in a submissive state. Angel was offered the woman for pleasure but, wary of her sexual background, the invitation was declined. The woman lay helpless in the centre of the floor as each in turn abused her. Bored with this amateur display, Angel, with a smile on his lips went and lifted the limp carcass from the floor. Still she smiled, ready to please. His large hands grasped her throat tightly and crushed the larynx. Even as she died the smile remained. As the last breath left the body, he discarded it like a used rag and walked away.

The next morning, Angel, immaculately dressed in a lightweight suit of pure silk, boarded the flight to Jakarta, the capital of Indonesia. Once in this authoritarian state, his disappearance had been arranged. The machinery was in motion but it was his right to collect the proceeds. After sunset a helicopter would land at a small village and transport him to the base camp. The villagers had been told to stay in their huts. In the distance the throb of rotor blades carried across the still night air. The man with Angel fired a small rocket, and for the few moments of its bright life, it gave the aircraft a heading to follow. As it came near, portable ground lights illuminated a cleared area. Its wheels barely brushed the dust as Angel leapt into the open cab. Once his safety harness had been secured, the pilot pushed the power lever to full, the gas turbines gulped fuel and dragged this beast of the air away until they became part of the night.

The man on the ground counted his earnings - $5000 American dollars, cash in hand for doing nothing. Corruption in this land was more than a way of life, it had become existence. The rich became richer and the poor died. Once he had paid off the local police, a substantial sum would remain.

The pilot concentrated on the demanding task of flying in the dark at treetop height. His associate navigated the craft unerringly through valleys and across stretches of open sea that separated islands. The monotonous beat of the rotor blades sent their passenger to sleep. As they approached their destination, a gentle touch by the co-pilot woke him. To antagonise Angel was certain death. He was in a good humour when they landed and so greeted Chung Wahh as a friend rather than a minion to do his bidding.

"Is everything ready?"

Chung knew this would be the first question and instantly answered with a loud "yes".

"I'm pleased. Now tell the pilots that I intend to visit the *Kia Hua* at first light. How many hours sleep will I manage before we leave?"

Chung talked to the pilots, then advised Angel as he accompanied him to his tent that he could get at least three hours sleep. With a sigh he lay on top of his bed and closed his eyes. In situations such as these he never truly slept, there were too many people who would pay a good price to see him dead.

A few hours later Chung entered Angel's tent with a cup of hot steaming coffee. At the sound of the tent flap being drawn aside, Angel rolled to the floor and was already cocking his pistol and aiming it at the intruder. "For Chrissake, Chung, this is the middle of the fucking jungle, not the Hong Kong Hilton—shout the next time you enter." He gulped down the hot coffee.

With fear in his voice Chung spoke: "The helicopter is ready to start its engines."

"Right, let's go."

When the two men were seated, the whine of the starter motor filled the air until the power of the engines made them self-sustaining. Lift-off was as smooth as any bird taking flight. The pilots knew their job and flew low over the choppy sea. A bird strike at this height would be fatal but neither of them thought about such things; it would be pointless anyway. At maximum speed it was going to take at least an hour and a half. Angel made himself comfortable and rested. Chung hated flying in these noisy uncomfortable machines and only money compensated for his misgivings. They droned on, the pilots skilfully maintaining almost zero altitude. As they neared the rocky coast the pilot announced it over the internal radio net. Angel sat and flexed his muscles before he moved towards the cockpit. All he could see were the red cliffs in front of him and a stream of brown water below.

He peered forward: "Where is it?"

"If the location you gave was correct, about five miles to go," smiled the co-pilot.

"It had better be there or you're pig food," grimaced Angel.

The helicopter started to gain altitude to clear the cliff face that barred their approach and as they rose into the air Angel glimpsed the bay ahead. His pulse rate quickened: "It must be there," he thought. As they gained height the *Kia Hua* came into view. It was almost high-tide and small waves lapped across of the upper bridge. Angel ordered the pilot to hover above the rusting steel deck that remained clear of the water. Nature was reclaiming its right: half a dozen huge crocodiles were laid across the deck, raising their body temperature. It was not a place for a mere man to be. Chung handed Angel a high-powered single-shot rifle. Raising the weapon, he rammed the stock into his shoulder and paused, his eye tuning itself to the telescopic sight. He lined the cross-hairs up on the brain of the largest crocodile. Momentarily he held his breath and, squeezing the trigger gently, shot it through the left eye with surgical precision. In less than a second he reloaded and fired again, this time the animal's brain disintegrated into a mangled mess of bloody flesh. With a moment of thought he carefully placed in the firing chamber a cartridge with an exploding head. As he rammed the bolt home he could see the animal's body twitching. Angel aimed for a point just between the creature's shoulder blade and fired again; the carcass split in two as if hit by a giant axe. Angel tapped the pilot on the shoulder and smiled. The helicopter began to rise into the air, and the pilot had a clear view of a mass of crocodiles twisting and turning in the water as they devoured their companion. As with the outward journey, Angel curled up in the bucket seat and rested. Chung held on to his seat and wished the journey was over, all he wanted to do was retrieve the harvest, get paid and go home.

+++

Sergeant David Jones needed a helicopter and called in a lot of favours. His constant pleas resulted in the Area Police Chief finally relenting. Even so the whole operation was described as a wild goose-chase relying on the ranting of a crazy drunk and two vagrants. The helicopter was to be made available for area reconnaissance work for one day only. David knew he was right and now he could prove it. The earliest the bird could be on station was late that evening. It didn't matter—after all, if the ship was there, it was not going to move. Feeling pleased with himself he went to the café for an early lunch. Terry was surprised to see him and queried the change of routine. David explained that he was on the verge of something big that would get him noticed and give him promotion.

"Promotion—what do you want that for? You've got it made here; no-one bothers you. The worst you get is drunken aborigines on pay night and they ain't no real bother."

"I need a change, something different and advancement would give me that." Rachel came and stood beside David as he leant against the bar, rubbing her left buttock sensually against his thigh. He didn't move, pretending he wasn't interested. Sex with Rachel or anyone else would have to wait until this was over.

That afternoon he cleaned two rifles and checked the ammunition. Then he told the aborigine who dreaded the thought of flying they were going for a ride in a helicopter. Soaring amongst the clouds was for birds not men, especially superstitious men. "Snake man, you're going to guide me to that ship, OK? If it's there you can get drunk for a week on my money. If it's not, you stay locked up for a week."

The snake-catcher called him all the scum names he could think of but realised that to David it made no difference, he had heard them all before. Charlie Metcalf, a constable, arrived at 1600 to take over the back shift, and was surprised to find his boss still there. David looked at him and asked if he wanted to go dragon hunting in the Kimberlies the next day.

"Why are we going up to that Godforsaken land?"

"As I said, dragon hunting." David's words were drowned by the noise of a helicopter. It landed with a clatter and a roar, creating a giant cloud of dry dust that blossomed and filled the surrounding air. Its arrival caused a momentary diversion in the town. The pilot welcomed the change from traffic duties in the city and was able to relax. In the office, David discussed his plan for the next day before they went for a meal and a few beers at Terry's place. Having drunk a couple of beers the pilot left. He had to be up early to pre-flight the bird. With a cheery "see you in the morning" and a wave he left David talking to Rachel. Their conversation covered a multitude of news items until she manipulated the dialogue to the topic of sex.

David looked at this young girl who should be a virgin but was most certainly not by the apparent diversity of her sexual knowledge. If she hadn't done it, she most certainly knew about it. Rachel had one of those smiles that promised everything.

"Will you walk me home?" Her lips were moist from the sensuous movement of her tongue.

David knew that if he wanted, she was available, no strings, just sex. "OK, when you're ready."

She shouted into the back room that she was leaving and a gruff "see you tomorrow" was the reply. The entrance hall to her apartment was dimly lit. During the walk to Rachel's home David had already decided to try his luck. He grabbed Rachel and pulled her close.

"My, my, if you feel that way." She kissed him passionately.

David's hands moved across her back and under her white cotton blouse to release her bra.

She giggled: "Not here, inside."

The flat was in darkness. Rachel held his hand, and, as though he were a small child, led him to the bedroom. She unbuttoned his shirt, ravishing and biting his chest. In an uncontrolled assault she attacked the remainder of his clothing until he was naked. He was fully aroused and she tormented him wickedly. Laughing at his eagerness she skilfully manoeuvred him until he tumbled onto the bed. In a wild motion he attempted to pull her down, but she moved to one side allowing her skirt to fall to the floor. With one movement of her hands, she removed her white panties and was on him.

David tried to sit up, but she wouldn't let him; instead she leaned forward while her hips moved with a gentleness that caused untold frustration and pain. When the moment came, the roar in his head became deafening. As he opened his eyes her face was inches from his, she smelt of sex and perfumed perspiration. Her cheap deodorant was working overtime. David realised that she knew how to please and torment. She smiled, her white teeth showing clearly in her sun-tanned face. With barely a body movement, she began to stimulate the muscles that held him tightly. He moaned as he became erect: "How do you do that?"

"That's for me to know and for you to enjoy," she giggled. This time as he kissed her, Rachel rolled onto her back, letting him take charge. Her compensation was in keeping with the magnitude of his climax—this time it was her cries that filled the night air. They fell asleep locked in each other's arms. It was the brightness of the sun shining through the window that caused David to wake. He moved the still sleeping form of Rachel. Gently he covered her naked body with a sheet and left the room. In a few minutes he was dressed and walking back to his own flat.

It was daylight and he had plenty to do this day and with luck he would find the ship. Not a cloud could be seen in the sky - it was going to be hot. He entered his office to find the pilot and his deputy, Charlie Metcalf, waiting.

"Thought we would have an early start," commented the pilot. "The sooner we start looking, the sooner we'll find this ship of yours."

David grinned, then looked at Fred Wills, another constable. "Get the abo out here."

"He's ready and waiting."

"Let's go." Three men and a very reluctant aborigine went through the back door of the station to the helipad and boarded the craft. The pilot completed his flight checks and started the engine. The whine of the gas turbine was low at first but soon the machine was in the air climbing to five thousand feet. They headed north across King Sound towards the Bonaparte Archipelago. Over the intercom the pilot asked where they wanted to start. David looked at the aborigine who now seemed quite at ease as they flew across his homeland. He looked down, shook his head and pointed. David was positive this man knew where the ship was but still the nagging thought went through his head that maybe they wouldn't find it. An hour passed and still the aborigine was pointing ahead. The journey was becoming pointless, and when the pilot advised that they would soon have to think about turning back, David felt despondent.

The pilot began the descent and attempted to follow the directions from his passenger. At a hundred feet above the surface he levelled the craft off and began moving towards the land. The aborigine suddenly poked him in the back—he was excited—and pointed downward.

The pilot noticed he was following the path of a muddy river outlet and had to gain some height as he approached the tree-shrouded cliff. They climbed into the air and once above the ridge the *Kia Hua* could be clearly seen. The receding tide had left her fully exposed. David was elated at the discovery and asked the pilot if he could land on the wreck.

"Let's have a look."

The speed and height were decreased as they hovered a few feet above the muddy water. David took pictures at every possible angle as they see-sawed around the wreck. He stopped only when his camera ran out of film. The pilot gave the thumbs up to David and swung the craft towards what was left of *Kia Hua*'s main deck. He eased the craft onto the buckled steel, ready to increase power if metal burst. The steel of the old ship was sound and held the burden placed upon it. The aborigine's scream defied the roar of the rotor blades as he pointed to the beach and the water. There were his dragons lazily moving towards the ship.

David shivered at the sight of these monsters as he gingerly left the safety of the helicopter. Charlie Metcalf followed him out as they moved cautiously across the deck towards the crew's quarters. Both men were more than wary about stepping into the darkness of the hull. Their powerful flashlights shone ahead as they carefully went about their business. David was looking for the captain's cabin. It took longer than either had anticipated as they wandered along dark slime-covered passageways. Although nothing was said, both were worried that at any turn one of those unfriendly crocodiles might be skulking.

They eventually found what they were looking for but the once highly polished door had swollen and jammed solid in its frame. Brute force overcame any resistance that held it shut. The smell of decaying meat and seaweed filled the passage causing both men to heave. David went straight to the desk, opened the top draw and found what he wanted - the ship's log. He didn't attempt to open it but gathered all the sodden paperwork he could find and placed it in a tray he retrieved from the floor. If nothing else he knew the value of preserving evidence. Charlie Metcalf was busy prising a brass plate off the far bulkhead that gave the ship's name and builder when his lamp fell onto the bunk. As he moved to pick it up, the shrivelled arm of Vaughan fell to the floor. The shock sent him reeling backwards into the far bulkhead. David wasn't so squeamish and moving the blanket very carefully uncovering the rest of the corpse. "Not a lot left," he remarked, "but a pathologist might be able to find out what killed him."

With their arms full they returned to the helicopter. The pilot shouted that he had started to get worried. It was only then that David and Charlie noticed that the depth of water around the ship had risen dramatically. "Another hour and those crocs would have been more than inquisitive," commented the pilot. "And if you think I was going to hang around you were out of your mind."

"I'm glad you didn't have to," shouted David above the roar of the engines as they rose into the air.

"Did you get what you wanted?"

"We know the name of the ship and these—" David pointed at the various books and bits and pieces "—should fill in the gaps. Looks like an insurance fraud—we did find one body. Damn, I forgot to shut the door. Looks like the crocs get a free meal."

FOURTEEN

Janice returned to her bedroom and realised that she could no longer deny her feelings for Adrian. She wanted his love and affection and to hear him say she meant everything to him. Sleep came and went as she thought about her life and the men that had shared some of it. Before the morning light began to shine through the curtains the decision she had tried so hard to avoid had been made. When the moment was right they would make love.

Mrs Duke was in the kitchen and was soon joined by Adrian. Moments later Selwyn entered and asked about her leg. She sat on a chair whilst Selwyn gently soaked the dressing. For a few minutes the warm water was allowed to penetrate before the bandages were removed. To Adrian's amazement the scald had been reduced to a slight reddening of the skin.

"How does it feel now that fresh air is getting to it?" asked Selwyn.

Mrs Duke looked at him lovingly and smiling in a motherly way replied that it tingled.

"Good; by this evening it'll have cleared completely."

"What was in that stuff?" asked Adrian.

"I'd rather not tell you, it's a family secret."

After breakfast, Adrian stood for a few minutes in the corridor waiting for Janice to appear. Last night he had spent a long time thinking why he loved her so much and he didn't have an answer. He was so engrossed in his thoughts that he did not hear her walk up and stand beside him.

"What were you thinking about?" she asked.

"You."

"What about me?"

Adrian raised his hands and held her face and gazed into her eyes. "I've said this before and I still don't know why but I love you very much."

The realisation of what he said frightened him. To Janice it was as if a door was opening and the sun was shining through; her world was changing.

During the next few weeks their love flourished. They visited the Yorkshire countryside, walked hand in hand along the beaches of Robin Hood's Bay, Filey, and Scarborough. On a headland high above the grey waters of the North Sea he stopped by the roadside. They left the car and walked to the edge of the cliff; standing with their arms around each other they looked down into a secluded cove. The only sounds to reach their ears were those of the sea—the rush of the tide as it moved thousands of small pebbles back and forth—almost drowned by hundreds of seagulls scavenging from the surf.

They played as adolescents, throwing seaweed at each other, skimming stones across the waves and kissing until they were gasping for air. But Adrian never tried to seduce or persuade her in any way. The last thing he wanted was to jeopardise the trust that had grown between them.

One evening, as they were strolling through the cobbled streets of Whitby, Janice entered a small shop. Adrian, holding her hand, followed almost obediently. The elderly gentleman behind the counter mentioned that the shop was about to close but if they were quick he would be pleased to serve them. Janice asked to see a pair of men's cotton pyjamas of suitable size for Adrian. The pair that was tendered were of a hideous green Paisley pattern. Janice laughed and asked for them to be wrapped as she handed over two crisp ten pound notes. Adrian said nothing until they had left the shop.

"Janice, why pyjamas?"

She looked at him, her eyes sparkling with the excitement of a young girl about to go on her first date.

"In case of fire—bottoms for you and the top for me. We're going to spend tonight together—no Mrs Duke to tuck us in and mother us, just you and me. Anyway, first things first, let's eat."

They found a small riverside restaurant and sat watching the fishing boats preparing to sail. Other boats tugged at their moorings as the incoming tide dragged at their tethers. The meal over, they wandered along to the largest hotel. A flock of sparrows swooped and circled across the darkening sky; for a second she gripped his hand tightly. He held hers in such a way that the instant of fear that had crossed her mind was eradicated. The receptionist at the Grove Hotel didn't even ask if they had any luggage but did require payment in advance. Adrian paid by credit card. The walk up the stairs to room 112 felt strange; neither were virgins and it wouldn't be the first time they had spent the night in a hotel bedroom. The room was adequate, clean and tidy with a small en suite bathroom. Janice faced Adrian, holding both his hands gently: "I love you and want you."

He kissed her lightly on the lips and let his hands undo the zip of her thin cotton dress. There was no resistance as it fell to the floor. She pulled back from him and removed her bra and panties and jumped into the bed pulling the covers up to her chin. "Come on. I'm cold. I want you to keep me warm."

Adrian sat on the edge of the bed, feverishly discarding his clothes into a heap on the floor. She lifted the covers, and for a moment there was hesitation, then, as lovers, they caressed each other. Adrian kissed her nipples and then, very slowly, every inch of her body, causing her to moan with pleasure. Janice could bear it no longer and reached down and felt for him. She was ready and she guided him. It had been a long time and the shear sensitivity of it made it all the more pleasurable. Together they climaxed, writhing in each other's arms as they did so. The rest of the night disappeared as they made love, rested in each other's arms and made love again. For a while they remained as one, enjoying the delights of being together until the need for sleep overtook them.

As the morning light filtered its way through the solitary window, Adrian woke. He left Janice sleeping whilst he went to the bathroom and showered. Janice took longer to bath and dress but having paid for breakfast, they ate it. They left the hotel and agreed that a walk would give them time to discuss their future. He slipped his hand over hers and looked at her slender fingers, then as they meandered along the cobbled streets around the harbour, began to discuss their future together. Janice was adamant that she wanted to continue as a news correspondent and maintain her flat in Southampton; Adrian was resolute that she should sell. An impasse was reached and for the moment they agreed to differ. They continued their walk along the shore holding hands; when they stopped for a moment Adrian wanted to do nothing else but hold her and kiss those soft lips.

"We shouldn't. People are watching."

He followed her glance and saw a man and his wife with two small children walking amongst the rocks.

"Who cares?" He held her tightly and kissed her full on the lips.

The fresh sea breeze gave them an appetite. Adrian knew of a small restaurant in the country a few miles away. Their pace increased as they returned to the car and drove out of Whitby.

Out of habit, Adrian turned the telephone on and immediately wished he hadn't. It was announcing a full memory of messages from Selwyn. He pressed the number for home. The telephone barely had the chance to ring before the receiver was lifted.

"Where the hell have you been?"

"Why all the phone calls?"

"Charles Dawning has been trying to contact you about the *Kia Hua;* I think they've found it."

"Where and when?"

"Somewhere in Australia from what he was saying. He wants to talk to you as soon as possible. Where are you now?"

"On our way home. We'll be about an hour. If you can, see what information you can wheedle out of Charles."

Selwyn laughed and rang off. Adrian contacted Charles Dawning as soon as he was in the house and the news was confirmed that the ship was the *Kia Hua*.

"An insurance fraud," commented Adrian with a touch of sarcasm in his voice.

"I don't think so," came an equally caustic reply. "Why, when there are areas of the world's oceans deep enough to sink a thousand ships?"

"Don't know and don't really care, Charles."

"Well you'd better begin to care; as far as I'm concerned you're still on the payroll. I've come to, let us say an amicable arrangement, with their Lords of the Admiralty. You're to be transferred to the Australian Navy for three months." He was laughing as he said it.

"You can't do that. You bastard."

"He who pays the piper always calls the tune. There's something peculiar about that ship and I want you around when it's searched by their navy—that is, providing you want your insurance to continue."

Adrian slammed the hand-set into the cradle and looked at Janice and Selwyn. After taking a few deep breaths he calmed down and told them what Charles had threatened. "It's not good."

Selwyn shook his head. "He has you over a barrel. If you refuse, Lloyds can simply withdraw cover and by the time they say it was a horrible mistake and apologise, you'll be out of business.

"So its heads they win and tails I lose."

Adrian picked up the telephone and called Charles.

"Hello Adrian, I thought you'd ring back. Now shut up and listen. The Admiralty has agreed to the transfer and you are to be appointed as the temporary executive officer in HMAS *Bunbury*. You have the choice of one further officer and a rating and I need to know who they are. Adrian knew exactly who he would choose but would have to ask them first. "I'll answer that question in ten minutes, I have to make a few telephone calls."

Jim Potts answered the call as if he was expecting it and was pleased that Adrian had asked him, but he needed twenty-four hours to arrange his business affairs. Adrian thanked him and suggested that he would let him have more details as soon as he had them.

The Buffer, Leading Seaman Peter Carrol, appeared to be out and Adrian started to leave a message. As he was about to ring off, a deep voice vibrated down the line. "Hello, Sir, sorry about the machine but I always leave it on. I'll pack me bags and be ready in half an hour."

Adrian was used to this type of response and waited a few seconds until he stopped chatting. "You have a bit longer than that; I'll let you know the arrangements tomorrow."

"Roger, Sir. I'll be ready to go when you give the word."

The line went dead as the Buffer rang off. The telephone was answered by Charles the moment it rang and before Adrian had a chance to speak he told him: "Fax me the names and official numbers of the officer and rating and leave the rest to me."

Adrian butted in: "I need twenty-four hours to sort things out."

"That's already been taken care off, your plane leaves London Heathrow ten o'clock in the morning the day after tomorrow. Three seats, first-class of course, have already been booked. All the information and paperwork you require will be waiting for you at the Singapore Airlines check-in desk."

Adrian wanted to shout at the audacity of this man who had figured out every move before the game had been played. He ended the call with, "I'll see you when I get back."

+++

Adrian and Janice waited for the appropriate moment when Mr and Mrs Duke were in the kitchen before they broke the news. They expected Mrs Duke to be surprised but she continued peeling the potatoes.

"How could you know?" asked a puzzled Adrian.

"The way you two have been behaving told me. Me and Mr Duke were young once, you know. The nice thing is we still love each other."

Mr Duke coughed, looked embarrassingly at his wife and left the kitchen.

After the evening meal, Adrian and Selwyn went into the office and discussed the next three months' business in minute detail. Mrs Duke had, with Janice's help, collected all of Adrian's uniforms together. She was more informed on naval dress than the best of stewards. Each item was packed with care until the cases were full. When they had finished Mrs Duke sat on the edge of the bed, motioning for Janice to sit beside her. "If you don't mind me saying, you two are good for each other. He's had women friends before but most of them were after the money they thought he had. As soon as they found out that he was almost broke, they ran as fast as they could. Mind you, since my Selwyn has taken over, it's a lot better. That's enough of an old woman's chatter."

Janice was amazed at this lady who had been a second mother to Adrian. "Thank you for being so nice about everything."

With that all knowing sparkle in her eyes, Mrs Duke smiled at Janice: "Have a good night."

Janice ran the bath and relaxed in its warmth as the thoughts of the man she loved made her feel safe yet sad because he was leaving. Tonight she would make it a night to remember. The hot bath had made her drowsy and as she snuggled between the crisp cotton sheets she soon fell asleep. Adrian tried not to wake her as he entered the bedroom but she opened her eyes as he began to undress.

He wanted a shower but she was out of bed and in his arms holding him tightly. He stroked her back and nestled his face in her hair. The scent of her perfume was overpowering. He pulled the ribbons that held her night-dress and she moved away, letting it fall to the floor. Then with great care he lifted her in his arms and placed her on the bed.

Janice, her eyes moist at the thought of missing the man she loved so much, teasingly said, "When you're away you'd better not forget me! I've heard all about you sailors!"

Whatever else she was going to say was lost as his mouth covered hers. Their love-making was tender and caring, each wanting to please the other. The morning came too quickly. There was a knock on the door and Mrs Duke walked in carrying a breakfast tray. She looked at Adrian and Janice and for an instant remembered when she was younger.

"Where would you like me to put the tray?"

Adrian pointed to the bedside table and muttered an embarrassed, "Thank you."

Janice looked at the man she loved more with each hour.

"That woman continues to surprise me."

"She certainly surprised me; I've never had breakfast in bed before." He poured two cups of coffee. Janice finished hers and laid back, placing her arms above her head. Adrian placed his cup to one side and bent over her, his hands caressing her breasts. The fire that burned inside her began to erupt with uncontrolled ferocity. Janice pulled him down, her strong legs wrapped around him, making him a captive in their embrace. They enjoyed each other and remained locked together long after the fire had subsided.

The telephone beside the bed rang; "Time you two were out of bed, there's work to be done." Selwyn chuckled as he replaced the receiver.

"Who was that?"

Adrian smiled: "Who do you think?"

As if reading his thoughts, she grinned: "We still have the rest of the day and tonight."

"It's not enough."

Adrian got out of the warm bed, walked across and opened the curtains and stared out across the peaceful Yorkshire countryside. Little had changed since he was a boy. It was not a bad day. Rain clouds still loitered in the sky but with luck they would blow away. He turned and looked at Janice; the moment was over—Selwyn was right. There was work to be done. Adrian had a quick shower that would allow Janice the luxury of taking her time while he discussed business.

Much to his amazement, it was well past midday when he strolled into the office. Selwyn smiled at his friend's entrance but did not say a word. It was a pleasure to see him happy. They finished those items that remained from the day before as Janice entered the room. Selwyn stood up and announced cheekily that Adrian was all hers.

"Go for a walk, get out of this place. For once be alone together."

Janice grabbed Adrian's right hand and dragged him bodily into the hall. She paused for a moment as she tossed a jacket to Adrian and pulled a coat from its hook for herself. The clouds were still there but it had remained dry. Hand in hand they wandered through the woods. They walked in silence; the only sounds were birds chirping and leaves flapping in the wind.

"Where are we going?"

They wandered on, Adrian carefully bending the occasional branch out of her way.

"I'm hoping to introduce you to an old friend."

"Who's this friend and why out here?"

Adrian stopped: "The difficulty is you never find old Joe, he finds you. He lives off the land."

"What do you mean? Is he a poacher?"

"No. Joe deals in supply and demand. If the police arrested him the sergeant would have to do without his couple of rabbits a week, and so would the magistrate."

"This Joe, does he smoke a foul-smelling pipe?"

Adrian was taken aback: "Yes he does. How do you know?"

"I've already met him, not far from the graveyard. At first I thought he was a gypsy but he seemed to know everything about us." Janice suddenly stopped talking as two facts joined together.

"It can't be true."

"What's wrong? You've gone as white as a ghost."

"That's just it, Adrian. There's a new headstone in the cemetery and his name was Joe and he lived off the land."

"It must be a coincidence—how could you be talking to someone one minute and reading his headstone the next?" Adrian was attempting to convince himself that it wasn't making sense. "Mrs Duke would have told me."

They were moving towards the graveyard; Adrian desperately needed to know. Stumbling, he almost fell down the moss-covered steps. As much as he did not want to believe, it was there in front of him: *"Joe, Died...Age unknown. He lived off the land."*

It was a shock and Adrian began to sob for the first time since his parents' death. His body shook with the stark reality of it all. He shouted out Joe's name and cried. Janice moved forward and placed her hands on his shoulders, more to reassure and comfort. He felt her fingers tighten as he placed a hand over hers; it helped but did nothing to fill the gap created by the loss of his friend and mentor. Slowly the tears subsided and the pain of grief began. He knew that this was not the way Joe would have wanted it.

As he stood there the smell of foul tobacco filled the air. "Hello Joe."

Janice also detected the acrid fumes but said nothing; however, her grip on Adrian's hand tightened significantly.

Adrian, his eyes full, looked at her. "Don't worry about old Joe, he's the last person to hurt you. You know he's here, don't you?"

Janice nodded; it was dreamlike to be stood in a country graveyard talking to a ghost. At first, one solitary drop spattered on the polished headstone; this was quickly followed by another. It began to rain heavily, culminating in a torrential downpour. They ran home, getting soaked before reaching the house. Mrs Duke chided them for being foolish and ordered Janice to take a hot bath. Adrian made to go with her, but was redirected to his own bedroom.

"There's only room in a bath for one," she said. Before leaving the kitchen, he asked Mrs Duke why she hadn't mentioned old Joe.

"I kept meaning to, but when you were both saying that you had seen him and talked to him, I didn't know what to do."

Adrian looked at her: "It's all right, Joe's at peace. He has the advantage now, by not getting any older."

That evening was tense. Selwyn attempted to lighten the atmosphere but the loss of Joe combined with Adrian's imminent departure, did little to help. Adrian and Janice eventually found themselves alone in the kitchen. For a while they talked; it was over an hour later when they made their way upstairs.

This night was different, for tomorrow she would be alone. They held each other tight and Adrian felt the moist warmth of tears on his cheek. Standing back he looked at her; her hands moved and began to undress him until he was naked. Janice remained motionless as he undressed her. He began by touching her, then his lips kissed each nipple in turn. Their mouths met and the passion exploded, her tongue went deep into his mouth entwining with his. She was ready and guided him towards the comfort of the bed. They tumbled, locked together, onto the soft duvet, and he was looking down on her, his breath mixing with hers. She whispered, "I love you," as he entered her. Having given themselves to each other completely they lay in a tight embrace, each afraid that the morning would come.

It was a bleak morning, the rain aided by the strong gale-force wind, battered against the windows. What moonlight remained was being filtered through dark storm clouds. The dull red glow of the digital clock displayed that it was passing five o'clock. Adrian knew that there was no choice, he had to get up and leave. Janice stirred as he went to shower. Mrs Duke had left all the clothes he needed neatly arranged in the bedroom.

As he dressed in the semi-darkness Janice spoke softly to him. "I can't stand goodbyes so before you leave come and kiss me and then go."

Adrian, for the first time in his life, didn't want to leave but he agreed it might be better if their parting was swift. To prolong the inevitable was foolish. Selwyn was already in the kitchen with Mrs Duke, having his breakfast when Adrian arrived.

Before he said a word, Selwyn let him know. "The car's packed and ready when you are. If we leave in just over five minutes you'll catch the six o'clock train. Any later and you'll be pushing it the other end."

Adrian knew he was right and ran back up the stairs to say goodbye. Janice grabbed him and held him tight, kissing him for all she was worth. Then she said, "Go," and rolled away.

Selwyn shouted that it was time.

As he left the house he was aware of that smell of tobacco that was so distinctive. Selwyn felt it and knew instantly that troubled times lay ahead. The journey to York was uneventful except for the weather. Selwyn, unlike Mr Duke, drove with the skill of a racing driver and covered the distance in record time. Once on the train, Adrian stared through the carriage window as the dimly-lit, rain-drenched station diminished into the distance.

The train arrived on time and a dozen or so black London cabs were waiting on the rank. As Adrian approached, the driver of the first cab got out, walked round the front and opened the luggage compartment. The suitcases were politely removed from Adrian's clutches and deposited in the cab. Before the driver had time to say a word, Adrian asked to be taken to Heathrow. The driver was overjoyed at his first fare of the day being long distance. Stanley was an East-Ender of London by birth and astute in the ways of the world; as he stated, "You see it all in this job."

His passenger found the patter that flowed ceaselessly through the glass partition entertaining and interesting. When on the odd occasion he was asked his opinion on a matter, he found that it was answered for him. It kept his mind occupied and at this moment he needed that. The traffic was horrendous but despite the foul-ups and incessant road works, Stanley made the airport in forty-five minutes. The fare came to forty pounds; Adrian gave him a fifty pound note telling him to keep the change. Stanley's cheery character had helped him to cope with leaving. He piled his cases on an abandoned trolley and began negotiating his way to the Singapore Airlines check-in desk. Jim and Leading Seaman Carrol were already there. Adrian asked the ground hostess if tickets had been left for them, only to discover they had not. The attractive dark-haired girl asked him to wait a moment whilst she made a telephone call. It was only seconds before she replaced the receiver and advised Adrian to proceed to the VIP lounge.

Their tickets were waiting, and their suitcases quickly removed. They had almost an hour to wait. Adrian and Jim settled down to cups of steaming black coffee and the morning papers. Peter Carrol found the bar. Jim had been keeping a wary eye on him and as the third double whisky made its way down Carrol's throat it was enough. Peter could hold his drink but when Jim quietly said, "No more!" that was it. Jim began to ask Adrian questions as to why a three month attachment to the Australian Navy was necessary. Adrian hesitated for a moment, then briefly mentioned that they were going to examine the wreck of the *Kia Hua*. This intrigued Jim who pressed for more information so he had no option but to tell him everything he knew. A stewardess came over and requested that they make their way to the departure gate in readiness for boarding.

Now in possession of some of the facts Jim was sufficiently stimulated to start feeling excited and soon began wondering what the next three months held in store.

FIFTEEN

Sergeant David Jones was in good humour and, as promised, he was buying the snake-catcher a barrel full of rum. Rachel was looking at him with eyes that distinctly said come to bed now. The Chief of Police had received all the information about the ship. The two survivors from the *Kia Hua* had been flown back to Perth for further questioning. He had achieved a result at long last that would get him noticed by the right people.

After locking up the aborigine for his own safety, he returned to Rachel's bed. Now aware that she was more sexually experienced than he had originally imagined, they explored many alternatives. Only when each had satisfied the other did they allow sleep to overtake them.

+++

Commander Elliott Adams of the Royal Australian Navy pulled back one of the bedroom curtains and looked at the beginning of a new day. The house facing theirs was very quiet - in this area of suburbia very few were obliged to get up and go to work so early. There was much to be done in the next thirty-six hours. His squadron of three patrol boats had to be made ready to sail.

HMAS *Bunbury* was to have three new crew members, two Pommy Officers and one rating. Elliott had agreed that the most prudent berth for these reservists was on his craft. What he hadn't bargained for was that the two officers were to be given temporary appointments as his executive officer and navigator. Despite objections, Admiral Bennie was determined that Commander Adams would, for once in his life, do as he was told. Time was passing as he left the bedroom to get washed and dressed. He would have breakfast on his boat. On returning to the bedroom he bent over and affectionately kissed his sleeping wife. As he passed his young daughter's bedroom she could be heard chattering away to her imaginary friend. Elliott didn't stop as she would want to be lifted out of her cot to play.

It was a twenty mile drive from the house to the HMAS *Stirling*, Fleet Base West, a journey that usually took him thirty minutes in light traffic. As he drove, his mind drifted; the squadron had been ordered to investigate an old abandoned tramp somewhere above King's Sound. Distracted by his own thoughts he did not see the car transporter turn across his path until it was too late.

The collision was unavoidable and as his car turned, it struck the steel frame of the monster and ground to a halt, firmly wedged under its chassis. It wasn't the pain that caused him to yell loudly but the sheer stupidity of his actions. The driver of the vehicle shouted that he was a stupid frigging maniac and shouldn't be on the road. Adams attempted a smile and without raising his voice ordered him to get some help. The driver, surprised by the command, used his

CB to notify the Police Rescue Squad. In less than ten minutes help had arrived, along with a crowd of unhelpful onlookers.

The paramedic checked his casualty: "Well, mate, you've broken your leg in at least two places, possibly your collar bone too and there's a few bruised ribs. Your face won't look too good for a week or two."

Elliott looked at this professional who took everything in his stride. "Thank you for those few kind words but I would appreciate it if you would get me out of here. It's not too comfortable at the moment."

"Before the boys start cutting, I'll give you a jab to kill the pain." He smiled sadistically as the hypodermic went deep into Elliott's thigh. After a few minutes a creeping sensation began at his thigh and slowly made its way to his toes. The medic had been right; as the pressure was released from his trapped leg the pain became excruciating. Elliott never uttered a sound. The ambulance whisked him directly to the Naval Base Hospital. Here rank had its privileges, but before the hospital staff were allowed to touch him, the use of a telephone was demanded. The first call was to his wife, the next was to Admiral Bennie. As he replaced the receiver he smiled at the thought of that silly old bugger Bennie trying to find a willing and competent Commanding Officer for his boat at such short notice. The young lieutenant knew his patient by reputation. Elliott was told that to set the leg properly it would have to be manipulated into its correct alignment.

"Well, get on with it, man, I haven't got all day."

The doctor looked at him and began. Blackness

and a pain-free world encompassed Elliott as the bones were moved into position.

+++

The flight from London to Perth consisted of too much food, drinks as required, films, sleep and your choice of duty free goods. Reality was when the seat-belt lights were illuminated for the approach to Perth. The landing was smooth, but, once inside the terminal building, they were no longer given any special treatment different from the other passengers. Peter had opted to push the baggage trolley that held all their luggage. His head was inflicted by a dull throb. His only regret was that an unlimited supply of free whisky did not happen often enough. They waited in the queue, moving forward as it did, when an airport official approached. "Commander Viper's party?"

"That's us."

"The Ministry has granted you priority clearance. Follow me, a car's waiting."

Jim looked at the buffer: "Buffer the bags, follow me."

"Roger, Sir, but where are we going?"

"To the car, it's waiting." Adrian listened to the banter between these two and fell in step with their guide. They wandered through doors, passages and rooms until finally they were in the fresh air but at the rear of the terminal. Just ahead of them was parked a gleaming black Ford with a female Petty Officer standing alongside, so engrossed in filing a broken nail that she failed to notice her passengers approaching. The Buffer shouted from behind so that all could hear: "That must be our car, Sir!"

The Petty officer jumped to attention and saluted Adrian who merely nodded. The Buffer loaded the suitcases into the boot. Adrian had already seated himself in the front passenger seat leaving the rear empty. They sped away and the driver, an Australian through and through, spoke: "I was told you lot are reservists. Is that right?"

The girl's manner was straight and to the point. "Yes we are, but why the question?"

She looked at Adrian. "Two hours ago your names were not on any scheduled pick-up list. This is the Admiral's car and I'm his private driver. I asked myself, why the VIP treatment and why would the old man want to see three Pommy reservists straight off the plane?"

"How far is it to the 'old man's' house?"

The driver laughed. "Don't let him hear you calling him that, he'll have your guts hung out to dry."

As they approached the Garden Island Naval Base the duty guard saw the driver and waved them on. After a few more minutes the car drew to a halt outside a large modern office block.

"Here we are, gentlemen, through those doors—take the lift to the fourth floor and then ask. Don't worry about your luggage, I'll take it down to the boat."

The car roared away leaving them standing in the road.

They walked into the air-conditioned interior and showed their identity cards to an insignificant-looking security guard sat at a desk. The man gave each card a cursory glance, whilst checking the visitors' list. When apparently satisfied he pointed to the lift and mumbled "Fourth floor."

"Thank you," said Adrian politely.

The lift whisked them to their destination. Once there Jim stopped a rating and asked the way to the Admiral's office. They were directed towards a room at the end of a long corridor. As they wandered in, three Wrens were busy moving files from one pile to another. A Wren Officer entered. With attractive features and steady hazel brown eyes, Jim was at once smitten by her engaging manner and shapely legs. She was very desirable and he felt his mouth go dry.

She looked at Jim, then Adrian, then the file in her hand. "Commander Viper?"

Adrian nodded.

"This way, Sir." She was slightly smaller than him and her perfume imparted instant reminders of Janice. As Adrian entered the room she closed the door behind her.

"Dana!" It was more of a command than a request. "When you have a moment could you arrange for some coffee?"

She smiled at the Admiral: "It will be about five minutes, Sir."

"Very good and make mine strong—none of that dishwater the staff drink," he responded, laughing as he did so.

She left the room, closing the door gently. Looking shrewdly at Jim and the Buffer she quickly surmised who was who.

"Would you gentlemen like a coffee?"

Both were dry and any liquid would have satisfied their thirst.

"Come with me."

Jim walked beside her but the Buffer walked far enough behind her in order to watch the motion of her backside. They were taken to the Officers' lounge where tea, coffee and sandwiches were available.

Back in the Admiral's room Adrian was not overawed by the situation but was suffering from jetlag. The Admiral, young-looking for his age, walked towards him and shook his hand. "Sit down and take the weight off your feet. I'm William Bennie, Bill to my friends and in private. I apologise for dragging you in here, but I have a problem." He perched himself on the edge of his desk. "Until a few hours ago everything was proceeding to plan and Anglo-Australian relations were at an all-time high—everyone was co-operating with everyone else."

Adrian sat tensely, waiting for the punch-line.

"This morning Commander Elliott Adams, your Commanding Officer and Squadron Commander, had a quarrel with a truck. Unfortunately for me he suffered some rather nasty injuries. That was his sister Dana, my PA, who escorted you in here. Bright young lady, should go far if she doesn't get herself anchored to some crazy boat driver. Where was I? Oh yes, this wasn't too bad as Lieutenant Commander Pat Briggs was eager to take command of the squadron. What I couldn't find at short notice, and, believe me, I looked, was a capable driver for *Bunbury*. I've discussed this with your people and mine. Don't worry—if you hadn't come up to scratch we wouldn't be having this conversation. I'm about to take a most unusual step by offering you the temporary command of HMAS *Bunbury*. What do you have to say about that?"

Adrian was caught off balance. It was the last thing he had expected and the shock of it almost overwhelmed him. "I don't know what to say, Sir." He paused for a moment and gathered his thoughts together. "I accept and thank you for the honour."

The Admiral stood, bent down over his desk and gathered up his papers, placing them in a neat pile at the edge, ready to pick up later. He looked at this man in front of him, remembering when he drove boats instead of a desk.

"It's not going to be easy; Pat Briggs is jumping for Commander and he could get it if he keeps his nose clean. The last thing he wants is an amateur, even a good one, spoiling his chances. He'll be demanding one hundred and ten per cent effort all the time, every time. I like you Viper, so watch your step."

At that moment there was a knock on the door and Dana Adams entered carrying a tray with two cups of freshly percolated, strong coffee. Carefully she placed the Admiral's at his side and handed the other to Adrian. She noticed that the Admiral's guest had shaking hands. As she quietly left the room she smiled; Dana knew he had accepted the job.

Adrian's mind was whirling like a top, he was eager to see his command. "What about Jim Potts and my Buffer, where are they going?"

"With you of course, as programmed—Navigator and Leading Hand, *Bunbury*'s executive officer will remain on board; listen to him and you'll avoid the obvious minefields. Must dash, lovely to meet you and good luck."

Adrian thanked him as they shook hands and left the room. As he entered the main office, Dana was receiving the full treatment from Jim. The Buffer had already made a date for that evening with one of the Wrens. Jim could see that his friend was deep in thought and asked him what was happening. "You'll never believe it but I've just been given command of HMAS *Bunbury*."

Dana moved forward to break up the celebration. "Gentlemen, my brother, despite his injuries, is waiting on board. We have twenty-four hours to complete the formalities and paperwork."

As they left the office Dana grabbed her tricorn hat, and as she did so, nodded to the Admiral's secretary.

The telephone on HMAS *Bunbury* rang moments later; the message was clear. "Your new Captain is on his way."

A car was waiting as they left the building and completed the short drive to the small ships' harbour where *Bunbury* was berthed. Alongside her were *Geraldton* and *Albany*. Adrian walked smartly across the gangway, whilst the Officer of the Day and the Quartermaster saluted. As his feet hit the deck the officer moved forward, "Lieutenant Bob Hopkins, your Exec, Sir." Adrian gave him the once-over and approved the preliminary demonstration of naval customs. "Bob, before all the formalities begin, would you take care of my two companions and direct me to the Captain's cabin?"

Dana butted in: "I'll show you the way—after all I've been there enough times."

Adrian's eyes were already scrutinising his boat; it looked clean, the men were well dressed and it felt right, there was about it the atmosphere of a happy well-run vessel.

Commander Adams was in his cabin and at his desk as Dana and Adrian arrived. "Excuse me if I don't get up but I had a bit of trouble with the car this morning."

"So I heard," remarked Adrian. They continued to chat about the flight and other insignificant details until the hand-over could not be avoided. Elliott, despite his injuries, did not like giving his command to a total stranger but knew it was not a matter of choice. He was now on the beach and would remain there until fit for sea.

"All the paperwork's in order and, although it's entirely up to you, the normal supersession reports and inspections have been completed by my Exec. I would suggest that such things as money and ammunition you check again."

Elliott asked whether he could leave and return to the Base Wardroom. Adrian apologised for his thoughtlessness and instantly realised that this man desperately needed rest. Elliott left with the able assistance of Dana and two duty men who physically carried him across the gangway to a waiting car.

Adrian, still in his travel clothes, began with the assistance of Bob, the arduous task of getting to know all he could about HMAS *Bunbury* and its crew. It was past two a.m. when the two men said goodnight. As he left the cabin, Bob turned: "Goodnight, Skipper, you're not bad for a Pommy."

The tiny travel alarm clock sounded, waking Adrian instantly but his body was tired. He rolled out of the bunk, placing both feet on the deck, his mind raced as the thoughts of the last thirty-six hours moved themselves into place correctly. In less than two hours' time he would be the Commanding Officer of HMAS *Bunbury*. He moved across to his suitcases and opened the largest, removing and hanging his best uniform with its gold lace and two medal ribbons. He shaved as close as is possible whilst listening to the sounds of the boat as it slowly started coming awake. The towel was Elliott's but he used it just the same and rubbed his whole body vigorously to stimulate some life into it. As he walked from the shower he knew something was wrong but for the moment it defeated him. Then he realised; his uniform was missing, not just the jacket and trousers, but all of it. He was about to shout for the First Lieutenant when leading Seaman Carrol stuck his head around the door. "Sir, the lads are pressing your uniform and cleaning your shoes. I had a word. Can't have their new skipper looking a mess for the change of command."

"Thank you, Buffer."

"Excuse me, Sir, but I'm not your Buffer this trip, just a gash hand."

"Point noted, Buffer."

Carrol laughed and told Adrian that as soon as it was ready he would be back with breakfast. Adrian smiled to himself; that rogue had been accepted already.

Breakfast arrived as did his uniform. By eight Adrian was ready; the paperwork only required a signature and the ship was his to command. Bob Hopkins was good, in fact very good. There was a knock on his cabin door and before he had a chance to speak, a tall, dark-haired, unsmiling Lieutenant

Commander stormed in. The voice that boomed from pencil-thin lips painted on a weather-beaten face filled the confines of the cabin: "Briggs, Pat Briggs, Squadron Commander."

Adrian felt like saying "not yet", but decided against it. The man's deep-set, dark brown eyes were studying him minutely. They stopped for an instant at the two ribbons. "Viper, I've been told that you know how to captain a warship. I have my doubts about you British part-timers."

Adrian retorted: "I think I hold the rank and have the experience to achieve a satisfactory result, Sir!"

Briggs turned and left without even the courtesy of a goodbye or good luck. Adrian had never met such an arrogant bastard. There was a knock on the door and he shouted at the top of his voice: "Wait!"

Bob Hopkins didn't wait but came straight in, closing the door behind him. "I see 'God' paid you a visit then. Pat's OK but if he doesn't make Commander this time he'll be passed over."

"That gives him no reason to talk to me in that manner," shouted Adrian.

Bob stood there letting the rage dissipate. At the right moment he barely whispered, "When you're ready, Sir, you have a boat to command and a good crew who need the best of skippers. Whether Pat Briggs likes it or not we're stuck with you and you with him. Shall we get the show on the road?"

Adrian knew then that Bob was ready to command. The handing over from one Commanding Officer to another can be a long or short ceremony; this was short. It began with the hoisting of the colours and ended with Commander Adams thanking his crew.

Three cheers was the order of the day. With a lump in his throat Bob Hopkins led the cat calls and whistles as the car sped away. Adrian said a few words to his crew, then had them dismissed. Pat Briggs had already begun to send signals about loose ropes hanging from the masthead and incorrectly dressed men on deck.

Adrian addressed all the officers in the wardroom. Bob and Jim asked to be excused but Adrian insisted: "For this once only we'll meet together; it might be the one and only time."

Bob commenced the introductions: "Sub Lieutenant Henry McGregor, under training, acting as Gunnery and Correspondence Officer. Last but not least Midshipman Edward Wilson, general dogsbody but definitely Entertainments Officer and Bar."

Adrian laughed at the comments on entertainment. "Gentlemen"—Adrian was interrupted by a knock on the door. Bob opened it, to be handed a message from the Squadron Commander. "All commanding Officers are to report for a briefing post haste." Adrian smiled at his officers: "It seems as if 'God' has called. I'd better get over there."

Adrian entered his boss's cabin; there sat on the sofa was the Captain of *Albany,* Lieutenant Commander Joe Eva. Before they had a chance to talk, Pat Briggs entered from his bathroom wiping his hands on a paper towel. He looked at Adrian and then pointed to a chair. "I hope you've completed the hand-over, Viper." Again those eyes scrutinised Adrian. "I understand that Commander Adams had a rowdy send-off. We'll miss him—he's a good man."

"I hope the noise didn't disturb you, Sir." Adrian's

sarcastic tone wasn't missed. Joe kicked him sharply on the foot, Adrian took the hint.

"Actually I was up early planning the evolutions for when we sail at fourteen hundred hours. "This—" he handed them a file containing sheaves of paper "—is the programme for the next month; naturally it is subject to change at short notice. I have been ordered to take this squadron north to find the wreck of an old tramp steamer. The Commanding Officer of *Bunbury* and I will formally identify this wreck and complete a survey. Joe, you will assist if divers are required."

Joe nodded.

"That is all gentlemen, be ready to sail.

As the two men got up to leave, Briggs in a hostile manner ordered, "Viper, wait."

Joe smiled at Adrian, shrugged his shoulders and went on his way. "From your sarcastic comment I gather you may not like me. I don't care what you or anyone else thinks of me. I require from you one hundred per cent effort, and for you to get the job done. You Brits may think your God's gift to the high seas with all your bloody history but you go against me and you'll be on the next flight home, Admiral or no bloody Admiral."

The tirade was over and Adrian stood up, holding his cap in his right hand. "Is that all, Sir?"

Briggs looked at him and gave a dry smile; "Carry on."

Bob and Jim were waiting for Adrian to return.

"My cabin, gentlemen please."

He scanned the upper deck; men were busy preparing for sea. Adrian gave them the details of the meeting and asked for their help and assistance to achieve whatever was required. Bob and Jim knew that it was not going to be an easy time. The few hours that remained before sailing disappeared in a blur of activities. Adrian, from the upper bridge, watched as Leading Seaman Carrol was controlling the storage of ropes and fenders. Sub Lieutenant McGregor was good—he knew what to do and where equipment belonged.

The Coxswain was already at his sea-station, the steering wheel, and talking to the engine room staff. "Sir, the engine room would like permission to start main engines."

Adrian's thoughts went to other ships at different times in his career but the preparations for sea were always the same. "Approved Coxswain, but do not engage propulsion clutches until ordered."

"Roger, Sir," came the crisp reply.

Adrian was aware that he had not yet had time to meet the senior rates or the rest of the crew. As soon as time permitted he would remedy that error. There was a rumble from beneath his feet as two sixteen cylinder diesels roared into life followed by a plume of black exhaust.

Bob Hopkins arrived on the bridge. "Ship's company all on board, Sir; we're in all respects ready for sea."

Adrian nodded. The plan was simple - leaving at two minute intervals, following the leader out of harbour. Adrian placed his cap firmly on his head. It was time to go. *Geraldton* slipped from *Albany* in a wide sweeping arc and was heading out of harbour in excess of twelve knots. Joe Eva waved as the last rope fell away. Adrian began to position *Bunbury* the moment *Albany* was clear. With cautious use of the engines Adrian held his vessel off the wall. The stern spring fell away exactly on time. It was going to be tight but Adrian let the boat move from the wall and then he spun *Bunbury* around on its engines; as the bow moved towards the required course he ordered both engines full ahead. As they responded, a dark plume of exhaust left the funnel, and the two propellers dug deep into the water, surging them forward. Bob very quietly said: "Fifteen love."

Adrian smiled. They were positioned correctly when he handed over to Jim. "All yours, Navigator."

"I have the ship, Sir."

A voice from the coxswain filled the air: "Pommy Nav has the ship."

Everybody laughed.

As evening approached, the boat settled into its passage north. Adrian was drained, wrote his night orders and went to his bed. Bob and Jim had decided, albeit against the rules, that the boss would only get woken up if it was absolutely necessary. With Jim keeping the middle and Bob the morning watch, HMAS *Bunbury* was in safe hands.

+++

Angel had spent all of the previous day talking with Chung Wahh. Time and again he had personally checked that the men and their equipment were ready. Then he made the decision that the operation was go. Chung had one helicopter filled to maximum with equipment required for the first stage. The second machine was to carry ten men, fully armed with heavy calibre rifles. It was their job to clear the area of crocodiles.

One helicopter was off the ground, its rotor blades churning through the pre-dawn darkness. Ten men jumped into the cab and spread themselves out over the worn aluminium flooring. Gently it lifted into the air and headed out over the sea. Angel was pleased that the retrieval of millions of pounds' worth of drugs had begun. The street value would be incredible. His associates would be completely satisfied with the outcome. Although there had been a few minor irregularities, some of which could have caused problems, he was content that this would be another successful venture. As the first machine flew over the crest of the cliff that hid the *Kia Hua*, the men were already aiming their sights at individual monsters. The slaughter was complete—after a century or more, generations of crocodiles were eliminated in less than twenty minutes. The craft landed among the corpses and the work of preparing the beach for the second helicopter began. Each monster was hoisted into the air and deposited into the sea. The pilot was mentally exhausted after flying for so long in a confined area and was grateful when the beach was clear. The second machine landed with fuel and stores for the camp to be established. Flying was to be limited to the early morning and late evening. Angel was not taking any chances that they might be seen. He appreciated that this consumed valuable time but he had considered the options and made his decision. No-one was in a position to argue. When the two machines returned that night to the base camp, they were loaded ready for the next day. Chung was ready to leave and take responsibility for the new camp. Angel, having discussed all the necessary details with his assistant, remained behind to control the delivery of supplies.

The transfer of tools, men and equipment from the base camp was progressed. In two days they would be ready to start removing the precious cargo from the hulk. The divers had already inspected the wreck and were making preliminary dives to check the current and visibility as the tide ebbed and flowed. Good working time was two hours before and after high and low water. This gave them at best sixteen hours a day if they worked at night. Angel had considered this—it would reduce the time span of the whole operation. It had been tempting but he decided that the better the conditions were for the divers, the less damage would result to the payload. The men under his control were professionals and preferred the safer alternative. He left the organisation of the salvage to Chung but insisted that both helicopters returned to base each night and were pre-flight checked before the pilots rested.

It was all going well, and very soon he could notify his contacts in Perth and all the other major cities that it was time to collect. The pick-up points had been agreed. Each associate would go fishing at pre-determined locations along the twenty metre line adjacent to Eighty Mile beach where there would be brightly coloured fishing markers with float and anchor. Attached to the wire would be millions of dollars of pure heroin. This method of recovery had been tried and tested around the world. In almost every case the haul was recovered intact. Only once had a few offerings been lost. As he entered his tent, he knew that this was another delivery that would enhance his position within the syndicate. One day he would be in the ever-powerful top group. He actually slept well that night.

+++

Chung was operating the men in shifts of two hours on and four off and it was achieving the results that Angel demanded. The task of cutting out the hull of *Kia Hua* was ahead of schedule. On the beach, protected by two of Chung's henchmen, was almost a third of the consignment. Considering it had been sealed in the hull for years, the wrapping was in perfect condition. One man alone controlled the packaging of the delivery bundles, that was Chung. Even he did not know when the delivery would be made. The whole operation was on a need-to-know basis. He was aware that to spoil any of the bundles would mean Angel's anger and that, without exception, meant that someone would die. The work was hard and dangerous as air-powered Steil saws bit into the heavily barnacled metal of the hull. The labour of cutting to a precise depth, inch by inch along pre-drawn lines, was arduous to all concerned. On the beach where the crocodiles once basked in the sun, diesel driven air-compressors filled the bay with engine noise, drowning all other sounds.

Those men not working attempted to rest, but found it impossible. By chance, one man realised that, by leaving the beach and clambering over the ridge to the rocky foreshore, he could get a few hours' respite from the bedlam that existed. Others were not long in following. The memories of the boredom that nearly drove them insane were past. Now there were not enough hours in the day, and all looked forward to those scant precious hours of peaceful sleep. Chung dare not let up the pressure; time was against them, the delivery date was critical. Angel, in the sanctuary and tranquillity of the base camp, was informed each morning and evening of the progress being made. As the hours elapsed he felt the thrill of another successful venture. It had been his idea to use old ships as a method of flooding the markets with cheap but high quality drugs, making addiction easy. When advised, his distributors would temporarily withdraw the supply, forcing the price to rise. Once hooked it was then a simple matter of reaping the harvest. His rise to power was almost guaranteed.

Sixteen

Janice was deeply concerned about Adrian. She was aware that he must be busy and that was why he hadn't called, but surely he couldn't be that far away from a telephone. Despite Selwyn's assurances, she worried and missed him terribly. With nothing else to do she went for a walk and found herself by a small stream that meandered through the woods. For a while she thought about her childhood, and tossed "Pooh Sticks" into the current and watched them float away. Adrian had discussed and wanted their relationship to have the permanency of marriage. It troubled her why she couldn't make such a commitment.

As she sat there, her knees pulled up under her chin, the smell of foul pipe tobacco filled the air. "Is that you, Joe?" There was no reply but she was sure that she could feel his presence. The hairs on the nape of her neck bristled and the temperature of the surrounding air dropped. What was it old Joe had said to her that day in the woods? Adrian was a good man and she did love him, but, after the disaster of her first husband and the death of her son's father, the fear of commitment persisted. From what seemed far away a church bell rang in the village. It was time to return home. That thought made her wonder why she had called it that. After all it was not her home but it could be if she wanted. Perhaps there was something wrong with her, maybe being single was the way it was meant to be.

She walked on, oblivious to her surroundings until the crunch of gravel returned her to reality. Not wanting understanding from Mrs Duke and reassurances from Selwyn, she went upstairs to the room they had shared and sat by the open window. Somewhere out there was the man she would marry. The shock of her own thoughts disturbed her as she attempted to argue with herself about marriage. As alien as it seemed, her point of view had changed. Was it this room or had old Joe influenced her in some way? All she knew was the atmosphere that surrounded her was changing dramatically; the room seemed to have taken on a warm glow as if everything was in its place. Before all else, Adrian had to be told.

Quickly she ran down the stairs into the office where Selwyn was busy collating data. He stopped and looked up, noticing a change: "You've made up your mind."

"Does it show that much?" Her smile filled the room.

"What do you want me to do?"

"Can we get a message to him?"

"That shouldn't be difficult. What do you want to say?"

Janice didn't have to think about it: "I will marry you. Arrangements being made for when you return."

"Is that it?"

Janice looked at this man who, in his own way, owed everything to Adrian but also understood exactly how she felt. "I think for the moment that will be sufficient. Don't you?"

Janice had no doubt about Adrian's answer and there was much to be done before his return.

Mrs Duke looked at Janice. "It's not my place to tell you what to do, but why don't you go to Australia and get married?"

As she finished talking, Janice jumped up, grabbed her and hugged her tightly. "Why didn't I think of that? I'll talk to Selwyn. It will be our wedding and honeymoon."

Mrs Duke had an uneasiness about her which was very obvious to Janice.

"What's the matter?" she asked softly."

Mrs Duke lowered her eyes before speaking: "It's something and nothing really, but Mr Duke and I have never been out of Yorkshire. You see, we are content with our lives and never needed to wander and the thought of travelling to the other side of the world is a bit daunting."

Janice found it difficult to comprehend the situation. "I would like you to be at our wedding. If you feel the journey could be an ordeal, I'll wait until Adrian comes home. He would never forgive me if you weren't there."

"I'm not sure and I must ask Mr Duke—if he says it's all right then I'm sure it will be."

Mrs Duke left the kitchen to find her husband. It seemed an eternity until the door opened and in walked both of them. For once Mr Duke took the lead: "Mrs Duke tells me you want to get married in Australia. Well, miss, young Adrian has always looked after us so I think it's only right that we're at his wedding. It'll certainly be a new experience, but Mr Selwyn will make sure no harm comes to us."

Janice had tears pouring down her cheeks, running into the edge of her mouth. She moved forward and held them both tightly and they shared her joy.

Selwyn was not so enthralled with the suggestion; it meant leaving the company to operate without direction. Once in a while it would make little difference but twice in such a short period was not good. There were other reasons but he felt that this was not the right time or place to let Janice know. When the whirlwind had passed she would know soon enough. Janice was determined to get her own way and Selwyn knew better than to argue, but he did manage, after much debating, to persuade her to delay their departure. His reasoning was that there was absolutely no point in travelling thousands of miles only to find Adrian was at sea or away from the naval base. Three months was too long for her to wait, she wanted to be in Perth making plans.

In her excitement she had neglected to tell her son Gregory the good news. It had been almost a year since they had last seen each other. It wasn't that she didn't love him but their lives followed different paths, almost in opposite directions. It was Mrs Duke who suggested that Janice invite Gregory to come and stay.

Janice telephoned Gregory at work and he agreed that he would love to come and see her the following weekend. For a moment he hesitated: "I'll be bringing my partner with me if that's all right."

"Of course. Let me know what train you'll be on and I'll pick you up. OK?"

The arrangements in place, Janice was moderately content to wait a while and enjoy some time with her son.

That evening she discussed her plans with Selwyn and Mr and Mrs Duke. Selwyn announced that he would enquire about the necessities of getting married in Australia. Janice thanked him and apologised for behaving like a spoiled brat.

Selwyn laughed and said he excused her as she was in love. "You've never told us about your son, would you mind?"

For the next hour or so Janice told the three of them an abridged version of her life, absorbing each with her story.

"You should write a book," commented Mrs Duke.

Janice laughed: "One day perhaps but I doubt if anyone would be interested in my life. You have to be a personality to get published these days."

"I'm sure you have some contacts in the media."

"Maybe, but writing a novel is for another time and place."

Mrs Duke made them a drink of hot chocolate before she and her husband left.

Janice and Selwyn chatted for a few minutes longer until she yawned and they agreed it was time for bed. She leant forward, kissed him gently on the cheek and said, "Thank you."

He looked at her, debating whether to say anything or not. "You must be very happy."

"I am," she responded with a smile that could have melted the coldest heart. She continued: "They say the grass is always greener on the other side of the fence. Then, if you're very lucky it is, if not you fall flat on your face into cowshit. This time Adrian was on my side of the fence and I didn't have far to travel."

Selwyn laughed at her analogy of life and kept his counsel.

After she had bathed, she drew back the crisp cotton sheets and lay flat on her back staring aimlessly at the ceiling. As her body cooled she pulled the covers up under her chin and tried to relax. Deep sleep evaded her until the early hours and then she dreamt that she was in a green valley looking into the distance. From it came a woman walking down a path towards her. A long coat, navy blue in colour, covered her body; the collar was turned up as if to keep out the cold. It was difficult for Janice to determine who she was but she had the distinct appearance of being beautiful. The dark hair and solemn steady eyes that could have been either blue or grey gave her face a peaceful serenity. She stopped and looked at Janice as if to speak but said nothing. For some reason unknown to her, Janice felt reassured by the presence of this stranger. After all it was only a dream.

"You are in our room, my son was born in this room. Remember he loves you and he is only a man." The woman's voice appeared soft and loving but it had a sad tinge to it.

Janice waited to see if she would speak again.

The scene changed rapidly and she was standing by a river watching the crystal clear water flow by. Adrian was standing on the opposite bank waiting for her to cross but the current made it impossible and she knew that she would never reach the other side.

When she woke it was getting light. She listened to the sounds of birds singing in the trees outside her window but the image of the dream persisted. The shower jetted sharp needles onto her skin, awakening every inch of her body. Dressed in only a housecoat she wandered downstairs to the kitchen. Selwyn was there, ready to begin the day's work. For a second she paused before relating her dream in its entirety to him. "Do you know what it means?"

He remained silent for what seemed an age, then he looked at her and gently held her hands. "It means that you are looking ahead and considering your present situation. Life is symbolised by the river with its twist and turns. The woman—I don't know. However, you see what you desire on the opposite bank which indicates a positive object but you must find a way to get to the other side. You should remember that there are more ways to cross a river than by swimming. It shows that, despite everything, you're prepared to take that chance. That's it in a nutshell; nothing to worry about, it was just your life, past, present and future."

Janice was uncertain but Selwyn was adamant that it positively indicated that the future was bright. In his heart he knew that the road ahead for Adrian was a treacherous one.

+++

The squadron remained in a close formation overnight whilst continuing their passage north. At dawn the early sunlight was obscured by a fast evaporating sea mist. Their patrol speed of fourteen knots meant five days on passage. Pat Briggs had calculated that if they completed all evolutions at high speed no time would be lost. The first signal of the day ordered a light line transfer, with the closing ship to use, when necessary, maximum speed. Pat Briggs, decided that *Geraldton* would be the receiving vessel for both operations, giving his crew the least work. *Albany* was to be first to make its approach. Joe Eva turned his boat to starboard in a wide sweeping ark, increasing speed as he did so. Adrian watched with satisfaction at her high speed approach. It was a text book display, until a huge plume of black smoke erupted from her funnel.

Superb ship handling avoided the almost certain collision between the two vessels. Pat Briggs had immediately recognised Joe's difficulty and pushed his engines to full ahead, allowing *Albany* to slide past his port quarter. *Bunbury* remained at a safe distance, only making slight headway to maintain steerage. Joe reported that there were major problems with his starboard main engine and that he had no option but to return to Perth. *Albany* was detached and ordered back to base, rejoining the squadron only on completion of repairs.

The formalities over, *Geraldton* and *Bunbury* continued their passage north. Adrian sat relaxed in his bridge chair and glanced forward as the two vessels sliced their sharp bows through the gently rolling sea. Below him, the boat went about its business as he waited for the next group of signals from Pat Briggs.

Henry McGregor had the watch and Adrian could hear him humming away to himself. The Signals Yeoman appeared on the bridge, his right hand tightly gripped the daily signal log. Pat Briggs was in good form and the pressure was still aimed at Adrian. Why did Pat resent him? Since leaving, they had completed evolution after evolution. Bob Hopkins was the best of executive officers and ran the boat as well as anyone could. Adrian was anxious and called Bob to his cabin; he needed someone to confide in and, for the first time, Jim was not the one.

"Bob. Why is Pat so hard on us?"

For a moment Bob sat and stared at his hands. "It's very simple—he's not happy with you being given command."

Adrian was surprised by his frankness; "Surely he must be aware that although it was offered I was practically ordered to take command." He continued to look at Bob who seemed tense.

"Sir, the truth is I was offered it initially and turned it down, and before you ask why, it's because I was scared. Pat Briggs would have eaten me for breakfast and spat out the pips. By refusing I made you the sacrificial lamb. I was fully prepared to support and help but I was wrong in assuming that you were one of the gin and tonic brigade."

Adrian listened intently; the questions he had asked himself had been answered. "Well, Bob, what do we do now?"

"What do you mean, Sir?"

"As my Exec you have supported me and so far we—the boat—have come out on top. I suggest we forget this conversation and get on with the task in hand and demonstrate to Pat-bloody-Briggs that this crew is the best there is."

"Is that all, Sir?"

Adrian looked at him, smiled a cheeky grin and merely said, "For the moment, but later we'll need to discuss your future."

Adrian watched Bob leave and then returned to the open bridge to let the warm wind clear his mind. Time had been Bob's enemy; he hadn't been ready for command and wasn't going to sacrifice his exemplary record by making a cock-up. He was determined to make him ready, and took some time to consider the situation. Bob Hopkins was not the kind of man to shirk responsibility but he did need a shot in the arm. He wandered down to the wardroom where he stood in the doorway waiting to be invited in; Bob, on seeing him, offered a seat and a cup of coffee.

Adrian said softly, "It's all a game and tomorrow you'll sit in my chair. If you need me I'll be in my cabin or wandering around talking to the crew." He sipped at his coffee before continuing: "I would like to see your programme for the day and use Jim as your Exec; he's very good and also capable of command. Between the two of you it should go well."

Bob sat silently, confused that a man who hardly knew him, was letting him take control.

Adrian left the wardroom smiling; "Night report before I turn in."

A faint "Aye, aye, Sir" was all he heard as he made his way to the bridge. Adrian sat back in his bridge chair and stretched his arms. The wind through the open windows was refreshing and for a moment he let his thoughts drift to Janice. All was well and he returned to his cabin.

That night he slept properly and rose at six in the morning. He showered and dressed in less than ten minutes and was soon on the bridge standing alongside Bob who had the watch. Adrian looked around and assessed the whole situation before he turned to Bob: "I have the ship."

Bob was taken aback and thought for a moment he was in the wrong, with the captain taking the boat from him.

Adrian smiled: "Bob, you have less than two hours to organise yourself and your day. Hand the watch over to me and get a breakfast—after eight o'clock I cease to exist."

Bob nodded, as he felt a pride in himself and the boat.

True to form, the day's evolution started exactly at eight. Bob and Jim worked well together. Adrian remained at a distance and studied the two officers: one an Australian, one as English as you could get, chalk and cheese in comparison, but they had united as a powerful force against Pat Briggs. The crew was giving everything and more to help. Problems were more often than not resolved before they had a chance to disrupt the proceedings. Once he heard a poor decision and faltered, wanting to say something but knew they could manage. If he interfered, they would see his action as a lack of confidence. The time passed without incident and together the three men dissected the day's performance. It was during this period that Adrian was requested to the communications office. Leading Radio Operator Boone was sat in his chair as Adrian entered.

"Personal signal for you, Sir, and congratulations."

Adrian took the message from his hand and read it slowly. He looked at Boone calmly: "Who else knows about this?"

Boone smiled wryly: "No-one yet, Sir."

Adrian grinned: "Well, make sure it stays that way."

He returned to his cabin where Bob and Jim were continuing their discussions on the day's activities whilst waiting. The signal was shown to Jim first and then Bob. Both men stood, slapped him on the back and shook his hand, congratulating him at the same time.

"When's the day then?"

"As it says, arrangements being made. Jim would you honour me by being my best man?"

The request was accepted with a jubilant "Absolutely".

Bob asked to be excused, leaving Jim and Adrian alone. "Some celebration! Still, would you insert my good news into the general comment on daily orders and issue an extra can of beer on my account to the crew."

Jim smiled: "Of course I will," and then made to leave but Adrian wanted him to stay. For once he wanted to talk but was acutely aware that Jim had the middle watch and needed a few hours' rest before taking over. Adrian desperately needed to do something so he went to the bridge and relieved Henry, advising him that he could rest but not sleep until midnight when his duty would have ended.

Once Henry had cleared the bridge, Adrian was asking the Bosun's mate to get some coffee. "Make it black and strong." Adrian was in his element, on the open bridge of his boat at night feeling the warm air rush past him. It helped to apprise the mind of the past, present and future. The hour and a half passed quickly and Jim, true to form, was standing beside him at fifteen minutes to midnight letting his eyes adapt to the darkness. Adrian handed over the watch and returned to his cabin. After a shower he lay on his bunk, thinking about his girl. Without any conscious effort, sleep overtook him as the most pleasant of thoughts filled his mind.

+++

HMAS *Bunbury* was moving gently in the rolling swell and Adrian was pleased with the new-found confidence that seemed to flow from his officers. Pat Briggs had finally run out of things to do. He returned to his cabin and dealt with the routine daily signals, making comments on some to be actioned by others. It was time to reply to Janice. He went to the communications room and handed his answer. It read: "***Pleased to accept your proposal of marriage. My life would not be complete without you in it. Adrian.***"

Pat Briggs had received the message from the naval base advising him that a police helicopter would be in the area to guide them. A warning of the tidal situation was given with precision; they were not, under any circumstances, to enter the bay until two hours before high tide and not to remain any longer than was absolutely necessary. Pat had the signal copied to Adrian. There was now less than thirty-six hours before they would be on station. His announcement to the ship's company that he was to be married was greeted with a few ribald comments and a rousing cheer for the extra can of beer. Each of them was content with his lot. His daily summary read: "The ship's company's *esprit de corps* is at an all time high."

His train of thought was interrupted by Leading Radio Operator Boone. "Message from *Geraldton*, Sir."

Adrian was handed the signal log; the message read, "Ships will come to a co-ordinated anchorage tomorrow night at a position decided by you and agreed by Squadron Commander. Position is to be suitable for rendezvous with police helicopter at 1000 hours local time. Captains will meet in my cabin one hour after completion of anchorage."

Adrian signed the pad, acknowledging that he had read it and handed it back to Boone. "Will you ask the Exec and Navigator to come to my cabin?"

"Aye, aye, Sir—I'll tell them to make it sharpish."

Bob and Jim arrived together and their boss gave them the news.

"Not a problem," commented Jim; "I'll get on with it right away."

That night Adrian lay on his bunk, listening to the heart of the boat, the mute beat of its engines and the rush of water passing along the side of the hull. His thoughts were far away but as if controlled by an unknown force he fell into a deep sleep. His eyes seemed to be open and he was watching a scene unfold before him that he had no control over. The picture was glowing—not sunshine but a white brightness, and what he assumed were people, moved around him but never touched. Then he saw old Joe and knew it was a dream—Joe was dead. It suddenly became confusing when Selwyn appeared and he knew that he was very much alive. Both these spirits were trying to tell him something but he couldn't hear the words; the more he tried to listen the more difficult it became.

Adrian awoke, shouting out loud in the red glow of his cabin.

He jumped as the squawk box above his bunk shrieked: "Captain, captain, Sir, *Geraldton* has stopped. I have reduced speed and am maintaining steerage way. Request you come to the bridge."

Adrian answered as he rolled off his bunk: "On my way."

He vaulted up the steps to the bridge; Jim as required, had followed the correct procedure and *Bunbury* was gently wallowing to the stern and starboard of the other vessel. Adrian waited for what he considered was sufficient time to elapse before he contacted *Geraldton*. His voice was crisp and alert: "217 Charlie Oscar to 213 Charlie Oscar." He waited.

Pat Briggs replied, his voice filling the confines of the small bridge. "217, I have a problem—out."

Jim had been busy taking a fix and in the darkness he heard Adrian mutter, "A man of few words."

"Right, Jim, maintain your position at a minimum of one thousand yards and as you are to starboard. I would prefer to be out of his way if something else happens."

"Roger, Sir."

Adrian decided that, for the moment, he would remain on the bridge, and sent one of the hands for his dressing gown. *Bunbury* was not the best ship to be in with a gentle swell running from the port quarter. On more than one occasion he had to steady himself as the hull lurched and trembled.

"The bastard's increased speed," remarked Jim softly.

"I suppose whatever was wrong has been fixed. I'm off to bed; keep it steady, just in case he's playing at silly buggers," suggested Adrian.

"Roger, Sir." For the remainder of the night he slept soundly. There were no more dreams. The message had been clear, it had been a warning.

+++

A long, slow swell was hitting the ship head on, causing a motion that made standing difficult. Adrian had wedged himself into the shower and cursed every time the soap fell to the floor. Breakfast was a cup of coffee and a bacon sandwich. As he made his way to the bridge he heard an assortment of curses from the ship's company as items fell with a clatter, smashing themselves to pieces as they hit the deck. Bob was just coming to the end of his morning watch and declared that he would check the boat before he had breakfast. As he positioned himself in his chair, Adrian merely nodded. By midday the sea was crashing over the bow, soaking everything in sight but Pat Briggs had vehemently insisted that passage speed be maintained. Adrian had retired to his cabin and lay fully dressed on his bunk; it was the safest place to be.

It was nearly three in the afternoon when Midshipman John Wilson knocked on his cabin door, asking if he would approve the anchorage plan. It was to be in Admiralty Gulf to the south of the Osborne Islands, approximately thirty miles from the reported rendezvous point.

"Well, what have you left to do?" asked Adrian.

John looked at the chart and for a few minutes

studied it intently. "I'm sorry, Sir, I haven't a clue." Then with a cheeky grin that filled his face he replied: "Inform our Squadron Commander, Sir."

Adrian glanced at John and smiled: "Oh, by the way, well done—it's a good plan."

For the remainder of the day *Bunbury* and *Geraldton* ploughed their way steadily northward. The large rollers maintained their steady pace as they buffeted the vessels from stem to stern.

Food consisted of thick slices of buttered bread and soup if you wanted it, but most of the crew didn't bother. Bob knocked on Adrian's cabin door and as he grimly clung to its frame, advised him it was time. Adrian grunted his acknowledgement, as the boat fell into another trough. He knew that everyone would be grateful for a good night's sleep. With the skill of a seasoned seaman he made his way to the bridge. He gripped the arms of his chair and forced himself into it. Bob reported that all was ready and Midshipman John Wilson had the conn. It went according to plan and both vessels dropped their anchors at their designated positions.

In the shelter of the bay it was calm, the ship gave a final shudder, and an eerie silence filled the air as the engines stopped. Adrian looked to the shore and in the darkness could barely make out the outline of the land. Down below he could hear Bob telling the coxswain that he wanted the ship cleaned and ready for mess deck rounds after the evening meal. Life goes on; like the proverbial ticking of a clock, it never stops. At that moment the bridge radio burst into life.

"Viper, this is Briggs; report to my ship in fifteen minutes."

Adrian acknowledged: "Viper out," then asked Henry to organise the boat transfer. Going to the open bridge, he looked into the night sky and for the moment enjoyed the solitude. His peace was interrupted by the harsh tones of Leading Seaman Carrol, screaming encouragement to half a dozen hands as they readied the Sea Raider. He leant over the side and watched the boat swinging outboard and finally settle in the water.

The journey was quick and uneventful and the alongside manoeuvre completed with absolute perfection. Adrian ordered the coxswain to secure the craft and wait. He made his way to the Commanding Officer's cabin where Pat Briggs motioned for him to enter. He was sitting on the bed settee that covered almost one side of the cabin, drinking what appeared to be a very large scotch. Neither a drink nor seat was offered.

Pat looked at his visitor carefully: "Pretty good effort by your crew these last four days." The statement was made as if he was talking to a newly appointed officer. "It is possible that I underestimated your ability. Tomorrow a police helicopter will pinpoint the location of this abandoned steamer. Once I've established the entrance to this hidden bay, my fast raider will make the initial survey, checking the depth and width of the channel."

Adrian felt like saying that if a bloody big merchantman found its way in there, their boats should have no difficulty, but he thought it wiser to say nothing, simply nod appropriately.

"If everything's satisfactory, I'll follow my raider and enter the basin. You'll stand off at one mile and wait for my instructions. Is that understood?"

"Yes, Sir."

With that he was dismissed. He was seething and counting to one hundred as he left *Geraldton*. Bob, seeing the look in his boss's eyes used his discretion and said nothing. Adrian entered his cabin tossing his foul weather clothing into a corner.

Some thirty minutes later Bob arrived with two cups of hot steaming coffee. He knocked on the cabin door and pushed it open wide. "Want someone to talk to?"

Adrian sat up, grinned at his Exec and told him to come in and sit down. They chatted about everything and nothing. Bob knew when he was ready he would be told what was happening.

"Tomorrow will be a quiet day. Have Jim draw a transit line on the chart, five miles long, and let the Mid have the forenoon watch. Someone might as well benefit from our inactivity."

It was getting late and Bob, like everyone else, needed sleep. He collected the two empty coffee cups and said goodnight. Adrian went up to the open bridge to enjoy the clean fresh air that filled the night. Able Seaman Duncan was there teaching Seaman Hughes. Neither noticed Adrian; so engrossed were they in checking positions that they both jumped when he said good evening.

Adrian very quietly asked, "Everything as it should be?"

"Yes, Sir."

Duncan remarked, "It's quiet now. Earlier, around dusk, I was sure that a couple of helicopters were operating over there."

Adrian was intrigued: "Show me."

Duncan pointed just east of north. Adrian picked up the sliding rule and, allowing a five degree error either side of the general direction, he drew two lines. The thin pencil strokes captured the rough position of the *Kia Hua.*

"Well done. It may be something or nothing but it's quite unusual for helicopters to be operating in such a remote area. Adrian dropped down to the lower bridge and made contact with *Geraldton* by radio. Pat Briggs was not available so he passed his message to the duty officer. On completion he returned to the open air.

"Duncan, tell your relief and those that follow, that if they think they see or hear anything unusual they are to wake me immediately. Is that understood?"

"Aye, aye, Sir; I'll make a note in the log."

Adrian returned to his cabin and tried to equate the significance of a tramp sunk in a remote part of the world with the possibility of helicopters operating in the same area. As he stood in the shower what had been said in Charles Dawning's office all those months ago came flooding back. What if she were carrying an illegal cargo? That would explain why she wasn't sunk in deep water. The helicopters were an ideal method of transporting a reasonably sized payload. As he rubbed his body hard with a towel, the more he realised it made sense. Wrapping the towel around his middle he sat at his desk and began to write on a blank sheet of paper: ships disappearing without a trace—vessel not worth a great deal—possible contraband—helicopters being used for transportation—if helicopters in use, possibility that members of the ship in the vicinity. Why did two leave and get lost?—police didn't notice any activity when they found the ship—the decayed remains of one body.

Large pieces of the jigsaw were forming but the picture they represented appeared vague and fragmented. The situation was pondered over for an hour before he settled naked onto his bunk and fell into a deep sleep.

Adrian believed that he had only just closed his eyes when he was being briskly shaken. Someone far away was raising his voice: "Sir! Sir! Those helicopters are in the air again."

As the words registered he was instantly awake and running to the upper bridge. It took him seconds to fix the direction from where the sound of beating rotor blades emanated. Again he examined the chart and the bearing confirmed that someone was working or operating in the vicinity of the wreck. A snigger from the quartermaster and a cool breeze that wafted around his lower body made him realise that he was stark naked. As he turned to face Able Seaman Talbot, the sound of rotor blades altered. Adrian knew from experience that there were at least two craft flying. Whoever was stripping the *Kia Hua* had planned this operation for some time, of that he was sure.

Thanking the men, he returned to his cabin and added this observation to his now full sheet of clues. The puzzle was beginning to form a circle. Load the ship, scuttle it, unload the ship. It had to be something easily transported, not too heavy and worth a great deal of money. It had to be drugs—it was the only thing that fitted the plot. If this was as organised as it seemed, they would be prepared if a casual vessel passed by but how would they react to the Royal Australian Navy driving into their back yard? Adrian had no facts or evidence to convince Pat Briggs but he had to tell him. Carefully he wrote down the details as he understood them and when he was finished he placed the memo into a white envelope and sealed it, covering the flap with his signature. As with all confidential correspondence, he placed this into another larger envelope and repeated the process. Having done all he could, he had the Midshipman take it personally and deliver it into the hand of Lieutenant Commander P Briggs, RAN.

He waited until almost an hour had passed. Surely Pat would make some comment even if he thought it a load of rubbish. All that remained was to have a shower, get dressed and be prepared for whatever the day would bring. As Adrian ate his breakfast he contemplated on how he could be ready, just in case he was right: a small arms shoot and 40/60 Bofors gun drills. Pat may think his assumptions were out of order but he would OK a whole ship activity, it was just his style. He summoned Bob and ordered that all ammunition and weapons be prepared before they were underway. Bob was about to question his boss when Adrian looked at him: "Do it."

SEVENTEEN

Chung was becoming happier by the hour. In two more days they could leave this Godforsaken place and be on their way back to civilisation and all that money could buy. For him it was a modest flat in a better area of Hong Kong. The majority of the men would return from where they were found. Most would squander their earnings in a few months on extravagant living with some disease-infected whore who would depart as soon as the money had gone. If they were lucky, a few dollars would be left to enable survival at the bottom of the heap or until another job came along. Chung, having been in Angel's employ for a few years, knew that the good times never lasted and had made provision for his old age.

Angel often intimated that there would be a good bonus if they finished early but Chung cautioned him that if they made the planned schedule he should be thankful. The loads to be dropped had been well protected to prevent any damage when they plummeted into the ocean. After a few days anchored to the seabed they would be collected. Subsequently, they would be divided into easily transportable packages for distribution amongst the numerous safe houses in every town and city in Australia. About ten per cent would be discovered when stupid amateurs drew their sudden wealth to the attention of the police. Despite the abysmal conditions, the men continued to work hard, maintaining the momentum. Careful planning and checking were now paying off as not one piece of equipment malfunctioned. The only difficulties had been the lack of diesel fuel and drinking water that had to be delivered daily. Chung had ensured maximum supply but it was never enough. Several times the diving air compressors had come close to stopping. It had been an operation of logistics and strategy, of which, Angel knew from past experience, Chung was the master.

Chung was worried. For the better part of the day and at intervals during the evening, he had heard chatter over the airwaves from naval vessels operating in the area. He wasn't concerned that they might be discovered but it did represent a problem with the operation of their helicopters. Communication by radio to their base camp was no longer a viable option. One word and the warships would pick it up, they always kept a listening watch.

A message was sent to Angel on one of the helicopters as it went for supplies. His answer over two hours later was to stop the salvage operation until the vessels were out of the area. No-one was to do anything to attract attention. For the first time since they had arrived in the bay the men could relax and it felt good to sleep without the sound of diesel air compressors reverberating in their ears. Chung ensured that there was a good watch and the radio was monitored throughout the night. The morning presented no further information of any value. The radio crackled, the message was short and precise: "***Charlie Oscar to Charlie Oscar your story read and dismissed. Out.***" Chung was not concerned with the message. It meant nothing to him except that the ships were still around. It was his decision not to commence the operation. One more good day and they could begin to wrap this one up.

Angel sat with the pilot of the second helicopter, planning the drops on a chart. Each one had to be located precisely for collection or millions of dollars could be lost. He thought he would have heard from Chung but the silence reaffirmed his own suspicions - that another day would make little difference to the final outcome.

+++

Sergeant David Jones was content with his lot, by day a respected policeman, and at night sharing Rachel's bed. What more could a man want except promotion? He was pleased with the message from headquarters that he was to guide the navy to the wreck. The helicopter had been arranged to arrive the night before the navy entered the area. It slightly annoyed him that he had to be at the wreck for ten in the morning. Rachel didn't seem bothered and merely stated that he had better not wake her as he left. David asked himself what was so important as to involve the navy—it was only an old tramp past her best. If it meant a step up the ladder who was he to argue.

Rachel had tormented David Jones all night and made demands that he only ever imagined in his wildest dreams. She worked at it with a sexuality that guaranteed intimate satisfaction. Each time he climaxed she would climb on top of him and manipulate her body until he was, once again, aroused. When this failed she had more outlandish methods of obtaining her way. On David every one of these methods worked until he was completely drained; only then would she let him sleep. When it was time for him to leave, he dragged himself out of the rumpled bed. For a moment he looked at this woman who had tormented him to the limit and beyond. She sighed with catlike satisfaction and snuggled down beneath the cotton sheets. In a dream-like stupor David went for a shower. A full-length mirror displayed the deep scratch marks that progressed from the nape of his neck to his waist, inflicted by her nails. He knew that the bloody wounds would sting like hell. David dressed and made his way out of the flat towards the waiting helicopter. With luck he would be able to doze for a few hours before the navy arrived.

Mike Nailor, the Police Sergeant pilot, sat in his seat watching and waiting for him to arrive. The sun was bright in the sky and for him it was going to be an easy day. When his passenger had secured himself in the co-pilot's seat, he completed his checks and turned on the ignition. The gas turbines started to roar, waking those who slept close by as the machine reached full power. With a reverberating commotion the large, seemingly unwieldy, rescue craft lifted into the air. As if deliberately attempting to wake the dead, Mike flew lower than necessary across the town. David had fallen asleep within a few minutes of their being airborne. Mike looked at him and laughed.

+++

Pat Briggs was applying an unrealistic pressure on both boats by sending signal after signal. The air was full of his abusive comments and instructions. Adrian, having seen Pat down a few large drinks, concluded that the man must have a giant hangover to be in such a foul temper. He was glad an expanse of water separated them. The time passed and the rage subsided. Turning to Jim, who had just come on the bridge, he asked, "What time's high water?"

He answered immediately: "Around ten o'clock." The night before he had spent hours plotting the entrance to half a dozen inlets in the area.

His boss asked to look at the chart and between them two possibilities for the last resting place of the *Kia Hua* were identified. Both had deep water although an entrance to one could only be achieved for a limited period.

Adrian looked at Jim. "If we go in there we're stuck for about nine hours if we miss the tide."

"In all honesty, Sir, I'd rather not go in there at all."

Adrian stood looking out of the bridge window as they followed *Geraldton* out of the bay: "If our leader gets his way, we won't be going anywhere. What time is it?"

Before anyone could answer the radio burst into life: "***X-ray Tango Juliet two one seven, This is Gulf, Charlie, Mike, Two One Four radio check, radio check over.***"

Bunbury's communicator completed the mandatory checks. Before signing off Adrian asked him to obtain an ETA at the rendezvous. The reply was twenty minutes.

Captain Viper had a decision to make and now was the time. He sent the signal requesting permission to carry out a small arms shoot and 40/60 drills. *Geraldton* answered, "***Affirmative out***."

Ordering an increase of speed, he looked at the chart again. Which bay? He studied the contours of the land; they were very similar, except the entrance to the deepest was the narrowest. The decision was made, the most difficult, and if he was wrong he was only at best speed thirty minutes away from the alternative. As directed, *Bunbury* was one mile offshore patrolling its transit while *Geraldton* waited for their guide to arrive.

The huge machine appeared from inland and further north than expected, but slowly it began to move down the coast towards *Geraldton*. Whoever was operating the radio was not familiar with procedure as the transmit switch remained on. His commentary on the coast line was being heard clearly by *Geraldton* and Chung. This had the effect of cancelling any other transmissions.

The voice was pure outback Australian: "Not there mate, further down. How the hell do I know? You're the fucking pilot. Not there, mate," and so it went on. The sound of small arms fire filled the air as *Bunbury*'s crew aimed an assortment of weapons at a floating target that was quickly disappearing astern. Adrian realised that he would soon have to turn the ship to avoid losing it altogether. The surprised tone of the voice filled the bridge as it shouted, "Jesus Christ, mate, what the hell's going on down there?"

Geraldton attempted to communicate but it was useless; the lunatic's mouth was in overdrive.

"There's a helicopter, machines, a few boats and at least twenty men. Wait a minute, where are the crocs? Mike, take us down, I want to find out what's happening."

Another voice, more refined and educated, answered: "Where do you want me to land, smart arse? The only good position has already been taken by their machine."

A pause, then the reply: "On the top of the ship's bridge."

"*Geraldton* attempted to intervene but it was too late; the helicopter was already out of sight. Adrian had calculated the correct bay. He watched as *Geraldton* lowered its Fast Raider and prepared to begin its passage.

Mike Nailor descended slowly below the ridge that encompassed the bay. He was a good pilot but his instinct told him to get the hell out of there.

David's eyes were flitting from one area to another as he wondered what these men were doing. From the amount of equipment littering the small beach he could only guess. What on earth were they after?

Four men boarded an inflatable dinghy powered by a small outboard and headed towards the *Kia Hua*. The weight of the police helicopter settled and steadied itself as the wheels touched and gripped the large expanse of rusting steel that was the top of the old ship's bridge. Mike was uneasy but accepted it was safe so long as the rotors remained turning. The small boat came alongside. The men were obviously accustomed to helicopter operations as they carefully with heads down made their way towards them. David and Mike waited. As the men drew close, two of them suddenly produced pistols. The occupants of the helicopter knew that they were in the wrong place at the wrong time. Fear caused sweat to run freely as Chung's men dragged them out of the cab. Before either could say a word, the barrel of a pistol was placed against the nape of their necks and they were forced to kneel. Each expected the worst but before they had a chance to defend themselves they were battered into unconsciousness. With a final arrogant kick from their attackers, they were left lying in pools of blood.

Mike groaned and Chung shot him through the back of his head. He motioned to one of his pilots: "Can you fly this?"

"If it's got wings I can fly it," came the arrogant reply.

"Do as you're told and get in or we'll need another pilot."

Things were falling apart; Chung's mind raced like a mainframe computer looking for solutions to an escalating crisis. Given time he could resolve any difficulty but this was a commodity of which he had little. Two ideas were conceived; if the simplest worked it would solve all their problems. One of his men was an Australian and, if he could convince the navy that everything was all right, the operation might yet be completed without a hitch. The police helicopter struggled erratically into the air as the pilot became acquainted with the controls. The handling of this machine was not that different from his own but, unlike the old crates he was used to flying, this craft operated as it really should. They came out of the bay and headed for the *Geraldton.* Chung noticed the Fast Raider leading the larger vessel. If the navy entered the bay, it was over.

He screamed at the Australian, "Get on that radio and tell that ship the bay is empty except for crocodile hunters."

The man obliged and they waited.

Briggs, his gruff voice indignant in its tone, blasted the small confines of the pilot's cockpit: "I will decide what my boat does. I have orders. Out."

Chung had to have more time—half the consignment was ready. If he could only divert the navy, he might be able to escape. His survival was uppermost, the garbage was expendable. His alternative plan now dictated swift action. If he could salvage at least half the drug consignment Angel would not be too angry; after all half was better than nothing.

He lifted his high-powered rifle and checked the magazine; it was full. The men with him were ordered to fire at the *Geraldton* as the helicopter passed down its port side.

They looked warily at Chung; to take on the navy was tantamount to suicide.

"Just fire over their heads," screamed Chung; "I want to scare the hell out of them. That'll give us time to make our escape."

They nodded uncertainly.

Chung pulled open the starboard door to give him an unobstructed view of *Geraldton*. The pilot dropped down to just above sea level and adjusted his cruising speed. They began to overtake the boat, as it made its way guardedly towards the narrow entrance. For a moment the bridge team turned and looked at the police helicopter.

As the machine reached the stern of *Geraldton,* Chung roared "Fire!" and all hell erupted. Chung's men fired as ordered but his aim was premeditated and deadly. Pat Briggs died in his chair, and rapid shots hit the Exec and Navigator before they found cover. Several shots penetrated the thin metal skin, and one ricocheted around the enclosed bridge, seriously wounding the helmsman. It had been easy target.

The crew of the Fast Raider suffered an unmerciful onslaught. With no cover, Chung aimed carefully, eliminating them one by one. *Geraldton* veered rapidly to port, leaving the narrow confines of the channel. The hard coral of the reef tore at the metal, ripping it as a sharp knife passes through paper. The ruptured hull flooded rapidly from stem to stern until she hesitantly settled with her bows in the air and her aft end under water. HMAS *Geraldton* had found her final resting place.

Lieutenant Dave Cooper, with a lower right arm that hurt like hell, had been lucky. He was desperately attempting to regain some semblance of order. There was blood everywhere, injured men, and they were sinking. The rule book had missed this one out. Priorities—that was the name of the game. He started by getting those who were unhurt to move the injured onto the fo'c'sle.

Adrian had been listening to the radio out of curiosity when he heard the Australian's message. The clamour of his own weapons firing had masked the sound of slaughter but when he saw *Geraldton* veer suddenly to port, it was evident that something had gone very wrong. It also wasn't clear why Briggs had failed to reply to his messages.

With only assistance in mind, *Bunbury* was turned across the sea in a wide sweeping arc until she was heading up the muddy outflow. Adrian had just ordered full ahead when he witnessed *Geraldton's* bows rise high into the air before she slid backwards anchoring her hull onto the teeth of the reef. His thoughts at that moment were confused. It was Jim who spotted the flashing light from *Geraldton* and the Yeoman who read each letter as it was sent:

> "Have been attacked. Captain and several of the crew are dead. Serious hull damage. Stuck fast on reef. In no immediate danger."

The suddenness of what had happened shocked Adrian and his team. One moment it had appeared to be unfortunate accident and the next a major disaster.

"Yeoman, send this message to the Base Commander and make sure it's encrypted," ordered a surprisingly calm captain:

> "HMAS Geraldton attacked by unknown force. Am taking the necessary and appropriate action to protect and recover survivors- Viper RD RNR."

The Yeoman scurried away like a startled rat to his office.

"Action stations, Number One. I want two heavy machine guns mounted on this bridge **NOW**."

As the klaxon sounded and men moved swiftly to their nominated stations, Leading Seamen Carrol and Young arrived on the bridge, each carrying a heavy machine gun over their shoulders; they were closely followed by two able ratings carrying boxes of ammunition. Adrian looked at Young, then Carrol: "All right Buffer?"

"Yes, Sir, this reminds me of when I was off Borneo in the sixties."

"I don't think you'll get a medal for this escapade," remarked Adrian. He then turned to Young: "What about you, Young; OK?"

The Leading Seaman stared at him, astonished that at a time like this the captain could be so calm and cool. "I'm all right, Sir; be glad when it's all over." His voice quivered slightly as he tried not to show fear. If he got out of this, he would always remember the moment he and his mate were up there with the captain. A few beers would pass his lips and the story would ultimately grow in the passing.

Adrian slowed the ship down whilst the preparations were completed. Jim studied his charts and advised, "Sir, time is against us. The flood tide is almost over.

"Thank you."

Bob arrived on the bridge; "The ship is at action stations and the Bofors' 40/60 guns' crew closed up."

It was time to tell his team what he considered they were up against. Adrian looked up at the unblemished sky; it was a beautiful shade of blue and the sun was getting far too hot for men to be fully dressed for action. The short message was precise and clear; these people, whoever they were, had to be stopped. As he replaced the microphone in its retaining clip, he questioned his own motives. All he had to do was rescue the crew of *Geraldton* and get the hell out of there. No-one would reprimand him for avoiding a confrontation with an unknown force. Why risk the lives of his crew? Who cared? Adrian planted the image of Janice in his mind; it would be easy to leave. The thought of the woman he loved so much gave him the answer he already knew. The reason was life itself. If he didn't end it here and now, whoever was behind this would be free to repeat more atrocities. If it was, as he suspected, drugs, many young lives would be destroyed with what this ship contained.

+++

Chung was having his own problems. After his attack on the navy, the men refused to obey his order to load containers into the helicopter. He didn't have the time to argue, so he shot the most argumentative full in the chest. At close range the impact tossed the bleeding carcass into the mass of renegades. The pointed weapon ensured that packages were tossed with indifference into the freight compartment. Not for an instant did Chung remove his eyes from the mob. They would now kill him given the slightest opportunity. The pilot was hurriedly completing his pre-flight checks and winding up the engines. Over the clamour of men and machine he advised his boss that he would not be able to take many, if any, of the men if he continued to load the way he was. Chung glanced sideways at him with murder in his eyes. The pilot knew when it was wise to shut up.

"If they shift themselves, they can use the other machine," Chung shouted; "your friend Di Song can fly it."

The pilot shrugged his shoulders. If the men co-operated they could escape. Pushed on by the thought that they still might get away, the men continued, albeit grudgingly, to load the packages. It was taking longer than Chung had anticipated.

+++

Adrian had Carrol cut down the canvas awning that protected their heads from the scorching sun. He wanted an unobstructed view all round. If he was to be attacked, he needed to see the enemy.

In less than three minutes HMAS *Bunbury* was battened down and ready for action. Adrian looked at Jim: "Two and a half hours of good water left, Sir."

For effect, Adrian leaned on the forward bulkhead and ordered slow ahead both engines. In his mind he was clear that he had to eliminate or capture whoever were responsible for the death of innocent seamen. At the same time he had to ensure the safety of his own crew.

Slowly they approached the resting place of HMAS *Geraldton*. She was firmly gripped by the reef and unless the sea state changed dramatically she was in no danger. Adrian could see Dave Cooper. The signal light began to flash; he and Jim read the individual letters together, and it caused them to smile wryly. It was not exactly naval protocol but it read, ***"Get the bastards."***

Adrian turned to Jim: "I want all spare hands with submachine guns on the port side—they're not to fire until I give the order. Is that understood?"

"Yes, Sir!"

Jim made his way down into the ship and gathered the spare hands and briefed them. The coxswain, normally part of the medical team, took charge. With an arrogant grunt of acceptance he bawled at the top of his voice at the five men to shut up and follow him.

Knowing he was taking a gamble, *Bunbury's* captain increased speed to twenty knots. From the chart there appeared to be ample room for him to manoeuvre the boat at high tide but unfortunately the ebb would soon be on them. There was an air of uncertainty about the whole situation. The thin line of the cliff face appeared to be almost covered by dark green foliage, but through that seemingly tiny gap a freighter had for a time disappeared. The noise of the diesel engines was beginning to reverberate off the cliffs as they made their approach. Adrian rested his elbows on the forward bulkhead and levelled his binoculars at the gap. He was navigating by instinct and knowledge. He looked at the 40/60 guns' crew as the aimer and trainer moved the black painted barrel across the bow from port to starboard. They were ready.

The gorge grew in size as they drew nearer and nearer and then their returning bow wave helped centre their passage through the channel and shoved them gently into the bay. Whip aerials slashed at the foliage that had begun to revive and conceal the entrance from the sea. As *Bunbury* entered this natural harbour, the *Kia Hua* was dead ahead. Adrian ordered port thirty and reduced the speed to slow ahead as they slid neatly passed the stern of the sunken vessel.

For the moment the rusting hull of the old tramp shielded them from any danger but Adrian was aware that, in less than a minute, they would be moving into open water. Quietly he ordered his men to be ready. Each member of his crew was tense as they waited for the order to open fire.

Chung and his men were momentarily stunned as *Bunbury* burst through into the bay - it was the last thing they had expected. The dread of capture gave a predatory strength to each man. In a last desperate hope that there would be room on the helicopter, some ran towards it. Chung was, as always, one step in front of the mob and without any remorse he raised his rifle, took aim and began firing indiscriminately. The rush faltered and fell back. Chung screamed at the pilot to take off. Others, desperately attempted to scramble up the steep sides of the bay and make a run for it. The professional flotsam collected their weapons and prepared to make a stand. The police helicopter was ready for take off, yet remained untouched on the bridge of the *Kia Hua*. Unnoticed, Di Song had swum for all he was worth to get to the ship. Out of breath, he had great difficulty in climbing the ropes that hung from her deck, but slowly as the adrenaline pumped through his veins he gained height. With luck he could start the machine and get clear away.

Fighting broke out as desperate men took decisive action. Chung sat with his legs dangling over the edge of the cargo bay as the helicopter rose into the air; carefully he raised his rifle and began to shoot the men he had worked with, then he fired randomly at *Bunbury*. His hope was to cause confusion and detract attention from himself. For once his underhanded methods did not produce the required result. As the first bullet struck the hull of *Bunbury*, Adrian ordered open fire. The heavy machine guns operated by Leading Seamen Carrol and Young began to traverse along the water's edge until they identified the source. An uncanny line of bullet holes began, as one followed the other, first into the underside and then with precision across the fuselage. This controlled accuracy by the two men almost cut the helicopter in two.

For a few seconds it clung, unmoving, to the air, its dead pilot's hands locked to the controls. As its upward momentum ended, it fell like a stone into the water. For an instant it seemed to float, its wide eyed, blood stained pilot bizarrely staring into the distance. Chung was still alive but the hurriedly loaded cargo had not been secured and had moved forward as the craft plummeted, pinning him against the forward bulkhead. He screamed and shouted but even if he had been heard there was no-one who cared. Entangled and unable to free himself from the jumble of cargo, the wreckage slipped below the surface silencing his screams.

Carrol and Young had independently selected alternative targets and were traversing the beach methodically. All hell was erupting as tracers hit fuel tanks and air bottles exploded, flinging themselves violently into the air. The wretched defenders of the bay fired wildly at the ship in the hope it would retreat. Adrian leant over the forward bulkhead of the bridge and roared at the 40/60 to fire. As he did so his body was spun about and then knocked backwards. Briefly the bay resounded to the dull throb as ten rounds of high explosive struck the cliff, detonating on impact. The red earth erupted with dust and flame, and many of those attempting to escape were buried with stones and earth. Those that survived were still clawing at the ground but a few more bursts of machine gun fire stopped them in their tracks. One final burst from Carrol's gun ensured all weapons were dropped and hands went up.

Their brief act of resistance was over. A short time in jail was preferable to death or a life sentence for murder in an Australian prison. They would all swear that it had been Chung who had done the killing. Adrian dragged himself up with his good arm: it was over. He shouted to Bob to take the Fast Raider with the coxswain and five armed men to the beach, while the ship covered them. It was Young who noticed the blood dripping from his captain's arm: "Sir! Sir! You've been hit."

Adrian's right arm had been numb; now that the blood flowed freely, it was beginning to hurt like hell but there was still a lot to be done.

+++

Angel Andrias sat with his pilot on the bare earth as they listened to the open channel on the radio. Chung had left it in the transmit mode to warn him. The mayhem they could only imagine. Success had been hours away—what had gone wrong? It no longer mattered; the entire shipment, one whole harvest from all those years ago was now unavailable. He would have to answer for his failure. With a last look at what remained of the base camp he climbed into the cockpit of the waiting helicopter. The pilot completed his pre-flight checks and as soon as the engines reached full power he was in the air. With a gentle acceleration he flew towards the village from where he had collected Angel. At least he was still alive. He was the lucky one.

Di Song lay on the steel deck of the *Kia Hua,* his lungs at breaking point; gasping, he dragged in air as a thirsty man gulps water. After a few minutes he was sufficiently recovered to stand, albeit shakily, and walk towards the waiting machine. On the beach all hell was breaking loose but with luck, in a few minutes, he would be away from this damned place. He clambered into the pilot's seat and spent valuable moments adjusting it. Ready, he started the engines, his eyes watching the RPM counter as it rose. The bullet went straight through his head, a neat little hole on entry, a gaping chasm on exit.

David Jones had lain on that steel deck since the return of the helicopter, not daring to move just in case the madman put a bullet in him. When he saw Di Song making for the cockpit he knew it was now or never. The severe beating and loss of blood had taken its toll and it had only been the pilot's concentration that had prevented David from being seen. It had taken all his reserves of strength to focus his eyes and hold the gun steady but it had been enough. As he fell back into unconsciousness, he witnessed his enemy topple out of the cab and lay motionless on the deck. Without a pilot in control, the RPM of the helicopter's engines reduced to an idle.

Bob found no opposition to their arrival as the Fast Raider's hardened keel ground onto the soft sand. The men on the beach were well aware of the damage a heavy machine gun pointed in their direction could inflict at such a short range. The coxswain fired his machine gun into the air and then roared at the top of his voice, ordering the rogues into a small but controllable area. They all looked at this bearded monster and reasoned it was best not to argue. Furthermore, he had them place their hands on top of their heads. Then, much to the amusement of Bob, he grabbed a nervous Seaman Tomkins. At the top of his voice he explained to the prisoners that if they as much as moved to scratch their bums, he would not be surprised if one machine gun went off and killed everyone of them. The coxswain turned around and winked at Bob as he made his way down the beach with the others, collecting discarded weapons as they went.

Jim had been constantly reminding Adrian that time was running out and now recommended they leave. The skipper, with his right arm strapped and a few pain killers to assist, agreed. "Jim, get a message to Bob to make himself at home—we'll pick him up on the next tide. In the meantime, if he can get someone to the *Kia Hua,* could he shut down that bloody helicopter?"

He waited until Jim returned and gently operated the engines until he faced the centre of the passage that exited the bay. This time it was more difficult as a strong current was pushing *Bunbury* from the stern and the depth of water was dangerously low. Power was the answer: the engines were increased to maximum. The twin propellers bit deep into the muddy water, accelerating them forward, creating a black mass of mud and debris in its wake. The power surge caused all on board to stumble. With grace, *Bunbury* passed through the gap into the open sea. The ebbing tide had left *Geraldton* high and dry and the recovery of the crew was the next priority.

Standing off at a safe distance, Adrian anchored *Bunbury* and, leaving Jim in charge, boarded the Fast Raider for the journey to *Geraldton*. Dave Cooper was waiting on the edge of the reef. He smiled at his boss and cheekily remarked, "So the bastards got you as well."

With a trace of sadness in his eyes, Adrian looked towards the wreck that was now clear of the water and the huge gash that scarred her port side. "How many casualties, Dave?"

"Five dead, including the captain; four wounded, none serious and most of us with cuts and abrasions from when we struck the reef."

"Well I suppose we should be grateful it's not worse. Can she be patched and floated off?"

Dave looked at *Geraldton* before answering. "My chief reckons it's a dockyard job just to patch the holes. She's split from stem to stern on both sides. If the weather holds she might stay there until the rescue crane appears but if the sea starts to get a bit choppy it will be an underwater salvage job."

Adrian agreed that she would never see service again. "OK, Dave; start getting your crew ready to transfer—one holdall of kit or personal possessions is the limit. It'll be a bit cramped but I'm sure we'll manage. I'm going back now, have your wounded return with me."

Dave shouted out four names, and in response each man and his helper carefully made their way across the reef to the waiting Fast Raider.

Jim was lingering around the gangway as Adrian returned and was unusually agitated. "The signal office is buzzing with the navy wanting to know what you mean by necessary and appropriate action."

Adrian winced with pain from his arm: "It's a bit bloody late for that, don't you think?"

"I suppose it is. I shut them up with a sitrep—a concise statement of the facts with a footnote that more details would follow."

"What you mean, Jim, is you got me out of the shit again. You're right but sometimes the paperwork comes second to procedures. Don't you agree?"

After a moment's reflection, Jim's answer was the obvious one: "It's easy for me to agree, Sir—you're the captain."

Adrian looked at his friend: "I suppose I'd better get some messages in the air; after all we do need some help to clear this mess up."

Both men walked forward to the signal office.

+++

David Jones returned to consciousness and felt the down-draught of the rotor blades. With determination he crawled on his hands and knees to the craft, dragged himself into the cockpit and flicked the fuel pump shut off switches. In a few minutes the engines, starved of fuel, stopped. It was the silence that Bob noticed first. The coxswain looked and could see a body slumped in the cockpit of the craft.

"Look, Sir, somebody's up there, Sir! You can see him," he shouted as if everyone was deaf.

Bob ordered two seamen to get themselves on board the *Kia Hua*, "Don't take any chances, shoot to kill if you have to." He handed them one of the spare radio handsets.

"Let me know what you find." The men were young and agile and it wasn't long before they were reporting. The only survivor was a police sergeant. Bob ordered that they get him back to the beach as best they could. It took time and a lot of effort, but eventually Sergeant David Jones was lying on the beach having his wounds treated by one of the noisiest people he had ever met.

EIGHTEEN

Janice woke suddenly, her whole body shaking with dread. For a few seconds she lay still; her eyes moved around the room. Once assured that the nightmare was over and reality took a grip, she jumped out of bed. Like a frightened child she grabbed her dressing gown and ran to Selwyn's room. "Selwyn," she cried as she pounded on his bedroom door.

The door opened and, surprisingly, he was up and dressed.

She grabbed hold and held him tight, sobbing uncontrollably.

Selwyn let the storm pass before he said anything. "You've had a bad dream about Adrian and you're scared."

"How could you know?"

"I had the same dream. There is no time for explanations but please believe me when I say he'll be all right. He's hurt, but not badly. Some of his comrades have not been as lucky."

"I must go to him."

"Get packed; I'll book the tickets through the company. We'll be on the first available flight to Australia."

Selwyn obtained two first-class tickets to Sydney and connecting flights to Perth. No time was wasted and, with a tearful farewell to Mrs Duke, Janice and her "knight" were on their way to Heathrow. When they had checked in, he suggested that they go and have a meal and a coffee to pass the time. She was grateful for any distraction. What she failed to notice was Selwyn dropping a small pill into her coffee. Its principal ingredient was a sedative that would reduce her stress level, and if, when they were on the aircraft, he could administer another, she would sleep for most of the journey.

+++

Adrian had been in radio communication with the naval base at Garden Island for over an hour explaining in detail what had happened and what action he had taken. There were no recriminations and no advice given. In fact, the lack of orders or information seemed odd. He was commanded to remain at anchor and wait. At best, the duty officer declared, assistance would arrive but it would be limited. The transmission ended by stating that the rescue of *Geraldton's* crew was the priority. Already the transfer of men was progressing well. Jim had organised officers and ratings into sentry details. Food and shelter for the prisoners were not a problem. To assist the guard detail, a cook and an engineer were dispatched. The Fast Raider was now operating a ferry service as armed men and equipment went to and from the bay. Bob returned on board and debriefed his Captain. The precious cargo was, as Adrian had suspected, a major drug shipment, but even he had failed to imagine the enormity of it. A great deal of it was in the helicopter at the bottom of the bay and would need to be retrieved.

Adrian was tired; his damaged arm was unusable and he felt awkward about having to ask the steward to do everything for him. Bob and Jim suggested that he should rest. The advice was refused; for the moment it was not even a consideration.

Henry MacGregor knocked on the cabin door and informed the trio there was a low flying Hercules circling the ship. The pilot was asking for Adrian over the radio by name and rank. The communication was to the point. A troop of soldiers was ready to parachute into the camp. The requirement was simple; they needed flares spaced at 100 metres distance, in a square formation as a drop zone. Adrian questioned the logic of such an action but was advised it wasn't a request but an order. The radio crackled as the coxswain loudly informed him that a landing site would be cleared and marked in less than ten minutes. The injured captain acknowledged, and the pilot confirmed that he had copied. The flares were placed in the sand and the sky glowed from their phosphorescence.

The labouring giant of the sky began its approach. Adrian found he had the company of both crews as they stared into the night sky. The outline of the plane appeared to drift across the star-splattered night. Without the use of the night-sight all found it difficult to see if the soldiers had jumped and they awaited confirmation of a successful drop by radio. ***"This is Major John Duncan, officer in charge. 'A' troop parachute regiment. My men are on the***

ground and I have taken over the security of camp and wreck. You will be receiving orders directly after I have notified the comcen of my arrival. Out."

Adrian could now consider the problem of his overcrowded vessel. The Fast Raider returned from shore with the armed guard and one well-bandaged police sergeant. Those who were wounded were given bunks to rest in; the remainder shared what was left or slept on cushions spread out on the deck. The dead were placed in an aft store. Cramped and tired, every man was glad it was over.

The signal Adrian was waiting for arrived; it directed HMAS *Bunbury* to proceed at best possible speed to Broome to land the dead, wounded and *Geraldton's* crew. On completion they were to depart and return to Fleet Base West for debriefing. Bob, on being told the contents of the message, advised Adrian that the wounded included him. By way of response his boss slumped down on the bed settee in his cabin and started to laugh. Bob looked at him and wondered if the large dose of pain killers administered earlier had affected him in some way.

"What's so funny?" Bob was more concerned than amused.

"You. What you tried to avoid has come full circle. Whether you like it or not you're in command. According to the rules, I am unfit and you have no option but to relieve me."

The full reality of what Adrian was saying struck home but now Bob was ready and, although only temporary until a new commanding officer was appointed, he relished the challenge.

"You have the best of teams to support you. Now, please ask my steward to come and help me get ready for bed. You have the ship, Number One—I'm tired and need sleep."

Bob left the cabin and almost fell over Jim who, waiting in the wings, had overheard most of the conversation.

"Sir, I presume you would like me to assume the duties of Exec?" Bob feigned a punch at Jim who obligingly ducked.

"Number one, get Commander Viper's steward to help him into bed."

Laughing, Jim acknowledged and went about his business. It was almost midnight when the boat finally settled down to something resembling normal routine and began a fast passage to Broome.

Their arrival was an anti-climax. Two ambulances and a staff car were on the jetty waiting. Once alongside and secure, Bob made his way down to the gangway.

He was about to walk across when a middle-aged man dressed in a smart charcoal grey suit moved to the other end and barred his way. "Commander Tomlinson, security," came the crisp well-spoken voice. This man knew how to make an introduction: "Lieutenant, no-one is to go ashore. The wounded will be escorted by the waiting medical orderlies. Now where is your commanding officer?"

Bob was startled by the stranger whose authoritarian manner did not sit well with him. "Sir, I am the acting commanding officer and before I agree to anything, can I see some ID?"

It was produced with a swiftness that could have

only come from much practice. "Lieutenant, we need to talk in private."

"Yes, Sir; Commander Viper is still in his cabin but a cup of coffee in the wardroom with the door closed should serve your purpose."

The Commander looked at this young man and smiled inwardly; the boy had the guts to stand up to him. Many a spoilt brat had buckled under his questioning manner. As they entered the wardroom, they found Henry relaxing over a cup of freshly brewed coffee. Bob told him to report to the First Lieutenant and asked that he ensure that the wounded were given all the assistance needed. He knew that his comments were not necessary but he had to show that this was his command.

The conversation was very one-sided, the Commander talked and Bob listened. Someone somewhere had moved fast and was bolting all doors before they had a chance to open. The meeting was blunt and to the point and the Commander terminated it as Adrian, his arm in a sling, walked into the wardroom.

"Viper, you are to come with me. There is a light aircraft waiting to take us directly to Perth. During the flight you will debrief me on the events that led you to open fire on civilians."

Adrian was in pain; the bluntness of the statement seemed undeserved and intimated more was to come. Before he was given a chance to say a word he was almost pushed out of the mess. Knowing it was useless to resist, Adrian refused the offer of assistance and with his good arm, carried his own bag. The speed of his departure almost caught midshipman John Wilson napping but protocol was maintained. Bob followed, and, as soon as the two men set foot on the jetty, he ordered Jim have the gangway taken inboard. Bob looked at him: "Don't ask."

In less than five minutes HMAS *Bunbury* was leaving Broome and heading at best possible speed for home. The removal of the dead and wounded had given extra space but it was evident that unless strict discipline was maintained from the start, arguments and fights could soon erupt. Once clear of the harbour, Bob decided that it was time to tell everyone what he knew. It was not much, only that someone had decided that a news blackout was to be maintained. He sympathised with the men being so cramped, but stressed that if all went well, they would be home in three days.

+++

Angel arrived back in Seoul with only the clothes on his back; he stank of body odour and was in the foulest of moods. His mind was in turmoil. Explanations were necessary as to what had happened and why it had gone wrong but the answers were not readily available. His luck had run out. As he opened the door to his penthouse suite he saw that it was still in immaculate order; there had been no visitors. For him, this was home and it was good to be back. His future hinged on the options available. He could run and hide, living off the money he had accrued, or he could face the wrath of the syndicate. For the moment all he wanted was to relax under a hot shower and have time to think. As the powerful jets massaged his skin he began to reason with himself. Over the years he had been successful and made a great deal of money for his bosses; they must surely take that into account. The cargo could have been lost at any time; it wasn't his fault that the bloody navy turned up. As he relaxed he began to convince himself that, although his elevation into the hierarchy might be delayed, there was still a great deal of good he could do for the syndicate.

Washed and feeling relieved at his own diagnosis of the situation, he opened a hidden safe and extracted his supply of cocaine. This was high quality stuff and he needed a good shot to restore confidence in his own ability. Before snorting the fine powder, he telephoned his pimp and demanded his two favourite girls. Tomorrow was another day which he would face when it arrived. Tonight he would satisfy his own sensual needs. It had been far too long since he had fulfilled his fantasies.

The drug began to have its effect and as the girls entered his lair he tore at their thin cotton dresses until they were naked before him. Obedience and subservience pleased Angel and, to tantalise his ego, they began to address him as master. With a faked tenderness one opened his bathrobe and then fell upon him. The other caressed his body. Angel was high and savoured their attentiveness. They guided him gently to the huge bed and mounted him in turn until his heart was pumping neat cocaine into every pore of his body. Now they stroked his skin and rubbed in scented oils with such tenderness that in his sensitised state he failed to notice what was happening around him.

The tranquil world he was in suddenly changed; two men were grabbing at his arms and pulling him off the bed. His confused mind failed to comprehend their actions. He even smiled at the two girls who held the balcony doors open. Angel stood naked, his feet not feeling the coldness of the polished granite floor; even the fresh air felt good as it embraced him. The men positioned him so that he was leaning over the wrought iron parapet, then, with just a gentle nudge, he found himself toppling over. For what appeared to be infinity he became the all-powerful soaring Eagle swooping to grab its prey. The moment died when his body hit the pavement.

Terry Rouse watched as the crowd gathered around the lifeless form. He tapped his driver on the shoulder and the car moved swiftly away. The local police knew Angel and what he did but had never been able to prove it. Suicide was a suitable explanation for the corpse that lay in a bodybag at the morgue.

+++

Adrian was beginning to reason that, for his actions, he had been judged, convicted, sentenced and there appeared to be no court of appeal. After treatment by the medical team he had been almost dragged into the waiting staff car and taken to the airport. Commander Tomlinson said nothing and acted like a jailer.

The airport was limited and at the far end of the main runway, well away from peering eyes, the army transport already had its engines operating. As the car drew alongside, a sergeant saluted the Commander, but ignored Adrian as though he were unimportant. Once seated, the two gas turbines roared, the brakes were released and they charged down the runway. With an almost imperceptible lift, they were in the air and turning towards Perth. During the journey Adrian told his side of the story as the Commander made notes. When this was over, Adrian attempted to converse but was at once advised, "I would get some rest if I were you. You may not get a chance later."

After nearly three hours of wondering what the hell was happening, Adrian, with one good arm, grabbed Tomlinson's jacket and demanded to be told.

"Look, I have my orders. I had to collect you personally, get you on this plane for debriefing. That's all I know; I can assure you I'd much rather be in my comfortable office in Sydney than with you on this bloody bone-shaker."

Adrian apologised for his behaviour but still asked what it was all about. Tomlinson didn't know. The airstrip at Perth was busy with its daily activities and no-one was at all concerned with yet another military aircraft landing. Once on the ground, the craft taxied to a remote part of the field before allowing its one passenger to disembark. Adrian stood and made his way to the door and, as he was about to walk down the exit ladder, he noticed that the sergeant was now sat next to the Commander.

"Aren't you getting off?"

The sergeant turned: "No."

The Admiral's driver was waiting with the car door open. "Been in the wars have we, Sir? The governor's waiting, cancelled everything. Most unusual."

Adrian smiled at her and thought, "You don't know the bloody half of it."

The car stopped outside the building where it had all began. Adrian moved to open the door but found it secure. The driver saw the look of puzzlement on his face but remained where she was. Within moments of their arrival, Admiral William Bennie walked from the building. He opened the nearest door and positioned himself next to Adrian on the rear seat, "Well, young man, what have you been up to? I've been ordered to place you under house arrest. You can tell me all about it on the way."

Adrian was now totally confused. The journey to the Admiral's residence was brief but during that time William Bennie listened intently.

Once inside, it was the Admiral's turn to comment. "It would seem to me that you did what you had to do and by your statement, did it well. Anyway, it's rare for me to be directed to do anything so there is much more to this than meets the eye. Furthermore, *Bunbury* may think she's returning to the base but I'm aware she's been ordered to investigate a suspicious vessel a few hundred miles to the west of her present position. I also know that this vessel is fictitious. The government body controlling this is making time for its own reasons. We're into a world of intrigue where we don't belong, young Adrian. It may be best for us if we sit this one out."

Adrian had to agree.

He was free to move around and enjoy the comforts of the Admiral's house but that was it. The afternoon had almost gone when the base doctor arrived to inspect Adrian's arm. He was pleased with the way it had been dressed but stitched the torn flesh to ensure better bonding.

"I'm curious, young man—where did you get this bullet wound?" Before Adrian had a chance to utter a word, the Admiral appeared.

"Time for you to leave, Doc, and if you whisper a word to anyone you'll be serving the rest of your time treating frost-bitten penguins. Understood?"

"Yes, Sir." The doctor packed his bag and hurriedly left.

Adrian felt weary. "Sir, would someone please show me to my room and may I be excused dinner?" It was only then that Adrian realised that the Admiral seemed to have no staff. His flag officer, a man who was usually crawling around the Admiral's backside, was nowhere to be seen. The house was empty apart from the Admiral and his wife.

Adrian was shown his room by Bill. He sat on the edge of the bed, removed his shoes, lifted his feet, spun around and rested his head on the pillow. Sleep came quickly, but rest was another matter; his brain remained active conjuring up strange visions of the past. The image of a large gibbet kept repeating itself. On this frame were hanging the bodies of executed men and he seemed to be waiting in line. As he lingered on the edge of the platform, the crowd he could not see would cheer, then go silent.

"Adrian, Adrian." The voice seemed far away, almost at the back of the crowd but then he returned to reality and realised where he was. His clothes were soaked with perspiration and he felt like death. The Admiral and his wife were standing by the bed. "Helen thought that you might like some supper but I think the doctor should give you something to reduce your temperature—you're sweating like a pig and you look like hell." Troubled, he looked at his wife and asked if she would telephone for the duty doctor.

"You will find his name in the book." Bill helped Adrian undress and pulled back the rumpled covers and told him to get in.

"No point in having a shower."

Almost as soon as the covers rested on his skin, Adrian returned to a restless slumber. The doctor diagnosed fatigue, shock, and an infection of the wound he had dressed earlier. Bill Bennie suggested in a more than officious manner that any treatment should have been administered earlier rather than later. The doctor wanted to say something but decided his career was not worth it. Cleaning a small area of skin he injected what he referred to as a cure-all.

Bill's wife remarked on Adrian's change for the better when she looked in before going to bed. But the next morning Adrian found it a struggle to get up. Helen entered the room just as his feet touched the floor. "And you can get right back in that bed or I'll have Bill order you."

Adrian spent that day and night being treated as a small boy. The doctor came and dressed his wound and pumped some more antibiotics into his system. Helen Bennie spoon fed him thick vegetable soup. The Admiral stayed out of the way and completed the routine mountain of paperwork that had been delivered from his office.

+++

It was late that evening when the taxi containing Janice and Selwyn arrived at the main gate of HMAS *Stirling*, Fleet Base West. Without a pass or someone to vouch for them, they were denied any useful information. Janice realised that the police were only doing their job and in a friendly manner she asked if there was anyone in authority she could see to explain the situation. The senior duty officer was not well pleased at having to visit the main gate. He had been relaxing in his cabin before having to undertake security rounds of the whole base. He eventually arrived, and his attitude changed when an attractive woman apologised and smiled at him. Janice employed her talents as a journalist and as his guard dropped she began to fire questions at him. As she talked he picked up the ships' movement list and checked it. "I'm sorry ma'am but HMAS *Bunbury* is still at sea and is not due in."

"Are you sure?"

"Ma'am it's my job to know where ships are and I can assure you that *Bunbury* is not in, will not be in and is not expected in."

"It's all wrong. I was convinced something had happened to Commander Viper."

A despondent Janice was about to leave but fate made its move as in walked the doctor.

The duty officer looked at him dourly: "What are you doing out tonight, Doc? Is there something going on that I should know about?"

"Oh, there's some Pommy up at the Admiral's house who's been shot and his dressing needed changing."

The duty officer frowned: "Surely that's a job for a nurse."

"Look, if the Admiral says jump, I don't ask how high."

Janice smiled; there couldn't be that many Pommies on the base. She smiled at the officer, said thank-you and left. It had to be Adrian. She ran back to the taxi which had now clocked up a large bill. Selwyn thought that the odds of Adrian being the guest of an Admiral were remote, but he agreed to go along with the idea. The house was easy to find as it was clearly signposted. In less than ten minutes they were being driven up the long drive. Janice left the taxi, Selwyn following close behind, as they ran the remaining few yards to the main door. After ringing the bell rapidly at least five times it was opened by Helen Bennie. Before she could utter a word, Janice stated firmly, "I'm Janice Porter. I was told by the duty officer that my fiancé, Commander Adrian Viper, is with you."

Helen was taken aback; "I'm afraid that you have been ill-informed."

"I know you have a Pommy house guest who has been shot and it's my Adrian," cried Janice in anguish.

Helen realised that there had been a security leak and for the moment it would be better if this woman were inside rather than out.

"Come in. He's not well at the moment. I'll take you to his room."

Bill Bennie, disturbed by the sound of voices, left his study to be greeted by his wife Helen and two strangers.

"Helen, who the hell are these people?"

"There's no need to swear, dear. They're friends of Commander Viper."

The Admiral was far from pleased. "Right you two, come into my study now." Bill Bennie glanced towards the heavens as his wife departed. The situation was not of his making and had to be dealt with quickly before more damage was done.

"Well, you had better come in and, before I allow you to see Adrian, some explanations are necessary."

Janice made the standard introductions and asked Selwyn if he would mind paying the waiting taxi. Helen arrived with tea and some sandwiches, interrupting her husband's narrative. Bill asked his wife to prepare two more rooms as Janice and Selwyn would be staying.

With a little smile on her lips she replied, "Yes dear," and left.

Selwyn, who had patiently waited for the opportunity to speak, began to ask some searching and very pertinent questions to which the Admiral clearly stated he did not know the answers.

"What in hell's name are you doing here?" came a voice from behind them. Janice jumped up, turned and looked directly at Adrian. His face had a few days' growth of beard, his arm was in a sling, and he looked like death. But at that moment nothing mattered; he was there and alive. All she wanted to do was hold him close. They embraced and tears of joy flowed from her eyes.

Helen broke the spell: "He's still weak and should return to his bed but I thought a few minutes together would be better than all the medicine in the world."

Janice thanked her and ordered Adrian back to bed.

"I'll go if you come and tuck me in." Holding hands they left.

Bill turned to Selwyn: "Whether you like it or not you're now my house guests."

Selwyn laughed: "At the moment a bed anywhere would be a blessing, I'm dog tired."

Helen showed him to a room and then advised her husband that it was getting late and he should be thinking of bed as well. Admiral or not he knew when his wife was talking good sense.

Janice spent some time with Adrian before kissing him goodnight. Helen was waiting and walked with her the few yards to the room she had prepared.

The next two days passed quickly. Helen was the ideal hostess, whilst her husband continued to undertake his duties as best he could without leaving the house. Adrian grew stronger, and when it was known that he and Janice were to be married, Helen left them alone as much as possible.

On the fifth day the Admiral's Flag Lieutenant arrived and Adrian was summoned. For a while the three men were in discussion until Bill left the room and requested the others to join them. When they were all present, Adrian was given the honour of reiterating the gist of the signal Bennie had received. "It would seem that after *Bunbury* sailed for Broome, the army meticulously combed the area for useful information; they investigated every item in and about the camp. The interrogation of every prisoner succeeded in a breakthrough. It was evident that the majority of the drugs had been removed from the *Kia Hua* and were ready for shipment, even if a great deal, thanks to my gunners, was at the bottom of the harbour."

All sat mesmerised by the incredible story that was unfolding.

"Anyway, they found a detailed index of the amounts and drop-off points along the coast. With time at a premium their goal was achieved. As directed by a special forces unit, each package was dropped according to the schedule. Once this had been completed the police units positioned themselves discreetly on shore and waited. Oh—I almost forgot—they placed a homing device in every package before it was dispatched to the deep. As they hoped, the collectors arrived, not all together of course, and recovered their assigned shipment. From the contents of the signal, I understand this has been the biggest drugs haul since seizures began. There have been numerous arrests, some very prominent business people amongst them. That's the summary of the facts. I understand there will be a full press release later. Naturally this will be the official version."

Janice asked if she would be allowed to contact her newspaper.

Bill Bennie looked at her and smiling gently advised her that, along with the rest of the media, she would have to report what they were told. "Obviously, my dear, there are still a lot of loose ends to tie together and Lloyds, along with the various authorities would not be pleased if you revealed all."

When the news broke and the local press and television channels learned that an officer involved in the drugs bust was at the house it became besieged. It was suggested by Bill Bennie that Adrian hold a press conference. Dana Adams, the Admiral's PA, was now an almost permanent fixture. At first she wanted to know about Jim. Adrian assured her a dozen times that he was fine. Satisfied she set to and prepared standard but credible answers for the press. All the media present were invited into the house but they left disappointed. It was apparent that Adrian had been well briefed and was toeing the party line. The bulk of the inquiries were centred around why a reserve British Naval officer had become involved in the action. Adrian side-stepped the main issue by replying that he was part of a continuing exchange scheme. By the end of the day he was utterly exhausted and fell asleep in a comfortable armchair; he was woken by a kiss on the lips from Janice who announced it was dinner time.

HMAS *Bunbury* arrived at the naval base the following day and everyone, with the exception of the bare bones of a duty watch, was whisked away for debriefing. Each man was advised of the Official Secrets Act and its implications if they revealed to anyone the details of the incident. Special counsellors were recruited to deal with stress and the anxiety of some of the men. The majority were happy to be alive and able to get gloriously drunk in the Fleet Amenities Centre. After they had consumed ample amounts, the bar was shut. Unable to stand, all were escorted by the military police to a barrack room previously readied.

Once debriefed, the officers were taken to the Admiral's house where they were advised of the official press release. On completion, *Geraldton's* officers were returned to the wardroom where, on a temporary basis, they had been allocated cabins. *Bunbury*'s officers wondered for a moment why the need for segregation. Bill Bennie, as was his manner, was brief and to the point. Adrian, because of his injuries was relieved of his command; Bob Hopkins was appointed in his place, the position to be confirmed later by signal. Jim Potts, subject to confirmation and until relieved, would be the First Lieutenant. *Geraldton's* navigator would be re-appointed to *Bunbury*. Before they left, the Admiral commended all of them for the way the operation had been completed and that Adrian had been recommended for a decoration.

The unassuming British commander was amazed by Bill's statement and after the congratulations and backslapping, the new commanding officer of *Bunbury* and his officers returned to their boat. Jim wanted to speak to his former captain but the opportunity did not present itself. With the formalities of the official hand-over of *Bunbury* complete, much of Adrian's time was consumed by the demands of the seemingly endless media interviews. When *Bunbury* was in harbour, Jim and Dana became inseparable; he would conjure up any excuse, no matter how feeble, to visit her office. The Admiral was known to have frequently commented in passing that Jim spent more time in his office than he did. The day they had all been dreading arrived - the funeral of Pat Briggs. Pat's family had been the navy and he was to be given a military burial with the honours befitting an officer who died performing his duty. Every member of his crew had volunteered for the honour guard; those not chosen formed a line to the church as the cortège passed. For once the base church was filled to capacity for Pat was a man they had all known. He was a member of the old school.

Adrian was given the task of assistant Base Officer, or as it was more generally known, the "shitty little job's officer." For the moment it was a convenient task: it left him available for interviews and physiotherapy.

Selwyn spent his time ensuring that their business continued to run smoothly in their absence. He also spent a great deal of time with Adrian and Janice discussing private matters.

Helen continued to ask when the great day would be but Janice just smiled and said when Adrian was fully recovered.

Once the media had another story to chase, the Admiral held a dinner party for all the officers from *Bunbury, Geraldton* and *Albany*. It was a semi-formal occasion and when the meal was over Adrian asked the Admiral if he could propose a toast. Bill Bennie was about to say something when he felt his ankle being softly kicked by his wife.

Adrian stood and holding his glass in his right hand thanked his friends old and new, with a special mention for the Admiral and his wife. The toast was to the Queen and her Royal Australian Navy. When the table thumping was over he looked at Janice and she moved towards him and held his left hand. Adrian's head lowered before he began to speak. "As you all know, Janice and I intend to get married. Well, thanks to a damaged wing, I have some sick leave owing. If any of you can spare the time you are all welcome to attend our reception tomorrow at the Park Royal Hotel."

Selwyn quickly rose from the table, moved and whispered in Jim's ear. Both men moved behind

Adrian, grabbed him and hoisted him onto their shoulders. Helen, Dana, Janice and the other ladies present decided it was time to let the boys play.

Janice resisted for a moment until Helen in her worldly way said, "Tonight he belongs to the navy. Tomorrow he's all yours."

THE END